HEIRS *of* EDEN

by HAROLD GERSHOWITZ

ISBN: 1484099036
ISBN 13: 9781484099032
Library of Congress Control Number: 2013907366
CreateSpace Independent Publishing Platform
North Charleston, South Carolina

CONTENTS

ABOUT *HEIRS OF EDEN*

Bantam Books originally published Harold Gershowitz's first novel, "Remember This Dream." The book became a Chicago Tribune Best Seller and won the 1989 Friends of Literature Award for Fiction. On the twentieth anniversary of its original release, Mr. Gershowitz reissued the book utilizing the print-on-demand publishing division (now CreateSpace) of Amazon.com.

The trade paperback edition of "Heirs of Eden," is also a publication of Amazon.com's CreateSpace publishing division.

Heirs of Eden is a work of fiction. One should not search for real-life counterparts to the central characters of this work, other than the well-known historical personalities who are, from time to time, referenced throughout the text. The fictitious incident in Heirs of Eden involving the Israeli town of Maalot in 1957 should not be confused with the massacre that took place there twenty years later.

DEDICATION

To Diane, my loving wife of nearly thirty years, without whom this project would have neither been conceived nor completed. And to Bayla, my dear late wife and our son Steven, both of whom were lost so very young. And, finally, to our children Amy and Michael and Larry, Danny and Jill.

ACKNOWLEDGEMENTS

The idea for Heirs of Eden was born shortly after Bantam Books purchased my first novel, Remember This Dream. I was searching for a subject for a second book at the same time my wife Diane was researching a paper pertaining to the Middle East. It was during our many discussions of the seemingly endless conflict between Israelis and Palestinians, and by extension, the antipathy between Arabs and Jews, that a storyline began to germinate. With the patient assistance of numerous individuals with whom I met on both sides of the cultural divide here in America and in the Middle East, Heirs of Eden finally emerged.

Jenny Chandler and the entire editorial and creative team at Amazon.com's CreateSpace publishing division were a pleasure to work with. Individually and collectively they performed as professionally, thoroughly and responsively as any publishing professionals with whom I have ever worked.

In addition to Diane, I extend great thanks to those who read and reread drafts of Heirs of Eden including my daughter Amy Lask, my son Michael Gershowitz and Diane's son Danny Kite. I am ever grateful for their comments and suggestions, which contributed greatly to the final version of this book.

Thanks also to Patricia Butler, a fine writer, who made many valuable suggestions during the early drafting of Heirs of Eden.

Very Special thanks to my friend Judge Abraham Sofaer for the time he spent with me in Jerusalem and for opening so many doors for me in Israel and on the West Bank during the first Intifada. I first met Judge Sofaer in Chicago at the signing of the Genocide Treaty when he was the Chief Legal Officer at the US State Department under Secretary of State, George Schultz.

The many courtesies extended to me as I met with Israelis and Arabs in Jerusalem, Bethlehem, Tel Aviv and Jaffa are greatly appreciated. The many hours they spent with me contributed mightily to my understanding of the characters I was about to create.

I am deeply indebted to Rema Saadeh Manousakis who shared with me the story of her family's odyssey from Jaffa, through the Middle East, and ultimately to America. Her story greatly influenced my story.

I am indebted to Yitzhak Segev, Israeli Brigadier General (Ret.), who spent many hours with me in Jerusalem and on the West Bank providing a one-on-one, unforgettable tutorial on the Middle East conflict.

There are no words to express my appreciation to the late Teddy Kollek, former Mayor of Jerusalem for the time and patience he extended to me during the time we spent together discussing this project.

It is difficult to adequately convey my appreciation to the late Israeli historian and biographer Amos Elon for patiently sharing with me his perspectives on the Middle East.

I owe special thanks to the late Elias Mitri Freij, former Palestinian Mayor of Bethlehem, who gave so generously of his time to meet with me on the West Bank during a very tense time. He spoke to me passionately of his dream for peace in the region and of his vision of the prosperity that would follow. Sadly, that is still an unfulfilled dream.

The fathers have eaten sour grapes,
and the children's teeth are set on edge.
—Jeremiah 31:29

PROLOGUE:

It was both appropriate and absurd at that time and place.

That was when Noah Greenspan first thought he was in love with Alexandra Salaman, the Palestinian Arab girl from Jaffa. Appropriate because the place was the "Lovers of Peace" Congregation. Absurd because everyone knew the place only by its Hebrew name, Ohev Shalom Congregation, the old inner-city orthodox synagogue in Washington, DC.

It was a time when Jews and Arabs were hardly embracing one another as "lovers of peace." And besides, it was at Noah's bar mitzvah, of all times and places.

This was supposed to be the day Noah's thoughts were of his religious manhood and his ancient Jewish heritage; but this was the day his thoughts turned to the Arab girl seated with her mother, Samira, and Noah's mother, Esther. They sat in the balcony overlooking the sanctuary in which Noah and his father, Hyman, were seated alongside Alexandra's father, Sharif, and her brother, Yusuf.

To understand how these peculiar bonds were forged, and where they were destined to lead, we must turn the pages of our story back two years.

CHAPTER ONE

SEPTEMBER 1948

Noah shielded his eyes from the sun as the softball climbed to the peak of its trajectory and then, after a moment's hesitation, came plunging down toward him.

"I've got it!" he yelled, shagging in the fly ball that Mike McGovern had hit with an old, splintered Louisville Slugger.

Noah hurled the ball back to Mike and grinned when it dropped squarely in the middle of the schoolyard's home plate, an outline someone had traced on the concrete with yellow paint.

"Nice throw, Greenspan!" Mike shouted.

"Nice hit, McGovern!" Noah yelled back.

It was the first day of school, and Noah and Mike were among the first to arrive. N. P. Gage was one of the smaller white elementary schools in the nation's still-segregated capital, and it grew smaller each year as more and more white families fled from the growing black encroachment.

The area east of N. P. Gage was virtually all white, while the neighborhood to the west, known as LeDroit Park, was all black—or colored, as Noah and his friends would say. Well, almost all colored. There were the corner grocers, mostly Jews and perhaps an Asian or two, who worked and lived there—tiny, mostly white islands surrounded by a sea of black.

Old Griffith Stadium, built in 1911, towered over the area, and the clock tower at Howard University stood as a proud symbol of black achievement during a time when a black man couldn't buy a hamburger at one of Mister Marriott's Hot Shoppes.

It hadn't always been like that, though. Seventy years earlier, LeDroit Park had been one of Washington's first suburbs, an exclusive, gated, guarded community where well-to-do white folks could live secure and comfortable only a short buggy ride from all the tumult and the politicians, wheeler-dealers, and assorted riffraff who were always flocking to the nation's capital. Then, about a year after Ulysses Grant thrashed Horace Greeley in the election of 1873, angry students from Howard University tore down the fences, and twenty years later Octavius Augustus Williams, a black man who cut the white politicians' hair in the Capitol barbershop, moved into the all-white neighborhood. And that's about the time the white folks started leaving.

Noah was the only child of Hyman and Esther Greenspan, or "Mr. and Mrs. Hy," as the black customers who shopped in their tiny grocery store called them. The For You Market was poorly lighted by yellowing and often flickering fluorescence, and its pungent aroma of kale and collard greens, intermingled with the acrid smell of salt mackerel and dill pickles floating in small, brine-filled wooden vats in front of the meat case, assaulted the senses. The store was a demanding, pathetic little enterprise that drained all the energy its owners brought to it ninety-five hours a week. The Greenspans had purchased the store two years earlier for $7,500 with money borrowed from Hy's father, a retired immigrant tailor, who mortgaged his Baltimore row house so Hy could have his own business.

During the week, Noah worked alongside his parents from the time he finished his homework until the store closed at nine o'clock, and on Saturdays he spent the entire day either in the store or on the street delivering groceries.

The Greenspans had waited nearly six years to start their family and never intended that Noah would be an only child. They only planned to wait until life was a little less demanding. They were still waiting.

In the meantime, their only son had grown into a fine young man with an inquisitive mind, curious about almost everything. Dimpled cheeks exaggerated an infectious smile, a gift from his father. From his mother he had inherited large, deep-brown eyes that sparkled with energy and enthusiasm. Noah was keenly aware of how hard his parents worked and for whom they toiled, and he understood much earlier than most children how central he was to his parents' very sense of purpose.

It often fascinated Noah that during his ten-minute walk to school, he almost never saw a white person west of N. P. Gage or a black one east of the school. Reaching the small, segregated school from the ghetto was, Noah thought, like entering a foreign country—different culture, different skin color. You could even hear the difference in the way people spoke.

Now, as Noah ran to his right to catch another pop fly, he heard his classmate Paul Suitland trot over to him from his blind side.

"Get a load of that," the tall, blond boy called.

"Get a load of what?" Noah asked as he gloved the ball and fired it back to Mike.

"That!" Paul said, gesturing to the sidewalk on the other side of the chain-link fence bordering the playground.

The boy looked about his age, eleven, and the girl about the same. She was thin and gangly and, Noah thought, looked a little frightened. The two adults, no doubt parents accompanying their children to their first day at school, surveyed the schoolyard. They, too, seemed apprehensive.

Several other boys stopped what they were doing to watch the newcomers. Foreigners were an oddity in the neighborhood. And these people, with their dark complexions, drab dress, and uneasy stares, were foreigners for sure, no doubt about it.

"You think they're niggers?" Paul asked in a low voice.

"Yeah, they came from your direction, Noah," one of the other boys said.

"Come on, you guys," Noah replied. "Cut it out."

"They ain't niggers," Mike replied as he joined the others. "They look like Indians to me."

"Punjab!" Paul called under his breath.

"Shut up, you guys," Noah whispered, without taking his eyes off the new boy, who stared back at Noah through the chain-link fence.

"Hey, Noah, maybe they're A-rabs," Mike said.

Paul laughed. "Yeah, the A-rabs are comin' to get Noah."

"Boy, they don't look none too happy to be here, do they?" one of the boys observed.

"How happy would you be if you were being stared at by a bunch of jerks like us?" Noah replied.

"Where do you think they're from?" Paul asked, turning serious for the first time.

"Beats me," Noah answered as he raised his hand and slowly waved to the boy. The young foreigner stood still for a moment and then hesitantly returned the gesture. Then the bell rang, and the man nudged his two children forward, urging them and their mother to go on through the gate at the end of the schoolyard.

**

Noah made his way to one of the desks at the front of the classroom and smiled as he scanned the etchings that had, over the years, been carved into the desktop.

"Quiet please!" Agnes Eastlack, Gage's sixth-grade teacher, yelled over the din.

A hush settled over the classroom, and Noah looked up and saw the new boy standing next to Mrs. Eastlack. She was one of the older teachers at Gage and reminded Noah of the newspaper photographs of Eleanor Roosevelt, with her tall, slight frame, toothy smile, and gray hair brushed back over the tops of her ears.

"Class, this is Yusuf Salaman, and he is new to our school this year," she said to the now-quiet classroom. "In fact, he is new to our country, so I know you will all want to make him feel welcome."

Yusuf stood awkwardly for a moment and then turned his attention to the other students. His eyes immediately locked on Noah, his expression softening as though he had spied an old friend.

Yusuf Salaman was uncommonly handsome for his age. His penetrating, dark-brown, almost-black eyes and his thick, wavy black hair made him a striking figure. He was one of those boys who at adolescence already looked like the men they would one day become.

"Yusuf, why don't you select one of the empty desks," Mrs. Eastlack said, pointing him toward the vacant desks at the rear of the room. "Shall we call you Joseph now that you're in America? What do you think, class?"

"Yeah, we'll call him Joey," one of the boys called out.

"How does that sound to you, Yusuf?"

The boy hesitated a moment as he made his way to one of the empty desks, a small frown tugging at the edge of his mouth.

"If you like," he finally said with hardly a hint of an accent.

"Splendid!" Mrs. Eastlack replied warmly. If she noticed the boy's displeasure at her easy usurpation of his name, she gave no sign of it. "Now, Joey, tell us something about you. Where are you from?"

"I am from Jaffa."

"You're from Israel!" Mrs. Eastlack exclaimed. "Oh, how exciting!"

Noah saw Yusuf Salaman's eyes widen, a hint of red rising across his face.

"I am *not* from Israel!" he protested. "I am from Palestine!"

Noah turned in his seat. "Shit!" he murmured under his breath. "They *are* Arabs!"

***

At the sound of the lunch bell, Mirs. Eastlack's class bolted from the room like warriors scurrying to man battle stations. All but Noah, who rose and walked back to Yusuf's desk.

"Hi, I'm Noah. Noah Greenspan."

"I guess I am Joey," Yusuf replied, only half smiling.

"Who do you want to be?" Noah asked.

"I suppose Joey is fine…at school here anyway," he answered.

"OK, then. Where do you live, Joey?"

"We live on Oakdale at Fourth Street."

"Fourth? You live at Fourth and Oakdale? Then you must've bought the Izumis' place!" Noah said, referring to the grocery store two short blocks north of the For You Market. Izumi's had been run by an elderly Japanese couple but had been empty for nearly six months, ever since Mr. Izumi had been pistol-whipped by thugs angry about the paltry sum they found in the store's cash register. After Mr. Izumi was released from Freedman's Hospital, the Izumis had just closed up the store and vanished.

"Yes, yes. That was the name of the market my father owns now. Do you know it?"

Noah could barely contain his excitement. "We have the store two blocks down Fourth Street, at Fourth and U. Our place is called the For You Market. We're neighbors!"

"You live in the colored section too?" Yusuf asked.

Noah nodded. "Are you going home for lunch?"

"Yes. My parents want my sister and me to come home. Are you?"

"Yeah. My mom likes me to come home during the first week or two of school. Come on, I'll walk with you."

***

Alexandra Salaman barely nodded when Yusuf introduced her to Noah on the school steps. Yusuf explained that while they were twins, she was a grade behind because the girls' school she attended in Jaffa had been closed due to fighting that broke out in the city the year before they left. Noah's glance lingered on the girl's simple attire, a neat, dark-green plaid skirt and a crisp, sleeveless white blouse that contrasted smartly with her olive complexion. His eyes lingered a moment on the small gold cross dangling from a necklace just above the top button of her blouse. Sensing Noah's gaze, the girl shot him a quick glance, and for a moment their eyes met. He was intrigued by the sea-green color of her eyes. She said nothing as they made their way into the ghetto. Noah reciprocated, making no effort to speak to her.

"So how long have you been in the States?" Noah asked as they crossed Second Street into the LeDroit Park ghetto, where they alone comprised the entire white adolescent population.

"For only three days," Yusuf replied. "We were brought here by my uncles. I think they bought the market for my father."

"Did your father have a food store in Jaffa?"

"No. He grew oranges in Jaffa. We had a small citrus grove that had been in our family since the turn of the century. I think he will go mad in that tiny store. He already hates all the cars and trucks that go by our home all day long. He hates everything about this place. He says the air suffocates him here."

Noah, unsure how to respond, said nothing.

"Come inside for a minute," Yusuf said when they arrived at the store. "I'll introduce you to my mother and father."

Noah glanced up at the sign on the top of the plate-glass window. Where it used to read "Izumi's Market," it now said "Crescent Market."

As the children entered the store, Joey's mother called out, "Sharif! Come! Yusuf and Alexandra are home from school!"

Noah had not paid much attention to Yusuf's mother earlier at the school, but now he thought Samira Salaman was just about the most beautiful woman he had ever seen. Her long, braided, dark-brown hair hung over her left shoulder, and her almond-shaped eyes were hazel-colored, not quite green and not quite brown. She had high cheekbones and full lips. Her smile was warm and genuine, revealing straight, chalk-white teeth that glistened as radiantly as did the whites of her eyes against her flawless olive complexion. She was almost as tall as Yusuf's father. Noah thought she looked like a movie star.

"Ah!" Sharif Salaman appeared from behind the meat counter, wiping his hands on the white apron he wore. "How are my two students? Smarter than when I left you three hours ago?" he asked with a broad smile.

"Father," said Yusuf, "this is my friend Noah. He is in my class."

"Yes, yes, I remember you," the boy's father said with a wide grin. "You were on the playground when we arrived at the school this morning. You waved at Yusuf."

"Father, Noah's parents have the store two blocks down the street at U Street."

"Ah, I see," Yusuf's father said, looking curiously at the youngster his son had brought home. "So, you are my competitor?"

Noah grinned, not knowing what to say. Sharif Salaman was grinning too, arching his eyebrows in a friendly but taunting way.

Sharif Salaman was an imposing figure, about six feet tall and with the same olive complexion as his wife and children. His eyes were coal black like Yusuf's, and a neatly trimmed, short-cropped beard covered a strong square jaw. His hair was thick, jet-black, and wavy, also like Yusuf's. Noah noted the unmistakable resemblance between father and son.

Noah shifted his weight awkwardly. "Well, I'd better go now. My mom will have lunch waiting for me."

"Noah, why don't you come home with Yusuf after school?" Sharif Salaman suggested. "I am sure Yusuf will have many questions that you can answer for him."

"Um, I can't," Noah answered awkwardly. "I have to be somewhere."

"Well, maybe tomorrow then. All right?" They stood there smiling, waiting for Noah to reply.

"I go to a special school after I leave Gage," he finally said, his voice betraying a hint of nervousness. "I have to go to Hebrew school every Monday, Tuesday, and Wednesday."

Their smiles vanished suddenly, in unison, as though someone had waved a wand over them.

"Well, see you later," Noah said.

"Yes, yes, Noah," Sharif Salaman said as he ushered Noah toward the door. "You must leave now." A chill was now evident in his voice.

Outside, Noah turned and looked back at the Salaman family through the steel-mesh-covered glass door. Yusuf's mother, covering her mouth with the tips of her fingers, turned a worried gaze toward her husband. Yusuf, too, looked up at his father, concern etched on his young face. Only Alexandra looked back at Noah through the smudged glass. Her wide-eyed gaze stayed with him as he turned to make his way home.

***

Sharif and Samira Salaman looked into each other's eyes for a moment or two after Noah left.

"He was the only one to welcome me, Father. I had no way of knowing…" Yusuf said after a moment of awkward silence.

"There was nothing to know, Yusuf. He welcomed you because he was friendly and because he has been taught good manners. I think he is a good boy."

"But he learns Hebrew, Father. He is a Zionist."

"Yusuf, he is a young Jew. He studies the ancient language of the Jews. It is nothing."

Yusuf saw his mother reach over and gently take his father's hand into her own. Sharif Salaman closed his eyes and nodded.

CHAPTER TWO

No customers were in the For You Market when Noah burst in.

"Mom! Dad! I met the people who bought Izumi's! They have a kid my age. He was at school today. He has a younger sister, and I met his parents too!"

"Oh, how wonderful," Esther Greenspan replied, smiling. "What are their names?"

"Salaman." Noah answered.

"Solomon!" Hy Greenspan said. "Another landsman in the neighborhood."

"No, Dad, not Solomon—Salaman," Noah corrected, enunciating carefully. "They're Arabs. They just arrived from Palestine."

"Oh, my God!" Noah's mother gasped. "Arabs two blocks away!"

"Noah, did they say they were Arabs?" Hy asked.

"Yeah, they did. They're from Jaffa. They were farmers. I think they lost their home during all the fighting."

"Huh, how about that," Hy muttered to no one in particular.

"Oh my God, this is terrible," Esther whispered.

"For chrissake, Es, this is northwest Washington, not the Middle East. Let's not make a big deal over this."

"But it is a big deal. We don't need such people in the neighborhood," Noah's mother replied anxiously. "We don't need to have Noah in school with an Arab."

"Es, why don't you fix Noah something to eat and stop worrying about whether the Middle East armistice extends to LeDroit Park."

"This isn't funny, Hy. I don't like it at all," she replied.

Noah decided not to say anything about the Salaman family's reaction to his mentioning Hebrew school.

Esther Greenspan said no more about the new neighbors until Noah had finished his lunch and returned to school. "Who would have believed such a thing," she fretted under her breath.

"Es, you're being foolish over this Arab thing." Hy stocked a shelf behind the cash register with cartons of Uncle Ben's Minute Rice.

"I don't know what to think," she replied. "Who would have ever dreamed that an Arab family would move here, to this neighborhood?"

"I don't imagine they like being here any more than you like having them here."

"No good can come of it, Hy. It's going to mean trouble for us, and for Noah too."

"Damn it, Es, that's enough! You don't know these people from Adam. You've never met an Arab in your life."

"Hy, you don't have to meet an Arab to know how much they hate Jews. They've killed thousands of our people in Israel."

"We've killed thousands of their people too," he replied. "Don't forget, it was called Palestine before it became Israel."

"And what is that supposed to mean?" she shot back at him.

"What is that supposed to mean?" he repeated. "How the hell do I know what that's supposed to mean? All I know is that nothing, but nothing, is either black or white. Our people fought for land that their people felt belonged to them. A lot of people got hurt, Es. My guess is that those people got hurt too," he said, pointing toward Oakdale street.

***

Hyman and Esther Greenspan made an attractive couple. Hyman, standing about six feet tall, was built like a man used to a hard day's work. While not naturally gregarious, he had a warm, genuine smile and was well liked by most everyone who knew him. He combed his light-brown hair straight back with no part, which gave him a distinctively continental look. His pale-blue eyes suggested sensitivity, even kindness, which put people at ease. He didn't waste words with idle chatter either. When he spoke it was usually something worth listening to.

Esther was two years younger than Hy. She had been eighteen when they married. He met her at a social at the orphanage in Baltimore where the welfare people had taken her after her widowed mother died when she was nine years old. Hyman Greenspan fell in love with Esther Appelavitch the moment he laid eyes on her, but then, again, so did most men. She was a beauty. Her dark-brown hair, falling almost to her shoulders, framed a beautiful face. Her large brown eyes were arresting, and she had a warm smile.

Esther's delicate features, while quite beguiling, belied a pragmatic, sometimes hard, demeanor. Hers had not been an easy life. Meeting Hy Greenspan, she felt, was the only good thing that had ever happened to her. She saw him as a gift, a reward for the unjust harshness of her youth. She neither expected nor sought any further gifts of fate, and she resented anything that threatened to take from her what little she had.

"So, what are you suggesting," Esther asked, the stress gone from her voice, "about our new neighbors?"

"Let's just not jump to conclusions," Hy replied. "U Street is not the River Jordan."

At that precise moment, Samira Salaman walked through the front door of the For You Market. It was rare that anyone other than a black customer or a salesman entered the store, and for a moment Hy and Esther just stared at the beautiful woman who stood before them, her smile rich and radiant.

"Can I help you?" Esther asked hesitantly.

"I am Samira Salaman. My husband and I have just opened the store at Fourth and Oakdale. I wanted to introduce myself and bring you this little gift. It's just some pastry I made. I hope you like it." She handed the small napkin-wrapped offering to Esther.

"Oh, why…how kind of you!" Esther replied, flustered. "I…I don't know what to say. I should be bringing *you* something. After all, you are the family new to the neighborhood."

"It is nothing," Samira said softly. "Just pastry made with honey and nuts."

Hy rested his chin in his hand, unable to conceal the smile on his face or the sparkle that danced in his eyes.

"This is my husband, Hy Greenspan," Esther said, turning to Hy.

Samira walked confidently to him and extended her hand as they exchanged greetings.

"Is there anything you need to help you settle in?" Esther asked, surprised at her own cordiality.

"It is kind of you to ask," the Arab woman answered. "Right now we have our hands full just getting organized."

"Well, be sure to let us know if we can be of any help," Esther said.

"Thank you. I really just wanted to introduce myself. I am sure my husband will come by just as soon as he can. Your son, Noah, has been very kind to my Yusuf. I wanted you to know how much we appreciate that." Samira turned to leave.

"He told us he met your two children," Esther said. "You have a daughter too?"

"Yes. Her name is Alexandra. She is Yusuf's twin sister. They're both eleven years old."

"We look forward to meeting them both," Esther replied, managing a nervous smile.

Then as quickly as Samira Salaman had entered the store, she bid them good-bye and left.

Hy turned to his wife. He did not speak. He smiled, raising his eyebrows playfully as if to ask, "So what do you think of our Arab neighbors now?"

CHAPTER THREE

"Noah, may I have a word with you?" Sharif asked as Noah entered the Crescent Market with Yusuf and Alexandra shortly after noon on a Friday.

"Sure, Mr. Salaman," Noah responded.

Whatever concern the Arab family felt toward Noah had quickly faded away, and Noah now felt entirely comfortable around the Salamans.

"I wanted to ask you about these circulars." Sharif held one of the flyers advertising the weekend's "For You Market Specials" that Noah had distributed throughout the neighborhood the day before.

"Oh sure," Noah answered. "What do you want to know?"

"Where do you deliver these?"

"Everywhere," Noah replied. "I mean all over the neighborhood."

"I see, I see," Sharif said, stroking his goatee. "I was wondering about the prices advertised on the circular. Your father is selling food for less than I can buy it. Look here." He pointed to the circular. "Your father is selling bread for eleven cents a loaf. I pay twelve cents. How can he do that?"

"Oh, that's Mary Jane Bread," Noah said. "That's a CGW brand."

"CGW? I don't understand. What's CGW?"

"CGW stands for the Consolidated Grocers of Washington. They have their own brands that are cheaper than the national brands."

"Your father does not sell the big names?" Sharif Salaman asked.

"Sure, we sell them too," Noah answered. "But CGW has its own warehouse, so they buy wholesale. The members pay what the wholesalers pay. Most of the small grocers have to buy from the wholesalers, so they pay more than the CGW members."

"Noah," Sharif said thoughtfully, "do you know how one becomes a member of this CGW you speak of?"

"Um, no, I really don't," Noah replied honestly. "Why don't you ask my dad?"

"He will not mind?"

"Why would he mind?" Noah shrugged. "He's a very friendly man, Mr. Salaman."

"Of course, of course, I understand that, Noah. It's just that sometimes competitors aren't anxious to help one another."

"The CGW members help each other all the time," Noah replied. "My dad says he could never compete with the chains if it weren't for the CGW."

Sharif Salaman nodded, absent-mindedly stroking his neatly trimmed beard.

"Perhaps I will speak with your father as you suggest," he said somewhat reluctantly.

Noah knew his friend's father was troubled. It had to be very difficult, he thought, losing your home and having to come to a strange neighborhood in a strange country to try a new business.

As he turned to leave, Noah called from the open door, "See you later, Joey."

Sharif smiled and waved half-heartedly as Noah took off toward U Street.

Samira slipped up behind her husband and wrapped her arms around his chest. "What is troubling you?" she asked.

"It is nothing," he murmured.

"I know better," she said, squeezing him gently in her arms. "I heard you from the storeroom. You are reluctant to speak with Noah's father, aren't you?"

"It's not that, Samira. I just don't want to have to ask him for anything."

"Because he is a Jew?"

Sharif Salaman quietly contemplated her question for a moment. *Leave it to Samira to get to the heart of the matter.*

"Is it because he is a Jew?" she pressed. "Is that why you do not want to ask him about this association of small grocers?"

"Samira, I simply do not want to ask anything of them. I bear them no ill will, and I seek no quarrel with them. I just do not want to ask favors of them. I don't want to be beholden to anyone."

"Especially Jews?"

"Especially Jews," he whispered.

Yusuf interrupted them. "Father, here is the telephone number of the Consolidated Grocers of Washington. I found it in the telephone directory. You don't have to ask Mr. Greenspan about belonging if you don't want to. You can just call the CGW yourself."

"Look, Samira," Sharif said, taking the small piece of paper from Yusuf. "We have the number for the grocers' association."

Sharif Salaman was uneasy about the call he was about to make. Samira and Yusuf stood watching him as he gazed at the telephone number.

The door opened, and Alexandra walked into the store from the street.

"Sorry I'm late," she said. "Mrs. Wallach wanted to talk to me about an assignment."

"You're not late at all, Alexandra," Sharif replied. "Samira, why don't you take the children back into the kitchen and fix them something to eat."

"Their lunch is on the table. They—"

"Samira…please!" he interrupted, making clear his desire to be left alone.

Samira, stung by Sharif's rebuke, turned and walked to the living quarters at the rear of the store. Yusuf and Alexandra, aware of the tension, followed their mother.

Sharif studied the telephone number once again. He looked down at the phone next to the old Victor hand-cranked adding machine on the front counter. He sighed apprehensively as he snatched the receiver from the cradle and slowly dialed the number.

"CGW," a thick voice answered.

"Yes. Ah, this is Sharif Salaman calling. I have the Crescent Market at Fourth and Oakdale Northwest, and I am calling to inquire about membership in your organization." Sharif said, irritated by the tightness in his chest and the nervousness evident in his voice.

"Gimme dat name again!"

"Salaman," he repeated.

"You new in the business?"

"Yes, my family has just moved to America," Sharif replied.

"Where ya from?" the thick voice asked.

"Jaffa," Sharif answered softly.

"Jaffa!" the voice shouted excitedly. "You'd be our first member from Israel! Let me be the first from the CGW to welcome you to the business!"

Sharif Salaman closed his eyes and sucked in a deep breath.

"Thank you," he replied, barely above a whisper.

"What? I can't hear you. You still on the line?" the voice asked.

"Yes, yes. I said thank you," Sharif said.

"You Israelis made us proud over here," the voice continued. "Goddamned Arabs wanted every inch for themselves, didn't they?"

"About membership," Sharif pressed.

"Yeah, yeah, shouldn't be no problem. We need every member we can get. Where you located again?"

"Fourth and Oakdale," Sharif answered.

"Hold on a second while I check the map."

Sharif Salaman ran his free hand through his hair as he straightened up and arched his back. At that instant he wanted no part of the CGW and regretted having placed the call.

"Hello, Solomon."

"Yes," Sharif replied, not bothering to correct the man on the other end.

"Listen, we got a little problem. Our bylaws say we can't take a candidate whose business is within a mile of another member without that member's approval. According to our map, we got a member two blocks south of you at Fourth and U. You know the store? It's called the For You Market. Hy Greenspan's place. You know Hy?"

"His son and my boy are schoolmates," Sharif replied matter-of-factly.

"Well, you tell Hy that you spoke to Morrie Berliner from the CGW warehouse. Hy's as good as they come, but this will be a tough one for him. He'd rather cut off his arm than see someone rejected from the CGW, but we never had two members within two blocks of one another. We got plenty whose businesses are within a mile, but two blocks…that's pretty tough."

"Thank you," Sharif replied quietly and slowly placed the receiver back on the cradle.

"What did they say?" Samira asked from the door at the rear of the store where she had been standing, observing her husband's telephone conversation.

Sharif sighed. "We can't join if there is another member within a mile unless that member approves."

"So what will you do?"

"I don't know. I think we should forget about it."

"Why? Perhaps Mr. Greenspan will not mind. You should go to him and ask."

"He will mind, Samira."

"Because you are a competitor?"

"That's part of it."

"There is more?"

"Samira, these grocers are all Jews. You should have heard the man from the CGW when he heard we were from Jaffa. He thought I was a Jew named Solomon. He said Greenspan might let me in when he realized I was from Israel. He said the goddamned Arabs wanted every inch of the place. Can you imagine that, Samira? They think *we* wanted every inch of the place!"

"Sharif, this Mr. Berliner doesn't speak for Mr. Greenspan or anyone else. Maybe Mr. Greenspan hates competitors and maybe he hates Arabs, but the only way you are going to find out is to talk to him."

"I won't grovel before them, Samira. I won't!"

"Before who?" she demanded.

"Before them!" he shouted holding up his clenched fist with the piece of paper containing the CGW telephone number. "I won't grovel before them, not any of them!"

"Sharif, Sharif!" she cried, moving to her husband and embracing him. "Are we going to go through life either hating or fearing Jews? Is that what we are going to teach Alexandra and Yusuf?"

Sharif pulled back just enough to look down into her eyes. He could see the dread she felt in her heart.

"Please, Sharif. I beg you. Do not begin our life here this way."

"Samira, we compete in a tiny area. Greenspan has an advantage over me with this association of his. That's why he joined this association— to have an advantage over the other grocers. Why would he ever share his advantage with me? What do you think he will say when his competitor two blocks away asks him to approve his membership in the very association that gives him the only advantage he has?"

"I have no idea what he will say, Sharif," Samira said, placing a hand gently on her husband's cheek. "I will wait for you to tell me what he says."

CHAPTER FOUR

Hy Greenspan leaned into the stiff wire brush with all his weight, pushing it briskly back and forth over the rough surface of the butcher block and scraping away the blood that the porous wood had absorbed since early morning. He heard the entrance door open and, wiping his hands on his apron, hurried around the refrigerated display case where assorted meat and fish were featured.

"Can I help you?" Hy asked, greeting the stranger with a smile.

"Yes, I am Sharif Salaman," said the visitor haltingly.

Hy could see he was uncomfortable.

"I am Yusuf's father—the children call him Joey—and I believe you met my wife. I wanted to introduce myself to you."

"Mr. Salaman! I'm pleased to meet you. I was hoping you would come by." Hy grasped Sharif Salaman's hand enthusiastically. *So,* he thought, *this is Samira Salaman's husband.*

"I would have come sooner, but we have been so busy trying to get the store organized," Sharif replied with a smile, his nervousness dissipated by Hy's greeting.

"How can we help you, Mr. Salaman?" Hy asked, anxious to put his guest at ease.

"I beg your pardon?"

"How can we be of assistance to you? Is there anything we can do to help you settle into the neighborhood?"

"Well, perhaps…" Sharif said and reached into his apron pocket. "I wanted to ask you about this." He handed Hy a folded copy of the circular Noah had delivered a day earlier.

"Ah yes. My weekend specials. What would you like to know?"

"I don't know about these things, so please tell me if I am being presumptuous…"

"Mr. Salaman, it's all right," Hy replied, growing a bit uncomfortable himself. "What is it you wanted to know?"

"You advertise merchandise at prices lower than I can buy the same items for," Sharif continued, reassured by Hy's friendliness. "I was talking with Noah. He explained about your association with other small grocers."

"You mean the CGW?"

"Yes, that's it, the CGW," Salaman said anxiously. "Noah said you couldn't survive without the CGW."

"Well, I'm not sure I wouldn't survive, but the CGW is very important to my business, yes."

"Without the CGW you wouldn't be able to advertise these low prices on your circular?"

"Well, that's true," Hy agreed. "I wouldn't even be able to afford to print the circular without the CGW. You see, several of us run the same specials, and the printer merely changes the name and telephone number and address at the bottom of the circular. None of us could afford to run a few hundred circulars. Together, we get a price on several thousand."

"I see," Sharif said.

Hy grew more uncomfortable discussing the considerable advantage he had over LeDroit Park's newest corner merchant.

"I suppose it must have been difficult for Mr. Izumi to compete with you," Sharif finally said, breaking the awkward silence.

"I…I don't know," Hy said, not sure where the conversation was headed. "We rarely ever saw the Izumis. There was trouble at the store, and they just closed the doors. But it had nothing to do with the CGW."

"Trouble?" Sharif repeated. "What kind of trouble?"

Hy slowly drew in a deep breath. Apparently no one had told Sharif Salaman why the store he occupied was vacant.

"Nobody said anything to you, then?…About the Izumis, I mean."

"I have no idea what you are talking about," Sharif replied, a puzzled frown tugging at the corners of his mouth.

"Mr. Salaman, there was trouble at Izumi's store. Some hooligans came in and demanded money."

"I see," Sharif said quietly. "Did the Izumis give them the money?"

"Yes, of course they did. But they still…" Hy's voice trailed off.

"There is more?"

"Even after they got the money, the bastards pistol-whipped old man Izumi," Hy answered quietly.

Sharif Salaman's back stiffened ever so slightly, the warmth in his eyes only moments earlier gone. He raised his eyebrows and breathed a sigh of resolve.

"I will buy a gun," he said softly.

"You don't want to do that," Hy replied. "These thugs are experienced, dangerous street toughs. Do you know anything about guns?"

Sharif Salaman smiled. "Mr. Greenspan, let's just say I may get shot someday, but I will never be pistol-whipped."

Hy nodded hesitantly. Who knew what the Salamans had experienced before they left Jaffa?

"Look, I'm sorry I had to be the one to tell you about Izumi," Hy said, trying to steer the conversation away from the violence that had occurred at what was now the Crescent Market.

"You needn't be sorry—I asked. Besides, I didn't really come to discuss Mr. Izumi. About the alliance…"

"Yes, of course," Hy replied. "But I'm afraid I don't really know what else to say about the CGW."

"Perhaps there is nothing to say. You are fortunate to have it."

"It's the only edge I have over my competition."

There was another uncomfortable pause, which Hy hurried to fill. "The CGW's rules allow only one member within a mile of another member. I know that sounds terrible, I mean me saying that to you, but it's the truth."

"Yes, the truth…is what it is," Sharif said, smiling again, recalling his conversation with the buffoon Berliner.

"I don't know what I would do without the CGW," Hy added weakly.

Another small silence ensued, this time broken by Sharif. "Mr. Greenspan?"

"Yes?" Hy replied as the smile faded from Sharif Salaman's face.

"What should I do? I am a farmer. I have grown oranges all my life. I know nothing about running a market."

Hy paused awkwardly, resenting the guilty feeling Sharif Salaman's question imposed. Hy knew perfectly well that he alone could open the CGW to the Arab, and without the CGW, he knew, his new competitor couldn't possibly survive. He had long believed that his own small store would have failed but for the CGW.

"I don't know, Mr. Salaman," he answered softly. "It will be difficult."

Sharif stared at the Jew for a moment. When Hy Greenspan showed no sign of saying anything more on the subject, Sharif simply nodded.

"Well, thank you for taking the time to talk with me."

Hy smiled and nodded back. He did not speak as Sharif Salaman turned and left the store.

***

Samira knew the moment her husband walked through the door that his conversation with the Jewish grocer had not gone well. Sharif went into the storeroom without speaking and emerged a moment later with a broom and began hastily sweeping the floor. He always did something like that when he was angry.

"Mr. Greenspan was not friendly?" Samira asked.

"He was friendly, Samira. He was very friendly," Sharif answered as he continued sweeping. "We talked about the association of grocers. He said he didn't know what he would do without this CGW of his."

"And...?"

"And that their rules allow only one member within a mile of another member," he answered.

"He told you that?"

"Yes, he told me that."

The sarcasm in his voice did not escape Samira. She regretted having urged her husband to meet with Noah's father.

"But what he didn't tell me," Sharif continued, "is that any member can approve the membership of a candidate whose store is within a mile of his store if he chooses to."

"I understand," she whispered.

"Obviously, Mr. Greenspan has no intention of doing that," he said.

"I'm sorry, Sharif. I know you're upset."

"Samira, I'm not upset with Greenspan. He would have to be insane to allow us into this CGW."

"Then why are you angry?"

"I am angry with myself. I had no right putting Greenspan in the position of turning me down," Sharif replied bitterly.

He had stopped sweeping, and Samira saw his knuckles turn white as his grip on the broom tightened.

"Don't you see? Greenspan stood there listening to me make a fool of myself with my childish questions, and when it was all over, he dismissed me with a half truth. It was degrading, Samira. I was degraded by...by..."

"A Jew," she whispered.

Sharif resumed his furious efforts with the broom. He made no effort to contradict her.

***

Hy Greenspan had not a reason in the world to be wrestling with his conscience over his conversation with Sharif Salaman. At least that's what he kept telling himself. Hadn't he joined the CGW to better compete with the other corner grocers in LeDroit Park?

The welcome sound of the phone ringing diverted his attention.

"For You Market," Hy answered, reaching for a pad of paper as he trapped the receiver between his shoulder and ear.

"Hy, is that you?" Morrie Berliner asked.

Hy rolled his eyes and grimaced as he recognized the familiar voice. He had little patience for the swarthy, overweight former grocer. Morrie Berliner had no interests in life whatsoever outside the CGW, and Hy Greenspan, unknowingly affirming Sharif Salaman's assessment of the man, considered him a bit of a buffoon. "Hi, Morrie. What's up?"

"Hy, just wanted to let you know we heard from your new neighbor. I think he said his name was Solomon."

"Salaman," Hy corrected, smiling at Morrie's mistake.

"Anyway," Berliner continued, having missed Hy's correction, "he called to ask about membership in the CGW. I told him we couldn't take two members within one mile of one another. But I figured Solomon being from Jaffa that maybe you'd be willing to make an exception in his case. I mean, I knew you would really feel for one of our own from Israel."

"Morrie, what else did you say to Mr. Salaman?" Hy asked, a feeling of dread suddenly tugging at his gut.

"I didn't say nothin'. I mean, I said we couldn't take a member if we already have a member within a mile. I mean, unless the CGW member says it's OK."

"You told him that?" Hy groaned.

"Yeah, I told him that. For chrissake, Hy, that's what the rules say."

Hy closed his eyes and saw himself standing in front of the meat counter lying to Sharif Salaman who, he realized, had known of his deception the whole time and had said nothing. Hy felt both angry and ashamed.

"Morrie, Salaman has already been to see me. I told him our rules don't allow two members within a mile of one another," Hy said, his voice tinged with frustration.

"But the rules…"

"Morrie, you don't have to lecture me about the rules. I know what the goddamned rules say."

"Hy, I intended to call you before Solomon…"

"Salaman, Morrie! His name is Salaman. I'll spell it for you: S-A-L-A-M-A-N—not Solomon," Hy snapped into the phone.

"What the hell difference does it make how he spells his name, Hy? He's one of ours. You know what those people have been through over there. I thought you would probably want to help the Salamans. I mean, shit, they're Israelis, for chrissake. They're the salt of the earth."

"Did he tell you he was an Israeli, Morrie?" Hy asked.

"Yeah, Hy, I told you he was from Jaffa. Didn't you know that?"

"Yes, Morrie, I knew he was from Jaffa," Hy said with exaggerated patience, as though speaking to a dimwitted child.

"What I asked you was whether or not Mr. Salaman told you he was an Israeli."

"What the hell's wrong with you, Hy?" Berliner responded in genuine confusion. "Don't you know where Jaffa is? For chrissake, there's been a war over there, you know."

"Really, Morrie?" Hy said, fighting to hold back his irritation. "And who's been fighting?"

"You know damn well who's been fightin'. Jews and Arabs, that's who. Don't you even care? This poor Salaman family goes through all that shit and tries to make a new life for themselves here in America, and you're lucky enough to have them two blocks away…"

"Morrie, they're not Israelis!" Hy shouted into the phone.

"Huh?"

"They're Arabs, Morrie! They were on the other side!" Hy wished he could see Morrie Berliner's face at that moment.

There was a brief silence.

"You shittin' me, Greenspan?"

"No, Morrie. I'm not shittin' you," Hy answered, sarcastically. "Mr. Salaman is an Arab from Jaffa." Hy grinned at the ensuing silence and tried to guess what Morrie Berliner's next words would be.

"That fuckin' son-of-a-bitch!" Morrie yelled.

Hy had guessed correctly.

"Hy, I had no idea. So help me, I had no idea!" Morrie insisted.

"I know you didn't, Morrie, but what difference does it make?"

"You know damn well it makes a big difference."

"Why?"

"Why? Because the bastard's an Arab, that's why."

"Morrie, a moment ago he was the salt of the earth. When did he become a bastard and a no-good son-of-a-bitch?"

"You know somethin', Greenspan? I can't figure you out. First, you're upset because I sort of lobbied for this Salaman, and now you're hassling me because I got pissed off when I found out he's an Arab. Just what do you want? I mean, what are you going to do?"

"I'm sorry, Morrie," Hy sighed. He knew he was taking out his anger at himself and his own deceit on the hapless Berliner. "It's just that you put me in an awkward position, and I'm not sure how to get out of it. I have to think."

"What's there to think about? You don't believe an Arab could get into the CGW do you? Especially an Arab that just came over from the fighting?"

"Morrie, thanks for calling," Hy answered, ignoring his question. "Like I said, I have to think."

"Listen, Hy, do me a favor. Let's not say anything about this to any of the other members, OK?"

"Sure, Morrie, it will be our little secret," Hy replied, a touch of sarcasm in his voice.

***

His conversation with the Arab nagged at him.

"What should I do?" the Arab had asked. "I know nothing about running a market."

Even worse, Hy was embarrassed by the way he had answered Salaman.

The CGW had nearly a hundred members, and not one of them would consider, for even a moment, allowing a competitor whose business was only a block or two away into the organization—not one. While true, the reality brought no peace to Hy's troubled conscience.

Around nine o'clock, he walked to the door with the last customer of the evening and flipped over the sign hanging on the door so that it read CLOSED from the outside.

"I'm going out for a breath of fresh air," he yelled as he stepped into the darkness.

Hy walked the few steps to the corner and leaned back against the streetlight, oblivious to the steady flow of traffic making its way through the ghetto toward the white neighborhoods uptown. After all these years, he was all but deaf to the urban roar that rushed by every day. He closed his eyes and let the warm breeze soothe his face.

Is this where we will live out our lives? he wondered, thinking of all the old men he saw every day at the wholesale markets. These men had sacrificed their youth to a lifetime of ninety-five-hour weeks in wretched corner grocery stores not unlike his own. When he opened his eyes, he saw the tiny, pathetic store the Salamans now occupied two blocks to the north.

Poor bastards, he thought, shaking his head. *They'll never make it.* He was still watching a few moments later as the greenish-white fluorescent glow of the Crescent Market flickered out and darkness enveloped the Arab's store.

***

Samira knew her husband needed her that night. His conversation with the Jewish grocer had bruised his ego and depressed his spirits. Sharif was a proud man who had grown up running through the orange groves of Jaffa. His family had planted roots on the Mediterranean coast of Palestine in 1892, the year the railroad linking Jaffa and Jerusalem was completed. They had been drawn to the ancient city known as "The Bride of the Sea" by the promise of the new citrus groves being established throughout the area. Before moving his family to Jaffa,

Sharif's grandfather Ibrahim had been a shepherd on the Judean Hills overlooking the Holy City, as had his father and his father before him. Now, barely a half century later, there were no Salamans in Palestine, and Sharif found himself trapped with his family in the last place on earth he wanted to be. Samira knew her husband hated what had happened to his home and to his land, hated what was happening to him and his family.

Sharif was propped up in bed with the *Washington Post* folded on his lap as he waited for Samira. The unrelenting rumble of traffic on the street below distracted and irritated him. He slapped the paper angrily as a horn blared its insult through the streets of LeDroit Park.

Samira entered the bedroom, her hair wrapped in a towel and her body cloaked in a white terry-cloth robe. She smiled as she walked to the bed and sat facing him, tucking her legs under her body. She pulled the towel from her head and absently rubbed it through her still-damp hair cascading below her shoulders.

"We do not need their association," she said, reaching out and laying her hand on his arm.

Sharif smiled. He reached out and took hold of the lapels of her robe and gently but firmly pulled her toward him. Samira dropped the towel and grabbed his arms to keep from being pulled off balance as their lips met. Sharif held her tightly against his body.

"It will be all right," she whispered.

"We will get out of this place, Samira. I swear to you, we will get out of this place," he murmured, burying his face in his wife's damp, fragrant hair.

"I know, I know," she replied.

"We must find a way to tolerate this existence in the meantime."

"We will tolerate this place as long as we have to," she answered confidently.

"We will, will we?" he said, smiling at his wife's fierce determination. "And what will make the intolerable tolerable?"

Samira lay with her head resting against Sharif's chest for a moment, listening to the steady, soothing pulse of his heartbeat. Then she looked up at her husband and smiled sensuously. Slowly, seductively, she pulled back the sheet that covered the lower half of his body. Sharif's eyes softened as his wife rose to her knees and then straddled his legs. Moving almost hypnotically, her eyes still probing his, Samira pulled loose the cloth belt that held her robe closed. With a graceful twist of her shoulders, the robe fell away, baring her naked and inviting body.

Moments later, Sharif lay with his head thrust back against the pillows, his eyes closed, as Samira summoned him to a fleeting respite in a utopia far, far from the grime and noise of the streets below.

CHAPTER FIVE

Over breakfast, Noah listened intently as his parents discussed the conversation Hy had had with Sharif Salaman the day before.

"What are you going to do, Hy, invite a competitor two blocks away into the CGW?" Esther asked, exasperation in her voice. "Why not invite Rosenblum from Fourth and T and Parks from Fourth and Elm to join too? They're struggling just like the Salamans."

"It's not the same, and you know it," Hy replied impatiently.

"No, Hy. I don't know it. I mean, why isn't it exactly the same?"

Hy Greenspan looked at his wife as he groped for an answer. He really wasn't sure why the visit from the Arab haunted him so.

"They're refugees, Mom," Noah interjected. "They lost their home and their family over in Palestine."

"Noah, I know all of that, and I am sorry for them, but what does that have to do with us? I mean, we're struggling too. There is no one to look out for us either. The CGW helps us survive by helping our tiny business attract a few extra customers a day. No one allows a competitor into the CGW whose business is as close as the Salamans' business is to ours, Noah. No one."

Noah stared down into his cereal, aimlessly scooping up milk with his spoon and spilling it back into his bowl. Hy looked at Noah for a moment, then glanced at his wife and shrugged.

"Haven't you ever been alone, Mom?" Noah asked. "I mean really alone like they are?"

Suddenly, Esther Greenspan's eyes filled with tears. "What?" she asked, shaken by his question.

"I asked if you knew what it was like to really be alone like the Salamans are."

While there may have been a lot Esther Greenspan had never experienced, she did know loneliness. It had been the ever-present companion of her youth.

"Yes, Noah. I have known loneliness," she replied in a soft voice. And there was no more debate on the matter.

***

Hy Greenspan had never visited the tiny grocery store when the Izumis owned it. He was surprised to see how small the Salamans' store was compared with his own. *It's half again as small as our place,* he thought as he walked through the door. The wooden floorboards creaked under his weight as he moved to the center of the empty store.

"Anybody home?" he called.

"Mr. Greenspan! What a pleasant surprise," Samira said, rushing into the store. "Welcome to the Crescent Market."

"Thank you. Thank you very much. Is Mr. Salaman here?"

"He's downstairs in the basement. He thinks a fuse needs to be replaced," she replied.

"Well, get used to it," Hy chuckled. "Something always has to be replaced in these old buildings."

"Sharif told me about his conversation with you. I'm pleased the two of you had a chance to meet," she said. "He really is worried. He knows nothing about being a merchant."

"It has become a difficult business, Mrs. Salaman. The chains are almost impossible to compete with."

"The chains? I don't understand."

Hy smiled and nodded sympathetically. "I'm sorry. I meant the big companies that own many stores all over town. They're opening in every neighborhood, and they have a hundred times the merchandise we do, all of which they sell at discount prices. You know the word discount?"

"You mean cheap prices?" she asked. "Noah explained to us how your association allows you to compete with these...these..."

"Chains," he offered with a smile.

"It is a strange word," Samira answered.

Hy's smile broadened as he nodded his agreement. He looked into her eyes for a moment without speaking. *She's beautiful*, he thought.

"Ah, Mr. Greenspan!" Sharif Salaman exclaimed as he climbed to the top of the basement stairs and entered the store. "To what do we owe this pleasure?"

"Mr. Salaman...I was not as...as..."

"Yes, Mr. Greenspan?"

"Mr. Salaman, I was not entirely candid with you yesterday. I thought we should talk some more."

"I see," Sharif answered. "Well, please, go on. What did you want to talk about?"

"The CGW," Hy replied.

"Ah, the CGW," Sharif said knowingly. "Well, Mr. Greenspan, you needn't explain. I understand the rules, and I understand the reason why the rules are as they are. I even told Samira I thought you would have to be crazy to let us into this CGW."

"I can't *let* you in, as you say. I can keep you out, but only a majority of the members can let you or any other candidate in. What the association's bylaws give me and every other member is the right to veto any candidate for membership whose store is within a mile of their own store."

"I understand," Sharif replied in a soft but serious voice. "Forgive me if this sounds impertinent, but surely you didn't come here this morning merely to explain the CGW's bylaws to me."

"No, of course not. I came to tell you that I would not veto your membership. In fact, I will sponsor your membership if you would like to apply to the CGW," Hy said.

"Sharif!" Samira cried out excitedly.

Hy looked from Samira to Sharif before continuing. "It will be difficult…maybe even unpleasant, Mr. Salaman. I want you to understand that."

"Sharif, this is…"

"Why are you doing this, Mr. Greenspan?" Sharif asked abruptly, cutting off Samira midsentence.

"You are going to fail on this corner, Mr. Salaman, without the CGW. With it, you have a chance."

"But isn't that the very purpose of the CGW?" Sharif asked. "To give its members an advantage over the competition?"

"Yes, it is," Hy replied. "That's its only purpose."

"So, again, I ask you. Why are you doing this?"

Samira waited breathlessly for Hy's response.

"We don't want to see you fail," Hy answered. "We know things have been difficult for you. There isn't a great deal we can do to help, but I'll be damned if I am going to deny you the only chance you have of making a go of it."

"And the other members of this CGW?" Sharif asked. "They will feel the same way too?"

Hy looked down at the tired old hardwood floor and then, after a moment, shook his head.

"No, I wouldn't say the others would feel that way."

"They would rather keep us out?"

"Probably," Hy answered candidly.

"But why?" Samira asked. "We do not compete with any member other than you."

"No one will resent you as competitors, Mrs. Salaman."

"But they will resent us as Arabs—is that it, Mr. Greenspan?" Sharif asked bitterly.

Hy nodded. "Yes, I think some will. At least at first anyway."

Sharif glanced at Samira, his cynical smile sending chills down her spine.

"Listen, Mr. Salaman, before you jump to any conclusions, let me tell you a little bit about the CGW," Hy said, sensing the rebuff that was about to roll off Sharif 's tongue. "The membership is almost entirely Jewish, probably ninety percent anyway. Every Jewish member of the CGW lost family during the last World War. Most of the men fought in Europe, and many of them saw unspeakable suffering. They know but for the grace of God, those zombies that walked from the death camps could have been their families, their children, their brothers and sisters. Some were. Many of them now have people in Israel. You hear stories how relatives they presumed had perished suddenly turned up in Palestine. Obviously, all of us have strong feelings for Israel, Mr. Salaman. Her survival is the only thing some Jews ever think about."

"And so they will recoil at the thought of a Palestinian Arab in their midst. Is that it, Mr. Greenspan?"

"Some may, yes. But mostly I think they will be, well…uncomfortable. It will take a little time and, if we're lucky, some simple reasoning."

"And how will you reason with them, Mr. Greenspan?"

"Well, I don't really know. I guess I'll tell them that you're no different than they are. That you're struggling to make a living and that you bear no hard feelings toward Jews. I'll tell them that you're a refugee just as most of them were, and that you're here, not over there making trouble."

"But that wouldn't be true, Mr. Greenspan," Sharif said with slow deliberation.

"Sharif…"

The Arab again silenced his wife with the wave of a hand. "It simply wouldn't be true, you see."

"I don't understand," Hy responded, taken aback.

"We are different, Mr. Greenspan. We are very different. I am not, as they were, a refugee," he said, all but spitting out the word. "Those people rejoiced when they escaped from lands in which they were threatened. We didn't choose to leave. I loved my home in Jaffa, and I dream of the day I will return to Palestine." Sharif drew out the word

Palestine for emphasis. "And, Mr. Greenspan, I detest the people who drove us from our home. The Salamans had been in Palestine since the time of Sultan Suleiman at the beginning of the sixteenth century. My immediate family had been in Jaffa since eighteen ninety-two. I do have hard feelings toward the people who drove us away. *This*, Mr. Greenspan," he said, waving his hand through the air in disgust, "this is not my home. It will never be my home."

Hy stood speechless for a moment as the Arab's words sank in. "And do you detest me?" he asked, barely above a whisper.

"No, Mr. Greenspan. I do not detest you. You are a decent man, and your family has been very thoughtful. Noah is a fine boy because he is the son of fine parents. You are always welcome in our home."

"We feel the same way, Mr. Salaman. Life will be difficult enough for you here. We do not want to be the source of any unhappiness."

"But we must also be realistic," Sharif responded. "You are who you are, they are who they are, and we are who we are. You and they are Jews, Mr. Greenspan. I am an Arab. I do not see the world as you see it, and my sympathies, at least where Palestine is concerned, will always be poles apart from yours."

"Perhaps we each have a little to learn about the other's points of view," Hy replied. "Meanwhile, I would like to sponsor your membership in the CGW. What do you say?"

"You say I will fail without the CGW. What do I have to lose?" Sharif said, smiling for the first time since Hy entered the store.

"You have nothing to lose, and I have an idea how we can both come out ahead."

"I'm listening," Sharif replied.

"Look, think of Elm Street, which is a block south of you and a block north of me as a line dividing LeDroit Park between north and south. Suppose I only promoted my weekly specials in the area south of Elm and you delivered the identical weekly specials circular to all the homes in LeDroit Park north of Elm Street—except your circular would have Crescent Market and your phone number at the top. We could each concentrate our efforts in a more condensed area. I wouldn't have to deliver all the way up to Howard University anymore, and you wouldn't have to run all the way down to Florida Avenue. If someone called me from your side of Elm Street to place an order, I'd refer them to you, and you could do the same when anyone calls you from south of Elm Street. We could each do twice the number of deliveries in the same amount of time. We'd both benefit."

Blithely oblivious to antitrust laws and with businesses too minuscule for the antitrust people to care about, the two corner grocers innocently conspired to improve their respective businesses.

Hy extended his hand to Sharif. Samira, choked with emotion, watched as the two men shook hands.

***

Sharif's application was approved at the next scheduled meeting of the CGW, making him the eighty-fifth member of the previously all-Jewish Consolidated Grocers of Washington. It hadn't been as difficult as Hy had anticipated. He asked, just before the vote was taken, for every member who would experience competition from Sharif Salaman's Crescent Market to raise his hand. Of course no one did. Hy told them that if their hands weren't raised then, they shouldn't be raised at all in opposition to Sharif—after all, he was the only member of the CGW Sharif Salaman could possibly hurt.

CHAPTER SIX

Having opened the CGW to the Salamans, Hy Greenspan quickly schooled Sharif in making the most of his membership. He shared whatever insight he had into the shopping preferences of the people of LeDroit Park and invited his Arab competitor to join him on his morning buying trips to the CGW's warehouse. Hy pointed out to Sharif which produce his customers favored, which fish they preferred, and the most popular cuts of beef and pork.

Sharif Salaman's Crescent Market would not have survived that first year had it not been for Hy Greenspan. The intense resentment Sharif had brought with him to America slowly began to subside, and he began to think as much about the life he and his family might build in this new land as he did about all they had lost in Palestine. For that, he was grateful.

Hy and Sharif soon began to enjoy the time they spent together pursuing the business arrangement they had created. A real friendship slowly developed that neither of them had sought or anticipated. A similar bond quickly evolved between Esther and Samira. Esther, despite her initial reticence, was slowly won over by Samira. Her strong reservations about a Palestinian Arab neighbor in LeDroit Park diminished and then simply disappeared.

Meanwhile, Yusuf and Noah formed a solid friendship of their own. As with their parents, their relationship at first evolved out of necessity, since the two boys were the only N. P. Gage students who lived in the LeDroit Park ghetto. But beyond the ease of proximity,

Noah and Yusuf found they shared common interests. Walking to and from school together became a daily routine, and they made almost nightly telephone calls to share whatever one had heard or read that he thought might be of interest to the other.

They even shared that great moment together in the bleachers at Griffith Stadium when Mickey Grasso completed a triple play at home plate for the Washington Senators. It was Yusuf's first baseball game when the Senators' right fielder Bud Stewart made that sensational catch of Jerry Coleman's line drive to right field and fired the ball to Eddie Robinson at first base, who caught Yankee Phil Rizzuto trapped between first and second and then fired the ball to Washington's rookie catcher, Mickey Grasso, who tagged out Fred Sanford trying to score from third base. It was all over in less than ten seconds, and it made an instant fan of the Palestinian youngster.

Both boys, hoarse from screaming, made their way home after the game.

"So, you guys coming to my bar mitzvah?" Noah asked.

"What, are you kidding?" Yusuf said, his face deadpan. "Four Palestinian Arab Christians? If we weren't in synagogue, where would we be?"

Despite Yusuf's lighthearted answer, the Greenspans' invitation to Noah's bar mitzvah had caused the Salamans more than a little concern. They were uneasy at the prospect of participating in a religious service where only Jews would be present, but there was no doubt they would join the Greenspan family at the synagogue. The invitation was, they knew, recognition of the warm relationship the two families had developed.

***

The Greenspans warmly greeted the Salaman family at the entrance of the old house of prayer on I Street, just two blocks from the Seventh Street corridor, a rundown retail section of the city no more than a half-mile from the nation's Capitol.

The synagogue reminded Sharif of a scaled-down version of the Basilica of the Holy Sepulcher in the Old City of Jerusalem. Built late in the nineteenth century, Ohev Shalom hinted at the majesty of Europe's grand old synagogues, with its domed roof sheltering a large sanctuary where muted sunshine streamed through stained-glass windows. The place exuded warmth amid the hodgepodge of deteriorating dwellings and the hustle and bustle of automobiles and trucks racing east and west along nearby New York Avenue. A neighboring shelter festooned with a bright-red neon sign proclaiming "Jesus Saves" stood immediately adjacent to the synagogue around the corner on Fifth Street.

Inside, subdued incandescent lighting warmly illuminated the cream-colored plaster walls. From the entry to the sanctuary, Sharif observed a lighted candle flickering in a red, flamed-shaped glass lantern hanging from the ceiling. The candlelight accentuated the immense ark that dominated the bimah from which the service would be conducted.

"It's the eternal flame," Hy said, noticing the direction of Sharif's gaze. "It is never extinguished. It is a symbol of hope, even during the worst adversity."

"It's lovely," Sharif replied softly.

Hy, draped in a white-and blue-striped prayer shawl, handed Yusuf and Sharif the traditional yarmulkes. Father and son looked uneasily at the skullcaps.

"We always cover our heads when in synagogue," Hy said, his hand still outstretched. "It's our way of showing respect to God." Sympathetic to their discomfort, Hy added with a nervous smile, "The orthodox cover their heads all day long."

Sharif hesitated another moment, then nodded his understanding and placed the skullcap on his head. Yusuf, no less uncomfortable, did the same.

Relieved, Hy ushered Sharif and Yusuf into the sanctuary to join Noah. They took their seats in the front row before the ark, which held the ancient holy scrolls comprising the first five books of the Old Testament.

As Samira and Alexandra moved to follow them, Esther slipped her arms around their shoulders and instead motioned them toward the stairs leading to the balcony.

"The women sit separately from the men," she explained. "We're not supposed to be a distraction."

Seated between her mother and Noah's mother, Alexandra surveyed the scene below. It was a curious sight. Men and boys were deep in prayer, bobbing and weaving to their own rhythm, some chanting aloud, some moving their lips silently, some with eyes open and transfixed on the prayer books they held, some in deep concentration with eyes closed. An older man stood on the bimah in front of the congregation, leading the chanting worshipers. Few, it seemed, were paying any particular attention to the man as they prayed, often aloud, at their own pace. Alexandra at first found the service a confusing jumble, with some congregants standing in somber prayer next to others almost convulsive in their entreaties to the Almighty. Finally, after what seemed an eternity of nonstop and, to the Salamans, completely unintelligible communal worship, Hy and two other men were called in succession to the bimah for their aliyah, or the honor of reciting the Birachu, which declares the blessedness of the Lord.

Alexandra inched to the edge of her seat for a clearer view as Noah was called to the huge podium. She watched as he stood and without hesitation made his way onto the bimah. As he shook hands with the cantor and the rabbi and turned to face the congregation, Alexandra felt an odd sense of bewilderment. *This is Noah*, she thought. *This is Yusuf's friend Noah.* Somehow the handsome young man she saw standing so confidently before the congregation seemed quite different from the boy she knew from school.

Although Noah was dwarfed by the men standing around him and the great and imposing ark housing the scrolls, which towered over the bimah, he betrayed no fear or hesitation when he took a slow, deliberate breath and then chanted the same prayer his father and the other men had recited moments earlier. Noah, she thought, seemed to deliver the words with a more practiced ease and a more even intonation than had the older men before him. Then he picked up an ornate, silver pointer and peered down at the Torah scroll that lay open before him.

He took the corner of his prayer shawl and touched it to the parchment of the Torah, then brought it to his lips and kissed the material. As Noah recited from the Torah, the men standing around him at the podium read along with him silently and respectfully, one or another occasionally nodding approvingly at Noah's mastery of the text. Noah chanted these verses from the Hebrew bible just as Jewish boys had done for thousands of years—as Jesus had done one afternoon in the Holy Land on a day still recognized as sacred by some Christians. Despite his youth, Noah managed to chant the ancient words like a seasoned yeshiva student. From her vantage point in the balcony, Alexandra could see her father and Yusuf sitting below, watching, obviously fascinated.

So this is what's been taking all his time lately, Yusuf was thinking as Noah continued to chant flawlessly. Although Noah had explained to his friend that bar mitzvah symbolized a Jewish boy's emergence as a man, an adult with adult responsibilities to his faith, Yusuf, like Alexandra, now understood that they were observing more than mere ritual. It was as though they were watching Noah transform from the boy he was to the man he would become. Thirteen-year-old Noah stood there as an equal among the men around him and those sitting in the sanctuary, many in rapt attentiveness as he continued chanting the week's Torah portion. This was a Noah Greenspan Yusuf hadn't known before—accomplished, mature, commanding the respect of men many times his age.

When Noah finally finished, he shook hands with those around him; then he and his father walked the few steps to the high-backed chairs positioned at the back of the bimah and sat down among the synagogue's clergy and the elders of the congregation.

Noah looked up and perused the sanctuary. He gave a slight nod of recognition to Sharif and Yusuf. Then he raised his eyes to the balcony. It was the first time he saw Alexandra sitting between Samira and Esther. It was also the first time he saw Alexandra as the attractive, lovely young woman she had become, a youthful version of her mother. His eyes locked on hers, and his face surrendered a faint smile.

In the balcony, Esther returned her son's smile until she realized it was not directed at her. Her smile faltering, Esther followed the direction of Noah's gaze to Alexandra. The young girl's face seemed alight in response to Noah's attention, and Esther also was struck for the first time by the girl's blossoming beauty and maturity. When she turned her face back to her son, her tears were of both joy and foreboding.

At the conclusion of the Torah service, the rabbi rose and offered his congratulations to Noah, then turned to address the congregation.

"Our Torah portion this week commemorates the arrival of B'nei Yisrael, the Nation of Israel, at Mount Sinai. It is at this place and it is at this time that God gave to Moses the Ten Commandments. This is the moment our history really begins. This is the moment that our people were forever joined to the quest of establishing the Land of Israel. It is only the third month of the exodus from Egypt and it is the day our ancestors arrived at the Wilderness of Sinai. Arguably, this is the moment from which all the great Western religions sprang. While it is true that we, along with those of the Muslim faith, trace our beginnings to Abraham, this is the moment that we became the people of the book. This is the moment we became *the chosen*. This is the moment that God commanded us to become a light unto the nations of the world. This is the moment the Western world's great religions have looked to for guidance, and they have continued to look centuries after God revealed his word to our forbears at Sinai."

Sharif and Yusuf, two Palestinian Arabs sitting among the congregation of Jews, were riveted on the tall, bearded rabbi as he continued.

"It has not been easy being a light unto the world. Others have tried to extinguish that light time and time again. We have been conquered, vanquished, enslaved, and nearly annihilated over the millennia. But always we came back. We remained faithful throughout the ages to the land God promised us at Sinai. Never has there been a time when Jews have not dwelled in the Holy Land. God willing, never will there be such a time."

At these words, Yusuf stiffened. He thought of all that he and his family had been forced to leave behind so that Jews might fulfill this promise they felt they were given. And what of the Salamans and all the others displaced by this promise? What were they owed in return? With fire in his eyes, Yusuf glanced up at his father, expecting to see his own anger reflected there. But as Sharif turned his face toward his son, Yusuf saw not anger, but rather an unexpected gentleness softening his gaze. Yusuf's anger turned to puzzlement. As though to answer his son's unspoken question, Sharif glanced at the congregants around him, who were all absorbed in the rabbi's words. His gaze touched on Hy, moved to Noah, then finally returned to his son's troubled face. Yusuf looked thoughtfully into his father's eyes. The resigned expression he saw there lessened the anger in his own heart. In its place a germ of understanding was born. Smiling sympathetically at his father, Yusuf nodded ever so slightly. These people were not the enemy; every struggle had a context. A lesson had been taught and learned without a word being spoken.

The rabbi turned and gestured to Noah that his time had come to address the congregation. Noah rose and walked confidently to the massive podium. Though this was the first time Noah had ever spoken in front of a large audience, he felt oddly at ease.

His parents, from their differing vantage points in the synagogue, were prouder than they could ever have believed possible.

Noah began, as all bar mitzvah boys do, by thanking the rabbi for teaching him about Torah and thanking his parents for their love and support. He then turned his attention to his Torah portion and spoke of the simple eloquence of the Ten Commandments.

"Has any people given the world a greater gift than the Jews did when they brought the Ten Commandments out of Sinai?" he began. "These commandments are the basis for the civilized world's most important laws and the ethic that we know as the Golden Rule; to love others as you love yourself, to treat others as you would like to be treated, is the basis for ethical behavior everywhere.

"So how are we doing?" he continued. "Well, the daily news headlines seem to answer that question every day. We're not doing so well. In our time—in fact just in the thirteen years that I've been alive—we have seen Nazis, Klansmen, and other bigots. We read about apartheid abroad, Jim Crow at home, and an endless array of 'isms' all over the world, all committed to the hatred of someone, somewhere. Our language is full of words like nigger, kike, spic, wop, and chink. Today people are killing one another in Korea, North Africa, the Middle East, Greece, and the Straits of Formosa. All of this hatred—all because of fear and distrust of people who are different, people who are strangers, people whose beliefs and customs are different. Maybe my generation can return some of the luster to the Golden Rule. Mankind has tarnished it long enough." Noah glanced up at his audience and paused for just a moment. "Thank you," he concluded and returned to his seat.

⁂

The reception after Noah's bar mitzvah was held in the synagogue's small, drab, and tired social hall. The celebration was simple and inexpensive—nothing like the more lavish parties Jewish parents in the tony uptown neighborhoods threw for their sons. There was an assortment of delicatessen potato salad and coleslaw, pastry, and coffee for the adults and punch for the children and teenagers. That was it.

The guests gathered around Noah with their congratulatory compliments. As he stood shaking hands with members of the congregation, almost none of whom he knew, he spotted Alexandra standing off to the side with Yusuf and her parents. He became momentarily oblivious to well-wishers crowded around him as his gaze fixed on her. It was as though he had never seen her before. Had she always been this beautiful? How could he have been so near to her for so long and yet so distant—until this day?

Noah followed his parents over to the Salamans. He shook hands with Sharif and accepted a kiss on the cheek from Samira. He and Yusuf briefly embraced, and then Noah turned to Alexandra.

"Thanks for coming," he finally managed after a moment's hesitation. He had just addressed an entire congregation without skipping a beat. Yet now, with Alexandra, he felt embarrassingly tongue-tied.

"Thank you for inviting us," Alexandra responded, more calmly than she felt. She looked into his eyes, lingering for an extra moment. "I…I thought you were wonderful," she added.

"Thanks again," Noah said, his eyes still fixed on hers.

The eagerness of their brief exchange was not lost on either Esther or Samira, and the two women glanced knowingly at one another. They smiled nervously at Noah's sudden awareness of Alexandra's emergence as an attractive young woman and at Alexandra's newfound attraction to Noah. The implications sent a shiver through Samira's bones.

***

That evening, as Esther sat at her dressing table absently pulling a brush through her shoulder-length hair, she thought about Noah and Alexandra. She glanced in the mirror at the image of her husband propped up in their bed waiting for her, but her thoughts were of Noah, who was by now fast asleep.

"What did you think of the kids' behavior today?" Esther asked as she studied Hy through the mirror.

"You mean Noah and Alexandra?"

She nodded. "Yes. It was as though Noah suddenly discovered that Yusuf had an attractive sister. Did you notice?"

"I was waiting for that question." Hy laughed, locking his hands behind his head. "I think it's great. Alexandra is a delightful child. Let's not make a big deal over it. The fact that Noah couldn't take his eyes off of her doesn't mean they're getting married."

"Oh, thanks for clearing that up for me, Hy," she replied sarcastically. "I thought Noah and Alexandra had become engaged."

"Well, just what are you concerned about, Es?"

"I think Noah is at an age where his friendships will be more important—you know, more lasting."

"So?"

"So, don't you think it would be nice if he had some Jewish friends too?"

"He has Jewish friends. You saw all the kids who showed up today."

"They're not friends, Hy. They're Hebrew school classmates. He has no interest in them at all outside of Hebrew school.

"Es, his friends are nice kids. I've never heard of any trouble or problems with any of them, and I consider him lucky as hell to have those Salaman kids two blocks away."

"I do too. You know that. But before long, Noah is going to be dating, and there is almost no chance for him to get to know any Jewish girls, let alone date any."

"Someday he'll go away to college, God willing," Hy replied. "There will be plenty of time for him to meet Jewish girls then."

"His dating habits will be established long before he goes away to school, Hy," Esther answered, turning around to face her husband. "And it's not only *that*. It's this neighborhood too. Every time Noah walks out that door, I'm afraid until I see him safely home again. Have you forgotten what happened to the Izumis?"

"Es, what in the hell do you want to do about it?" Hy asked, a touch of anger in his voice. "What in the hell do you think we can do about it? This is where we live and where we earn a living. I'd love to be in some other business and live up on Sixteenth Street or in Shepherd Park somewhere, but this is probably where we are going to be for a long time, Es. It's not ideal, but we make a living, I'm my own boss, and we have a damn fine boy."

Esther looked at Hy for several moments and then lowered her eyes to her hands, which she held clasped together in her lap. "We don't belong here, Hy. This is no place for Noah to grow up." She lifted her eyes to meet his once again.

"Noah is doing fine, damn it!"

"He deserves better."

"We can't afford better!" Hy snapped, raising his voice for the first time. "We make a living, but we can't afford to pay rent here and pay rent somewhere else too. Maybe someday we can try another business, but that's years away from now, Es. We can make the most of what we have…or we can eat our hearts out."

"Please, Hy. Don't get upset with me. I want what's best for Noah, that's all."

"We both want what's best for Noah, and we're giving him the best we can with what we have. Es, that boy isn't going to suffer because of where his home is. We've made a good home for him, and someday he'll appreciate his accomplishments all the more because he'll remember growing up over a tiny grocery store in LeDroit Park. You'll see."

She smiled. "He is a good boy, isn't he? I was so proud of him today."

"He's a wonderful boy, and he hasn't done anything to cause us to complicate his life."

"I know that, Hy, and I know that Alexandra and Yusuf are fine kids too. It's just that…"

"What?"

"You mark my words, Noah's attraction to Alexandra is going to develop into something more than friendship someday soon."

"And that bothers you?"

"It worries me. I don't want to see either of those kids hurt. There's going to be a lot of pain in their relationship if it ever turns serious."

"You know, Es, earlier this evening at the reception I could have sworn I heard you saying something about how our two families are proof that people can be above politics. I was really impressed, but it was really all *meshuggaas*, wasn't it? You were saying it because it sounded good, not because you believed it."

"That's not fair. It wasn't foolishness at all," she replied, a hint of anger in her voice. "I was talking about our relationship as two families. We have a wonderful relationship with the Salamans, and it has been above politics. I would think having them at Noah's bar mitzvah today would be proof enough of that."

"But you want to draw the line at having our kids have too good a relationship. Is that it?"

"Are you oblivious to what could happen between Noah and Alexandra? Hy, they're not just Arabs—they're Christians too."

"Are you oblivious to what could happen if we try to manage and manipulate those kids and whatever relationship—as you call it—they might develop?" he countered.

"What are you talking about?"

"You want to guarantee something special between them? Well, just interfere, Es. You'll wind up strengthening their relationship and weakening our own relationship with our son, that's what you'll accomplish."

"Hy Greenspan, I don't understand you. You'd stand by and let those kids start down a path that can't lead anywhere but to heartache?"

"I won't concede that it can't lead anywhere but to heartache, but, in answer to your question, yes! I would trust those two kids to handle whatever they had to contend with on that path, heartache and all. Noah isn't going to meet any Jewish girls around here, and if he is going to have a girlfriend where he goes to school, you tell me where he could find a lovelier girl to be friends with."

"I wonder," she mused, suddenly changing the subject, "what the Salamans have been talking about tonight?"

∗∗∗

Samira and Sharif turned off the lamps on either side of their bed at about the same time the Greenspans darkened their room. Samira knew her husband had seen Noah's preoccupation with Alexandra that day and that the implications would weigh heavily on him. She waited for him to say something, to give her an opening to reassure him. But Sharif Salaman said nothing. He simply drifted off into rest-less slumber.

***

Noah, wide awake in the darkness, stared at the ceiling, oblivious to the deep concern his attraction to Alexandra had caused his—and her—parents. Despite his rite of passage that day, his thoughts were not of his accomplishments but of Alexandra and her blossoming adolescent sensuality. The more he thought about her, the more intense was the strange sensation that seemed to glow within him, energizing his body with anticipation and an inner tension he had never experienced before. Noah couldn't wait until morning when he would meet his friends at Fourth and Oakdale. But for the first time, it was Alexandra, not Yusuf, who Noah most looked forward to seeing.

CHAPTER SEVEN

By the time Noah and Yusuf began junior high school in 1951, American troops had spent their second wretched summer bogged down in Korea defending the Pusan Perimeter, and the nation was preoccupied with the Far East. Even the *Education Weekly*, which was distributed in seventh-grade civics and history classes, was filled with references to the Yalu River and the Thirty-Eighth Parallel and Formosa and to Chinese artillery pounding deserted Quemoy and Matsu and the Pescadores Islands. When news from the Middle East found its way into the classroom, photographs of Israeli farmers plowing their fields, rifles at the ready, were not uncommon, nor were the numerous references to Israel as the land of milk and honey and the place where pioneers were making the desert bloom.

Noah and Yusuf often studied together after dinner, alternating between the Greenspan and Salaman homes. Noah liked studying with Yusuf at the Salaman home, mostly because Alexandra would often join them.

One evening after Yusuf and Noah had finished quizzing each other on a Spanish assignment, Yusuf suggested they review the week's *Education Weekly* since a quiz on its contents was likely.

Both boys hunched over the newspaper after Noah spread it out on the floor. As they read, Alexandra came in. She peered down, steadying herself by leaning on Noah's shoulders.

"What is it?" she asked.

"It's the *Education Weekly*," Noah answered, acutely aware of the pleasant pressure of her hands on his shoulders, her breath softly brushing the back of his neck. "Want to join us?"

"No. It looks boring," she replied, continuing to lean on his shoulders. "What's it about?"

"I don't know," Noah answered. "I haven't really gotten into it yet."

"It's trash!" Yusuf suddenly burst out angrily. He got to his feet and scooped up the paper. "It's Zionist trash!" he shouted and crumpled it into a ball.

"Hey! What are you doing?" Noah cried out, stunned by Yusuf's sudden change in behavior.

"I'm throwing out the trash. That's what I'm doing," Yusuf snapped back.

"Hey, that's mine!" Noah leaped up and tried to grab the paper. "Come on, cut that out!"

"Yusuf, are you crazy?" Alexandra cried. "Give Noah back his paper."

"You want the paper? Here, take your fucking paper!" Yusuf yelled, and hurled the balled and torn tabloid at Noah.

"Joey! What the hell's wrong with you?" Noah asked as the crumpled paper bounced off his hands.

"What's going on in here? What's happening?" Samira demanded as she rushed into the room from the kitchen. Noah stood staring angrily at Yusuf.

"Yusuf, what's wrong with you?" Samira demanded once again.

The boy, red-faced and angry, just looked at his mother defiantly.

"Yusuf! I asked you a question. What's wrong with you?"

"Shit!" he murmured under his breath and stalked past her out of the room.

Samira, Alexandra, and Noah stared at one another in shocked silence. Then Noah looked down at the crumpled tabloid he'd picked up and slowly opened the paper. A moment later, he closed his eyes knowingly. He turned to Samira and Alexandra, almost apologetically, and handed them the paper. They looked at the lead feature.

The photograph showed rows and rows of orange trees heavily laden with fruit. Under the three-column half-tone appeared the week's main story:

JEWS' EFFICIENCY RESTORES LAND AFTER CENTURIES OF ARAB NEGLECT

Jewish settlers have performed a modern–day miracle throughout the ancient land of Israel by restoring thousands of acres of barren wasteland into one the most fertile regions in the entire Middle East. Experts from the United States Department of Agriculture, concluding a recent tour of Israeli citrus groves, called the progress made by the fledgling mini state "absolutely astounding" and said even the United States could learn from the experience of the Israelis.

"By comparing what the Jews have accomplished here in three years to what the Arab peasants accomplished here over a period of three hundred years, we see what determination and respect for the land can mean," said Dr. Raymond Lassiter, Associate Director of Research at the USDA experimental farm in Beltsville, Maryland.

The story jumped to the inside of the paper and went on to praise the accomplishments of the Israelis. Other than one scant mention of the need for the Jewish farmers to carry weapons to protect themselves against periodic attacks by dissident Palestinians, virtually nothing in the article suggested any Arab presence in the land at all.

"Noah, I'm sorry this happened," Samira said. "I hope you realize this had nothing to do with you personally. Yusuf still has hard feelings about what has happened in Palestine."

"Momma, it was stupid," Alexandra said. "You should have seen Yusuf. He behaved horribly. He had no right to take out his feelings on Noah."

"I'll talk with him," Samira said wearily.

Noah nodded and knelt to put his books back into his book bag.

"Noah, you don't have to go," Alexandra said. "I can quiz you on your homework."

He got to his feet. "May I have the paper back, please?" he asked, extending his hand toward Samira.

"What? Oh, yes, of course," she answered, handing him the badly creased *Education Weekly.* "Please don't be upset with Yusuf, Noah," she added, almost pleadingly. "You must understand that this has nothing to do with you."

"Yes it does, Mrs. Salaman," Noah replied, walking toward the door. "It has a lot to do with me. I'm proud of what the Jews have accomplished in Israel. They should be left in peace."

Samira closed her eyes as Noah disappeared through the door.

"Oh, I could kill Yusuf!" Alexandra said tearfully.

Samira turned, confronting her daughter. "Don't you ever say that again, Alexandra!" she said, glaring at her. "Not about Yusuf or any other member of this family!"

"Yusuf was wrong to treat Noah like that," the girl replied defiantly.

"Yes, he was," Samira answered. "But he is not wrong to mourn for his home, and he is not wrong to be hurt by stories that glorify those who have taken it."

"Momma, Jaffa is not our home anymore," Alexandra argued. "This is our home now. I want to be an American. I don't want to fight with people like Noah because the Arabs lost the war in Palestine."

"I don't want to fight with people like Noah, either, Alexandra. But Noah and Yusuf are going to have to deal with this matter themselves. Yusuf is like his father. There's a fire burning in their hearts that neither you nor I can extinguish."

"But Yusuf and Noah have been best of friends," Alexandra reasoned. "I can't believe a dumb article could end that."

"The article has nothing to do with it, Alexandra. Until now, Yusuf and Noah have been drawn together by those things they have in common. Now they will be forced to see that there are things they don't have in common, things about which they have very different views."

"You mean a piece of land that means nothing except where we once lived."

"The *piece of land*, as you call it, is a lot more than where we once lived, Alexandra. The piece of land doesn't just identify where we lived. It identifies who we are. When our land was lost, we lost our identity too. Yusuf wants his identity back, just as his father does."

"The Greenspans didn't steal our identity," Alexandra argued.

"No, they didn't, Alexandra," Samira replied. "But their hearts and souls are with those who did."

"So, we can't ever be friends with the Greenspans or people like them? Is that what you're saying?"

"I don't know the answer to that question, Alexandra. I don't think anyone does. Maybe it will take a lifetime to answer."

"Noah is my friend, Momma. He's been a good friend to Yusuf too. Politics shouldn't interfere with friendship."

"No, it shouldn't." Samira smiled sadly as she reached out and took her daughter's hand. "But it does," she said, "and it always has."

***

Noah, still smarting from Yusuf's attack, grew angrier and angrier as he walked home that night. It would be up to Joey, Noah decided. He would not apologize nor plead with his friend to not be upset with him. Joey would have to decide whether he wanted to be friends. *Who in the hell was Joey anyway?* Noah asked himself bitterly. *An Arab named Yusuf pretending to be an American named Joey…a newcomer… someone with a chip on his shoulder…a fair-weather friend who turned on him for no good reason…Alexandra's brother.*

***

Hy and Esther listened carefully as Noah described the fight with Yusuf.

The shoe finally fell, Esther thought as Noah finished. "I guess it had to happen sooner or later," she said, "A leopard never changes spots."

"What the hell is that supposed to mean?" Hy snapped.

"Alexandra doesn't feel the way Joey does, Mom," Noah interrupted. "She was really embarrassed by Joey's behavior. Mrs. Salaman seemed real upset about it too."

"Look, Noah, I know you're upset," Hy said. "And maybe Mom's right. Maybe it did have to happen. After all, the fact is we do come from different worlds. They see things very different from the way we see things. But this doesn't have to mean the end of your friendship. It just means that there are areas around which you kids are going to have to tread very carefully."

"Dad, I'm not looking for a fight with Joey. But I'm not going to apologize for what the Jews have accomplished either."

"No, I don't think you have anything to apologize for," Hy agreed.

"Joey owes me an apology," Noah continued.

"Noah, I don't want to interfere, but if I were you I wouldn't worry too much about whether or not Joey apologizes. If this friendship of yours is worth having, it doesn't require apologies. "

"I know, Dad, but I could never be friends with someone who hates Jews."

"Don't jump to conclusions, Noah. I'm not so sure Joey or any of the Salamans hate anyone who hasn't hurt them."

"You should have seen him, Dad!"

"Noah, think of how he must have felt. The Salamans believe their home was stolen from them, and here he sees a picture of an Israeli farm—a citrus grove no less—in a school publication along with a story that praises the very people who took what they really believe is their land."

"*Did* we take their land?"

"Well, some Jews have always been in the Holy Land, and in the last hundred years, many more Jews settled in Palestine, and the fact is people like the Salamans were there before those Jews arrived."

"Then who did the land belong to?" Noah asked.

"A relative handful of wealthy Arabs and Turks actually owned a lot of the land," his father explained. "They had no intention of working the land, so they allowed tenant farmers to live on much of it as long as they would work the land and take care of it. Many of the wealthy landowners raised money by selling property directly to the Zionists. In the years before the war, the Jews paid top dollar for land in Palestine."

"I get it," Noah said. "The only problem was that there were already people living on the land…right?"

"That's right," Hy answered. "But you know, there are families who live in these buildings around here who have no idea who owns their homes. Someday, the owners of these properties will probably sell them, and the tenants who live in the buildings won't know a thing about it until they receive an eviction notice telling them to move."

"Could that really happen? Here? In LeDroit Park?"

"Of course it could happen," Hy replied. "It happens all the time."

***

Yusuf lay on his bed staring off into space, his thoughts far from the black ghetto that was now his home. He could almost feel the warm breezes that would blow in off the Mediterranean and "kiss the young orange blossoms," as his grandfather Ibrahim used to say. What did the *Education Weekly* know about orange groves? How could they write about Arab neglect of the land? Didn't his father and grandfather plant every seedling by themselves, and didn't they all work from morning to nightfall when the oranges would grow heavy with what his father called the sweetest citrus juice in the world? What did the *Education Weekly* know about respect for the land? Could any man on the face of the earth love the land more than his own father?

Yusuf remembered Sharif kneeling on the ground, stroking the turf affectionately after he had laid Ibrahim to rest. The old man had been buried, according to his instructions, in the shade of the orange trees clustered on the mound from which a person could see the blue waters of his beloved Mediterranean.

Yusuf remembered the pain in his father's eyes the morning they left their home in Jaffa. His father had stood on the high ground alongside his mother, himself, and Alexandra. Together, they somberly watched the sand-colored cloud below hovering over the people moving slowly eastward toward Ramallah. Behind them, Jaffa's harbor lay still and abandoned. It had been a ghost port ever since the Jews fled and built their own port in Tel Aviv after the Arab riots in the spring of 1936. Yusuf cast his eyes over to the maze of narrow streets and alleys of the old town, nestled behind the clock square. He then glanced toward the opposite hillside, where the Franciscan Monastery stood, sun-drenched against the pale-blue sky. It seemed aloof and oblivious to the turmoil.

"So, the Jews have won!" his father said.

The Jews had, indeed, won, just as Sharif had said they would. Sharif had known that the Arab reflex of rhetoric and riot would not stop the return of the Jews to their promised land. The sweep of history was, for now, with the Zionists. The Arabs would pay dearly for the political and economic stagnation that had, during their tenancy, fallen on the land known as Palestine, the land the Jews called Eretz Israel.

"What will become of them?" Samira asked, looking off in the distance at the sandy pall of dust. It hung over the evictees like a curse as they made their way from Jaffa toward the newly proclaimed armistice lines and the territory now claimed by Jordan.

"They'll be back," Sharif replied. "They may come one at a time, crawling on their elbows and knees, but they'll be back."

Any hope his father had harbored that the Jews would allow his family to remain had been dashed when the authorities told him he had been classified as *present absentee*, one who had abandoned his property and later returned to reclaim it. Abandoned property had been confiscated by the new state, and apparently that meant property abandoned by residents like the Salamans who fled only temporarily to seek refuge from the fighting. Besides, Sharif had been unable to produce a deed or other proof of title after being advised that the parcel, which included the Salaman orange grove, was actually part of a larger land holding that had been sold to the Zionists.

Yusuf's father told him they were among the lucky ones. Sharif's uncle on his mother's side, Anwar Khadari, who had fled to America in 1918 when the British came, had sent for them. The old man forwarded passage on the Greek freighter *Aphrodite* and had even leased a business for his sister's only son. Sharif and Samira Salaman would own a food market in America.

"How many people does it take to make such a cloud on the horizon, Father?" Yusuf asked as he gazed wide-eyed at the vista before them.

"It takes an army of people, Yusuf," Sharif answered sadly. An entire army of homeless, stateless victims; victims of circumstances they neither understood nor were responsible for; victims of the thoughtless, hateful exhortations of local Arab demagogues and distant politicians whose disastrous leadership had left an entire people in ruin. "There are more than one hundred families making their way to the frontier," Sharif continued. "There must be four or five hundred people out there."

The Jews had not been without provocation. Even Yusuf knew that. But the mass expulsion of so many Arab citizens of Jaffa was unconscionable, his father insisted. It was true that many of Jaffa's Arabs had been quick to riot against the Jews. And much of the lawlessness, which was endemic in the old town, had been directed against the Jews. In fact, the Arabs of Jaffa had at one time actually marched on Tel Aviv. Sharif had expected severe retribution to be directed at those who had engaged in hostile activity. Jaffa's Arabs, not unlike Arabs everywhere these days, were easily moved to violence, and on more than one occasion, Jewish blood had been spilled by rampaging mobs from the city.

Now, almost overnight, it seemed, the Jews had turned Jaffa into a nearly Arab-free suburb of Tel Aviv. Jewish immigrants new to Palestine moved into abandoned Arab houses as fast as their terrified owners vacated them. In many cases, pathetic Jewish refugees, the stench of Hitler's Holocaust still fresh in their nostrils, took possession of Arab houses within hours of when the owners had been ordered out. Most of the newly dispossessed Arabs had nowhere to go in Jordan or on the so-called West Bank, which lay between the River Jordan and the territory held by the new state of Israel. The new Israeli army simply put them on the road and ordered them toward Jordanian lines. As far as the authorities were concerned, these families would no longer exist once they crossed into Jordanian territory.

Yusuf knew his father shared their humiliation. While he had been spared the insult of being marched from his home into oblivion, Sharif Salaman had been stripped of his home and the land on which they had toiled for half a century. He had been unable to protect his wife and children from the disgrace of eviction. Fifty years of Salaman dominion over the land had come to an end.

When the time came for them to leave, Sharif lingered, unable to turn and simply walk away from the orange grove and the house he and his father, Ibrahim, had built with their own hands.

"It is time," Samira had said softly and sympathetically. "We must go."

Slowly, they made their way down the grassy knoll toward the dirt road that led to the harbor. There a waiting trawler would take them to the port of Athens, where the Aegean meets the Mediterranean. Then, aboard the *Aphrodite*, they would depart from the only world that they—and all the Salamans before them—had ever known.

They did not look back until they reached the edge of the orange grove and stepped onto the uneven, rock-strewn road. There would be no return. Sharif, at that moment, stepped off the land of his birth, the land where his father had been laid to rest. Heartsick, he paused and then knelt down in front of his son and daughter.

"This may be the last time you ever see our home," he said, his eyes peering into theirs, alive with brilliant intensity. "Take a moment to look and to remember."

Yusuf and Alexandra had turned and looked over their shoulders at what had, for more than five decades, been the home of the Salaman family. The orange trees stood in proud and precise formation, biding their time until the moment was ripe for them to yield their treasure. Only this time, the harvest would not be for those who had nurtured the grove for so many years. This time, the harvest would be for strangers.

"Promise me you will not forget your home!" Sharif demanded as he tightened his grip on their shoulders. "Promise me!"

They turned back to face him. Alexandra nodded, not really understanding, but frightened by the sharp edge of her father's voice.

"We will not forget!" Yusuf had replied.

***

Langley Junior High School was about a twenty-minute walk from Fourth and U, and each morning Yusuf would stop by the For You Market, where Noah would join him for the short hike to school. The first morning after their argument, Noah left the store at eight-twenty as usual, but the sidewalk was empty. As he turned to go back inside to wait for his friend, he saw Yusuf already at the far end of the block, almost to T Street.

"Joey!" Noah called.

Yusuf turned and stood motionless as Noah took off at a trot toward him.

"Why didn't you wait?" Noah asked as he caught up to his friend.

"It was late, and I thought you had already left," Yusuf answered.

"It's eight-twenty, Joey. It's the same time we meet every morning."

Yusuf turned to Noah. "Do me a favor, Noah. From now on call me Yusuf, will you?"

"I'll call you anything you want, damn it! Now tell me, why didn't you wait for me?"

"What the hell difference does it make? I forgot, OK?"

"Listen Jo—Yusuf," Noah said, "are you going to make a big deal over that business in the *Education Weekly*?"

"No, I'm not going to make a big deal over it," Yusuf replied bitterly. "I'm just going to remember who I am and where I am."

"What's that supposed to mean?" Noah asked as they rounded the corner onto T Street.

"It means I'm an Arab living in a country that doesn't give a damn about what happens to the Arabs," he answered. "It means I'll have to get used to reading that Zionist crap."

Noah felt anger welling up inside but didn't say anything. He wished he had let Yusuf walk ahead of him, as his friend obviously preferred doing anyway. As they waited at the stoplight at Rhode Island Avenue, Noah looked up the T Street hill. They were about to cross out of the ghetto and into a formerly all-white neighborhood that was rapidly changing as the whites fled northward. Across the street stood the Sylvan Theater, which had just announced its conversion to integrated status. That meant it would soon cater to an all-black audience because the white people in the neighborhood would stop going as soon as it began admitting Negroes.

"Things are changing all over the world, Yusuf," Noah said, careful to use his friend's Arab name. "People around here are all moving too. Nobody's happy about it, but that's the way it is."

"What's that got to do with me?" Yusuf snapped.

"I didn't say it had anything to do with you. I'm just saying people are on the move everywhere."

"My father doesn't belong in LeDroit Park," Yusuf responded, his anger and frustration not yet spent. "He's here—we're all here— because our land was taken from us by Zionists with a piece of paper that said our land was theirs." He turned to face Noah. "Can there ever be justice when people can do that?"

"How did they get the paper, Yusuf?" Noah probed. "How did they get ownership of the land?"

"What difference does it make?" Yusuf answered angrily. "My father didn't give it to them."

"But someone did!" Noah replied, raising his voice. "Someone had the paper because someone else sold it to them, someone else who had legal ownership of the land."

"You don't know what you're talking about," Yusuf said. "You don't know anything about what happened over there. My father didn't sell the land to anybody."

"Yusuf, maybe it wasn't his to sell."

"No one should have the right to sell someone's home and someone's livelihood to someone else," Yusuf replied indignantly. "No one should be able to do that."

"How do you think your uncle was able to lease Izumi's place for your family?"

"What are you talking about?"

"Yusuf, the Izumis' landlord leased the property to your uncle when Mr. Izumi was in the hospital. He leased Mr. Izumi's home and livelihood. Now it's your home and your livelihood."

Yusuf stared hard into Noah's eyes as he tried to collect his thoughts. "Who told you that?" he asked.

"My dad mentioned it when Izumi was still in the hospital. I think one of the salesmen told him. He said Mrs. Izumi didn't know what she was going to do."

"Why would the landlord do something like that?" Yusuf asked.

"I don't know," Noah answered. "I guess he was worried about whether the Izumis would be able to run the business. He probably got nervous when they closed the store and missed their rent payments when Mr. Izumi was in the hospital. And I'd be willing to bet your uncle offered to pay more than Izumi was paying."

"What ever happened to the Izumis?"

"I don't know," Noah shrugged. "They just sort of disappeared from LeDroit Park."

Yusuf nodded knowingly. "Yeah, like we disappeared from Palestine," he answered bitterly.

By now the boys had reached the entrance to the school.

"Well, we'd better hustle or we'll be late," Noah said pulling open the doors.

"Yeah," Yusuf replied as he turned and walked down the long, dimly lighted corridor toward his homeroom. Noah stood for a moment and watched his friend navigate his way through the crowded hall. Things would be different now, he thought sadly. He wasn't sure exactly why, but he knew they would be.

CHAPTER EIGHT

As it turned out, Noah and Yusuf's friendship didn't suffer that much from the *Education Weekly* incident. Just as Samara had predicted, they didn't brood for very long. Their brief altercation forced them to recognize their differences, as well as what they shared in common. Both boys understood that each had sensitivities that could either be accommodated or exacerbated but not ignored. As the years passed and they moved on to high school, they remained close, and nearly everyone thought of them as best friends. As different as their respective backgrounds were, Noah Greenspan and Yusuf Salaman had more in common with each other than they did with any of their other classmates.

While Noah plodded through adolescence, Alexandra seemed to glide effortlessly toward womanhood. She had the same rich brown hair that framed Samira's face, and her large, brilliant green eyes tantalized almost everyone. By the time she was sixteen, Alexandra was slightly taller than Samira and as generously proportioned as her mother had been when she had married Sharif. Alexandra's innocence and beauty melded into a winsome but alluring sensuality, and Noah reveled in his friendship with her.

Noah towered over his mother by the time he reached high school, and at just a fraction over six feet, he was one of the taller boys at McKinley Tech. His hair, which he now combed into a small wave, had darkened, and he had grown into a handsome young man.

Noah and Alexandra did not actually date until one November afternoon during Noah's junior year when he asked her to be his date on a hayride and cookout sponsored by a high school fraternity he had joined early in his freshman year. Her mother, she knew, wouldn't object. But she wasn't so sure about Yusuf and Sharif.

"Your father and brother wouldn't want you to go on the hayride with me?" Noah asked incredulously.

"I've never been on a date," Alexandra explained. "A girl beginning to date is a serious matter in Arab families." Alexandra chose not to share with Noah the issue she feared most.

"For pete's sake, it's just a hayride," Noah said.

"It's still a first date, Noah," Alexandra replied. "I think it will be all right, but I have to ask first."

"Well, tell them all we're going to do is sing songs, roast marshmallows, and incinerate some hot dogs and hamburgers."

"It wouldn't be the marshmallows, hot dogs, or hamburgers they would worry about."

"Alexandra," Noah said, turning serious, "tell your dad I'd be glad to talk to him…you know, about how much I respect you."

"Oh, Noah…"

"No, I mean it. I know your folks are concerned. I want them to know that I understand and that I would never do anything that would cause them to worry."

Alexandra reached up and kissed Noah on the cheek, thinking to herself how little he really understood.

***

Sharif Salaman was not in a good mood when he sat down with his family at dinner that night. During his morning buying rounds at the Florida Avenue Market, a poultry wholesaler, Armand Peshkin, had refused to sell him his last crate of broilers. Peshkin had instead sold the chickens to another customer who had arrived at the wholesaler's just after Sharif. The man, Peshkin claimed, had called in and asked to have a crate put aside for him. Sharif caught the wink that told the other grocer that Peshkin would take care of him.

Sharif had paused just outside the door as he left Peshkin's and listened to their amusement inside. "So, *nu*, I'm going to sell to him before a landsman?" the wholesaler had said with a laugh.

"Thanks, Armand. All I'd need is to start the weekend without any broilers," the other grocer had replied.

Now, Samira, sensitive to her husband's dark mood, felt her pulse quicken when Alexandra, beaming from ear to ear, told her family about her forthcoming date with Noah. Sharif froze. Alexandra, sensing her father's displeasure, abruptly excused herself from the table, explaining she had homework to complete. Sharif's fork remained suspended halfway between his plate and his mouth. He stared at the meal before him without speaking.

Yusuf finally broke the awful silence that had descended over the dinner table. "Alexandra will not do this!"

"What are you talking about?" Samira asked anxiously, dreading the argument she knew was coming.

"She will not go to this party with Noah," Yusuf answered vehemently. "She will not do this to our family."

"You don't want your sister to go out with Noah Greenspan?" Samira asked. "That's crazy."

"This is a matter of honor," Yusuf replied.

"It's a matter of honor for Alexandra not to go on a hayride with Noah?" Samira pressed on incredulously.

"Mother, this fraternity of Noah's consists only of Jewish boys."

"What has this to do with Alexandra? If the other members are as nice as Noah, what is there to be concerned about?"

"These are boys from families that support the Zionists," Yusuf said, exasperated at his mother's failure to understand the gravity of the situation. "They would refuse me membership if I were interested in joining their club. Their families all send money to the Jews in Palestine, like the ones who stole our land in Jaffa. We must remember our home. We can't do that by going to parties and socializing with the very people who financed the theft of our land. Besides, Alexandra would be the only Arab there. Everyone would have something to say about Noah's Arab." Yusuf's temper was rising.

"Alexandra is not 'Noah's Arab,' Yusuf," Samira replied, her voice rising. "She is Noah's friend as, I believe, you are. Noah doesn't care about all this political business. He cares about your sister, and she cares about him. Let me ask you something, Yusuf: would you join their fraternity if they invited you to join?"

"No. Of course not," he replied.

Sharif, who had been silently observing the exchange between mother and son, finally spoke. "Perhaps they care too much, Samira," he said. "They will both be hurt if they care too much."

"Noah would never do anything that could hurt Alexandra," Samira responded.

"They will hurt one another. It is inevitable," Sharif insisted. "If Alexandra goes to this party, she will be a curiosity, just as Yusuf has said. I do not want my daughter to be a curiosity for Noah's Jewish friends."

"Sharif, Yusuf, this is terribly unfair to Alexandra—and to Noah, for that matter," Samira said. "Noah is a decent young man. You both know that. His intentions are honorable, and to ask Alexandra to turn her back on him because of events far from here that in no way involve him is wrong."

Sharif listened silently while his wife argued. She was defying both her husband and her son over a matter involving the honor of the family, behavior unheard of in most Arab women.

But Samira was, after all, only half Arab. Her father, a captain in the British army, had come to Palestine with his Egyptian wife when the British Home Office had transferred him to Jaffa at the beginning of the Mandate. Samira's mother had died of influenza shortly after the small family had arrived in the old city, and not long afterward, her father had been killed in an automobile accident on the road to

Beersheba, not more than fifteen kilometers south of their home. The orphaned Samira, little more than a toddler, had been taken in by an Anglican order and was raised and educated at the Anglican boarding school just outside Jaffa. Whether it was her English blood or her English education, Samira had grown up to be fiercely independent and far more outspoken than any of the Arab women of Jaffa. Yet it was that very combination of her alluring beauty and her confident, independent nature that Sharif Salaman had first found so irresistibly attractive in the woman who would become his wife.

Still, there were times, such as now, when his daughter was exhibiting her mother's same fiery independence, that Sharif longed for the unquestioning obedience of the traditional Arab wife. Samira had certainly never hesitated to speak her mind, and now, Sharif thought ruefully, his only daughter was proving to be just as obstinate.

Though Sharif often found Samira's independence appealing, having something as important as this decided by the women was quite another matter. Yusuf had been right in his objection.

Sharif stood to leave the table. "You will tell Alexandra she cannot accompany Noah to this party, Samira," he said, a ring of finality in his words.

"Sharif!"

"Enough!" he shouted, throwing his napkin to the table. "You will do as I say!"

"What?"

"You will do as I say!" he repeated.

Samira rose to confront her husband. Her cheeks were tinged with angry scarlet and her eyes full of fire.

"No, Sharif, I will not do as you say! If you choose to punish your daughter and her friend for the tragedy of Palestine, go ahead. But don't ask me—command me—to convey the anger in your heart."

"What are saying?" Sharif asked, dumbfounded by his wife's defiance, extreme even for the outspoken Samira.

"There have been enough victims, Sharif. We don't need any more casualties in this family. If you want to continue the battle, I can't stop you; I won't even try. But I won't join you. You will have to fight with Noah and with your daughter yourself. The Greenspans have done nothing to offend us. I will do nothing to offend them."

"I don't wish to fight with anyone," Sharif said quietly.

"Then don't forbid Alexandra to go to this party with Noah."

"It is not the Arab way," Sharif answered in a soft and pained voice.

"Sharif, look at where we are. In America, people don't feud endlessly for no reason."

"No reason!" She had gone one step too far. "How dare you!" Sharif yelled, bracing himself on the table and leaning toward his wife. "You call the loss of our home no reason? You call the eviction of thousands upon thousands of Arabs no reason?"

"Oh, Sharif, what is happening to us? The Greenspans didn't take our home! They didn't evict our neighbors! Are you going to make Alexandra an instrument of your anger?"

Yusuf, who had been silently witnessing the confrontation between his parents, interrupted. "It is a question of honor, Mother. Someday Alexandra will have to face her countrymen who have lived under the Zionist yoke. What will she answer when they ask about her life in America? Will she tell them that she went to parties with the Jews?"

"My countrymen are Americans, Yusuf," Alexandra said, walking back into the room.

She had been standing in the hallway, silently listening to the entire argument. Now she was going to be heard.

"We live here," she said angrily. "I don't ever plan to live anywhere else. I haven't done anything to shame this family, and I never will. Going out with Noah does not dishonor this family!"

Sharif watched, speechless, as his daughter moved to her mother's side.

"Alexandra, you are an Arab," Yusuf replied, a cold finality in his voice. "You can live in America all your life, and you will still be an Arab."

"That's because I share a common language with other Arabs, Yusuf," Alexandra replied, "not because I share a common hatred with them. I detest what happened to our land, but neither Noah nor his friends had anything to do with that. You cannot ask me to hate them. And you cannot force me to, either."

Sharif watched and listened as his son argued with his daughter. Such a confrontation would never have taken place in an Arab land. Samira and Alexandra, independent enough before stepping foot off Arab soil, now seemed totally Americanized.

Yusuf, fighting to maintain his Arab identity, saw in his sister's actions a threat to his sense of honor. In her defiance, he saw a threat to his very manhood.

Patria Potestas, Sharif thought, recalling the Arab principle that requires the father to restore honor to the family should a daughter bring shame or disgrace to the household. The daughters of Arabia had far more to risk than the loss of an argument. Behavior that embarrassed the family had cost more than one Arab girl her life in the vast sandy reaches between the Euphrates and the Mediterranean.

"Enough!" Sharif declared, bringing his fist down on the table, rattling the glassware and cutlery. "If this is really what you want, Alexandra, it will be your choice. I will not interfere with your decision. However—" Sharif held up a hand to stop his son, who had begun to protest his father's decision. "However," Sharif continued as Yusuf crossed his arms sullenly, "I will not allow anyone to compromise the honor of this family. You will bear the consequences of your behavior, Alexandra. Honor is a great responsibility. You believe you can live as an American, do as the Americans do, and still preserve your honor as an Arab, then by all means, go your own way and do as you please. But you will be held accountable. No darkening of this family will be tolerated. At home, I would decide such matters of honor. But here we'll do it the American way. Behave as you choose, Alexandra. From this moment on, your decisions will be your responsibility. But do not forget, the honor of this family is my responsibility. Do nothing with this newfound responsibility to provoke me."

"But—"

"Enough!" he yelled, pounding the table with the open palm of his hand. "Enough," he repeated somewhat more softly and less belligerently. "You shall have your way. We will see how well you handle this responsibility you seek."

Samira caught Alexandra's eye and shook her head, silently counseling her daughter to not pursue the matter further.

***

"See, I knew it would be OK," Noah said when Alexandra burst into the For You Market to tell him she could go on the hayride with him. "Your dad didn't have any problem, did he?"

"Well," said Alexandra, "let's just say it took some coaxing."

"Really? He really objected?"

"As I told you, Noah, these things are more complicated then they seem."

"Did you tell him I would talk with him…you know, about how I feel about you and how I'd never…"

"Dishonor me?"

"Well, yes. I mean it's hard to believe that in the nineteen fifties a guy has to promise to be honorable to ask a girl out, but I'd be glad to talk to him."

"No, I didn't mention your offer, but I think it would be a very nice thing to do. It might reassure him."

***

When Noah entered the Crescent Market the next morning, Samira resisted the urge to give him an affectionate hug. She knew, of course, why he had come, and she admired his courage.

"Alexandra told me about your concern over the hayride," Noah said to Samira and Sharif.

"You understand, Noah, it has nothing to do with you," Sharif replied.

"Noah, we think the world of you," Samira said. "We would never want you to be hurt by anything we did."

"Unfortunately, there are other issues here, Noah," Sharif continued.

"Look, I understand how you feel about me and Alexandra. I know you think my friends, I mean my Jewish friends, might not be nice to Alexandra."

"Yes, that's right, Noah," Sharif answered. "We are concerned about that."

"Well," Noah said thoughtfully, "if I was concerned that anyone would be mean or rude to my daughter, I guess I'd do whatever I had to do to protect her too. I really don't think my friends would ever make Alexandra uncomfortable, but I understand how you feel, and I want you to know that I wouldn't ever let that happen, Mr. Salaman."

"And?" Sharif asked.

"And...well...and I like Alexandra more than any girl I've ever known," Noah continued, choosing his words carefully. "I respect Alexandra a whole lot, Mr. Salaman, and I don't want to cause her any trouble. But I'm not going to stop being her friend. Mr. Salaman, I know Alexandra would stop seeing me if you insisted, and I guess I'm really here to ask you not to do that. What I mean is, please don't do that."

Sharif, reflecting on Noah's words, did not reply immediately.

"Noah, no one in this family would even think of asking you and Alexandra not to be friends," Samira said. "Alexandra would miss you terribly, and so would we."

"Tell me, Noah, what kind of relationship do you wish to have with Alexandra?" Sharif asked. "I think it's fine that you two study together and that you are friends in school. But tell me, what about this dating business? What goes on between these young men and women?"

"Sharif—"

"Please, Samira. I asked Noah a simple question," Sharif said.

"It is not a simple question," Samira replied impatiently.

"Yes, it is, Mrs. Salaman. I don't mind answering Mr. Salaman's question," Noah said, trying to avoid the confrontation he saw developing. "It really is simple. I want Alexandra to be my...friend. And I'll do whatever I have to do to keep you from worrying."

"Noah, I don't think you can begin to understand the things that worry me," Sharif replied.

"You're a handsome, likable young man," Samira said. "There will be a hundred girls who will want to be your...friend. You belong to this fraternity Alexandra told us about, and they will have lots of parties and dances. Why do you want to complicate your life?"

"Because Alexandra is the only girl I...I ah...I'm interested in," Noah replied.

He had wanted to say, *Alexandra is the only girl I love.* Samira, of course, knew that and felt only affection for Noah at that moment.

"Noah, this is much more complicated than you realize," Sharif said. "I don't want to see either of you hurt, but that is exactly what is going to happen. I do not want to interfere with you and Alexandra, but where is all of this is going to lead?"

"Sharif..."

"Please, Samira. It is not an easy thing. You know that."

"I know, Sharif, but I think we should let Noah go on to school. As long as we trust Noah and Alexandra, there is nothing to worry about, is there?"

Sharif said nothing, but Noah knew by the look on his face that his concerns were unchanged.

CHAPTER NINE

The other couples were huddled near the rear of the two open trucks when Noah and Alexandra pulled into the Glen Echo parking lot in the heavily wooded Maryland suburb of Cabin John.

Alexandra had been confident until the moment they arrived. Just another bunch of kids, she'd convinced herself. But as Noah maneuvered his Chevy into a parking space opposite the rear of the trucks, Alexandra stared nervously at the teenagers waiting for them.

"Come on, I'll introduce you to everybody," Noah said, opening his door. Alexandra saw the others turn to look at her when the interior light of the car illuminated her face in the dusk of early evening. She took a deep breath as Noah came around the car and opened the door for her.

"You OK?" he asked.

"I'm scared to death," she whispered. "I don't know if I'm shaking because it's cold or because I'm so nervous."

"Relax. They're just like any other kids," he said with more confidence than he felt at the moment.

"Hey, guys! How's it going?" Noah asked cheerfully as he and Alexandra joined the rest of the group.

"Going great, now that you're here, big man," someone answered.

"Hey, everybody, this is Alexandra. Alexandra, this is, um… everybody," Noah said.

"Oh, great introduction, Noah," responded an attractive girl who Alexandra thought to be about her own age.

"Hi, Alexandra, I'm Robin Ratner," the girl said with a friendly wave.

"Hi, Robin. Good to meet you," Alexandra replied, thinking to herself that Robin Ratner could have been a relative from Jaffa. Her dark, wavy hair hung to the tops of her shoulders, and her deep-brown eyes sparkled in the light of the November moon.

One by one, the others all introduced themselves. While a few of the couples were somewhat reticent, most were, Alexandra thought, genuinely friendly, and her anxiety quickly began to subside.

"Let's move it!" someone yelled impatiently.

They all climbed onto the two flatbed trucks, which had been rigged with wooden side panels and piled with hay. A stack of olive-drab flannel blankets sat folded in a corner.

"Oh yeah!" one of the boys yelled as he pulled a blanket from the pile and wrapped it around himself and his date. Others quickly followed suit and, within minutes, the entire group, it seemed, was cuddled in pairs under blankets as the truck lurched forward.

Alexandra and Noah were in the second truck, sitting with their backs against the side panel, their blanket draped over their shoulders for warmth. They could hear laughing and singing in the lead truck as the small caravan made its way toward their destination. As soon as the group in the lead truck began a song, those in the second truck with Noah and Alexandra would join in. By the time they neared the rustic warming house in Sligo Creek Park several miles to the east in Silver Spring, they had raucously worked their way through "If I Had a Hammer," "The Sheik of Araby," "Hang Down Your Head, Tom Dooley," "Down by the Riverside," and the never-ending "John Jacob Jingleheimer Schmidt." They even tried to do "Moonlight Bay" in rounds, but every time the lead truck rounded a bend in the road, they would momentarily lose contact and be totally out of sync by the time they caught up. It was a spectacle—loud, tumultuous, silly, but most of all, fun.

When they all finally arrived at the warming house, Noah's friends could not have been nicer to Alexandra. Whether it was because Alexandra was the curiosity Sharif and Yusuf had feared she would be or because she was so attractive, she was the center of almost everyone's attention throughout the evening.

"They all love you," Noah said softly in her ear as they slow-danced to "My Secret Love."

"They hardly know me," she whispered, moving her arms affectionately around his neck.

"But to know you is to love you."

"Noah, you're the smoothest talker ever to come out of LeDroit Park," she said playfully.

You know we're made for one another, Alexandra. We really are. We're like a great love story."

"Yeah, Romeo and Juliet," she replied, the humor not as evident in her voice.

"Do you want to be a Capulet or a Montague?"

"At the end of the story, it didn't make much difference, did it?"

"Well, that's not the ending they're going to write about us," he replied.

"What's it going to say?" she whispered playfully into his ear. "And they lived happily ever after?"

Noah stopped dancing and took her gently by the shoulders. "If that's what we want it to say, that's what it will say," he answered. And he believed that to be true.

***

By the time they boarded the trucks for the ride back to Glen Echo, the temperature had dropped into the low forties. Noah and Alexandra found a spot at the forward part of the flatbed and sat down with their backs propped against the rear of the cab. Within moments they found themselves to be the only ones sitting up; virtually every other couple lay entwined under their blankets. There was very little talking amid the subdued murmurs and the occasional moans that broke the stillness on the floor of the truck.

Alexandra's eyes roamed across the flatbed from one blanketed couple to the next. Most were just lying there embracing and occasionally kissing. One or two couples, judging from the twisting and heavy breathing, seemed oblivious to the rest of the group. Alexandra didn't care what any of the couples were doing as much as she was surprised that they were doing it so openly. There was no privacy. Anyone could see or hear. There was no shame or humility—no honor. Then, she thought of her brother and father. "You will be held accountable. No darkening of this family's honor will be tolerated," Sharif had said.

"C'mon," Noah said, dropping down onto his right elbow while he held the blanket up for her. "I'll keep you warm."

"You can keep me warm sitting right here," she replied, pulling the blanket back.

"Aw, c'mon," he urged playfully.

Alexandra leaned down toward him and spoke in hushed tones. "Noah, I am not going to lie under a blanket with you on the floor of a truck with twenty other kids necking all around us. That may be your idea of fun or of romance, but I think it's just plain dumb."

"Hey, relax," he said, repositioning himself next to her. "You're right, it is kind of dumb...fun, but dumb." He smiled devilishly. "It's just necking. You know, hugging and kissing. It's not like they're *doing it*."

"How would one know?" Alexandra gave a chagrined glance at the few writhing mounds in the shadows around them.

"Alexandra, these are great kids...most of them are, anyway. I mean, everyone likes to neck. It's normal."

"Normal for them...maybe normal for you, but I don't ever think it will be normal for me."

"What is it that will never be normal for you? Necking? Or necking on the floor of a truck with ten other couples?"

"If I thought something could darken my face or my family's name, I wouldn't do it," she replied.

"That's no answer. You have to tell me what you think would darken your face."

Alexandra took several moments to consider her reply. Then, she turned to look into his eyes before she spoke. "I think you know what would darken my face. I mean, that's why you're so special to me. Caring for someone enough to never darken their face is what love is all about, isn't it?"

Now, it was Noah's turn to consider his reply. "Yeah, I guess you're right," he finally said.

At the Glen Echo parking lot, Robin Ratner hurried over to Noah and Alexandra as soon as they climbed down from the truck. "Hey, will you guys come to my sweet-sixteen party the week after next at Indian Springs? I'm having about ten couples. You'll like all the kids who will be there," she said, looking almost pleadingly into Alexandra's eyes.

Noah turned to Alexandra. His subtle shrug signaled that it was her call.

"Sure, why not?" Alexandra replied with a smile.

"Oh great!" Robin said, hugging Alexandra. "See you guys in two weeks," she called as she ran back to her date.

"Have you been there?" Alexandra asked.

"To the country club? Yeah, I've been there. It's really nice. I mean, the people seem very nice."

"But…?"

"But what?"

"I don't know. You tell me. I feel a *but* coming," she replied.

Noah smiled as he opened the door of his Chevy for her. "You really read me like a book."

"So?" she said after he'd come around the car and slid in next to her.

"So, I've always had a problem with Indian Springs. Well, not Indian Springs, I guess. I think I'd have a problem with any country club."

"What is a country club anyway?" she asked.

"It's a private club in the suburbs—you know, what used to be the country. They have golf and tennis and swimming and a clubhouse for dining."

"So, what's your problem?"

"I guess it bothers me to know that my parents will never belong to a country club," he answered as he pulled out of the parking lot. "I've been out to Indian Springs a few times with friends whose parents belong. I always felt guilty as hell. I mean, I see all these people sunning themselves around the pool, and I think of my folks in that hot grocery store, sweeping the floor or waiting on customers or cleaning fish or something, and I get this awful feeling. And when I've been there for dinner, I watch everybody laughing and having a great time, and I know my folks are still in the store and will be until eleven o'clock. I know it's wrong, but I think I resent being there."

"Well, then, why are we going?"

"Like I said, the people I've met there are really OK. They're not snooty or anything like that. I can't expect them not to belong to a club like Indian Springs just because my folks can't."

"But if it makes you uncomfortable, you shouldn't go."

"Look, Robin is a great kid. How could we say no to her because of my hang-up?" Then he began to laugh.

"What's so funny?"

"Alexandra, I guess you should know—Indian Springs is also a Jewish country club."

"Oh great!" she sighed. "*Now* you tell me!"

***

Sharif was chopping cutlets from a loin of lamb when Alexandra mentioned her plans to go to Robin Ratner's sweet-sixteen party with Noah. He didn't say a word when she told him, just seemed to pause ever so briefly, then continued chopping, a little harder and a little faster. His silence said it all; Alexandra knew her father was unhappy.

***

Indian Springs was an unpretentious place as far as country clubs go. The membership consisted mostly of middle-income Jewish families; more affluent Jews preferred to socialize at the prestigious Woodmont Country Club. Most of Noah's fraternity brothers and the girls they dated were from families that belonged to Indian Springs.

As Noah and Alexandra walked up to the clubhouse from the parking lot, he pointed out the pool area and tennis courts.

"The first hole of the golf course is on the other side of the clubhouse," he said. "During the day, you can watch the golfers tee off while you're having lunch."

"People come here all week long?" she asked.

"Sure. It's always open."

"It must cost a fortune to be able to live like this," she said.

"I don't think so. I don't know what it costs to belong here, but I know there are clubs that are much more expensive."

"For Jews?"

"Uh-huh."

"And they wouldn't let a gentile join?"

"Actually, I don't know. I mean, Indian Springs is always referred to as a Jewish country club. I just assume it's only for Jews. Besides, I don't think a gentile would want to join Indian Springs. They have their own clubs, and they sure don't invite Jews."

Noah and Alexandra checked their coats and walked toward the dining room. Alexandra was wearing a white satin dress that accentuated her olive complexion. Her hair hung to her shoulders, gracefully framing her face. She had never looked more beautiful, Noah thought, and he told her so, putting his arm around her as they entered the dining room, which was alive with the din of chatter competing with music from a dance band playing on the opposite side of the cavernous room.

"Noah! Alexandra! Over here!" Robin waved to them from the far side of the large, noisy room. Waving back, they negotiated their way through the maze of tables.

"Thanks for coming," Robin said, hugging them both. "C'mon, I want to introduce you both to my folks." Robin's parents greeted them warmly, if curiously.

"We're delighted you could join us, Alexandra, Noah."

Alexandra thought Robin's parents were about the same age as her own parents. They seemed very pleasant and put her at ease almost immediately. The other teenagers were, as Robin had promised, as friendly as they had been on the hayride, and all were eager to talk with Alexandra.

Indian Springs Country Club fascinated her. She had not known such places existed. She now understood the discomfort Noah had expressed earlier, as she found herself imagining what her parents were doing while the music played or as a course was served or whenever she and Noah got up to dance. It was her first evening in such a different world, one that was both friendly and alien, she thought.

After dessert, Noah leaned over to Alexandra and whispered, "Ever been on a golf course?"

"I've never seen one," she admitted.

"Come on, then. Let's go out to the eighteenth hole. It's right behind the clubhouse."

When they stepped into the brisk night air, Noah took off his suit jacket and draped it over Alexandra's shoulders.

"You'll freeze," she said as they walked onto the eighteenth green.

"Nah, I have fire in my blood," he joked. "I'm fine."

"The grounds are beautiful," she observed.

"So, what do you think about all of this?" he asked with a sweep of his hand.

"I understand what you meant," she said. "You know, about feeling sort of resentful because it's all for them but not for our families."

"Yeah. It's probably not fair of us. I mean, I'd love my folks to be able to join. It's just that I know they can't and probably never will be able to live like this. That's what really bothers me."

"It's really interesting, isn't it?" Alexandra mused. "I mean we're constantly reminded of how unrealistic our relationship is—I hear it from my folks, you hear it from your folks—yet you and I have more in common with each other than we do with any of those kids in there."

"It is ironic, isn't it?" Noah said with a wry grin. "We're like visitors from another culture here. These people take all of this for granted."

"I'm sure I'm the first Salaman in history to stand on a golf course," Alexandra said with a laugh.

"Hey, that's right! No one in my family has ever played golf either."

"Hold me, Noah, I'm freezing," she said suddenly.

Noah embraced Alexandra for a moment and then kissed her softly on the lips. He gently, slowly pulled her tight against his body, her breasts pressing against his chest. The sound of "The Tennessee Waltz" wafted, distant but audible, across the green from the dining room. That moment was the closest thing to rapture Noah had ever experienced. In the still autumn air, it seemed that the orchestra played only for Noah and Alexandra as they clung to one another and swayed gently to the music.

CHAPTER TEN

Every year on the Monday before Memorial Day, the Consolidated Grocers of Washington held its open meeting for the election of officers. Refreshments were served afterward and everyone socialized, so wives of the members also attended the meeting. This year Hy and Esther Greenspan had asked the Salamans to accompany them. Since Yusuf was in Gettysburg on a two-day school field trip, they agreed that Noah and Alexandra would stay together at the Salaman house until the parents returned later that night. Neither the Salamans nor the Greenspans wanted to leave the young people home alone; the neighborhood just wasn't that safe anymore.

Sharif and Samira were both in high spirits when the Greenspans arrived to pick them up.

"So, Noah, I leave you in charge of the Salaman home," Sharif announced as they prepared to leave.

"It will be here when you return, sir." Noah smiled.

"Alexandra!" Samira called upstairs to her daughter. "Come say hello to the Greenspans."

Alexandra greeted them all as she entered the kitchen. She looked especially radiant that evening, having just applied fresh lipstick and a touch of color to her cheeks. Both Hy and Esther noticed the color Alexandra had added to her lips. Samira, hugging her daughter, also caught the faint scent of perfume.

"Are you going somewhere?" Sharif asked, the slightest hint of disapproval in his voice.

"Father!" Alexandra said, a real blush accenting the light dusting of artificial color on her cheeks.

"See you later!" the two young people called to their parents as they made their way to the door.

"Make sure the door is locked, Noah," Sharif said. He paused for a moment and once again glanced anxiously at his daughter. Then he turned and followed Samira and the Greenspans onto Fourth Street.

Noah engaged the bolt on the lock and lowered into place the heavy wooden two-by-four that further barred entry to the Salaman's store and home. Stillness filled the air and, for several seconds, only the hum of the refrigeration compressors broke the silence.

They were alone.

"Let's go upstairs," Alexandra said as Noah turned to face her.

Noah nodded and followed Alexandra into the kitchen and up the narrow staircase that led to the Salamans' living quarters. The second-floor layout was almost identical to that of the Greenspan home. There was the same long corridor no more than four feet wide, which seemed dark and drab despite the fresh coat of beige paint Yusuf and Sharif had recently applied. Old gas sconces still protruded from the walls, even though, long before the Second World War, the gas company had sealed them. Noah and Alexandra walked past two tiny bedrooms and the larger bedroom her parents shared. Then the corridor jogged to the left and brought them to the living room, which was about a third again the size of Sharif and Samira's bedroom. An old and modest oriental carpet covered the floor, its colors having long since lost their richness. The couch, covered with royal-blue and cream-colored fabric, had embroidered doilies on its overstuffed arms. Two comfortable, deep-blue wingback club chairs sat in the corners of the room, and a twelve-inch black-and-white Admiral television stood against the wall opposite the couch.

"Do you want to watch TV?" Alexandra asked, sitting on the couch.

"No," Noah answered, taking his place next to her. "Do you?"

Alexandra shook her head. "No."

"Do you want to kiss me as badly as I want to kiss you?" he asked.

Alexandra looked into his eyes and nodded ever so slightly. Noah reached out and gently pulled her close to him. They explored one another's eyes for a moment or two more before he leaned toward her and kissed her on the lips.

Slowly leaning back against the couch, Alexandra pulled Noah with her. They embraced and kissed, joined in each other's arms for several moments. When they finally separated, Alexandra smiled up at him, reached out, and traced the contours of his face with her fingertips.

"What's going to happen to us?" she asked in a whisper. Noah straightened up, took her hand from his face, and kissed the backs of her fingers.

"I don't know, Alexandra. I guess that depends on us, I mean how much we want each other."

"I love you, Noah," she answered softly. "But I'm afraid for us. I don't know what we should do or what is going to happen."

"I love you too, Alexandra," he whispered, taking her in his arms again. They held onto each other for several moments before Noah again kissed her softly on the lips. Then he brought his hand to rest on Alexandra's breast for a moment and gently caressed her cheek with his lips.

"Maybe we should just let time take its course," he finally said.

"Do you think things will get better?"

"Hey, before you know it, we'll be through with high school and in college. We'll be free to do what we want without worrying so much about what our parents think."

"And what will we want when we're free to do whatever we choose?" she asked.

"You mean besides marrying one another?"

"Did you just propose?" she teased.

"No," he answered seriously, "but I will one day."

"OK, what will we do other than marry one another?"

"Good question. I'm sure I'll wind up in business, but I haven't the slightest idea what kind of business it will be. What about you?"

"I want to be a journalist. I love writing for the school paper. I think I'd enjoy writing about important people and events, and I think it's what I should do for a living someday."

"The University of Maryland has a good journalism school."

"There are a lot of good journalism schools."

"Do you know where you want to go to school?"

"Maybe Syracuse or Columbia if I could get in. Maryland would be OK too, I suppose. What about you?"

"I don't know for sure. The schools here in the Washington area are pretty good."

"Noah, with your grades you could go anywhere you wanted."

"But can I afford to go anywhere I want? That's the question."

"Where would you go if you could go anywhere you wanted?"

"Oh, I don't know. Harvard, I suppose, or maybe Yale or Princeton or Stanford. They're supposed to be the top schools in the country."

"Maybe you can get a scholarship."

"Fat chance."

"You never know. Somebody has to get them. Who has better grades than you?"

"Probably a few million kids."

"OK, so let's say it's nineteen sixty and you've just graduated from Harvard or Stanford. Then what?"

"You mean before or after we get married?"

"Really, Noah, I'm serious. What do you see happening then?"

"If I had two nickels to rub together, I'd want to put them into my own business. I don't think I would want to work for anyone else. You know my parents, and yours too, work outrageous hours just to be their own bosses. I think it gets in your blood. My dad is fiercely independent. He doesn't make much money, but being his own boss means a lot to him."

"You'll do well, Noah. I know you will. You're so damn smart, and you have a way of seeing things clearly that are confusing to many of the other kids."

"Well, what about you? You're not exactly a low achiever, you know."

"I'll make a good reporter someday. I'm curious about what's happening around me. I'm not sure it's realistic, but right now I'm trying to figure out how to make it happen."

"And I can say I knew you when." He smiled.

"Great. Now that we know we're both going to be successful, all we have to do is hope the world holds together until we make our mark."

"Oh yeah, the world," Noah sighed. "I almost forgot about the world. Why did you have to bring up such a depressing subject?"

"Isn't reality a pain in the ass?" she said, pulling Noah down just enough to kiss him tenderly on the lips.

At about eleven o'clock that evening, Noah thought he heard a car pull up in front of the Salaman store. He went to the window that looked out on Fourth Street and pulled up the shade. Alexandra came over and put her arm around his waist as they looked out into the darkness. As they stood there, Hy Greenspan's blue Chrysler pulled up in front of the store, and Hy tapped lightly on the horn.

"We'd better go down," Noah said.

"Wait just a sec, Noah. I'd better put on some fresh lipstick," Alexandra replied.

At the top of the stairs Noah reached out and took Alexandra's hand. Standing on her toes and reaching up to him, she gave him a kiss on his cheek. Noah gently pulled her into his arms and kissed her, once again, on the lips.

"I love you, Alexandra," he whispered.

"I love you too," she said, gently pushing him away, "but I just put on fresh lipstick."

He laughed. "Smeared lipstick, the universal sign of shame."

She smiled and squeezed him for a moment before he turned and hurried down the stairs.

The Salamans were waiting at the entrance when Noah lifted the wooden bar and unlocked the door.

"Hi, Noah," Samira said, reaching up and kissing him on the cheek just as Alexandra had done only moments earlier.

Noah smiled warmly. Samira Salaman had never done that before.

***

Sharif stood in the doorway and watched Noah get into the Greenspan car, then he waved to them before closing the door.

"So tell me, Samira," Sharif asked in a low voice, "how close does a young man have to get to a girl before he can carry off the scent of her perfume with him?"

"About as close as you've gotten to me tonight." She laughed as she reached up and nuzzled her nose into his ear.

"I kissed you tonight!" he said, a sharp edge to his voice.

"And I think Noah probably kissed Alexandra tonight," Samira answered. "Frankly, I can't think of a nicer boy to have kissed her."

"You really feel that way, don't you?" he said.

"Of course, I do," she answered. "Would you rather she were kissed by someone else?"

"Is it written somewhere that she had to be kissed by anyone tonight?"

"Yes," she said with a laugh, "in the stars."

"Samira, I don't consider this a funny matter." Sharif followed her into the kitchen.

"I think you're making it a very funny matter, Sharif. Alexandra is sixteen, and one of the most thoughtful boys I've ever met probably gave her her first kiss tonight. Now, how big a crisis do you want to create over this?"

"You keep making this a personal matter between me and Noah," Sharif said, pulling a chair out from the table and straddling it so he could lean forward against the back of the chair. "I've told you it has nothing to do with Noah."

"Oh, Sharif, that's nonsense. It has everything to do with Noah. Do you think you can depersonalize this by talking about Arab honor? You want those kids to sacrifice their relationship in the name of Arab honor?"

"Samira, as God is my witness, I have nothing but affection for that boy. I would protect him as I would protect my own son if I thought he were in danger. But I do not want Alexandra to be with a Jew. Any Jew! Not Noah, not anyone. The Jews have humiliated the Arab people. Arabs cannot ignore that."

"But Noah has not humiliated anyone!" Samira answered, upset that they were having a disagreement for which there had been no provocation.

Alexandra leaned on the railing at the top of the stairs and listened as her parents argued about her and Noah.

**

The next day, Noah and Alexandra met, as they usually did, for lunch in the school cafeteria. He had made a major decision the night before and was anxious to discuss it with her.

"Noah, over here!" Alexandra called as soon as she spotted him. He had come into the crowded lunchroom late, and when he finally saw her waving to him, he hurriedly made his way to her table.

"Hi!" he said, kissing her on the cheek.

"Hi. I was worried you weren't coming," she said. "Everything all right?"

"Everything's great. I just had to talk with my advisor for a few minutes. Listen, we have to talk. There's something I want to do."

"You want to get something to eat first?" she asked. "I've already had a tuna sandwich."

"I'm not hungry. I'll grab something later."

"What's up?"

"Let's get pinned."

"What?!"

"Let me give you my fraternity pin. Let's tell the world, including your parents and my parents, that we're going steady, that we're a couple."

"Noah, I don't think that's a good idea. Why upset them more than they already are?"

"Because we *are* a couple. Everybody knows it. I don't go out with anyone else, and neither do you. The only reason we don't say it openly is this damned Arab-Jewish business. Sure, your dad will piss and moan, and so will my mom. So what?"

"They'll forbid it."

"They'll forbid what?"

"My being pinned to you."

"Look, if worse comes to worse—I mean, if they really get emotional over this—they'll make you give me back the pin. So, what have we lost? We'll be exactly where we are now."

"It isn't that easy, Noah. We're not just another couple whose relationship doesn't have parental approval."

"But that's just it, Alexandra. We really are just another couple. You and I aren't hung up over this Arab-Jewish business. Why should we let other people make it a problem?"

"Those other people you speak of aren't exactly strangers, Noah. We're talking about our mothers and fathers. We're talking about my brother, and we're probably talking about every aunt and uncle and cousin you have."

"Damn it, Alexandra, the only people we're not talking about is you and me! Nobody loves his parents more than I do, but I'm not going to turn my back on you without one hell of a fight."

"Nobody's talking about turning their back on anyone," she said. "But I don't think throwing down the gauntlet to our parents is a very smart idea. All it's going to do is create a huge issue."

"You know they're just sort of humoring us," Noah said. "They're positive we'll outgrow each other if they can just keep us at arm's length long enough. They're tolerating our relationship, and they probably figure we'll each find someone more suitable when we go away to college."

"Most parents with teenage kids who are going steady figure that."

"Alexandra, if I give you my fraternity pin, will you turn it down?"

"Please don't put me in that position, Noah. Please don't do that."

"For chrissake, Alexandra, all they could do is say no or insist that you give it back. What have we got to lose?"

"Plenty. Maybe they *are* just humoring us, but I'd rather have them humoring us than fighting with us."

"Wait a minute!" he said, grabbing her hand as she rose to go. "What about what we've been talking about?"

"Don't do this to me, Noah," she said again as the bell rang.

"Alexandra…"

"I have to go," she said. With a wan smile, she gave his hand a reassuring squeeze, then turned and hurried away.

"Shit!" Noah yelled, slamming his books down on the table.

***

That evening, Noah stayed late working on the senior class yearbook and didn't leave school until after five o'clock. It was turning dark as he headed down the deserted hill on T Street. As the evening shadows lengthened, Noah walked briskly, anxious to make his way to the busy intersection at Rhode Island Avenue just two blocks away. He never heard the furtive footsteps approaching him from behind.

"Hey, Jew," someone called out.

Noah spun around to confront whoever it was who had followed him from school. Before he knew what was happening, he was thrown to the ground, his head banging into the pavement. As he struggled to maintain consciousness, he felt rough hands going through his pockets. Suddenly, pushing through his fear and pain, he struck out blindly with his feet and fists. His foot connected with something solid, and his assailant cried out in pain. But the triumph was short-lived. Lying on the ground, head throbbing from his fall, Noah was no match for his attacker, who was enraged by Noah's attempts to defend himself. A fist was rammed viciously into Noah's midsection, causing him to double up in pain. Then a volley of kicks came at his face, head, and groin with a fury that continued even after Noah had, mercifully, passed out.

When he finally came to, choking from a combination of blood and vomit, Noah had no idea how much time had passed. Struggling to his knees, he gasped for air. He was in an alley, just a few short feet from where he'd been walking. There was no sign of his attacker, beyond Noah's extensive wounds and bruises and his missing watch and wallet.

After resting a few minutes, Noah managed to get to his feet, each movement filling him with agony. He slowly gathered up his books and stumbled back onto the street. By the time he'd hobbled home, his right eye was swollen shut, and the blood that had been running from his nose had begun to congeal.

Esther screamed in horror as Noah staggered into the store, his swollen, blood-covered face badly bruised. Hy rushed in from the back room where he had been unpacking groceries. The sight of his son struck terror in his heart.

"What happened?" he shouted. "My God, what happened to you?"

Hy and Esther got their son up the stairs and onto his bed. Esther tried as best she could to gently wipe away the blood from Noah's wounds as Hy raced for the phone to call the police. Right after he reported the attack, Hy called the Salamans.

Moments later, just as a squad car with two policemen pulled up, Sharif and Yusuf rushed into the store. Hy led Sharif, Yusuf, and the two officers up the stairs to Noah's room. Noah was lying on the bed, Esther holding an ice bag to his swollen face. His knees were pulled up tightly toward his abdomen to relieve the pain that still pulsated through his groin.

Esther, tears streaming down her face, just shook her head when she saw Sharif and Yusuf. "Why?" she mouthed to them.

As the police began to question Noah, Hy signaled Sharif and Yusuf to follow him from the room. "Noah was walking home from school. Whoever the bastard was who did it simply called him a Jew and jumped him from behind when he reached the alley on T Street."

"Why would anyone do it?" Yusuf asked. "Noah doesn't have an enemy in the world."

"Who the hell knows?" Hy answered.

"Mr. Greenspan, can I see you for a moment?" one of the policemen called to him.

"Yes, officer." Hy sighed and walked back to the entrance of the room.

"Mr. Greenspan, this appears to be nothing more than a mugging by someone who doesn't like Jews. It could have been another student or someone who guessed he was a Jewish boy. Most of the white kids live east of the school. They may have just guessed that a white boy walking into the Negro neighborhood must have been a Jewish kid who was from one of the retail families in this area. It's happened before. Does Noah have any enemies at the school?"

Hy shook his head. "Absolutely not. Noah doesn't have any enemies."

"Are you sure?"

"I'm as sure as you can be," Hy replied. "I mean, how do you ever know about these things? If anyone has a grudge against Noah, I've never heard about it."

"Noah doesn't have any enemies at Tech," Yusuf offered. "I would know. There's nobody better liked than Noah."

"Well," the officer said, "there you have it. We'll want to get a statement from the boy when he's had a chance to recover, but I have to tell you, the odds of us ever catching this guy are pretty remote. I'm really sorry."

As the two policemen were leaving, Alexandra passed them on the stairs. She had run to the Greenspans as soon as Samira told her of the attack on Noah.

"Noah!" she called, rushing up the narrow stairs.

"He's in the first room, miss," one of the police officers called up to her.

"Noah!" she gasped as she ran into his room. "Noah, what happened?"

Noah waved feebly to Alexandra, trying for a grin, which came out instead as a grimace of pain.

"What happened?" she cried again, bringing her hands to her face in horror.

"Someone attacked Noah, Alexandra," Yusuf said.

"But who would do this?" she cried.

"We don't know," Esther said, her face white and drawn with fear at the sight of her only child so badly beaten. "Whoever it was snuck up behind Noah when he was walking home from school."

"But who would do such a thing?" Alexandra asked again, looking frantically about the room from face to face, her eyes begging for an explanation.

"There are plenty of vicious and sick people in Washington," Hy answered angrily. "Don't forget the thugs who attacked the Izumis."

"Whoever did it called Noah a Jew just before he attacked him," Esther said, barely above a whisper.

Sharif and Yusuf glanced at one another. Sharif, an expression of pain on his face, closed his eyes and simply shook his head. Yusuf took a step toward the bed. "I'm sorry, pal," he whispered.

"Oh, Noah," Alexandra murmured as she moved to the edge of the bed and kissed him on the forehead. Noah reached out, took her hand, and squeezed it gently. Hy and Sharif glanced uncomfortably at each other as they watched the exchange between their children.

"Noah, I'd love to wear your fraternity pin," Alexandra suddenly said with fierce determination, tears streaming from her eyes. "I'd be the luckiest girl in the world!"

Noah forced his eyes open and looked up at her. A smile touched his lips, again bringing an immediate wince of pain. Bending low,

Alexandra heard him murmur through his swollen, blood-caked lips, "Gee, if I'd known this was what it was going to take…"

The room fell silent as Alexandra sat down on the edge of the bed and gently took Noah in her arms. As the two embraced, it was hard to tell whether the expressions of concern on their parents' faces were for what had already occurred that night or for something else that might very well lie just ahead.

CHAPTER ELEVEN

Noah lay with his head in Alexandra's lap, looking up into the puffs of white billowy clouds floating in the sky above Rock Creek Park. They had driven there after school, as they did frequently that spring. Earlier in the year, they had discovered a special spot, a flat outcropping of rock high above the road, less than a quarter mile from Pierce Mill, the old flour-mill landmark in the park. The rock was accessible only by a narrow footpath that snaked its way up a steep hill overgrown with thick, almost impenetrable foliage. It was to this private paradise that the young couple escaped and spent a few uninterrupted hours whenever they could.

In years to come, Noah would often recall and savor images from these special interludes with Alexandra. Every sight, every sound, every aroma reminiscent of that bucolic place would, invariably, summon wonderful memories with vivid clarity: the soft, slow sound of Alexandra's breathing and the distant, faint roar of the creek cascading against the rocks; the sweet, heady fragrance of the wildflowers that blanketed the ground around them, mingled with the clean aroma of Alexandra's silken hair; the shadow of Alexandra's lashes on her cheek as her eyes closed in anticipation of Noah's kisses. But right now they were here, together, the world reduced to just the two of them. Noah reached up to pull Alexandra down toward him. Her hand tenderly caressing the side of his face, she yielded to the gentle tug of his arms.

"I love you, Noah Greenspan," she whispered.

"And I love you, Alexandra Salaman."

"You'll be going off to college soon," she said, "and that scares me."

"There's nothing to be afraid of, Alexandra. I'll be home for Christmas. We'll write or call every week, and the time will fly by. You'll see."

She smiled and lightly traced the contours of his face with her fingertips.

"Stanford's a long way from Washington," she said. "I'll be sharing you with a thousand distractions."

"You think and speak poetically. Did anyone ever tell you that before?"

"I think and speak like an Arab," she replied. "We're all poets at heart."

"Doesn't it seem as though we're a thousand miles from LeDroit Park?" he mused.

"It's like paradise," she replied. "It's the only place you and I are ever alone."

"It's kind of sad that we have to escape in order to just be ourselves, isn't it?" he asked.

"Well, we're ourselves now, aren't we?" she answered, leaning down to kiss him again.

Noah embraced Alexandra and held her tightly for a moment as they kissed. Then, their desire mounting, they rolled over, and Noah, for the first time, felt Alexandra's body under his own. She looked up at him, momentarily startled. He slid his hand under her head to protect her from the hard surface of the rock. Her eyes smiled up at him as he again brought his lips down gently onto hers. Then Alexandra tightened her embrace and slowly pushed her lower body up against his.

Noah lifted himself up just enough to look into her eyes, his gaze full of affection, while her soft, unbroken stare silently but eloquently spoke of her love for him. Alexandra spread her legs as much as her skirt would allow so that he easily slid between the contours of her thighs. She felt the firmness of his excitement pressing against her and, almost frantically, she pulled his head down to hers and pressed her lips against his.

"Make love to me, Noah," she suddenly said.

"What?"

"Make love to me."

"When? Where?" he asked, pulling himself up so he could look into her eyes.

"Now…here…in the woods…in the mill—I don't care."

Noah rolled off her and propped himself up on one arm.

"Alexandra, I love you and I want to make love to you, you know that. But I looked your father right in the eye and told him I intended to keep seeing you, but that I wouldn't give him any reason for concern."

"We were just kids then. You're getting ready to go off to college, and you have kept your word to my father." She turned on her side to face him.

"Alexandra, I intend to marry you someday. We both know it's not going to be easy. We don't have to create problems for ourselves now."

"Is that what you think making love to me would be: creating problems?"

"No. Making love to you would be wonderful. It would be sheer ecstasy. But it would absolutely destroy your father if he knew."

"I don't intend to tell my father."

"Parents sense those things. Besides, I have to look him in the eye every day. If I so much as flinched or did anything any differently, he'd pick up on it in an instant."

"We're not going to be together forever," she said matter-of-factly.

"Don't say that!"

"But it's true, Noah. Everything is against us."

"Not everything. We're in love. People in love stay together. Why are you so certain we won't last?"

"Our parents pray we'll break up sooner or later. Yusuf hardly talks to me because I'm wearing your fraternity pin. He thinks it's a disgrace.

Today we're neighbors in the heart of a Negro ghetto, but soon you'll be out in California, surrounded by bright and attractive girls and probably lots of them Jewish too. It's not going to last, Noah. You know it isn't."

"Don't ruin it, Alexandra!" Noah rose to his knees. "Start believing we're going to break up, and you'll make it happen. Is that what you want?"

"You know that isn't what I want. It's just that I can't imagine how we could ever get married. Can you imagine what our parents would do?"

"Marriage is years off. Things can change. The world can change. You have to believe that."

"Do you believe that things are going to change? That four or five years from now, the world will be so different that you and I could marry?"

"Yes! Yes, I do believe that. And do you want to know why I believe that? Because I can't imagine going through life without you. You can't imagine the circumstances where we'd be able to get married, and I can't imagine the circumstances where I'd ever be with anyone else."

"I love you, Noah, but I think you're a dreamer."

"Look, you're seeing the whole world the way it is now. Maybe you're right. Maybe things will be no better five years from now. Maybe they'll even be worse. We'll have to cross that bridge when we get to it. But maybe—just maybe—things will be better. Meanwhile, let's not even think about breaking up."

"I wasn't suggesting breaking up. I just think I'm more realistic than you are about the future, that's all."

"Our future is up to us, Alexandra. Five years from now, if you still want to marry me and I still want to marry you, then that's all that should matter. I don't want to hurt my parents any more than you want to hurt yours, but if they can't understand that, then that's going to have to be their problem—not ours."

Alexandra smiled at Noah. "You're one in a million, Noah Greenspan," she said as she reached out with both arms and grabbed him by the shoulders.

"Hey!" he yelled when Alexandra pushed him over backward and threw herself over his body.

"Alex—"

She pressed her lips firmly against his mouth, silencing his protest. He responded, embracing her tightly as their tongues touched and explored. Then, as she had done earlier, she pressed her body firmly against him. Noah slid both hands under Alexandra's sweater and, after a moment's awkward fumbling, unfastened the clasp of her bra. The touch of her bare skin under her sweater sent his senses reeling, and as they rolled over, his hand closed gently over her breast. Noah could feel her heart beating under the warm flesh. Her erect nipple pressed into the palm of his hand, electrifying him.

"We're going to make love before you go away to school, Noah. I don't want to just be your girlfriend when you leave. What we have is more special than that."

"I know," he whispered.

***

Samira knew something was on Sharif's mind. He was unusually pensive. The last time she could remember him being so distracted was during the weeks leading up to his decision to leave Palestine and move to America. She sighed. Her husband would reveal his thoughts when he was ready.

Sharif knew it would be futile to insist that Alexandra and Noah stop seeing each other. Alexandra was too much like Samira. He was sure they had both inherited a strong stubborn streak from Samira's British father. The girl was too determined and inquisitive and bright to be dictated to, and he would only drive her away if he interfered too much. He knew that. And while that would be preferable to the disgrace she could bring to their family, he hoped to find a better way to deal with his high-spirited daughter.

Yusuf approached the dinner table, shuffling through several letters he had received that morning. "I'm still receiving mail from colleges that have openings for the fall term," he said.

"You should be flattered," Samira said. "They're still after you."

"Anything interesting?" Alexandra asked.

He laughed. "Not as interesting as a full scholarship to Yale," he said, referring to the scholarship in architecture he had been awarded. His academic achievement had been a godsend for Sharif and Samira, who would not have been able to afford Yale on their own.

"Who have you heard from?" she asked.

"Wheaton College in Massachusetts, Haverford—I think that's near Philadelphia—and the Phoenicia University at Beirut," he replied, sifting through the envelopes once again.

Sharif suddenly grew serious, his eyes drawn to the envelope Yusuf held in his hand. "You received a letter from Beirut?" he asked.

"Well, from the school there, the Phoenicia University at Beirut," Yusuf replied.

"What does it say, Yusuf?"

"Nothing much, they're just inviting me to apply. That's all."

Sharif nodded. "It is a good school?"

"Yes, I think so. One of our counselors said it's the best school in the Middle East. He probably sent them my name because we're Arab."

Alexandra shifted her eyes to her father and watched him apprehensively. Sharif, deep in thought, lowered his eyes to the table for a moment and then turned his attention to his daughter.

"Phoenicia," he said softly, referring to the beautiful, ancient land that now included the country known as Lebanon.

Alexandra nodded her understanding.

"It would be a wonderful place to study," he said, his eyes still on his daughter.

"It's good the children of Lebanon have such schools available to them," Alexandra replied carefully. "Of course, we're even more fortunate here in the United States with so many excellent institutions."

"Yes, the children of America have such fine schools available to them," he said. "They're very fortunate if their parents can afford to send them."

"Yes, *we* are very fortunate," Alexandra said, a defiant edge to her voice.

"Alexandra, come help me serve!" Samira interrupted, trying to break off the conversation before the rising tension between Sharif and Alexandra got out of hand.

***

Samira always worried when Sharif withdrew when he was deep in thought. He became unapproachable and pensive until he was ready to discuss whatever was on his mind. This time, his mood changed the moment Yusuf mentioned the university in Beirut. He said little more at dinner and remained uncommunicative the rest of the evening. It was not until Samira joined him in bed that he revealed what was on his mind.

"This Phoenicia University at Beirut could be a godsend to us, Samira. It is the perfect place for Arab children to be educated."

"Sharif, Yusuf has a full scholarship to one of America's finest universities. You saw for yourself that he had no interest in the school in Beirut."

"I wasn't thinking of Yusuf."

"Alexandra! You would suggest that Alexandra go all the way to Lebanon to study when there are so many wonderful institutions here in America?"

"It would be the one opportunity we have to expose her to some semblance of Arab culture and Arab values. She could enjoy an excellent education in an environment that would give her a chance to meet bright young Arabs."

"Would you be so interested in having Alexandra go to Beirut to study if it weren't for her friendship with Noah?"

"Friendship! Is that what you call it? If we don't do something, that child is going to disgrace us forever."

"Sharif, listen to yourself. What are you saying? There is nothing about Noah that could ever bring disgrace to this or any other family. He is a wonderful young man who treats our daughter with love and respect. Besides, he's going to college in California. Alexandra will go away to school somewhere else, and they will hardly ever see one another during the next five years. There is no reason to send Alexandra halfway around the world for her education."

"If we're going to send her away anyway, what difference does it make whether it's halfway across the country or halfway around the world? What's wrong with a university that will educate her, and do it in an Arab environment as well?"

"Nothing at all unless you're doing it just to separate her from Noah," Samira replied. "Alexandra will resent any suggestion that she study in Beirut. She will see it as an attempt to interfere in her life. I beg you, Sharif, don't propose this to her. The child has another year of school left. Don't worry her with this idea now, please!"

"There's no need to discuss it now, Samira. But I disagree with you entirely. I think it is a splendid idea. I think any Arab child that has been forced to live outside the Arab world, as Alexandra has, should be thrilled to be able to go to this university in Beirut."

"Alexandra is an American now, Sharif. She will want to go to school with other Americans," Samira insisted.

"She is an Arab, Samira. She will always be an Arab. She should take advantage of an opportunity to live and study among Arabs."

"If she chooses to apply to the university in Beirut, that's one thing. But Alexandra is a young woman now. It should be her choice to make. We should not force this upon her."

Sharif shrugged his shoulders. "Have I said anything about forcing this upon Alexandra?"

***

The Greenspans and the Salamans celebrated the graduations of their two boys from McKinley Tech with dinner together at Hogates, an old seafood restaurant on the Maine Avenue waterfront across the river from Haines Point and Washington National Airport. Yusuf brought a date to dinner, an attractive blue-eyed blond named Maggie Kieley. Maggie had had a crush on Yusuf throughout high school, and everyone thought she had selected Hartford College in Connecticut just to be near him while he studied at Yale. Yusuf and Noah had made plans with Maggie and Alexandra to go after dinner to the old Shubert Theater on Ninth Street to see a road-show performance of *Kismet*. It was a relaxed and delightful dinner.

Sharif was in fine spirits listening to the boys talk of their plans. Yusuf had decided on a career in architecture, and Noah said he wanted to develop real estate—to build things in the nation's capital.

"Maybe someday Yusuf and Noah will work together," Hy speculated. "Yusuf will design skyscrapers, and Noah will build them."

"That sounds great, but skyscrapers aren't allowed in Washington," Noah said.

Sharif laughed. "So, you'll build small skyscrapers."

"Alexandra, Maggie, let's hear about your plans," Esther said.

Sharif looked at Esther, annoyed that she had interrupted. "Yes, of course. Have you decided on a career, Maggie?" he asked.

"I plan to get a BA in education and eventually teach school."

"Ah!" Sharif exclaimed. "Very good!"

"And what about you, Alexandra?" Esther asked, just as Sharif was about to redirect the discussion back to the boys.

"Alexandra has time," he answered for his daughter. "She still has a year of high school left."

"I plan to major in journalism," Alexandra replied, ignoring her father. "I hope to go to the University of Missouri or to Syracuse. They both have excellent journalism schools."

"And when was this decided?" Sharif asked.

"I've been interested in journalism ever since I began writing for the school paper," she replied. "I love to write, and it's what I want to do after I'm through with school. My English teacher nominated me for a summer position at the *Evening Star*. I probably won't get the job because they have applications from all over the city, but it's an honor just to be considered."

"She's really a great writer, Mr. Salaman," Maggie said. "Everybody thinks Alexandra's stories are the best in the school paper."

"I think journalism is a wonderful career," Esther said encouragingly. But it was clear Sharif wanted to hear no more about his daughter's plans, and before long the conversation once again centered on Noah and Yusuf and their plans for the future.

***

After dinner, while Hy and Esther drove the Salamans home, the two young couples made their way over to Ninth Street in Noah's Chevy.

Kismet was the first Broadway show they had seen, and they loved it. "I think I'll spend the rest of my life singing 'Stranger in Paradise,'" Maggie said as they walked to the car after the performance. "Wasn't it beautiful?"

"Take my hand, I'm a stranger in paradise..." Noah crooned as he opened the door for Alexandra.

"Noah," Yusuf whispered as soon as he closed the rear door after Maggie. "Let me take your car when you get to our place to drop off Alexandra. I'd like to take Maggie home alone."

Noah grinned. "You got it."

When they arrived at the Crescent Market, Noah got out of the car and tossed the keys over the hood to Yusuf, who was circling the car to take Noah's place behind the wheel.

"Sorry, I removed them by force of habit," Noah said. "Keep the keys. I'll come by for them in the morning."

"Bye, Alexandra. I'll call you over the weekend," Maggie said, waiting awkwardly for Alexandra to get out of the car.

"Good night, Maggie," Alexandra replied. "And see you tomorrow, Yusuf," she added with a touch of irritation.

After Yusuf and Maggie had driven off up Fourth Street, Alexandra turned and handed Noah her key to the door of the Crescent Market.

"Your mood certainly seems to have headed south," Noah said as he unlocked the door and held it open for her.

"It irritates the hell out of me," she replied curtly.

"What does?"

"The fact that my father couldn't care less that Yusuf has gone off with Maggie tonight."

"What's the big deal about Yusuf taking Maggie home?"

"You know damn well he's not just taking her home. They'll drive over to Pierce Mill and make out for a couple of hours before he drops her off. It's fine for Yusuf to do that, but my father would be seething inside if he thought you and I were parked somewhere."

"Don't you think most fathers have a double standard when it comes to sons and daughters?"

"That's not what I'm talking about," she replied sharply.

Noah sighed. "I know. It really doesn't make much sense, does it?"

"Oh, it makes perfectly good sense to my father. Yusuf can't really disgrace the family by his relationship with a girl. But my relationship with you is a different matter. Did you notice how interested he was in what you and Yusuf were planning to do with your lives? It hadn't even occurred to him to ask what my plans were."

"Aren't you being a little hard on him? After all, we were all together because Yusuf and I just graduated. It was natural for the discussion to be focused on us."

"Noah, I informed my parents of my career decision tonight. You saw the expression on my father's face. It was as though I had interrupted an important conversation. He just didn't consider my news worth discussing."

"I think you're overreacting a little bit. He just looked a little surprised to me, that's all."

"Oh, he was surprised all right. He's always surprised when I don't conform to what he expects of me."

"And what do you think he expects of you?"

"He expects me to be a good Arab daughter. But I'm not just an Arab and not just a daughter. I'm also an American and a woman with a mind of her own. My father simply can't relate to any of my aspirations. He has no problem with Yusuf's developing independence, but I think he feels threatened whenever I display any of that same independence."

"He'll get used to it, Alexandra. He wants what's best for you, just like any parent."

"That's bunk, Noah. My mother is not like that at all. She won't fight with my father, at least not in front of me or Yusuf, but she totally disagrees with his paranoia about you and me."

"Has she told you that?"

"No, not directly, but I can tell. His obsession with our relationship upsets her very much."

"You don't think she would be upset if we were planning to get married?"

"She would worry whether or not we could be happy, but she certainly wouldn't feel it's the disgrace my father thinks it would be."

Noah opened the Salaman refrigerator. "Have anything to drink?" he asked.

"Sure, I think we have some orange juice on the top shelf. I'll have a glass too."

Noah took the half-full juice jar from the refrigerator.

"My father drinks a glass of orange juice every morning," Alexandra said. "It's a ritual."

"So do millions of other people."

Alexandra smiled. "It's different though. He drinks it because it reminds him of our citrus grove in Palestine. You should see the look on his face when he has his juice. He closes his eyes and savors the taste. It's like a religious experience with him. He stands there for a moment, concentrating while the taste is still fresh in his mouth. It's almost as if, momentarily, it takes him back to our home in Jaffa. He's almost in a trance for several seconds."

"He does that every morning?"

"Every morning," she replied.

They moved to the kitchen table and sat down with their glasses of orange juice. As Alexandra set her glass on the table, she noticed the letter addressed to her father. It was from the Phoenicia University at Beirut.

"Oh God!" she said in a whisper.

"What's wrong, Alexandra?" Noah asked.

"That!" She sighed and cast her eyes to the envelope in front of them.

"What is it?"

"Read it."

"I can't do that, Alexandra. It's addressed to your father."

"He left it here on purpose, Noah. He wanted me to see it and read it."

Noah looked at her, hesitating for a moment. Then he picked up the unsealed envelope.

"Go on, read it," she said.

Noah paused a moment longer and then removed the letter.

Dear Mr. Salaman:

Enclosed you will find the application and catalog you requested. We shall be delighted to receive an application from your daughter, Alexandra, in the autumn, and will look forward to having her study with us should she be admitted and decide to enroll at the University next year.

Salaam Alaikum

Basil Haddad, Director of Admissions

"What the hell is this all about?" Noah asked.

"Just my father trying to arrange my life for me. Now do you understand what I've been talking about?"

"He wants you to go to college in Lebanon?" Noah was dumbfounded.

Alexandra smiled as she peered into his eyes. "You read the letter."

"He can't be serious!"

"Oh, he's serious. That's why he was so taken aback at dinner when I talked about studying journalism at Syracuse or the University of Missouri. I was interfering with his grand scheme."

Noah leaned back in his chair and stared up at the ceiling for a moment, trying to comprehend what he had just learned.

"I can't believe it," he moaned.

"Don't worry. I don't plan to go to school in Lebanon," she said. "Nothing could make me do that."

"I don't understand," Noah said, his voice unsteady. "How could he do this?"

"It's perfectly logical to him."

"There is nothing logical about wanting to send a daughter all the way to Lebanon when some of the world's best schools are right here in America," he replied angrily.

"It's not a school he's looking for. It's an entire culture he's trying to establish contact with."

"Promise me you won't go, Alexandra," Noah implored. "You have to promise me you won't go all the way to Beirut."

"Noah, there isn't an argument that could ever convince me to go to school there," she replied.

"Do you think your father was just inquiring, or do you think he really intends to push the issue?"

"I'm not sure, but I think he's very serious about this. He gets very emotional about the loss of our Arab identity. He doesn't seem to give a damn about what Yusuf does. I mean, he seems delighted about Yusuf going to Yale, and Maggie certainly doesn't seem to present the dilemma to him that you represent. He's not worried whether Yusuf is serious about Maggie—he knows he's not. But I think it is important to him that one day I give him Arab grandchildren. You're a threat to that. Almost anyone I could ever hope to meet here would be a threat to that, but you're a particularly big threat. I tell you, my father worries himself sick that because of me, our family will be stigmatized in the eyes of the Arab world."

"Because I'm a Jew."

"Because you're a Jew."

"And he thinks that sending you to college in Beirut would prevent that from happening?"

"He thinks it could," she replied.

Noah felt queasiness in the pit of his stomach. "Sometimes the odds do seem insurmountable, don't they?"

Alexandra reached over and squeezed his arm affectionately. Their eyes locked. "They may be, Noah," she said with sad resignation.

CHAPTER TWELVE

Alexandra could not have been more surprised when the call came from the personnel office of the *Evening Star*. It had been weeks since she had applied for one of the summer jobs that Washington's leading evening newspaper offered aspiring high school journalists. Alexandra was overjoyed, as were all the Salamans. As soon as she heard, she left for the For You Market to tell Noah and the Greenspans that she got the job.

While she was gone, the letter from Beirut arrived. It advised Sharif that, yes, the Phoenicia University at Beirut had a school of journalism and furthermore, his daughter might well be eligible for a four-year, full-tuition scholarship. Sharif folded the letter and slipped it into the pocket of his apron to await an appropriate moment to tell Alexandra the news. He dreaded the confrontation he knew was coming.

***

Alexandra began working at the *Star* on the last Monday of June 1956. She began her new job at the very time Gamel Abdul Nasser became president of Egypt. She thought it was a good omen.

Alexandra soon found herself keenly interested in world affairs as she made her rounds, checking the various wire service machines, tearing off each hour's developing stories to distribute to the appropriate news desks. She was fascinated by the news of Marilyn Monroe's marriage to Arthur Miller the last week in June. News came from Algiers about the war raging between the French and the Arab rebels who were fighting to free Algeria from European domination. And only days earlier, Great Britain, after a seventy-two-year presence, had sailed out of Port Said, leaving the Suez Canal's defense in Egypt's hands.

Alexandra quickly became the Salaman family's authority on world events. A ritual developed at dinner each night: Sharif would question Alexandra, and Samira and Yusuf would listen to her answers. Alexandra's status within the family was enhanced by her job, and Sharif genuinely relished the discussions each evening. He was particularly eager to discuss President Nasser, who he saw as the most important figure in the entire Arab world. After years of impotent leadership that had brought havoc to the Middle East, a new personality had walked onto the pages of history and lifted the dignity and morale of every Arab.

***

Franklin Markazie, wire service editor for the *Evening Star*, knew from Alexandra Salaman's first day at the paper that she was special. The other kids were little more than couriers running back and forth all day to carry messages and dispatches to the various editors and reporters. But Alexandra was different. She read every item. Markazie watched her absorbing every story and searching the paper each day to see how the reporters and editors had treated the raw material she had brought them from the wires. Frank Markazie asked all the "summer kids," as he called them, what they saw in the dispatches. Alexandra's responses were always head and shoulders above those of the other summer staffers.

One time he asked Alexandra what she thought of the news about first the United States and then Britain withdrawing their offers of support for building the Aswan Dam in Egypt; the stories had run on successive days, July 19 and 20. Alexandra shrugged and said, "We missed the point."

"Explain," Markazie demanded.

Alexandra told him she thought Nasser could use the American and British actions as an excuse to take over the canal. Everyone knew

Nasser intended to make a grab for the canal; he had been threatening such a move all summer.

So when the president of Egypt announced six days later that he was nationalizing the waterway to fund the High Dam at Aswan, Frank Markazie was impressed. There had been no speculation in the press that American or British backpedaling on Aswan might provoke such a move, and he felt Alexandra's assessment showed real journalistic promise.

Sharif, exhilarated by Nasser's bold move, proclaimed at dinner that night that European meddling in the affairs of the Arabs was over.

"What does the press think about all of this, Alexandra?" he asked. "Are they ready to start showing the Arab world the respect it deserves?"

Alexandra shook her head and smiled sympathetically at her father. "No, they're not showing respect for what President Nasser has done, Father. They think he has overplayed his hand."

"Overplayed his hand? He is taking what is his."

"It's not that simple," she replied. "There are agreements and treaties. The British built the canal, not Egypt, and all the major powers say the canal should be internationalized because of the international dependency on the waterway."

"And should the new Saint Lawrence Seaway be internationalized, too?" he asked indignantly. "Maybe Egypt should call for the internationalization of the Saint Lawrence Seaway."

"America and Canada can protect their asset," Alexandra answered. "Egypt can't."

"So the people at the paper think the British and the French will interfere?" he asked.

"Mr. Markazie says our people in Europe think there will be war if President Nasser goes ahead with the nationalization plan."

"What do they think the United States will do if there is war?" he asked.

"They say the American secretary of state, John Foster Dulles, would like to stop President Nasser. If President Eisenhower encourages the French and the British, there will be war," she said.

Then Yusuf asked, "What about the Israelis? What do they say about the Israelis?"

Alexandra shrugged. "I haven't heard any news about the Israelis, although Mr. Markazie says he thinks Israel would love an opportunity to take the canal. They're furious that the use of an international waterway could be denied them."

"What does Noah have to say about all of this?" Yusuf asked. "Do the two of you have much trouble discussing the affairs of the Middle East?"

"Yusuf!" Samira interrupted.

"Mother, I'm not trying to antagonize Alexandra. I'm really curious. Noah is my friend too. I've had some conflicts with him, but I still consider him my friend. We really are worlds apart over this business. We worship Nasser, and the Greenspans probably think he's another Hitler. I'm really curious. What does Noah have to say about all of this?"

"His views are similar to what I hear from most people at work. They view Nasser as a troublemaker. He has sworn to destroy Israel, and whether we like it or not, most people in the United States support Israel. Noah thinks Nasser will embroil the entire Middle East in a war."

"He thinks Nasser is a Hitler?" Sharif asked.

"He's never spoken of Nasser in those terms," she replied, "but I think he views Nasser as a very evil man. Most of the people I come in contact with believe Nasser is trying to control the Arab world."

"*Lead* the Arab world," Sharif insisted. "He is not trying to control the Arab world, he is trying to lead it. And I ask you, does it not need leadership?"

"One man's hero is another man's despot," Alexandra answered philosophically.

"Alexandra, doesn't it bother you to wear the fraternity pin of someone who sees President Nasser as a despot?" Yusuf asked.

Alexandra sighed. "No, not really. Not because it doesn't matter, but because I try hard not to think about these things too much when we're together. The mess in the world doesn't change the fact that Noah is a wonderful person."

"I don't think you're being realistic, Alexandra," Yusuf said, more with affection than with anger.

"You know, Yusuf, I'm not sure we're being realistic either. Time will tell. But I'll tell you what I *am* sure of," she said looking him in the eye and choosing her words carefully. "I'm sure there is absolutely nothing shameful in my relationship with Noah. There is nothing about Noah that could ever bring dishonor or disgrace to this or any family. Maybe our respective heritages will be more than our relationship can endure, but if that turns out to be the case, the real tragedy will be the destruction of that relationship, not the relationship itself."

No one spoke. Sharif and Samira exchanged brief glances. Yusuf, after a moment's hesitation, smiled faintly and nodded his understanding.

***

It was an eventful summer. Alexandra's ambition to become a journalist hardened into zealous determination as she stood in front of the teletype machines and watched each day's news unfold. She felt a sense of power being part of the process through which history is given expression. Alexandra read with cold businesslike detachment each dispatch as it clattered out of the machine. Only later would she let herself react to the information as an emotional reader. When the Teletype paper fed through her hands the early details of the collision off the coast of Nantucket of the *Stockholm* and the *Andrea Doria*, it was merely information to be reported. But at home later that evening, she was horrified as she read the story in the paper about the fifty-two people who had died in the disaster.

Alexandra followed the nominations of Eisenhower and Nixon and Stevenson and Kefauver on the Teletype machines, and she winced at the news of Jackson Pollock's death hours before most of the rest of the world learned about the rebellious artist's fatal automobile accident. Standing before those noisy mechanical messengers of history each day, Alexandra knew she would, one day, be one of those creating the stories that would pass through teletype machines around the world.

Alexandra trusted Frank Markazie. He was the worldliest man she had ever known, and she credited him with all she learned working at the *Star* that summer.

Late one morning, Markazie stuck his head into the teletype room, where Alexandra was skimming the various wire stories.

"C'mon, I'll buy you a tuna sandwich," he said. "I'll take you to Pe-op'-oles—best Greek cuisine in town."

"Really!" she said, laughing as she accepted his invitation to a counter lunch at the nearby People's Drugstore.

Frank Markazie was tall and trim, and Alexandra guessed his age to be about fifty. He had wiry, gray hair, striated with dark tinges. His steel-blue eyes could rivet a colleague's attention or coax a smile in a lighter moment. Markazie always wore a bow tie, but he invariably worked in shirtsleeves, regardless of the season.

"So, you still want to be a journalist?" he asked as they claimed two adjacent stools at the counter.

"Oh yes!" she replied. "More than ever."

"Good! You're going to be famous someday."

"Oh, without question!" she said facetiously.

"You think I'm teasing you?"

"Aren't you?"

"Not a bit, Alexandra. I can spot a newshound. You don't know it yet, but you were born with printer's ink in your blood. You are a natural journalist. Any other career will be a waste of your talent."

"Do you really mean that, Mr. Markazie? Please don't kid about this."

"Alexandra, I'll tell you a little secret. You're the best summer kid I've ever had at the paper."

Alexandra beamed from ear to ear. "Do you think I could come back next year?"

"If you commit to journalism as a major when you're ready for college, the job is yours."

"Oh, that's great! I'd love to have a chance to write for the paper!"

"How about now?"

Alexandra's eyes widened. "What would you like me to write about?"

"What would you like to write about?"

"I…I don't know. I mean, I'm not exactly an expert on anything. I mean, not yet, anyway."

"Oh, I beg to differ, Alexandra. I think you have rare and interesting areas of expertise."

She looked at him quizzically. "I do?"

"Yes, you do. You're an all-American girl, Alexandra. Now, we both know that that's not a story in and of itself. But you're an *immigrant* all-American girl. What's more, you're a *refugee* all-American girl. Now we're beginning to home in on something that might just be a story. But you're not just an immigrant and a refugee; you're an Arab immigrant-refugee all-American girl. Now that, Alexandra, is a story."

"You want me to write about me?" she asked, surprised by Markazie's interest in her.

"Yes, you and your immigrant family and um…"

"And what?" She was surprised to find Markazie tongue-tied, even for a moment.

"Alexandra, we did a story no more than a year ago about a high school fraternity that raised a ton of money for muscular dystrophy—several thousand dollars, as I recall."

"Yes?" she replied, curious.

"Well, the boys we interviewed wore the same fraternity pin you're wearing."

"I know—Upsilon Lambda Phi. I'm pinned to one of their members. They raise money for muscular dystrophy. But what does that have to do with me?" she asked nervously, beginning to anticipate the focus of his curiosity.

"Alexandra, while you are writing about your family's immigrant experiences in America, you might want to include some copy on how an Arab girl fell in love with a Jewish boy."

Alexandra sat stunned for a moment. "Can I think about it?

"Sure, think about it," he said with a wry smile. "But while you're at it, think about this too. I can take you back across the street and show you three hundred seasoned reporters who would kill to be in a position to do this piece. Not one of them can. You, Miss Summer Intern of 1956, and you alone, have the knowledge and the talent and, I'd bet, the pain and heartache to do this story."

Again she stared back at him, speechless.

"Two tunas with coffee!" the waitress said, interrupting them.

CHAPTER
THIRTEEN

"Well, old man, it won't be long before I'll be calling New Haven home and you'll be hailing from Palo Alto, California," Yusuf said as Noah tossed the packet he had received from Stanford across the Greenspans' kitchen table toward his friend.

"Boy, it looks a hell of a lot nicer than New Haven," Yusuf continued as he thumbed through one of the descriptive booklets.

"A lot of water's gone under the bridge since your folks first brought you and Alexandra to Gage back in forty-nine," Noah mused.

"Hey, man, do you realize you've been my best friend from the time we met that first day?"

"And you've been mine," Noah said. "That's never going to change either. We'll always be able to pick up wherever we've left off, even if we don't see one another for months or years. I really believe that."

"We have to keep in touch while we're at school. We could really drift apart if we don't make a real effort."

"We'll keep in touch. I don't have any doubt about that. I'll be curious as hell about what you're doing."

"College is going to fly by. Before you know it, I'll be an architect and you'll be starting some business here in Washington. It's going to happen just like that." Yusuf snapped his fingers.

"From your lips to God's ears, buddy."

"I'm so damn excited to get on with this next stage of my life," Yusuf went on. "Do you realize, LeDroit Park will be just a place we come to during school breaks? Soon we'll leave these dingy markets for school and never return, except to visit our folks."

"I guess I never thought of it that way," Noah answered. "I mean, it's home. It's the pits, but I still have pretty warm feelings about this place."

"You're kidding."

"No, I mean it. I hardly remember anyplace else. I grew up here. I met you and Alexandra because we were here. I was sitting right at this table when I learned I won a scholarship to Stanford. Whatever I am, I became...here."

Yusuf smiled at his friend affectionately. "You're a piece of work, Noah."

"Hey, you guys," Alexandra called to them as she made her way up to the Greenspan kitchen from the store. "Can a girl join this party, or is this an exclusive men's club?"

"Hi, babe," Noah said, lifting his face to kiss her on the cheek.

"Hi, sis," Yusuf muttered absently as he thumbed through the Stanford course catalog.

"All that stuff from Stanford?" she asked.

"Yeah, it came in today's mail," Noah replied, making little effort to conceal his excitement.

Alexandra feigned enthusiasm too, but excitement wasn't what she felt as she huddled with Noah and Yusuf over the material. Rather, she felt a sense of dread, and only the smile she forced kept her from bursting into tears.

***

Samira and Sharif looked at each other anxiously as Alexandra picked at her dinner later that evening.

"What's troubling you, Alexandra?" Samira finally asked.

"Nothing," Alexandra answered, shaking her head. "Really it's nothing."

"Noah got his dorm assignment from Stanford along with all kinds of information about the school year," Yusuf interjected.

"Ah, I see," Sharif said.

"There's nothing to see!" Alexandra snapped back. "What's the big deal about Noah getting some mail from Stanford?"

"No one said it was a big deal, Alexandra," Samira replied. "It's just that you haven't been yourself since you returned from the Greenspans'. You were fine when you left here, but you've been miserable ever since you got back. It's apparent that something happened over there to upset you."

Alexandra lowered her head onto one hand and tried to collect her thoughts. Sorting through everything she was feeling as the entire family sat there watching her was more than she could manage at that moment. She didn't want to cry, nor did she want to discuss Noah or Stanford.

Sharif broke the silence. "I received another letter from the Phoenicia University at Beirut," he said softly.

Samira's eyes darted to her husband, reproaching him for his poor timing.

Alexandra lifted her head and turned to her father, staring at him in frustration and disbelief.

"Alexandra—"

She cut him off, jumping to her feet and throwing her napkin down on the table. "I am not going to school in Lebanon, Father! Don't tell me anymore about that university in Beirut. There are plenty of schools here in America, and they can offer everything that the school in Beirut offers. There is no reason for me to go to school there."

Sharif sat back in his chair, his eyes reflecting both hurt and sorrow.

"Alexandra—" he tried again.

"No, Father. Please! I don't want to discuss Beirut. There is nothing there of interest to me."

"But there is, Alexandra," he answered softly. "There is."

"There is nothing in Beirut I can't find here, accept maybe other Arab students," she snapped.

"And, perhaps, a scholarship," he said. "Mr. Haddad, the admissions director, has invited you to apply for a scholarship. He says they have identified several children of Palestinians to whom they may want to offer full scholarships."

Words failed her as Alexandra tried to grapple with the new information her father had just conveyed.

"My God, Alexandra! That's wonderful!" Yusuf exclaimed. "Congratulations."

Samira's eyes were wide with delight. "Alexandra, a scholarship!" She beamed.

"They are only awarding four or five such scholarships, Alexandra. I wrote to them and explained that you had mostly Bs and a few As, and they wrote back that you seemed to qualify for their scholarship program for Palestinian children. Mr. Haddad said they would need more information from your school but that you seemed an excellent candidate for their program. They are looking for Palestinian Americans."

She looked from her parents to her brother, sharing neither their joy nor their excitement. Unable to find an acceptable response and unwilling to sit in silence as her family waited for her reply, Alexandra turned and walked from the room.

Samira found Alexandra lying on her back with her hands clasped behind her head in the dimly lighted bedroom. Alexandra's eyes did not stray from the spot on the ceiling, even when Samira closed the door behind her and sat on the side of her bed.

"I'm sorry, Alexandra. We all are. No one has been sensitive to your feelings about Noah leaving for Stanford," Samira said. "Your father couldn't wait to break the news about the scholarship to you. He wasn't intending to interfere."

"Mother, how can you say that?" Alexandra asked, finally turning her attention to Samira. "Father has taken it upon himself to correspond with the university in Beirut on my behalf without even telling me. I'm perfectly capable of applying for a scholarship if I want to. I don't want to be that far from Noah, Mother. I just don't."

"No one is going to force you to go to Beirut or anywhere else, Alexandra. You know that," Samira replied. "But let me ask you something. Do you really think there is much difference between being three thousand miles away and nine thousand miles away? Either way, you're not going to see much of Noah while he's at school."

"Momma, now let me ask you something. I love Noah. Noah and I are no longer adolescents. We can debate forever whether it was in our best interest for you and father and the Greenspans to have allowed Noah and me to see each other. But that's not the issue anymore. I'm in love with Noah. If you were in my place, would you agree to do this if you believed it would cost you something that meant the world to you?"

"Alexandra, asking you to consider a scholarship, if it's offered to you, is not the same as asking you to give up Noah or anything else. Your relationship with Noah is not going to be determined by the schools you two choose. You will have to deal with issues far more trying than that. Noah isn't letting the relationship you two have keep him from going across the country to Stanford, and you needn't hesitate to go to whatever school you believe is best for you either."

"I felt so out of control when I heard Father talking to me about that scholarship. It was as though everything was being decided for me."

"No one was deciding anything for you, Alexandra, but we're in no position to have you turn up your nose at a full-tuition scholarship. If you think you can win a scholarship somewhere else, then by all means try. But until then, I think your father has earned your gratitude by pursuing this scholarship business—not your scorn."

"Do you think Father is pursuing this because of the money or because he desperately wants me to go to school in the Middle East?"

"A scholarship to the university in Beirut would undoubtedly serve both of those interests for him. For the rest of us, perhaps the financial assistance is all that matters. What difference does it make? It's still a fine scholarship to a fine school."

Alexandra thought for a minute before responding. "You know I wouldn't ignore an opportunity to help the family."

Samira nodded. "I know. Maybe there are other scholarship opportunities, Alexandra. You have nearly a year. Why don't you look into it?"

"I have already, Mother. Ever since Father received that first letter from Beirut, I have been looking into scholarships in America. I never dreamed I might be offered one from Beirut, but I thought a scholarship here would end any further talk of my going to Lebanon."

"What have you learned?"

"Not a whole lot other than that my counselor doesn't think I am a very likely candidate. Except for my literature classes, I have mostly Bs. That's good enough to get into many schools, but not good enough for a scholarship to a really good school."

"Well then, you can see how fortunate you'd be should the university in Beirut offer you a full scholarship," Samira replied.

"I'm sorry I'm not enthusiastic about a scholarship in Beirut. I'm just not."

"Major decisions are always unsettling, Alexandra. That's why it's good that there is plenty of time for you to make up your mind. You don't have to feel rushed. You know what they say—haste is the devil's work."

Alexandra smiled. "You're still an Arab, Mother."

"And so are you, Alexandra" Samira replied as she reached over and hugged her daughter. "So are you."

CHAPTER

FOURTEEN

Markazie was pleased with the yellow-page draft of Alexandra's feature story.

"Not bad," he whispered aloud. He turned to the first page again and leaned back, propping his feet on his desk, for a more careful reading.

THE HEIRS OF EDEN
By Alexandra Salaman

Mine is a proud family. We lived on a citrus grove in Jaffa, a Mediterranean port city where my father and his father before him grew oranges. My grandfather used to say, before he died, that our grove produced the sweetest oranges in the entire world. I remember standing on the knoll near my grandfather's grave and looking out over the sea. I used to love watching the sun descend over the horizon in the evening.

There are no trees where we live now, and I can no longer see the sunrise or the sunset. We came to America shortly after the fighting stopped and the victors of that war renamed our beloved Palestine. Israel was to be her name now, and we were told our citrus grove no longer belonged to our family. Others had bought the paper from the representatives of the family that had, long ago in the last century, passed the land to my grandfather, Ibrahim. It was an absentee owner's way of rewarding him for the years in which he had looked after their land. But they had only given him the land and not the paper. Never mind that he planted the land and made it blossom; never mind that he and he alone cared for the land in the years before my father accepted that responsibility; never mind that every tree and every orange was there because they nourished every seedling and harvested every sapling. Other men came with the paper and said that because they had it, and not my father, we would have to leave. And so, shortly after the fighting ended, we arrived in America, having left our family home and our beloved grove and the grave of my grandfather.

My family owns a food market in the LeDroit Park section of Washington. We live above the market on a corner surrounded by hundreds of other dwellings in which thousands of other people live. There are markets on every corner.

My father misses Palestine, but he is grateful that we are safe and that we have a livelihood. He craves the culture that was ours in Palestine and mourns even the thought of its total absence from our lives now. He has no contact with the Arab world, and his best friend is a neighbor who owns the market two corners to the south. The friend is my father's competitor. He is a good man who, my father says, was our salvation when we arrived in LeDroit Park. The man's wife is my mother's friend, and his son was the first to befriend my brother. He is still my brother's closest friend, and he is the only boy I have ever loved. There is a bond between our two families. It ties us together, but it is a bond that strangles us too, for they are Jews.

There is an Arab saying that teaches, "The friend of my enemy is my enemy." Our good neighbors have been our friends. As my father says, "They were our salvation," but they are also friends of Israel, and Israel is our enemy, and the friend of our enemy must be our enemy too. But this is the family that refused to let my father fail in his business. This is the family of the boy who became my brother's pal. This is the family of the boy with whom I fell in love.

We feel love for these people, and they feel love for us, but they are the friends of our enemy, and our honor demands that they be our enemy too. But what does our honor say about returning the friendship of a true friend?

Can a good and decent boy who showers me with respect and love be my enemy? Can the boy who was the first to befriend my brother be his enemy? Can those who came to my parents' aid and taught them how to survive in America be their enemy?

How do we reconcile the irreconcilable? Here are people who have earned our love and respect and who reciprocate with their love for us, but they have prayed for two thousand years to be able to return to Jerusalem, and they cheer those of their fellow Jews who have. They do not thrill to the words of Gamel Abdul Nasser the way we do, and the yearnings of our people to return to Palestine threaten them as though they were the yearnings of a foreign invader.

These neighbors worried about our loneliness, agonized over the possibility of our failure. Their son saw my brother and me as strangers in a new land and gave us friendship. He felt his heart stir when I looked into his eyes and remained loyal to those stirrings despite the cultural chasm that strikes fear and dread in the hearts of our families. We look into each other's eyes and see the love there and know that it is good. But we also look into the eyes of our loved ones and see that, to them, it should not be.

And I ask He who reigns over the Paradise we lost and over the Paradise to which they returned whether ours is a love forbidden in his design or whether ours is a love pleasing in his design. Over the millennia, Eden has watched our comings and our goings, but are we not still the sons and daughters of Eden? Are not both our families the rightful Heirs of Eden?

Franklin Markazie sat up at his desk and stretched so he could see over the solid partition and through the glass that comprised the upper half of his office wall. He saw Alexandra walking through the newsroom with wire dispatches for the editors and reporters. *We're really fucking it up good for her generation,* he thought.

"Alexandra!" he called out as she walked by his office door.

"Yes, Mr. Markazie," she replied with an anxious smile.

"Congratulations. It's terrific."

"You've read it…already?"

"Yeah, it's been a slow news day. Nothing much has happened, except the city sold the whole damned transit system to some guy named O. Roy Chalk…Really, Alexandra," he continued, turning serious. "It's a great piece."

"Thank you! Thank you, Mr. Markazie." Her smile blossomed into a wide grin.

***

Alexandra watched nervously while Noah read her story in the *Star.* Everyone had been impressed with the feature, even Sharif, but it was Noah's reaction she anxiously awaited. She had brought several copies home with her, hot off the press. She wanted her family and

Noah to see it before it appeared on the newsstands. Now she sat in the Greenspan kitchen waiting for his reaction to the story in which he and his family were the central characters.

"Alexandra, it's incredible," he said, his eyes still riveted to the text. "I'm so proud of you."

"Do you really like it?"

He looked up from the paper and smiled warmly. "It's beautiful."

"Can you get away for a while?" she asked.

"Sure. Why?"

"Let's go to our place in Rock Creek Park before it gets dark. We have so little time before you leave for Stanford. I want to be alone with you for a while."

Noah nodded and got to his feet.

***

As evening approached, the lush green park seemed their own private Shangri-La. The sun was low on the horizon, and the oppressive August heat had largely dissipated as the day drifted slowly from dusk to darkness.

"Look—you can see the moon already," Alexandra said.

"I ordered it a little early tonight," Noah quipped.

"Ah, you're such a romantic," she murmured as she sat next to him and snuggled against his chest.

"Listen, I have an idea," Noah said. "It's going to sound silly, but I'm serious. Here's what we should do after I leave for Stanford. Every evening at eleven o'clock your time, I want you to look up at the moon if it's out and think about me, and every evening at eight o'clock my time, I'm going to do the same. That way we'll both be looking at the same spot in the universe and thinking about one another at the same time."

"OK!" she replied. "I like that."

"I'm serious!"

"So am I."

They sat there without speaking for several minutes, looking out over the vast expanse of Rock Creek Park.

Alexandra was the first to break the silence. "Do you think we'll ever come here again?"

"What kind of question is that?" he asked.

"A realistic one. I think so much is at stake with all the changes that are about to take place in our lives."

"The only things that are going to be at risk are the things we put at risk. I don't intend to put us at risk. Do you?"

"Life puts things at risk, Noah. You and I have never known less about what's in store for us than we do right now."

"What would you like to be in store for us?"

She looked at him, her expression serious, her eyes tender and loving. Then she reached up and kissed him passionately. He put his arms around her and pulled her firmly against his body, and they slowly lowered themselves to the ground. Their tongues caressed as their bodies strained against each other's.

"Oh, Noah," she cried softly when he touched her breast. He slowly unbuttoned her blouse and after awkwardly loosening her bra, leaned down and gently kissed her bare nipples. The touch of Alexandra's taut flesh against his tongue sent shivers coursing through his body. They pressed desperately, breathlessly together.

"Make love to me, Noah," she whispered.

This time there was no hesitation. Without further discussion, Noah moved to his knees and in silence lowered his trousers while Alexandra removed her panties and pulled her skirt above her waist.

"I don't have any protection," he whispered, settling down between her legs.

"I just had my period. I won't get pregnant," she replied, guiding him, impatiently, with her hands.

He did not penetrate her easily during that first lovemaking, and her muffled cry was one of pain far more than ecstasy. But it was not pleasure they were seeking that August evening. Their lovemaking was to be the bond that would hold them together during the many months they would be apart.

CHAPTER FIFTEEN

By the time Noah boarded the cavernous plane that would carry him from the narrow confines of life in LeDroit Park to the tantalizingly unknown world of Stanford University, he and Alexandra were drained from the emotional tension that had been mounting as the day of their separation grew nearer.

Noah had never been on an airplane. He was going to fly from Washington National to Midway in Chicago and from there on to Denver and then San Francisco. It should have been an exciting time, but it wasn't. His sadness at leaving Alexandra far outweighed whatever enthusiasm he felt at that moment.

Once he was in the air, the lush green landscape unfolding below and the beauty of the cloud formations all around him proved welcome distractions. Several times he tried to get into the book *A Tree Grows in Brooklyn*, which he had borrowed from his mother for the trip. But while his eyes read, his mind wandered, and he soon surrendered to the futility of trying to read. He forced himself to think about Stanford and college life, and gradually the thrill of the adventure lying ahead began to seize him. Thoughts of what he was leaving behind began to recede into the clouds.

***

"Welcome to the Farm!" called the tall, dark-haired boy in the gray "PROPERTY OF STANFORD UNIVERSITY" sweatshirt. "You have to be Noah Greenspan because everyone else who's supposed to check in to Encina today is here." He smiled, then said, "Catch!" and threw

Noah the keys to his room with an arcing hook shot. "You're in room one-twelve. Your roommate checked in this afternoon."

"Thanks!" Noah replied, plucking the keys from the air. "Some farm," he added.

"Yeah, I don't know how Stanford got that name, but everybody around here calls it the Farm."

"I know—even the airport bus drivers," Noah answered.

"By the way, my name's Kendricks—Oliver Kendricks," the young man said, extending his hand to Noah. "I'm the official Encina greeting committee today."

"Good to know you, Oliver." Noah grinned as he shook hands with him.

"Call me Ollie," he said. "Everyone calls me Ollie. I'm from Des Moines."

"I'm from Washington, DC," Noah replied. "What year are you?"

"I'm a junior. It's a great school, Noah. You'll love it here."

"Thanks, Ollie. I'm really looking forward to it. I guess I should probably get unpacked. Which way is one-twelve?"

"Go down the corridor past the exit sign," Ollie replied, pointing the way. "It's on the right. You can't miss it."

The dimly lighted corridor was deserted. Other than muffled music coming from the end of the hallway, Noah could hear nothing but the sound of his own footsteps on the tile floor. About halfway down the corridor, he came to room 112, where an index card had been neatly taped to the door with Burns and Greenspan hand-printed in bold, black letters. Noah slipped the key into the lock and opened the door.

"Hey, Greenspan! How ya doin'?" The handsome boy spun around in his desk chair to greet Noah. "I'm your roommate, Rollie, from New York City. Good to know you."

"Hey, Rollie! I'm glad to meet you," Noah replied. "Ollie and Rollie…If the next person I meet here is named Mollie, I'm leaving." He laughed.

"My name's really Roland—Roland Elliot Burns to be exact—but most people call me Rollie…well, everyone here anyway. Back home my friends call me the Reb."

"The Reb?"

"Yeah, you know…Roland Elliot Burns…R-E-B."

Noah grinned and grasped his new roommate's hand. "I think I'll just stick with Rollie."

"Most of my friends back home are Jewish too."

Noah laughed at his roommate's unexpected candor. "I'll still call you Rollie."

"You are Jewish, right?"

"Yes."

"I'm sort of Jewish too," Rollie said, again taking Noah by surprise. "Well, actually, we're not much of anything, but my mother's Jewish and my father; well, he thinks religion is more trouble than it's worth. "

Noah liked Rollie Burns. He was tall and trim and clean cut, almost to a fault, and dressed more like the kids from Georgetown Prep in Bethesda than any of the public school kids Noah had known in Washington. Rollie spoke in a relaxed, colloquial manner, but his diction was precise and flawless.

"What does your old man do?" Rollie asked.

"He has a grocery store in Washington, DC," Noah answered. "We live over the store."

Rollie nodded his understanding. "My old man is the vice president for service of Richardson Automotive. They make auto parts—you know, fuel pumps, spark plugs, batteries, and all that sort of stuff."

Now it was Noah's turn to nod. Noah knew Rollie wasn't nearly as interested in what Noah's parents did for a living as he was in using the conversation to establish his own father's accomplishments.

"What's your major, Greenspan?"

"Economics," Noah answered. "What's yours?"

"Same thing, man. Maybe we can study together."

"Sounds good to me," Noah replied as he threw his suitcase on his bed. "So tell me about your family, Rollie. I'd like to hear more about your folks."

"You mean, how a nice Jewish girl from Queens wound up with a Christian athesist from Detroit?"

Noah, his back turned to Rollie, closed his eyes in exasperation. He turned and faced his roommate, who stood with his arms across his chest, a big grin on his face.

"No, that thought hadn't crossed my mind," Noah said quietly.

"Hey, it's no big deal, Greenspan. After all, my mom is a nice Jewish girl from Queens, and my dad is a Christian atheist from Detroit. It just means he doesn't believe in God."

"I know what it means, Rollie."

"OK, OK," Rollie said, holding his hands up, laughing. "I like you, Greenspan. Friends?"

"Don't mind me, Rollie," Noah said, relaxing slightly and holding out his hand once again. "I'm just beat. It's been a helluva long day. Don't worry—I'm sure we'll get along fine."

Grinning, Rollie grasped Noah's hand again with an energetic slap. "You're OK, Greenspan. You're OK," he said.

Noah began laughing too, as he shook his head in friendly exasperation.

***

The next morning, Noah and Rollie left the dorm to meet Ollie at one of the students' favorite eateries, the University Deli on Camino Real. Noah spotted Kendricks as soon as they entered the noisy restaurant. He didn't see the girl sitting next to Ollie until he reached the booth where they were seated.

"Hey, Ollie, how's it going?" Noah asked as he and Rollie slid along the bench opposite Kendricks and the girl.

"Everything's cool, man." Ollie turned to the girl next to him. "Karen, say hi to Noah Greenspan and Rollie Burns."

"Hi!" she said, smiling across the table at the newcomers.

Kendricks turned back to the other two men. "Guys, say hi to Karen Rothschild."

"Hi!" the two said in unison. Noah reached over to shake the girl's hand. Rollie followed suit.

Karen Rothschild was about Noah's age and a real looker. Her hair, which she had parted sharply on the left, was a shade lighter than brown, but not quite blond, and it hung to the top of her shoulders. She had a peaches-and-cream complexion and pale-blue eyes.

"Are you from around here?" Karen asked Noah after a polite acknowledgment of Rollie's presence.

"Nope. I'm from Washington, DC," he replied.

"Long way from home."

"Scholarship," Noah answered. "I guess you go where they take you. Where's home for you?"

"Chicago. Well, actually Highland Park. It's a suburb on the north shore." Then, circling back to Noah's remarks, she added, "I met a girl last summer from Washington. She went to Coolidge High. Did you go to Coolidge?"

"No," said Noah. "I went to McKinley Tech. I live in LeDroit Park, and McKinley's the school for LeDroit Park."

"LeDroit Park," said Karen. "That sounds pretty fancy."

Noah grinned. "Right, it does sound sort of fancy, doesn't it?"

"Is it?" she asked, returning his grin.

"Well, it used to be the home of the Senators," he answered with a perfectly straight face.

Rollie's laugh let them know she was being teased.

"Inside joke, huh?" She smiled gamely.

Noah laughed. "Well, the Senators are a bit of a joke. They used to wind up in the basement every year when LeDroit Park was their home."

"Ah! The Washington baseball Senators," she said. "I get it."

"Yeah," Noah said. "My folks have a grocery store a block from the old stadium where they used to play."

"So not so fancy," she said, nodding her understanding.

"Not so fancy."

After breakfast, Noah and Karen paired off to walk back to the campus, and Kendricks and Rollie departed to catch a matinee in Palo Alto.

"You're Jewish," Karen said, more a statement than a question.

"Yep."

"You know it's funny, but the only worry my mom had about me going to Stanford was that I wouldn't meet very many Jewish guys. Wait until I write her that I met the first one before classes began."

Just imagine what she'd say if you wrote her that the first Jew you met at Stanford is in love with an Arab, Noah thought.

***

In Washington, Alexandra stood under the streetlight on the corner of Fourth and Oakdale, her eyes riveted to the illuminated clock tower at Howard University. At precisely eleven o'clock, she shifted her gaze to the crescent-shaped October moon that hung over LeDroit Park and closed her eyes for just a moment, as she had done each evening since Noah's departure.

"Alexandra, please come in now," Samira called from the Salaman store entrance. "I don't want you out on the street this late."

Alexandra nodded and paused to gaze at the moon for just an extra moment before rejoining her mother.

"Good night, Noah," she whispered to herself.

***

Three thousand miles to the west, Noah excused himself from the convivial chatter in the living room at the recently established Taube Hillel House, slipped out to the front steps, and looked up into the heavens.

"Greenspan, what are you doing out here?" Karen Rothschild called, leaning out the front door. "Come on inside," she coaxed, waving at him with the Coke she was clutching.

He sighed. "I'm coming—just wanted to get some fresh air."

"Hey, don't give me that, Greenspan. I see the way you sneak out wherever you are at eight o'clock every night. The only other person I ever saw with as severe a moon fixation was Lon Chaney."

"Graaaa," he snarled and approached her, hands clawing at the air.

"Just my luck, the first guy I get to know here turns out to be a werewolf," she said. "Come on, they're serving pizza inside."

CHAPTER SIXTEEN

The Hillel House emptied out around nine thirty most nights, after which the students scattered to reconvene at Rossotti's or Kirk's or Stickney's, where they would continue socializing over beer or ice cream or maybe a late hamburger. One Friday evening late in October, Karen Rothschild and Noah left together. They hadn't planned to leave together, nor did they have any place in particular to go. But Noah waited around for Karen, who had lingered a few moments to throw away some paper plates and soda bottles. Karen, pleased that he had waited, threw her sweater over her shoulders and grabbed his arm as they left the house.

"Rossotti's or Kirk's?" he asked as they walked out into the balmy fall air.

"Lagunita," she answered, squeezing his arm.

"What?"

"Lagunita. I want to go to the lake."

Lake Lagunita was on the edge of the campus, just across Junipero Serra Boulevard from the Stanford golf course. By late spring the lake would reach depths of seventeen to eighteen feet and students could canoe or sunbathe there. But it dried up during the summer, and by the time the freshmen arrived for their first semester in September, it looked more like a shallow crater than a lake. The lake wouldn't begin to fill in until January or February. But now, in late October, its claims to fame were the huge bonfire students ignited in the center of the dry lakebed before the UC game and its seclusion, which made it a favorite make-out spot.

"What's going on at Lake Lagunita?" Noah asked.

"I just thought it would be fun to walk across a dry lake," Karen said.

"It's dark as hell out there."

She smiled. "Yeah, that's why I thought it would be fun. Besides, the moon is out. It's not all that dark."

Noah turned and looked at her. She smiled back at him and lifted her chin, daring him to chicken out.

"OK!" he finally replied.

She reached for his hand. "Let's stop by my dorm and grab a blanket. We'll have a moonlight picnic. I have some Cokes, and I think there're some cookies and potato chips in my room."

It was not quite ten thirty when they made their way around the deserted wooden beach house and onto the rim of the lake bed. Noah carried the shopping bag into which Karen had hastily stuffed a blanket, a couple of Cokes, and a half-empty bag of Oreo cookies.

They stood for a moment, holding hands and looking out into the black hole that had been Lake Lagunita. Noah's pulse quickened and his mouth turned dry as they began moving toward the center of the void that stretched before them. They were engulfed by the serenity and stillness of the lake bottom and the seductiveness of the mysterious, fantasy-like world they had entered.

"Do you think anyone else is out here?" Karen whispered.

"Why are you whispering?" Noah asked, whispering himself.

They turned to one another and burst out laughing.

"Shh, don't make so much noise," she said.

"Karen, who do you think we're going to disturb out here?"

"You never know," she replied softly.

After feeling their way a bit farther into the still darkness, Karen stopped and took the shopping bag from Noah. She pulled out the blanket and smoothed it over the rough ground.

"I feel like we're a million miles from civilization," Karen said, snuggling close to him.

"Yeah, I feel the same way," Noah replied, suppressing the guilt he felt as he put his arm around her.

Karen pulled two bottles from the bag.

"Want a Coke?" she asked, handing a bottle to Noah. "Here's an opener."

He pried off the tops and handed one back to her.

"Don't you feel as though we're the only two people in the world right now?" she asked. "I mean, have you ever felt so secluded?"

"It's hard to believe we're in the middle of a large university, isn't it?"

There was a moment of silence as the two sipped their drinks and contemplated the stars overhead. Then Karen asked, "Do you believe in fate?"

"What do you mean?"

"I feel a real sense of destiny when I'm with you," she said, her voice still hushed. "I really get this feeling that fate placed us in the same place at the same time for a reason. Do you feel that way too?"

Noah felt only awkwardness at that moment. He didn't want to tell her the truth and spoil the mood of the moment, but he didn't want the conversation to get too heavy either. He enjoyed being with Karen and felt the excitement and anticipation of the romantic encounter he thought was about to take place. He wanted to take her in his arms and kiss her because they were in the middle of the empty lake and it was pitch black and the idea of embracing her seemed so inviting. But he didn't want to pretend that they were in love or anything like that.

"Well, do you?" she asked, then suddenly turned and rested her head on his lap.

Yeah, I guess so," he said reluctantly. "I mean here we are alone on the lake bed, and a few weeks ago I had never heard of Karen Rothschild."

"Hmmm," she murmured. "I've never been on a bed with a man before. We ought to make the most of it."

He laughed. "What? What did you say?"

"You heard me." She reached up and grabbed Noah's sweater by the neck and pulled him down until she could kiss him.

Noah continued kissing Karen as he gently lifted her head off his lap. He maneuvered himself to a reclining position and took her in his arms. After several minutes of embracing and kissing, Noah pulled her firmly against his body.

"I think I'm falling in love with you, Noah," Karen murmured.

Noah wanted to say *I love you too*, but the words stuck in his throat. He knew it was what she wanted to hear, but he couldn't bring himself to make the right sounds. Instead, he pretended he hadn't heard her and began, again, to kiss her.

Responding to Noah's urgent kiss, Karen suddenly twisted her body and rolled on top of him, pressing herself against him as hard as she dared. Their kissing continued with even greater intimacy as their tongues caressed and their bodies moved against each other's. Then, as though a thought suddenly invaded her mind, destroying the mood, Karen pulled away from his embrace. Propping herself up on her forearms, she peered intently down at Noah. The reflection of the moon in his eyes reminded her of Noah's nightly moon-gazing ritual.

"You never responded," she said.

"Huh?" he murmured.

"I just told you I loved you. You never said anything in return."

Christ, women are complicated, he thought. "Karen, I think you're great…you know that…I mean…"

"Shit!" she snapped and jumped to her feet.

"Karen! What's wrong with you?"

"Give me the goddamned blanket," she said angrily, tugging at it in an effort to pull it out from under him.

"What did I do?" he protested. "Will you tell me what the hell I did to make you so angry?"

"You didn't do a goddamned thing, Noah. That's the trouble. You were lying there hugging and kissing me and thinking of someone else. You have a girlfriend back home, don't you?"

Noah sighed as he rolled onto his back.

"Look, I'm sorry," she said. "I just don't want to make a fool of myself. If you're committed, that's fine. Just tell me."

"Yes," he said quietly. "I have a girlfriend…back home. Her name is Alexandra."

"Oh," Karen replied softly. "Serious?"

Noah nodded. "Yes, it's serious. We've been together for a long time."

"I see," she whispered. "What's her last name?" she asked, hoping against hope that her competition wasn't Jewish and therefore not likely to hold onto Noah.

"Salaman," he answered.

"My luck," Karen said sarcastically.

"Her family and my family are very close, and her brother Yusuf is my closest friend."

"Yusuf?"

"Yeah, Yusuf."

"What kind of a name is Yusuf? Yusuf Solomon?"

"Salaman, Karen. It's Salaman. They're from Jaffa."

"Israel?" she asked, quizzically.

"Well, they would say Palestine."

Karen sat there as his words sank in. He thought he could see her mouthing the word Palestine.

"Oh, shit!" she finally said, falling onto her back.

***

Despite their encounter at Lake Lagunita, Noah and Karen slowly became almost constant companions as their first semester at Stanford progressed. Most of their classmates assumed they were going steady, but they were only steadies by default; they simply didn't date anyone else. Karen wouldn't think of dating anyone who wasn't Jewish, and there were precious few Jews at Stanford in 1956. To Noah, Karen was an absolute godsend. She was great company, exceedingly bright, and full of curiosity. She was spunky, comfortable, and confident, and any gathering seemed more lively and interesting when she was present. She was simply liked by everyone. Even though Noah had told her about his relationship with Alexandra, Karen still seemed eager to be with him.

As he was about to return home for Christmas, Noah realized that the thought of leaving Karen saddened him about as much as the thought of seeing Alexandra excited him. Life was not quite as simple as it had been before he met Karen.

***

With his head pushed against the tiny window, Noah gazed intently toward the terminal as the airplane rolled to a stop at Washington National Airport. The biting winter air had cleared the gate area of family and friends who had come to greet arriving passengers, but Noah knew Alexandra would be there with his parents.

"I'll count the minutes until I see you walk off the plane," she had told him over the phone the night before. He was anxious to see her too, despite the nagging guilt he felt. He had never cared about anyone before Alexandra, but now there was Karen. Noah tried not to think of Karen and love at the same time, but he sure knew he liked her—very much. She was, after all, very easy to like.

Hy and Esther Greenspan embraced their son the moment he walked through the TWA gate. As he was hugging his mother, he looked over her shoulder and saw Alexandra standing a few feet away, waiting. Whatever doubt he had harbored about his love for Alexandra disappeared as soon as he laid eyes on her. With one arm still tightly grasping his mother's shoulder, he lifted the other arm, inviting Alexandra into the reunion. She moved to his side, throwing her arms around his shoulders, and kissed him.

Hy Greenspan, grinning from ear to ear, surveyed the scene before him—Esther, Alexandra, and Noah clinging to one another, laughter and tears intermingled.

The Greenspans and Alexandra peppered Noah with questions during the drive into the city. It was Alexandra who first asked about the friends he had made at Stanford, and she listened intently as Noah talked about one new friend after another, though he carefully omitted Karen's name. Meanwhile, Hy and Esther were particularly curious about Rollie. "Atheist roommates you could have had here in Washington," Esther said. "We sent you to Stanford to expose you to experiences you couldn't have here."

"Believe me, Mom, Rollie is an experience I couldn't have here—or hardly anyplace else in the world," he replied. "Besides, he's as Jewish as I am."

"You mean because his mother is Jewish?" Esther replied.

"Yeah," Noah replied. "That makes him Jewish, doesn't it?"

"It's not the same," she said. "He's only technically a Jew."

"Es, the boy's a Jew," Hy interrupted. "If he was born of a Jewish mother, he's Jewish. Why's that so difficult? He's a Jewish son of an atheist father and a Jewish mother."

"It's a contradiction," Esther replied.

"Mom, that's the most ridiculous thing I ever heard," Noah said, the humor suddenly gone from his voice.

Alexandra, uncomfortable with the family's preoccupation with Rollie's Jewishness and the way it excluded her from the conversation, pointed to the building that served as the headquarters for the DC library system.

"I'll be spending a lot of time there during the holidays, finishing a paper," she said, hoping to divert everyone's attention to safer topics.

"Noah, I don't like being called ridiculous," Esther snapped, turning in her seat to face her son. "Ridiculous, indeed!" she repeated, ignoring Alexandra's attempt to change the conversation.

Noah turned to Alexandra in time to see her roll her eyes and look out the car window in frustration.

The grandeur of the Federal Triangle quickly disappeared as they turned north off of Pennsylvania Avenue. Noah took in the seediness of the area as they crossed New York Avenue and drove through the city's Second Police Precinct, one of the toughest in Washington.

"Are you enjoying being a senior, Alexandra?" Hy asked, anxious to pick up on Alexandra's bid to change the conversation.

"Yes," she replied quietly, the enthusiasm gone from her voice. "I'm the managing editor of the school paper."

"That's nice," Hy said. "Your folks must be very proud of you. We're all proud of you, Alexandra."

"Thanks," she whispered.

The Salamans greeted Noah with nearly as much excitement as they had greeted Yusuf when he returned from New Haven only two days earlier. Both families were proud of the boys' success.

Noah spent much of the afternoon comparing experiences with Yusuf. It was as though they had never been apart—their rapport was so easily reestablished. They had covered only a fraction of all they wanted to talk about when Alexandra knocked on Yusuf's door.

"I hate to break up this talk-a-thon, but I don't want to starve to death just so you two can catch up on events at Yale and Stanford."

"I'll see you tomorrow, Yusuf," Noah said, extending his hand. "I promised your sister I would feed her." Yusuf clutched Noah's hand and held on to it an extra moment before pulling him into an embrace.

"You're like my brother, Noah," Yusuf said, slapping Noah's back affectionately. "I really missed you."

***

The parking area at Pierce Mill was deserted, as it often was when winter tightened its grip on the nation's capital. It was after nine o'clock by the time Noah and Alexandra left Caruso's, having lingered at their corner table to talk long after they had finished their pizza. They held hands during the fifteen-minute drive up Connecticut Avenue to Tildon Street, where Noah turned onto the dark road that descended into Rock Creek Park. The heavily wooded enclave, long a haven for young lovers, seemed pristine and undiscovered that cold December night. Noah parked, then slipped his arm around Alexandra's shoulder and pulled her close to him.

"Remember our last trip up there?" he asked, pointing in the direction of the rock outcropping that hung over the park.

"I remember," she replied, taking his hand and brushing the back of it lightly with her lips.

Noah gently turned her so she slid into his arms, cradled between his chest and the steering wheel of the car. He leaned down and kissed her, tentatively at first and then with greater urgency. In just a few moments, the windows of the car were coated with frost from the moisture in their breath freezing against the cold glass.

***

Karen Rothschild was the last person Noah expected to hear speaking when he answered the phone on a cold winter afternoon just two days before Christmas. She called to tell him that she and her parents were stopping in Washington for a couple of days on their way to Colonial Williamsburg. They were going to the reconstructed town for the holidays.

"It's supposed to be really great between Christmas and New Year's," she told him. "They celebrate everything the way they did two hundred years ago. Anyway, we're going to be there for the week before New Year's, and we're stopping in Washington for the weekend on the way. We have reservations at the Shoreham Hotel."

"That's not far from our place at all," Noah said enthusiastically. "I could get there in fifteen minutes."

"Oh great! I'm dying to see you, and I really want to meet your folks too."

"Huh?" Noah stammered, unnerved at the thought of Karen visiting LeDroit Park.

"Really, I want to meet your parents," Karen replied, then added, "and I'd like to meet Alexandra too."

Noah opened his mouth to speak but no words came.

"Noah?"

"Yeah, I'm here. I um…"

"Noah, I have to run. I'll call you a week from Friday when we get in. Maybe we can all have dinner together."

"Uh…Karen, we can't do that. I mean my folks are in the store until nine."

"Every night?"

"No, they're open until eleven on Saturdays. Maybe my folks could come to the hotel for dinner on Sunday. We close at four on Sundays."

"Too bad. We're leaving early Sunday afternoon. Well, it doesn't matter. You can bring me by to meet them at the store during the day on Saturday. OK?"

"Sure…sure, I can do that," he answered.

"Great. I'll talk to you next week. My folks are dying to meet you, Noah. Bye."

"Bye, Karen," he replied, looking around the interior of the For You Market. He winced at the badly peeling paint high on the wall over the front door. Tape shored up a two-foot-long crack in the plate-glass window behind the produce bins. The day's specials were advertised on the window, applied with a paintbrush dipped in soap and water:

HOG MAWS – .20 LB.
PORGIES – .19 LB.
COLLARD GREENS & KALE – .15 LB.
CHIT'LINS – .17 LB.

This was his family's livelihood. This was his home. He had never brought anyone here from the outside. Who did he have the most in common with: Alexandra or Karen? *Christ, how can I bring Karen here?* he thought. Then he winced, ashamed that he would even pose such a question.

Later that day, Noah met Alexandra in front of the main library. It was unseasonably warm, even though the sun had already set. They had made plans to have dinner at 823, a favorite hangout for locals looking for an inexpensive dinner, good beer, and a lively beer-hall environment.

They decided to walk rather than take the streetcar that made its way along Pennsylvania Avenue at a snail's pace, stopping at every corner on the way. Their walk took them past the Mellon Art Gallery, the Archives of the United States, the FBI building, the Museum of Natural History, and the Department of Commerce. The restaurant was on Fifteenth Street, around the corner from the White House itself. They strolled by the old Ford's Theater, where Lincoln was shot, and a few blocks farther, the National Theater, the oldest continuously operating theater in the nation.

"Quite a bit of history and culture for a twenty-minute walk," Noah said as he opened the door. "I almost envy you getting to go to college in this town."

"Who says I'm going to college in this town?" Alexandra replied, taking his arm as they went down the steps into the rathskeller and were seated at a waiting table.

"I just assumed..."

"There are many places to go for history and culture, Noah."

"Alexandra, am I about to have some momentous decision laid on me?"

Alexandra reached across the table and took his hand. "Poor Noah. I'm really not making you very happy, am I?"

"Alexandra, where are you going to school in the fall?"

"I got a scholarship, Noah," she said. She looked down at their entwined hands for a moment, as though steeling herself for what was to come. When she looked up again, she locked her eyes on his.

"I'm going to the school in Beirut."

"Beirut!" he exclaimed, the word falling like a sledgehammer. Alexandra nodded, her eyes remaining fixed on his.

"Lebanon?" he asked.

She nodded again. "The Phoenicia University at Beirut gave me a full scholarship."

"My God, this is terrible," he murmured, lowering his head into his hand.

"No, it isn't terrible, Noah. It's wonderful. It's a godsend for my parents, and it's a wonderful opportunity for me to study in an environment that's close to my roots. Besides, you'll be away most of the time I'm in school anyway. You've got three and a half years to go at Stanford. By the time you're ready to come back to Washington, I'll have almost completed my studies in Beirut. It's really not that big a deal."

"Bullshit!" he replied sharply, drawing glances from the other diners nearest them. Noah glared back at them but continued in a lower tone.

"You think we have trouble with our backgrounds now?" he asked. "You'll be so goddamned brainwashed after spending four years in the Middle East, we'll have nothing to say to one another!"

"Do you want me to forget that I'm from the Middle East, that I'm an Arab?" Alexandra snapped back, the color rising in her cheeks. "Is that what you think will make things right between us, Noah?"

Noah considered his reply before speaking. "Maybe…maybe the best hope for us is to get on with the job of being Americans and to end this preoccupation with your family's past. Going to the Middle East for college is not the way to accomplish that."

As soon as the words came out of his mouth, he knew he had not considered his reply carefully enough. Alexandra's eyes narrowed, and she pulled her hand away from his.

"I don't have an Arab past," she said angrily. "I am an Arab, damn it! And I intend to remain an Arab. I also intend to remain an American. I'm as American as you, Noah."

"I wasn't saying you weren't an American, Alexandra, and you know it. I'm trying desperately to hang on to what we have. You going off to Beirut is the last thing in the world I want. You can't pretend it's just going off to another school. It's insane! It's totally incompatible with…with us."

"Noah, there's a lot going on right now that is incompatible with us. My studying in Beirut is the least of our problems. Education isn't incompatible with anything. Remember, Stanford is not next door, either."

Noah knew the decision had been made. Their discussion could lead nowhere but to more argument. He knew it was pointless to pursue the matter; all he would do was infuriate Alexandra.

"Let's not argue, Alexandra," he said after a long pause. "We don't have that much time."

"Nothing has changed, Noah. Nothing," she replied, clutching his hands in hers. "No one will ever mean as much to me as you do."

"OK." He smiled, then changed the subject. "What are you doing this weekend?"

"Well, Saturday morning I have to finish my paper, but...nothing else. Why?"

"I have a friend from Stanford who's coming to visit this weekend. I thought we could all get together and do some sight-seeing Saturday."

"Oh, that sounds great. We can meet at the mall. What's his name?"

Noah's heart skipped a beat in response to Alexandra's innocent question, and he hesitated for just a moment before replying. "Huh?"

"I asked what his name was."

"Well, it's a *her*, not a *him*," he replied with studied nonchalance. "Her name is Karen Rothschild."

The smile slowly faded from Alexandra's lips. "Oh," she murmured.

"She's from Chicago. Highland Park, actually."

"You've never mentioned a friend named Karen before."

Noah shrugged. "No, I guess not. I mean, I have lots of friends I've never mentioned. It's no big thing."

"I...I didn't say it was. It just seems strange that you haven't mentioned her before. I mean all your letters and calls, and you never mentioned her. Rothschild...that's Jewish isn't it?"

"Yes, of course, Rothschild is Jewish. So what?"

"Well, there you are at a school with very few Jews, and you never mention her. Doesn't that seem strange to you?"

"No…no, not at all. There wasn't any reason to mention it."

Alexandra smiled quizzically. "Let me ask you something, Noah. Do you think you would have mentioned your friend to me if she had been a he? Let's say if the name had been Karl instead of Karen?"

"Alexandra, do you want to come sightseeing with us Saturday or not?" he asked, making no effort to hide his irritation at being put on the defensive.

Momentarily stung by his rebuke, she paused before responding. Then, her lips slowly curled into a slight, almost coy, smile. "Yes, Noah. I'd like very much to come with you…and Karen."

CHAPTER
SEVENTEEN

The Shoreham was one of the city's grand hotels. It sat perched atop Rock Creek Park like a fortress and was rivaled in size only by the immense Wardman Park Hotel around the corner, just off Connecticut Avenue, and Washington's downtown flagship hotel, the Mayflower.

Standing in the lobby, his six-foot frame erect and confident, Noah caught his reflection in the mirrored panel on the wall and was pleased with the way he looked. He wore freshly laundered khaki slacks and a new button-down blue oxford shirt his mother had purchased at a pre-Christmas sale at Hecht's.

"Noah, over here!" Karen called as she emerged from the elevator into the lobby.

"Hi, Karen," he called back as he spotted her approaching with her parents. She was wearing a dark-green-and-blue plaid skirt and a dark turtleneck sweater under a crisp, white cotton blouse.

Karen's parents made an attractive couple. Carol Rothschild had light-brown hair, almost identical in color to her daughter's. She wore only a slight trace of makeup, and her blue-green eyes were as inviting as her smile. She was no more than five and a half feet tall, and as she looked up at Noah, she squeezed his hand reassuringly. Paul Rothschild was slightly taller than Noah and mostly bald. What hair remained was black, without a trace of gray. His penetrating but friendly eyes were coal-black and set deep under thick eyebrows.

Karen introduced Noah to her parents, who made him feel comfortable and relaxed after barely a moment of easy conversation. As soon as they began walking through the hotel lobby, Paul Rothschild draped his arm casually around Noah's shoulder and engaged him in conversation as though he had known him for years.

"So, Noah, I understand your folks are in the food business."

"Well, not exactly, Mr. Rothschild. It's just a tiny neighborhood grocery store."

"Don't sell the neighborhood grocer short, Noah."

"I'd never sell my parents short, but I think the neighborhood grocery store is about to become extinct. I really worry about what the future holds for my folks. The chains are really squeezing the mom-and-pops."

"Today's mom-and-pops will be tomorrow's convenience stores, Noah." Rothschild waved a finger at Noah as he spoke, encouraging the younger man to mark what he was hearing. "It will be a whole new industry, national chains of mom-and-pop size stores. They'll attack the chains' weak spots. They'll open earlier and close later, and people will shop there when they need just a few things and don't want to wait in one of those damn checkout lines in a chain store."

"Paul, for goodness sake!" interrupted Mrs. Rothschild. "You've known Noah for all of two minutes, and you're already talking his ear off about business."

"I'm in brokerage, Noah," Mr. Rothschild continued, ignoring his wife's comment. "I know the food business like the back of my hand. Don't count the corner grocer out yet."

At the hotel entrance, Mrs. Rothschild turned to Noah and said, "You kids have a good time," and put a slim hand on her husband's sleeve in gentle, silent restraint.

"It was great meeting you both," Noah replied, wishing he had more time to talk to Paul Rothschild.

"Take care of my daughter, young man," Karen's father teased.

Noah smiled. "She's in good hands, sir."

Paul Rothschild shook Noah's hand again and winked approvingly at his daughter.

**

"Boy, your folks are really great," Noah said as he and Karen walked east on Calvert Street to Noah's car.

"Yeah, they really are," she agreed.

"Want to stop for a cup of coffee? We have a little time before we meet Alexandra."

"We just had room service," Karen answered. "Can we go by the For You Grocery? I really want to meet your folks."

"It's the For You Market," he replied, "not the For You Grocery."

"Excuse me!" Karen said and laughed.

"I mean, does anyone call the Ford Motor Company the Ford Car Company? This is big business, where names are important, Karen," Noah said with mock severity. "You're about to meet the president and the chairman of the board of the company. You can't go around making mistakes like that."

"You know, my father liked you the instant he met you," Karen said.

"You could detect that in the two minutes we were together?"

"Yep. He would have never put his arm around your shoulder like that if he hadn't had a good feeling about you. He only does that with people he likes."

Noah smiled. "Well, I really liked him too. I liked them both."

"Good, now let's go so I can meet your parents."

"Next stop, LeDroit Park!" he called out as the car pulled away from the curb.

The neighborhoods steadily deteriorated as they traveled away from the posh Connecticut Avenue area on the edge of Rock Creek Park and on through the Adams Morgan neighborhood toward LeDroit Park. Karen grew more pensive as they continued eastward into the tired and alien streets of the inner city. Noah sensed her growing concern.

"Is it safe to be driving through here?" she asked nervously. "There seem to be only Negroes around here."

"We've been doing it for as long as we've lived here, and no one has ever bothered us," Noah replied, a slight touch of irritation in his voice.

When they crossed Seventh Street, she asked, "Are we near your store?" To their left was Griffith Stadium, and to the right, just beyond a garish neon-emblazoned liquor store, stood the Howard Theater, one of the few cinemas in the city open to blacks. The apprehension in her voice hadn't been lessened by Noah's assurances.

"We're just a couple blocks away," he assured her, reaching over and squeezing her arm affectionately.

As Noah turned north off Rhode Island Avenue onto Fourth Street, a black couple on the corner caught Karen's attention. The sign above them read frazier's funeral home, and the man was trying to console a woman as she wept in his arms. Karen twisted in her seat to watch them as Noah drove by.

"They bury their loved ones and cry at their funerals just the way we do, Karen."

"I know that," she whispered, a touch of regret in her voice.

"Tell you what. I'll give you a quick tour of the neighborhood before we go in and meet my folks."

"Great!" she replied with forced enthusiasm.

Noah detoured by N. P. Gage, where he had first met Alexandra and Yusuf nearly a decade earlier, then drove a mile east to where Langley Junior High School and McKinley Tech stood side by side.

"Now you've seen the seat of all my wisdom," he said with a smile.

"Hardly. I expect the seat of your wisdom is behind a grocery counter at Fourth and U Streets."

"Ah, you say all the right things, Karen. My parents will love you."

Noah headed north toward Howard University. As they drove through the small, picturesque campus, he explained how Congress had established the school after the Civil War to provide an opportunity for the children of slaves to obtain a college education.

"That's Freedman's Hospital," he said pointing to the redbrick Georgian structure that formed the south perimeter of the campus. "*Freed man*. Get it?"

Karen nodded. "Got it," she replied.

Noah slowed the car to a halt as he approached Oakdale Street from the north, coming to a stop across the street from the Crescent Market.

"Want to meet some authentic, bona fide Palestinian Arabs?"

"What?" Karen asked, startled for a moment before she realized what he was up to.

"C'mon," he said as he opened his door and got out of the car. "I want to introduce you to some friends of ours."

"Noah!"

"Karen, trust me. You visited Israel and never met a Palestinian. Now you're in LeDroit Park, and I'm going to introduce you to a couple of authentic Arabs."

Karen hesitated for a moment, then sucked in a deep breath before stepping from the car.

Noah took Karen by the hand and ran with her across Fourth Street.

"Noah!" Samira called out to him as they entered the small, dingy store. "What a surprise! Sharif, come out here. It's Noah, and he's brought a friend with him."

Karen stood speechless as Noah kissed Samira and embraced Sharif Salaman.

"Mr. and Mrs. Salaman, I would like to introduce you to a friend of mine from Stanford, Karen Rothschild. Karen is visiting Washington with her parents. They're on their way to Williamsburg."

"Ah, Rothschild!" Sharif said. "That is a well-known name in my country." The Balfour Declaration, promising a homeland to the Jews in what had been a portion of Palestine, had been delivered by Balfour to the British Lord Rothschild.

Recognizing the reference, Karen smiled nervously. "No relation," she said.

Sharif took both of Karen's hands into his and grasped them warmly.

"Alexandra told us Noah had a friend who would be visiting. The friend of our friend is our friend," he said.

"I have heard a lot about you," Karen replied, disarmed by Sharif's warmth and awed by Samira's beauty.

"Can you have tea with us?" Samira asked anxiously.

"No, thank you, Mrs. Salaman," said Noah. "We're meeting Alexandra at noon, and I want to take Karen by to meet my folks before we head downtown."

"Where is your home, Karen?" Samira asked, placing one hand affectionately on Karen's arm.

"We live outside of Chicago in a suburb called Highland Park," Karen replied.

"Well, I'm glad you came," said Samira. "Noah is like a son to us. It is an honor for us to have him bring a friend from Stanford."

"Thank you so much," Karen replied, moved by the Salamans' affection for Noah and the warmth with which they had greeted her.

"I wish Yusuf were here to meet you," Samira said. "He and Noah have been best friends since we came to this country. He is a student at Yale, but he is studying at the library today. Even on holiday, he studies."

"I would like to have met him too," Karen replied.

***

Noah and Karen crossed Fourth Street and got back into the car without speaking. Before he started the car, Noah turned and looked at her. "Really screws up one's stereotypes, doesn't it?" he said with the slightest trace of a smile.

"Wow!" she whispered.

As he approached U Street, Noah again slowed the car to a crawl.

"There's the great facade of the For You Market," he said, pointing to the tired, drab store as they passed through the intersection of Fourth and U Streets.

Karen leaned across the front seat to get a better look at the tiny grocery store. The twin plate-glass windows on either side of the entrance couldn't have been more than eight feet wide. The ornamental wood moldings at the top corners of each window formed perfect frames around the name for you market, which appeared in large black letters in the upper-left panel, opposite the familiar red-and-white Drink Coca-Cola signature that graced the matching right-side panel. In the otherwise clear window space below these borders, Hy had written the daily specials in large, soapy lettering.

"Surprise!" Noah yelled as he and Karen entered the store.

They were greeted by the strong aroma of salt mackerel aging in a small wooden vat of brine in front of the meat counter. Fluorescent bulbs in fixtures that hung from the ceiling dimly lighted the store. An exhaust fan at the rear of the store whined annoyingly.

Hy Greenspan was busy at the butcher block, hacking with a cleaver cutlets from a loin of pork.

"Noah! This is a surprise!" Hy put down the cleaver and began wiping his hands on the front of his apron, further soiling the white fabric. "So this is Karen," he said with a grin, walking around the meat counter to greet her.

Karen smiled at the warm greeting. *My God, it's Noah's face*, she thought as Hy approached.

Esther was stocking the produce bins and was on her knees, hidden from view on the other side of the store. She shook her head in disbelief that Noah would bring Karen to the store without calling first. Her hands were red and chapped from the ice around the produce, and a trace of blood stained a cuticle on her right forefinger. A suggestion of the acrid aroma of kale and collards tinged the fabric of her sweater, and her right apron pocket had torn where she had snagged it on the head of a screw protruding from a bin.

Esther got to her feet and instinctively smoothed the front of her apron.

"Well, you could have called," she said to her son.

Karen and Noah turned, surprised by Esther's voice.

"Karen, this is Mr. and Mrs. Hy," Noah said. "That's LeDroit Parkeeze for Hy and Esther Greenspan."

"I'm so glad to meet you both," Karen replied, hugging each of them.

"So, Noah tells us you'll be here until Sunday," Hy said. "That's hardly enough time to see Washington."

"Well, it's just a quick stop on the way to Williamsburg," Karen replied. "Besides," she continued, slipping her arm around Noah's affectionately, "I really wanted to stop in Washington so I could see Noah."

"Listen, I know you kids are going to meet Alexandra, so you should be on your way or you'll be late," Esther said. Karen's clasp of Noah's arm had not escaped her notice. "Noah, why don't you run Karen by the Salamans? They would love to meet her."

"Beat you to it," he answered. "We just came from there."

"Well, Karen, tell your parents we hope they enjoy our city," Esther said. "Maybe next time we'll be able to meet them."

"Thank you, Mrs. Greenspan. I'll tell them. They would like that."

"You kids have fun," Hy called as Noah and Karen turned to leave the store.

***

"They're fabulous, Noah," Karen said as soon as she had pulled the car door shut.

"I agree." He nodded and inserted the key in the ignition.

"You know, it's amazing. We come from totally different backgrounds. I mean most of the kids I know would consider LeDroit Park to be another country, yet you and I have so much in common. I mean, we really connect with one another."

Noah nodded without speaking.

"I think you are the brightest guy I've ever met, and whether you like to hear it or not, I'm really crazy about you. And I know it kills you to admit it, but I think you feel the same way about me. I mean…it's almost a miracle that our paths crossed."

Noah, still silent as he drove toward their meeting with Alexandra, couldn't help but think that the real miracle would be just getting through the rest of the day.

***

As Karen and Noah rounded the corner, Karen spotted the beautiful young woman standing in front of the main entrance of the library. *God, I hope that's not Alexandra,* she thought.

"Alexandra!" Noah called.

"Hi, Noah," Alexandra replied, reaching up to kiss him on the cheek.

"Alexandra, this is Karen Rothschild," he said.

Oh God! I'm dead, Karen thought.

"I've been looking forward to meeting you, Alexandra. I've heard so much about you," she said, extending her hand.

"I've been looking forward to meeting you too," Alexandra replied, returning her firm handshake.

"Well," said Noah uncomfortably, "let's eat." While this introductory meeting between the two women was going smoothly, Noah had the feeling he'd just heard the opening bell of round one. "I thought we'd walk around to the Neptune Room next to the Warner Theater," he continued. "They have great seafood."

"Sounds fine," Alexandra agreed. "Do you like soft-shell crabs, Karen? We love them."

Karen smiled and nodded. The words *we love them* jolted her. Alexandra's use of the plural had found its mark—no way was Karen going to admit to Noah or his Arab girlfriend that she couldn't even stand to look at soft-shell crabs.

Karen was determined to be at her best in the presence of Alexandra Salaman. She really believed that if Noah could see them together, he would understand how much more he had in common with her than with an Arab neighbor with whom he'd shared a childhood romance. And besides, Alexandra was nearly a year younger than Karen and still in high school. Karen had been confident that the differences between her and Alexandra would be clear and that the comparison would certainly favor her.

But it wasn't working out that way at all. Alexandra was mature and poised and one of the most beautiful girls Karen had ever seen. As they ate, Karen was also disarmed by Alexandra's graciousness. She seemed genuinely interested in Karen, asking her about her home, her interests, and her travels. Karen avoided mentioning her visit to Israel when she talked about the places she had been.

"So, where will you be going to school next year?" Karen asked. *If she says Stanford, I'm going to get up and walk out right now,* she thought, smiling politely.

"Phoenicia University at Beirut," Alexandra replied, almost stridently.

Karen was dumbfounded. *Victory from the jaws of defeat,* she thought as she fought to subdue her joy.

"How...uh...interesting," she finally managed to say.

"They offered me a scholarship. It's also a wonderful opportunity to reacquaint myself with the cultures of the Middle East. I think it should be a terrific experience."

"Oh, I agree. I think it really sounds great," Karen replied, fighting the urge to grin. "Isn't that great, Noah?"

Alexandra's announcement of her impending enrollment in a school half a globe away from Noah had helped Karen relax, and as the busboy cleared the table, the two girls continued to engage in animated conversation.

Noah finally interrupted them. "Listen, we're going to run out of time, you guys."

He was startled to see these two women, so different yet chattering away as though there was nothing odd about this meeting. A stranger would never have known that the strongest link between the two women was their love for the same man. But Noah knew, and it unnerved him.

"Karen's in Washington to sightsee," he said. "Why don't we walk over to the Washington Monument?"

The trio spent the rest of the afternoon making their way from the Washington Monument to the Capitol, stopping at a couple of museums along the way. They left the Capitol at dusk and took a bus across town, where they walked a few blocks to Mickey Grasso's Italian Grotto. "Best pizza in town," Noah said as he held the door open for the two girls.

When conversation over dinner shifted to Stanford and Karen recounting the many experiences she and Noah had shared, a slight but discernible tension emerged. Alexandra listened carefully and responded with polite enthusiasm as Karen revealed just how much time she and Noah had spent together. While the two girls continued their now-strained conviviality, Noah was dying a slow death. Karen rambled on in a seemingly random but thoroughly calculated manner, divulging much more about their relationship than he wanted Alexandra to know.

It had not been a particularly enjoyable day for Noah. He understood that Karen and Alexandra neither liked nor disliked each other. They both knew they were each a threat to the other, and except for their interest in Noah, they had little in common.

Noah was also still upset at Alexandra's decision to attend school in Beirut. That plus the tension of the ongoing repartee between the two women had left him exhausted. To make matters worse, he knew Alexandra was irritated at his decision to drop her off first before taking Karen back to the hotel. She saw it as his choice of who he wanted to be with that evening.

Actually, Noah just hoped he would be able to see Karen's parents again before they left for Williamsburg. But they hadn't returned. At the door to her room, Noah apologized for being so tired and kissed

Karen on the cheek. "Sorry I missed your folks," he said. "Say good-bye for me."

"OK, Noah," Karen replied, reaching up and hugging him. "See you the week after next back at school."

"See you back at the Farm," he said.

Noah rubbed the back of his neck to keep alert as he drove east across Florida Avenue. He yearned for a quiet, uneventful week before returning to school.

***

Alexandra did not mention Karen even once during her brief conversations with Noah the last few days before he left for school. Alexandra knew, of course, that Karen was competing with her for Noah. She was frustrated and, perhaps, scared.

When Noah didn't call Alexandra during the first week after returning to Palo Alto, she knew his eyes were no longer turned to the same spot in the heavens that she gazed on each night. Alexandra did not feel defiant. Her love for Noah had not diminished. But she knew he saw her Beirut decision as a personal affront. Though she agonized over what she believed was the beginning of the end of their relationship, she never wavered from the decision.

CHAPTER
EIGHTEEN

Perhaps it was his frustration over Alexandra's decision, or maybe just his constant proximity to Karen, but more and more the young coed from Highland Park began to crowd Noah's thinking. The first warm breezes began rolling through the foothills of the Sierra del Monte Diablo Range and down through Palo Alto early that year, heralding the coming of spring.

On the first Sunday in April, Noah and Karen joined two other couples on a drive to Sausalito. There they spent the day strolling aimlessly along the waterfront, stopping from time to time to toss an old football. They found a park where they could relax on the grass and listen to the rich tones of a nearby tenor saxophone. The soothing and seductive music and warmth of the fresh air wafting in from San Francisco Bay intensified the bond developing between them.

As the sun began to descend on the western horizon, the three couples drove to Fisherman's Wharf in San Francisco, where, making their way from one vendor's stall to another, they dined on shrimp and calamari. They ended their brief excursion at Golden Gate Park. While the other two couples relaxed on the grass near the center of the park, Karen and Noah strolled along the sidewalk, savoring the few remaining moments they would spend in San Francisco that night.

As they passed a row of newspaper vending machines, their attention was drawn to a headline on the front page of the *Examiner*: ISRAELI FARMER AND SON AMBUSHED ON TRACTOR.

The shocking photograph showed the two corpses slumped over on a tractor where, according to the article, they had been cut down by Arab infiltrators on a kibbutz near the Gaza Strip. Karen and Noah stood grimly reading the story of the attack.

"God," he whispered.

Karen laid her head on Noah's shoulder. He put his arm around her as they slowly walked away. They continued halfway around the park in silence, their minds gripped by the sickening headline and photograph.

"I can't get that awful photograph out of my head," Noah said quietly.

"I know." Karen sighed. "It's terrible."

"Do you realize how much the Arabs must hate the Israelis to do something like that?" he asked.

"Face it, Noah. Arabs and Jews are deadly enemies."

He closed his eyes and sighed. She knew his thoughts were of Alexandra at that moment.

"You thinking of Alexandra?" she asked.

Noah shrugged. "I don't know what I'm thinking," he answered, a hint of impatience edging his voice.

"Where do you think Alexandra's sympathies lie, Noah? I don't mean with the murdered or the murderers we just read about. I mean with the Israelis who won the land or with the Arabs who are trying to push them off?"

"Christ, Karen. The Salamans feel it was the Israelis who pushed *them* off the land."

"Nobody pushed Arabs off the land. They abandoned their homes so the invading Arab armies could push the Jews into the sea."

"Oh, Karen, that's bullshit. I'm telling you, the Salamans were thrown off their land. And if *they* were, thousands of other Palestinians must have been evicted too."

"Noah, I don't want to argue with you," she said, stopping to face him. "Not after what we just stood there reading in the paper. If you think you and Alexandra have something in common, that's fine. But these are the issues that are shaping our world. You can't hide from them, and neither can Alexandra, and if you think the two of you could go through life pretending they won't affect you, you're kidding yourselves."

"I know that, Karen," he said softly. "I really wanted to believe that we were the couple that would change the world. You know, prove that we could overcome all this Middle East hatred. But Alexandra was always the realist. She always saw the obstacles."

Karen looked up at him, and her heart melted. "Remember what I said to you that first time out in the middle of Lake Lagunita?"

"Yeah," he said, laughing. "'Get off the blanket.'"

"What I said, you jerk, is that I love you," she answered. "I really do love you, Noah." She reached out to hug him, and Noah took her in his arms and kissed her tenderly on the lips.

"I love you too, Karen. I really do," he whispered.

The sadness she had felt only moments earlier eased as they embraced. A moment of shared sorrow had changed everything.

***

Alexandra hung up the phone and closed her eyes against the tears. When she hadn't heard from Noah for over two weeks, she had finally called him. But their exchange was distant. Then, after what amounted to no more than very polite conversation, Noah said he had to run—something about Karen waiting for him in front of MemChu, which Alexandra knew was Stanford slang for the campus's Memorial Church.

Alexandra was far angrier at fate than at Noah. After all, she had been the one who understood the hopelessness of their teenage romance. Hadn't she frequently referred to Noah as a dreamer for his belief that they could make it? And hadn't she burdened their relationship with new obstacles with her decision to study in Beirut?

***

There were no such obstacles between Karen and Noah. The emptiness Noah felt after Alexandra's decision to study in Beirut was, in time, filled by Karen's presence and warmth. One evening, after a dinner of hamburgers and fries at Rossotti's and watching Henry Fonda debate his fellow jurors in *Twelve Angry Men*, Karen and Noah drove along Alpine Road in the car Noah had borrowed from Rollie. Karen leaned over and kissed him on the cheek. He put his arm around her, and she slowly reached up and kissed him on the mouth.

"Hey, are you trying to get us killed?" he asked, pulling the car over to the side of the road.

"Let's go to the barn," she replied, an urgency in her voice.

The red barn was a landmark on the golf course side of Junipero Serra Boulevard. Lake Lagunita, which was directly across the boulevard, isolated the barn and golf course from the rest of the university. Noah turned off the road and drove slowly past another car parked near the barn.

"Damn!" Karen murmured. "Someone beat us here."

"There's a lot of here…here," Noah said, guiding the car toward a clump of trees by the side of the barn. Karen leaned forward and turned on the radio. Carol Lawrence was singing "There's a Place for Us." They both sat listening to the poignant lyrics from *West Side Story*. For a moment, images of Alexandra swept through Noah's mind. Then he turned to Karen, who was watching him anxiously, and he saw the worry in her eyes as the haunting music tugged at their emotions.

"I love you, Karen," he whispered as he slid out from behind the wheel and across the seat to embrace her.

Breathless, she flung her arms around him and hugged him as tightly as she could. Noah took her face in his hands and kissed her tenderly on the mouth. Karen groaned under her breath as their tongues probed and caressed.

"Oh God," she whispered, feeling Noah's hand gently cup her breast. "Oh God," she murmured again, and the warm pressure of his touch sent a shiver through her body.

"Make love to me, Noah," Karen whispered, kissing him frantically.

"What? What did you say?" he asked, pulling away from her.

"You heard me. I said I want you to make love to me. I want you to make love to me before you go back to Washington."

"Where? You mean here in the car?"

"We can do it on the back seat."

"On Rollie's back seat?"

"Goddamn it, Noah, do you have some other back seat?"

"We can do it on the grass," he replied nervously. "There are some trees over there by the side of the barn."

"I love you," she said, kissing him again.

"You sure you want to do this?"

"I'm sure," she answered, nodding her head.

Noah took a deep breath and reached for the door handle. "Jesus, look at the windows," he said with a laugh. "It's like a steam bath in here."

"You have any protection, hot breath?"

"What?"

"Noah, do you have a rubber?"

"Are you serious?"

"Of course I'm serious. Don't you have a rubber?"

"Karen, what the hell would I be doing with a rubber?"

"I thought all guys carried them in their wallets."

"What the hell would I do that for?"

"So you could *fuck*, you idiot!" she answered in utter exasperation.

"Karen, what is wrong with you? You're the only girl I date. We've never done that."

"I know we've never done that, but there's always a first time, Noah. You're supposed to be prepared. What do you think guys do when it finally happens? Say, 'You wait right here, I have to run down to the corner Rexall'?"

"Well, I don't have a rubber," he snapped defensively.

Karen looked into his eyes for a moment and burst out laughing.

"I'm glad you find me entertaining," he said.

"Oh God, you're wonderful." She laughed as she clung to him.

"Karen, what would you have thought if I had just reached into my wallet and pulled out a rubber? I mean would you have just said to yourself, 'Boy, that Noah's really prepared'?"

"I would have probably fainted."

"Were you really ready to do it? I mean if I had had a rubber, would you have done it?"

"It?"

"You know what I mean?"

"Say it," she teased.

"Karen…"

"Say, 'Would you have fucked me?'"

"Karen, I'm serious. Would you have?"

"I think so. I mean…I really do love you, so I don't see any real harm in it. It's not like the world would come to an end."

"What made you want to go all the way?" he asked.

"I told you…I love you."

He looked at her, unconvinced.

"It's been such a great spring, Noah. I dread you going back to Washington."

Noah knew she meant *going back to Alexandra.*

"And you think going all the way will make me love you more?" he asked quietly.

"I suppose," she whispered.

"Karen, I think the world of Alexandra. I love her and probably always will, but I've finally come to realize that loving her is the end of the relationship, not the beginning. I mean there is simply no place for us to go."

"But what would you do if your folks and her folks got together and said, 'Say, we've given it a lot of thought, and we've changed our minds. We think it would be great if you and Alexandra got married'?"

"If I hadn't met you, I'd say great and marry her as fast as I could. But I have met you, Karen, and I know you're more right for me than anyone else."

"I don't have to worry about you going home and being with Alexandra all summer?" she asked anxiously.

Noah smiled and pulled Karen tight against his body before answering. "No, Karen, you don't have to worry."

Karen lowered her head to his shoulder. "She's so damned beautiful," she said, making no effort to hide the envy in her voice.

"So are you," he whispered, closing his eyes to shut out the image of Alexandra that had invaded his thoughts once again. "So are you."

***

The following Saturday, Noah and Karen returned to the wooded area alongside the barn. This time, he assured her, he was prepared. He had made the obligatory trip to the Palo Alto Rexall, just in case they wanted to do *it*.

"Oh God," Karen said, as he removed the small, square packet from his wallet.

"Always be prepared," he joked nervously and carefully placed it on top of the dashboard.

Noah slid out from behind the steering wheel and across the car's wide bench seat toward Karen.

"Come here," he said, turning serious as he took her in his arms. The familiar feel of her lips on his and the mingling of their breath and probing of their tongues inflamed his senses. After a few moments, Noah pulled away and looked into Karen's eyes. Her return gaze gave silent consent. With trembling hands, he reached down to her blouse and began to negotiate the buttons. Their eyes remained locked as the blouse fell open and she shrugged it off. She reached behind her back to maneuver the clasp of her bra as Noah watched, transfixed. A moment later, following a twist of her shoulders, Karen sat before him, supple, inviting, half naked, offering herself unconditionally.

He took her gently by the arms and pulled her astride his lap so she was facing him. She put her hands on his shoulders and groaned as his tongue caressed her taut nipples. Noah then pulled her face down to his, again pressing his lips against hers, the intensity of their explorations escalating.

"I love you, Karen," he whispered.

Hearing those words, which he uttered so rarely, she squeezed him tighter and, almost involuntarily, pressed her pelvis down against him as firmly as she could.

"Oh God," he moaned as Karen, encouraged by his reaction as well as her own mounting excitement, slowly thrust herself in a rotating motion against him again and again. She moaned as Noah's hands slid slowly under her skirt. She wasn't wearing stockings. His hands moved over the warm, smooth flesh of her thighs to the gentle swell of her hips. His fingers hooked over the elastic of her panties and again he looked into her eyes for affirmation.

"I want you," he whispered.

In response, Karen raised herself enough to allow him to draw her panties down past her thighs. There was an awkward moment as the undergarment caught on her bent knees before she finally extricated one leg. Noah moved to free the panty from the other leg, but Karen pulled his face back to hers.

"Leave it," she said breathlessly as she brought her lips down on his again, leaving the bit of white silk dangling almost comically around her right ankle. She reached for the packet on the dashboard and gave it to Noah. He fumbled with his belt as she again lifted herself enough for him to lower his pants. Then he tore open the wrapping and removed the condom from the plastic package. Without either of them speaking, he put on the thin latex sheathing. Karen rose up on her knees and then tried to lower herself over him so he could enter her. After several awkward and painful attempts, which seemed to take an eternity, she was finally able to ease down over him.

"Oh my God, we've done it!" she gasped with mingled pain and pleasure.

"I know," he replied, all but hyperventilating as she began to thrust against him, again and again.

"Karen!"

"What?" she asked as she continued to thrust against him. "What is it?"

"Karen!" he called out again as he suddenly convulsed in an explosive release of tension and pleasure.

"Oh God, I'm sorry," he said breathlessly, embarrassed. "I just couldn't help…"

"Shh," she whispered, putting her finger against his lips to silence him. "It will get better and better. Besides, I couldn't have gone on much longer, anyway. The first time is difficult for a woman."

"Are you all right?"

"I've never been happier in my life," she replied, laying her head on his shoulder. "I'll never forget tonight."

It took but a momentary glance at the moon shining through the branches of the trees for thoughts and images of Alexandra to flood into Noah's consciousness.

"Neither will I," he said as he stared through the misty windshield and into the night.

**

Ironically, it was Karen's father, Paul Rothschild, who solidified the relationship between the Salamans and the Greenspans and dramatically changed their lives. Karen had written to her father asking what advice he would have for her *absolutely brilliant* young man who was determined to go into business and whose only business experience was confined to the tiniest of tiny corner grocery stores.

Paul Rothschild wrote back: "Tell Noah not to forget what I told him about the convenience store business when we met during the holidays. It's an ideal business for an entrepreneur who understands the neighborhood grocery business. He and his parents should buy out every damn corner grocer in Washington. The present owners will sell cheap because the chains are killing them anyway. The real estate alone is worth more than what they'd have to pay for the businesses. The future of the retail food industry in this country is chains and convenience stores."

***

In May, when Noah arrived home for the summer, his parents eagerly embraced him at the airport gate, but Alexandra wasn't there. It hadn't occurred to Noah that she wouldn't be there. He had spent most of the semester dreading the conversation he knew awaited them. He had rarely mentioned Karen to Alexandra when they'd spoken, but he had spent a lot of time worrying about how he would tell Alexandra that things were different. And now, in the hot, humid airport terminal, enveloped in the welcoming hugs of his mother and father, he understood that she knew.

They had been driving for several minutes before Noah asked about Alexandra. He wanted to ask whether she was upset with him or whether they had asked her to accompany them to the airport. Instead he just asked how she was.

"She's fine, Noah," his mother answered. "She's busy working on the newspaper. Samira says she's leaving in August for Lebanon."

Noah nodded and, deep in thought, stared out the car window before pursuing the matter further.

"Has she said anything about me and Karen?"

"No, of course not," Esther replied. "But I think she's very hurt. She used to stop in the store on her way home from school nearly every day just to say hello. She rarely does that anymore. What have you said to Alexandra, Noah?"

"Well, not much, Mom," Noah answered somewhat defensively. "I mean she knows things aren't the same between us, but I'm sure we'll always be friends. I just haven't discussed Karen with her."

"Oh, that's very nice, Noah," his mother said, a hint of irritation in her voice.

"What are you getting upset over?" Noah asked.

"Noah, your father and I are delighted that you and Karen are seeing one another. I think you know that. But you have to be very sensitive where Alexandra is concerned. She's really entitled to that. She knows about Karen, whether you've told her or not. She's too smart not to have sensed what's going on. Your not discussing it wasn't doing her a favor."

"I didn't know what to say."

"Well, you'll be home in about ten minutes, and you can bet she'll be waiting for your call," Hy said as he turned onto the Fourteenth Street Bridge and headed north over the Potomac River.

Noah sighed and looked out at the old railroad bridge that spanned the river just to the east. "I know," he replied softly.

***

"Hi, Noah," Alexandra said nervously as soon as she heard his voice on the phone. "Welcome home."

Noah closed his eyes and tried to calm his nerves, but all the resolve he had mustered when he left Karen seemed to evaporate.

"I missed you at the airport," he managed to say.

"I thought it would be best to let your parents have you all to themselves when you arrived."

"Can I come over? I'd like to talk to you."

Alexandra's heart sank. He wanted to come over not to see her but *to talk* to her.

"Sure," she replied. "I'd like to talk to you too."

Sharif and Samira both rushed to greet Noah as soon as he entered the store.

"My, you've changed," Samira said as she stood back to look at him after they embraced.

"You look more mature, and you've put some flesh on your bones."

"You mean I'm getting old and fat?"

"You're not fat, but you have put on some weight, and it becomes you, Noah. You're what the kids call a hunk."

"Hardly," Noah replied with a laugh. "How's Yusuf? I haven't heard from him since my birthday in February. He sent me a card."

"He's fine," said Sharif. "In fact, he should be home tonight. He finished finals yesterday, but he wanted to stay and try to find an apartment for next semester. He says good housing is hard to find in New Haven, at least near the university."

"Hello, Noah," Alexandra said, walking into the store from the kitchen. "You look great!"

Noah's heart raced as she came over to embrace him.

"You look great too," he managed to say.

"How's Karen?" she asked.

"She's fine," he answered, barely above a whisper.

"Why don't you kids go upstairs where you can talk," Samira urged, realizing they needed to be alone.

"Let's go to the living room," Alexandra said. "We can talk better up there."

Noah nodded his agreement.

Walking along the dark hallway toward the Salaman living room, Alexandra reached back and took Noah by the hand. His mouth turned dry when she gently squeezed his hand and smiled at him over her shoulder.

"Relax, Noah, I'm not going to seduce you." She squeezed his hand again.

The moment he had dreaded all semester was here now, and he was certain that Alexandra knew how flustered he was. She turned and, facing him, locked her hands affectionately behind his neck.

"I understand, Noah," she said with a warm smile.

He knew better than to try to speak at that moment.

"I don't love you any less," he finally managed to say.

"I know. I'll always love you too, Noah."

"It's all so damned unfair," he whispered.

"Do you love her?" she asked softly.

"She's a great girl," he answered, more evasively than he had intended.

"You are in love with her, aren't you?" she asked again, putting her head on his shoulder.

"Yes, Alexandra, I think so," he answered, stroking her hair.

"It had to happen. I know that. I've known that all along," she said.

"I really do still love you, Alexandra. I don't think that will ever change. It's just that we wound up at a dead end. I mean, no matter how hard I tried, I couldn't figure out how to make it work."

"I didn't make it any easier for us. I know, deep in my heart that going to Beirut is the right thing for me to do at this time in my life. It means everything to my father, and I think I'd regret it the rest of my life if I didn't go."

"It's not just Beirut, Alexandra. I realized we'd spend our entire lives climbing over obstacles. Sooner or later one of us would want to give up."

"I'm so envious of Karen," she said. "It's all so simple for her."

"If it will make you feel any better, she said the same thing about you."

"What are you talking about?" she asked, pulling away from him for a moment.

"She said she was so envious of you. She thinks you have everything."

"Everything but Noah," she whispered and rested her head on his shoulder once again.

"Alexandra, I don't ever want there to be a time when we're not close friends. I couldn't bear that."

"It's hard to even talk about it being over between us. The words just stick in my throat," she said as tears welled up in her eyes.

Noah tried to speak but finally just sighed.

"Do you know what you're going to do this summer?" she asked, more to change the subject then anything else.

"No. Not really," he answered softly. "I guess I'll just try to help my folks out in the store. I have some ideas I want to discuss with them. Actually, they're Karen's dad's ideas about the grocery business."

"I have my old job back at the *Star*," Alexandra said, showing no interest in Karen's father's ideas.

"That's great. I know things won't be the same between us, but I…" He really didn't know what to say.

Alexandra looked up at him, making no attempt to hold back the tears, and nodded her understanding.

"I know," she whispered. "I know."

CHAPTER
NINETEEN

Noah hadn't planned to mention Paul Rothschild's advice about the convenience store business to the Salamans. He had discussed it with his parents and was surprised at how interested his father had been. But neither he nor his father had a satisfactory answer when his mother asked where they would get the money to start buying any other grocers' businesses. He knew they would have to borrow the money, but he had no feel for what it would take to negotiate such loans with a bank. So, had it not been for a long and uncomfortable lapse in conversation between Noah and Yusuf the afternoon following Yusuf's return from Yale, the subject might have never come up.

The two boys were genuinely glad to see each other and spent about an hour discussing their experiences at their respective schools. Yusuf had called Noah as soon as he got home, and shortly the two were embracing and slapping each other's backs. They seemed to run out of conversation right after Noah asked Yusuf if he had met anyone special. Yusuf replied that he had done a little dating, but he caught himself just as he was about to ask Noah about his social life.

As the discussion trailed off into an uneasy silence, Noah mentioned that a friend's father had suggested the best thing an independent grocer with money to invest could do was go into the convenience store business. That jump-started the dying conversation. The boys spent the next two hours talking about the idea. The next evening, Sharif asked Noah to stay a few minutes longer so they could chat.

"Noah, Yusuf was telling me about this idea your friend's father had. You know, about this convenience store business. You think your friend's father knows anything about this business?"

"Sure he does, Mr. Salaman," Noah replied. "He's a very successful food broker in Chicago. You met his daughter last Christmas, remember?"

"Ah yes, the girl you brought by to meet us. She was here visiting with her parents."

"Yeah, her name's Karen. Her dad is the food broker. He says we should buy out some of the independent grocers here in Washington when I graduate from Stanford. Mr. Rothschild says the chains are killing them and they would sell for a song—you know, cheap. Mr. Rothschild says the real estate would be worth more than you would have to pay for the businesses."

"Rothschild? Your friend is really a Rothschild?"

"No, not really. I mean not one of *the* Rothschilds."

"It doesn't matter," Sharif replied, smiling. "It's just a name I haven't heard for a long time. So tell me, what makes these convenience stores so special?"

"Well, they're like miniature chain stores—you know, real modern and self-service, and they stay open from very early in the morning until very late at night. Except Mr. Rothschild says the profit margins are much higher than the chains get."

"And they can compete with the chains?" Sharif asked.

"No, I don't think the idea is that they compete with the big chains. They're sort of a backstop to the chains. People run into a convenience store to pick up a few items they forgot to get at the Safeway or the Giant, or maybe they've run out of something before they're ready to go back for their week's shopping. Having a chain of these small convenience stores, you would enjoy the advantage of bulk-buying discounts."

"Why wouldn't they just run back to the Safeway?"

"Mr. Rothschild says people go to a convenience store so they won't have to wait in a long checkout line just to pick up a bottle of milk and a loaf of bread. The convenience stores do most of their business early in the morning or late at night, when the chains aren't open."

"What if the chains start staying open late?"

Noah shrugged. "Good question. I guess they'd still have the checkout lines. Anyway, the convenience stores are set up like the chains. They're modern, and they have more variety than traditional corner grocers, and the customers can browse around a little, just the way they do in the chain store. I don't know why, but they just seem to like it a lot better than the For You Market and the Crescent Market."

"So he thinks that's what you should do, buy up the corner grocers?"

"He says that's what he would do if he were me and just starting out. Of course, he neglected to mention where I was supposed to get the money." Noah laughed.

"Well, maybe you can start with the For You Market," Sharif said with a laugh. "Tell your father you and he are starting your own chain."

"Who knows, maybe we'll need a partner," Noah said as he turned to leave.

As Noah disappeared out onto Fourth Street, Sharif stood scratching his chin for a moment and thinking about the young man's parting words.

In fact, Sharif thought about little else the rest of the week, and after a long talk with Samira, he called Hy to suggest that both families have dinner together the following Sunday. They agreed to meet at Hogates.

***

One could walk into Hogates blindfolded and tell that it was a seafood restaurant, so tantalizing was the aroma of lobster bisque, crab gumbo soup, and the variety of other fresh fish dishes frying and simmering in the kitchen or being whisked, piping hot, to tables.

When all seven of the Salamans and Greenspans were seated, Sharif wasted little time in getting to the point.

"Look, Hy, Noah told me about this convenience store idea of Paul Rothschild's. Now, you know I would never enter where I don't belong or may not be wanted, so if you plan to proceed with this idea, you have our best wishes. But if you don't think you can swing it on your own, I have a proposition for you."

"Sharif, it's just conversation," Hy said. "How could we ever manage such an undertaking? We don't have that kind of money."

"I think this fellow Rothschild is on to something," Sharif replied.

"Ideas are a dime a dozen, Sharif. Where would we ever get the means to do such a thing?"

"We could be partners."

"What!"

"I spoke with my uncle, Anwar Khadari, who brought us here in nineteen forty-eight. He is a wealthy man, Hy. He'll guarantee notes for us at the bank."

"He'd guarantee notes for us?"

"Yes, for us. He's knows you two are the people who saved us, who made it possible for us to survive here. He said Jews are good business-people and that Jews and Palestinians would make great partners."

"He said that?" Hy asked incredulously.

"Yes, he did, Hy, and besides, let's be honest: I am, at heart, still an orange grower, a farmer. You and Esther are the ones with all the grocery store experience. Together, I think we can build something great. If you want to do it and would like partners to share the risk and the work, Samira and I will be your partners. That is, if you want us."

Hy sat there for a moment, and then a large grin spread across his face. "What do you think, Es?"

"I think the Salamans and the Greenspans would make great partners," she replied without hesitation.

"Then it's done. We're family," Sharif said, extending his hand to Hy. "We'll look into this business, and if we like what we see, we'll do it together."

"You see, Noah, we're family now," Alexandra repeated, the sadness in her eyes contradicting the slight smile she managed. "The Salamans and the Greenspans are as one," she said, blinking back tears.

Noah looked at Alexandra and returned the pained smile.

"To the family," Yusuf said softly, raising his water glass, an ever-so-slight sardonic touch to his voice.

***

Hy and Sharif spent most of the summer of 1957 planning their new business. They began by compiling a list of all the CGW members whose business included enough property for them to convert the existing store into a convenience store and still provide parking for several cars. Of the eighty stores comprising the CGW, only twenty-two had the necessary space.

Noah and Yusuf drove throughout the inner city each afternoon, scouting for stores next to vacant lots or other property that could be purchased. By the Fourth of July, they had identified thirty-eight locations that met their requirements. Yusuf was given the assignment of designing various layouts for the stores, while Noah consulted with Paul Rothschild and then drew up a business plan that would provide direction on how Sharif and Hy were to proceed.

Given the two grocers' total lack of experience with such complex business dealings, the new venture should never have succeeded and probably would have failed had it not been for Karen's father. Intrigued by the unlikely partnership of an Arab and a Jewish family, he quickly became committed to helping in any way he could.

Noah called the Rothschilds every evening and, after talking with Karen for a few minutes, would speak with her father. Paul Rothschild cautioned Noah that the corner grocery stores he would be buying were worth no more than a year's revenue, given the deterioration of business caused by the chains' aggressive competition. He warned Noah that the independent grocers would place a value on everything—the real estate, fixtures, shelves, inventory, and goodwill—but he should keep in mind that except for the inventory and real estate, it was all next to worthless.

By the end of July, Noah and Yusuf had completed the list of candidate stores they felt were suitable for conversion. Yusuf had prepared several alternative store designs, and Noah had put together a first draft of a business plan, which he sent to Paul Rothschild to review. Five days later, Paul called and offered to meet with both families. He explained that he was coming to Washington for a meeting of the National Food Brokers Association and could arrange to stay for an extra day or two. He had some novel ideas to discuss with them, and he thought it would be better to discuss them in person. Both families readily agreed.

***

Their meeting went well. Paul liked them all. He was fascinated by the trust and warmth he observed between these unlikely partners and was eager to help them.

For their part, Hy and Sharif saw in Rothschild someone who could guide them through the unfamiliar maze they were about to enter.

In less than two hours Paul Rothschild had convinced them they could succeed if they followed certain guidelines. He urged them again to pay no more than one year's revenue for the stores. Many of the grocers would probably be willing to sell for the value of their inventory alone, he said. Inventory and fixtures were probably worth about half of annual sales, making an offer of one times annual sales very attractive to grocers who doubted their ability to survive at all in the face of competition from the aggressive chain stores. With the conversion to a modern convenience store layout, which Karen's father estimated would cost on average about eighty thousand dollars, the cost of acquisition and conversion would be no more than twenty-four months' revenue. Paul believed volume would increase substantially with well-planned conversions, and the payback would be extra-ordinary if they stuck to the one-times-annual-sales guideline.

CHAPTER TWENTY

Sharif agreed that Hy and Noah would make the first acquisition call. They had selected a small corner store in the southeast section of the city, not more than two blocks from the old Navy Yard and only about two miles from the Capitol. The area was still a slum, but there had been considerable urban renewal around the Capitol, and many people believed the area would someday attract young, affluent professionals and government workers from the Maryland and Virginia suburbs.

Oscar Weismann was a crusty loner who had been on the corner of Seventh and L Streets for over thirty years. He'd joined the CGW the year after his wife died, shortly after the war. He never socialized with other members of the CGW, but he paid his dues, purchased merchandise regularly at the CGW warehouse, and ran an efficient business, which, like most of the other independent corner stores, was failing in the face of the expanding chains. At sixty-eight, Weismann was in no mood to contemplate any significant change in his life. His ninety-five-hour week at Weismann's Market was all the life he had known for an entire generation. Like most of the city's corner grocers, Oscar Weismann lived above his store. Except for his daily trips to the market and regular attendance at CGW monthly meetings, he rarely left the corner where he had set up his business back in 1925.

The Greenspans and Salamans talked through their strategy one last time the night before Hy went to see Oscar Weismann. At Noah's suggestion, they decided to not mention the Salaman family's involvement in the venture. Sooner or later, they would want word to get out, but they all agreed that the more they could get done before the Arab family's involvement became an issue, the better. They also agreed they would offer Weismann 55 percent of his annual revenue for openers.

Hy's nervousness was evident as they drove east along Florida Avenue past the old market where most of the city's independent grocers did their buying.

"You know, this whole business could go down the drain at Weismann's," he said to his son as he turned south on Eighth Street for the last leg of the drive, which would take them all the way down to the Anacostia River and to Oscar Weismann's place of business. "Whether we make a deal or leave empty-handed, everyone in the business will know what we're up to."

"I thought we picked Weismann because he's such a loner," Noah replied.

"That's true, but he'll mention our offer to someone…sooner or later. That's all it will take."

"Well, I guess we'll have to make a deal then," Noah said.

"You're enjoying all of this, aren't you?" Hy asked.

"I really am," Noah replied with a smile. "Mr. Rothschild says it's an even playing field. He says they are no more experienced at selling businesses than we are at buying them."

"I don't know, Noah. I feel like I'm way over my head. I'm used to buying food to sell, not businesses to run."

"You bought the For You Market," Noah answered.

"That's different."

"What's different about it?"

Hy looked at his son and considered the question.

"Really, Dad. We may be trying to put a chain of stores together, but we're buying them one at a time, just like you bought the For You Market."

Hy shrugged. "I guess you're right. I never thought of it that way."

As they crossed Pennsylvania Avenue, Noah noticed a new, large Safeway store that had just opened. Then, at the next two intersections they crossed, he observed vacated grocery stores standing like ghosts of the dead enterprises that had once thrived there.

Hy pulled up in front of Weismann's Market and turned off the ignition. He sat with both hands on the wheel for a moment and then turned to Noah.

"I haven't been so nervous since I asked your mother to marry me."

"Relax, Dad," Noah said. "No matter what happens, I promise you're not going to have to marry Mr. Weismann."

"Very funny. Come on, let's go before I get cold feet altogether."

They stood on the sidewalk in front of Weismann's Market and surveyed the area quickly before entering the store. The neighborhood was hard and ominous, and Noah wanted to get into the store and off the street. Hy tilted his head in the direction of the empty lot next to the store, which Oscar Weismann also owned.

"Just the right amount of space," Hy said under his breath.

"Makes LeDroit Park look like Spring Valley," Noah said, referring to one of the most exclusive areas in the nation's capital.

"Hello, Oscar! Good to see you," Hy called out as he and Noah entered the small, dingy store.

"Good to see you too, Hy, but I wouldn't drive all the way up to LeDroit Park to tell you that," the old grocer replied. Oscar Weismann had the pale, gaunt look of a man who belonged in a sickbed. His thinning hair was mostly white, and he had a day's growth of stubble on his face. Noah thought he was about his father's height, but Weismann's slightly stooped posture made it hard to tell for sure. He wore thick glasses, and Noah noticed that the right earpiece was fastened to the frame with a paperclip where a screw belonged. The grocer's apron, which was both dirty and blood stained, was torn along the seam of the pocket. Noah decided he didn't like Oscar Weismann.

"Oscar, this is my son, Noah. I don't think you've ever met Noah."

"Hello, young man. Maybe you'll tell Oscar what this visit is all about."

"So how's business, Oscar?" Hy asked, more as a social nicety than a serious question.

"You have to ask?" Oscar answered.

"No, I guess not. I know things are tough for everybody."

"You going to make me wait all afternoon to tell me what this visit is all about?"

"No, of course not, Oscar."

"So?"

"So, how would you like to sell your business?"

Oh, shit. Noah moaned under his breath, cringing at his father's lack of finesse.

"What? What did you say?" Oscar asked with a laugh.

"I asked if you'd like to sell your business?"

"Who wants to buy?"

"Me."

"You want to buy Weismann's Market?"

"Yes, I do," Hy answered.

Oscar Weismann peered over the top rim of his glasses as though to see the two of them at closer range.

"Young man, do you know how to get to Saint Elizabeth's from here? It's really not that far," Oscar said, referring to the mental hospital on the other side of the Anacostia River. "I think your father has taken leave of his senses."

Noah smiled feebly. *You're blowing it, Dad,* he thought as he saw the look of nervous frustration on his father's face.

"Let me make sure I have this straight," Oscar said. "You brought Noah here so the two of you could offer to buy my business? Tell me, Hy, business so good up in LeDroit Park, you want to expand down here in Southeast?"

"I'm interested in buying your business." Hy answered.

"Your boy flunk out of school or something? Is that it? You want to put him into business? Because if that's what you're doing, you ought to have your head examined."

"Oscar, Noah hasn't flunked out of school, and I'm not looking to put him into business," Hy responded irritably.

Jesus, Dad, tell him you want to try out a new concept or something, but stop evading his question, Noah pleaded in silence.

"Hy, why don't you come back when you feel you can talk candidly," Weismann said. "I really don't like talking business when I don't know what the business is."

Noah agonized over the panic he saw on his father's face. He knew he had to do something.

"Mr. Weismann, that's really not fair," Noah said, surprising himself.

"Oh, really? Why is it not fair for me to want to know what this is all about?"

"It's perfectly fair for you to want to know what our proposition is all about, Mr. Weismann. But I'm sure what's confused my father was the doubt you were expressing over whether or not he was serious. I think we were both taken aback by the way you ridiculed his offer."

"I had no intention of ridiculing anyone," Weismann replied. "I just wanted to know what this wanting to buy my store was all about."

Noah glanced at his father, who nodded for him to continue.

"We're planning to open mini-supermarkets called convenience stores. We're going to buy several independent corner grocery stores to test the concept."

"You're serious?"

"Very serious," Noah replied.

"And what are you paying?"

"Four months' revenue," Noah answered without batting an eye.

"You want I should sell for four months' revenue? Why would I ever do that?"

Hy looked at Noah, dumbfounded by the conversation unfolding in front of him.

"Mr. Weismann, we think what we're offering will be a godsend to the small, independent grocers. Most of the independents are simply closing their doors and hoping someone will buy their inventory from them. That probably doesn't amount to two months' revenue."

"I'm not selling my store for four months' revenue, young man. I haven't slaved here for over thirty years to walk away with twenty thousand dollars."

"Mr. Weismann, you, my dad, Marcus up at Eighth and Penn, or Millman over at Eighth and H Streets are all in the same boat. You've all worked years and have all made a pretty good living, but times have passed you by. What do you think Marcus or Millman got for their businesses?"

Weismann's confidence vanished as soon as Noah mentioned the two grocers whose nearby stores now stood vacant. Weismann knew both had been forced to close their doors within two months after the opening of the new Safeway Noah and Hy had passed a short time earlier.

"Damn shame about Marcus and Millman," he murmured, suddenly drained of his feistiness. "I *am* ready to throw in the towel, Hy. The chains are killing us. The Safeway up on the avenue is squeezing me, and just yesterday I heard that a Giant is opening a few blocks east of here. I'm caught between two chains that will be fighting it out."

"I'm sorry," Hy responded. "We're in the same pickle, but instead of closing or selling out for inventory, we're going to try to invest in this new concept Noah spoke of. Maybe there'll be a niche for us."

"But Jesus, Hy. I mean, four months' revenue."

"Oscar, we want to start a new business and offer the independents, who we both know are going to fold anyway, more than they can get anywhere else. We really want to be fair."

"But four months, Hy! Jesus Christ, can't you do better than that?"

Hy looked at Noah, his expression pleading as much as Oscar Weismann's was.

"Mr. Weismann, I'm sure you realize how much risk we're taking with this idea of ours."

Weismann nodded his understanding. "I don't know whether I should admire you or pity you."

"What would you consider a fair offer to be?" Hy asked.

"I'd like a year's revenue, Hy."

Noah spoke up before Hy could accept Weismann's counteroffer. "Mr. Weismann, we can take Marcus's or Millman's store just by taking over the lease."

"Then why don't you?" Weismann snapped.

"You have a better corner, Mr. Weismann. You're just a block from the Navy Yard. We like that."

Hy's eyes darted to Noah, but Noah was staring intently at Weismann. Hy and Noah both knew that the Marcus and Millman stores were too small and offered no space for parking.

"It's not much for thirty years' work," Weismann said in a whisper.

Noah glanced at his father. He knew Hy was sharing none of the exhilaration he was experiencing at that moment.

"How about six months' revenue?" Oscar asked, defeat in his voice.

"Six months it is," Hy replied before Noah could say anything more. "Six months it is."

***

"Noah, where in the world did you learn to do that?" Hy asked as soon as they were in the car.

"I don't know. I didn't know any other way to get the discussion back on track."

"You saved the deal. I was absolutely going to blow the whole thing. I never expected Oscar to challenge me the way he did. I was at a loss for words. Our plan would have been dead in the water if you hadn't been with me."

"It was great. I can't wait for our next meeting," Noah replied.

"Noah, don't misunderstand what I'm going to ask, because I'm truly astonished at how well you handled the whole thing, but aren't you troubled at how unhappy Oscar is with the deal we made?"

"Dad, Oscar is unhappy because he's in a rotten business. You heard him. He said he was ready to throw in the towel. That's not our fault. There's no place in the world he could have gotten a better deal than the one we gave him today. What is there for us to feel bad about?"

"Why did you only offer four months? We had agreed earlier that we would begin with an offer of six months' revenue."

"That was before we passed Marcus's and Millman's stores and saw they had both gone out of business. It just seemed that Weismann's store would go for less given the deterioration of the business in this neighborhood."

"Well, where do we go from here, Noah?" Hy asked.

"I think we just wait for the telephone to ring, Dad. My guess is that when Mr. Weismann goes to the market tomorrow, he'll tell Morrie Berliner he is selling his business to you."

Hy laughed. "That will do it."

The next twenty-four hours made a prophet of Noah. The telephone began ringing off the hook, just as he had predicted. The transaction with Oscar Weismann established Noah as the primary negotiator for the Greenspan-Salaman convenience store venture. And Noah learned that he loved making deals.

CHAPTER
TWENTY-ONE

The summer of 1957 was a season they would all remember. The Milk & Honey chain of convenience stores was organized with Hy Greenspan as its president and Sharif Salaman its chairman. The name was Esther and Samira's idea. They thought they should use a name that symbolized something both families shared in common.

Hy and Noah got better and better at selling their convenience store conversion concept, and virtually all the transactions were concluded that summer at prices between six months' and a year's revenue. Sharif, with his uncle's guarantee in hand, had no difficulty securing the credit needed to finance the acquisitions and conversions. By Labor Day, eighteen independents had sold out to Milk & Honey, and another ten had signed letters of intent. In every case, the merchants were relieved to have found a buyer for their seriously ailing businesses. Yusuf's design for the stores was imaginative and, not surprisingly, characteristic of the innovative flair for which he would become widely admired in the years to come.

While Yusuf and Noah were busy helping their parents establish a new business, Alexandra continued to impress her editors at the *Evening Star*. She was clearly the most talented intern at the *Star*, and Franklin Markazie wasn't about to lose her entirely to Beirut. He had a big surprise for Alexandra, which he waited until her going-away party two weeks before she left for school to spring on her.

***

Markazie was the last of the invited guests to arrive at the farewell gathering being held in one of the banquet rooms of the Raleigh Hotel, just around the corner from the *Star*'s offices.

Alexandra was thrilled with the crowd that gathered to say good-bye. Many of the reporters on duty were there, as were nearly all the editors. They were giving her the sort of send-off they would have given a veteran journalist. It was a remarkable honor to extend to a summer intern, and she knew it.

Franklin Markazie rushed into the party with a newspaper under his arm and made his way to the bar in the middle of the room. He climbed onto a chair, placed two fingers in his mouth, and whistled. The room dutifully fell silent.

"I'm here for the same reason you're all here," he shouted, holding a bottle of Hedges and Butler Royal Scotch Whisky high above the crowd. "I'm here to drink a toast to our fair Alexandra."

"Hear! Hear!" someone yelled from the back of the room.

"Alexandra, can you come up here and help me with this?" Markazie said. "Somebody pull a chair up here so Alexandra can stand next to me."

As Alexandra made her way to Markazie's side, someone slid a chair across the room to where he stood. A nearby reporter held Alexandra's arm as she climbed up next to her editor.

"You know you made tomorrow's paper, kid?" he asked. It was not the kind of question that required an answer.

"Is the *Star* down to covering its own going-away parties?" she quipped.

"Hey, this is serious, kid. I mean this is important stuff," he said, grinning widely.

"Mr. Markazie, whatever are you talking about?" Alexandra asked, not quite taking him seriously.

"Hey, no more of this Mr. Markazie business, understand?"

"Why not? Have you changed your name?"

"Why not? I'll tell you why not. This is why not," he answered, handing her the local section of the newspaper he had been carrying. "Read it to us, Alexandra."

Alexandra slowly unrolled the paper and held it up to scan the page. There, just below the fold on the lower right side of the local news page, she saw it.

"Oh my God!" she whispered as she saw her picture under the single-column headline.

"Read it, Alexandra. I think your colleagues would like to hear the news from you directly," Markazie said, grinning from ear to ear.

Alexandra looked at him, tears brimming in her eyes. Then she looked back down at the paper and, her voice quavering slightly, began to read.

"Intern Lands Beirut Post. Alexandra Salaman, an *Evening Star* summer intern, has been appointed special Middle East correspondent, joining veteran *Star* reporter and Beirut Bureau Chief David R. Ellis when she arrives in the Lebanese capital in the fall to begin classes at the Phoenicia University at Beirut."

Alexandra tried to say something. Markazie put his arm around her and hugged her until she regained her composure. He then took the paper from her and read the rest of the brief story aloud. When he finished, the room burst into applause. Alexandra's tears gave way to laughter as the guests whistled and yelled enthusiastically.

***

The Greenspans took nearly as much pleasure in Alexandra's appointment as did the Salamans. Hy taped the article about Alexandra's appointment to the back of the cash register for his customers to read, just as he would have displayed a newspaper story about his own son's achievements.

The *Evening Star* story about Alexandra was also proudly displayed on a message board at the student union at Phoenicia University in

Beirut. The part about Alexandra studying in Lebanon was under-scored in red.

***

Noah and Alexandra had dinner together at Caruso's shortly before they left for their respective schools. They both wanted, more than anything, to preserve whatever they could from their relationship.

"Excited?" Noah asked as they took their seats at a window table overlooking the traffic on M Street.

"I have been, and I know I will be, but right now I don't feel very excited about anything."

"Yeah, I know," he said.

"Noah, I have to ask you something."

"Go on."

"If all of this Middle East business hadn't been a factor in our lives, do you think you would have still been attracted to Karen?"

"What you mean is, would I have left you for her?"

Alexandra nodded, her eyes riveted to his.

"No," he answered without hesitating. "I loved you…no, I love you as much as any human being can love anyone. But love has to be able to grow into something. It has to be able to blossom into a lifelong commitment, into marriage, into a relationship that produces children who bring joy to their parents and to their parents' parents. We love one another, but we could never climb over the barriers."

"That's true, but…no one will ever mean as much to me as you, Noah."

"You'll fall in love with someone, Alexandra."

"I didn't say I'd never fall in love. I said no one would ever mean as much to me as you do. I think you'll always be the most special person I've ever known."

"We'll have to manage to keep in touch while we're both away at school. We don't want to become strangers," he said.

"I'll try to send a copy of the *Star* to you whenever I have a story running," she said.

"That would really be great, but I want to hear from you, Alexandra. I want to know what's going on in your life, and I want to know that you're well."

Alexandra reached across the table and squeezed Noah's hand. "Do you think I'll ever look at the moon without thinking of you, Noah? I'll always be in touch with you."

Noah, fighting back tears, knew better than to try to speak at that moment.

"Alexandra, I'll answer every letter I receive from you," he finally said.

"And I'll do the same," she answered softly.

They sat hand in hand without speaking for several moments. Noah's throat ached, and tears now filled Alexandra's eyes.

"I guess it really is over," she said with great difficulty.

"We'll always mean a great deal to one another," he said, his words empty, devoid of conviction.

"It's over," she whispered. "I don't blame you, Noah, and I think it would have ended whether or not I went to Beirut to study."

Noah didn't reply. They had addressed it all so many times before. That events and tensions could reach out from across the seas and across the ages to smother the love they had once so strongly believed in distressed them both.

"Karen Rothschild must be the happiest girl in the world," she said softly and without bitterness.

"Karen admires you, Alexandra. She's not gloating."

"She's very lucky," Alexandra said. "The most thrilling fantasies I ever had were when I would think about us marrying someday and living like normal people. That was my dream."

"That was my dream too, Alexandra."

"But not any longer?" she whispered.

He looked at her, pain in his eyes. "No," he lied, "not any longer."

***

Alexandra began packing for her trip to Beirut the week before she was to depart. There was no joy or excitement in the process. She was still agonizing over her loss of Noah. As she thumbed through the letters he had written to her during the past year, she was tempted to call him, but instead she just dropped the correspondence into the wastebasket at the side of her desk. *What's done is done,* she thought.

Noah had resisted the urge to go to the Salamans' to say good-bye to Alexandra again. He had finally convinced himself that their separation was for the best. He fumbled through her letters to him, pausing here and there, aching as he read one expression of affection after another. Then, carefully, he snapped a rubber band around them and put them in a drawer where he kept other important papers. What was done was done.

CHAPTER
TWENTY-TWO

Alexandra arrived in Beirut exhausted after nearly twenty continuous hours of travel. Accompanying her were countless preconceived images of what she expected to find upon arriving in the city known as "Paris of the Middle East." She soon learned how quickly reality weaves its own tapestry.

Beirut was an inviting, sun-drenched city, pulsating with prosperity and energy. Alexandra was stunned by the wealth that seemed ubiquitous in Beirut and by the apparent universal preoccupation there with the accumulation of such wealth.

The first goodwill ambassador she met was a taxi driver who approached her as soon as she emerged from the airport terminal.

George Mitre was a gregarious Maronite Christian who owned more than a dozen cabs and who made it a point to personally spend one day a week driving, saying it made him a better manager to know what his drivers were experiencing.

"Let me help you with those bags," he said in perfect English as he gently, but firmly, took hold of Alexandra's two PUB-decal-emblazoned suitcases. "You'll start school a hunchback if you try to carry them yourself."

"Thank you," she said. "Are you from the school?"

"No, no," he said with a laugh. "But I'll take you there."

"You're a taxi driver?"

"Not just a driver, my friend. I own the company, but I like to drive too. Today, you are lucky. The owner of Beirut's finest taxi company is going to personally drive you to the university."

"I don't know if I can afford to take a taxi. I was hoping to find a jitney or something."

"A jitney!" he exclaimed, pretending to spit in disgust. "Are you trying to put me out of business?"

"No, no." Alexandra laughed. "I just want to get to the university as inexpensively as possible."

"You're an American?"

"I'm an American," she answered.

"George Mitre at your service," he said, half bowing. "Today, Americans ride half price. OK?"

"OK," she replied and extended a hand, which the jovial man clasped warmly.

"My name is Alexandra," she said. "Alexandra Salaman." She guessed George Mitre to be in his forties. He was a short, heavy man, with gunmetal-gray, thick, coarse hair that reminded her of steel wool, and his dark-brown eyes sparkled with intensity. He lifted her two bags easily and put them carefully in the trunk of his Mercedes. Opening the door for Alexandra, he touched her elbow, coaxing her into the back of the car.

"You're a Maronite?" she asked, watching the reflection of his eyes in the mirror.

He laughed. "You're psychic?"

"No, just observant. I noticed the cross you're wearing."

"Ah yes. It was my father's," he said as he turned onto the Corniche, the beautiful motorway that ran along the coast toward the center of the city. "And tell me," he added inquisitively, "your parents were born here in the Middle East?"

"Yes," said Alexandra, "and so were their children."

She saw his eyes dart to the rear-view mirror.

"You were born here?"

"Yes, in Jaffa."

"Ah, a Palestinian Christian," he said, searching the mirror again to get another look at his passenger.

"What makes you so sure I'm Christian?"

"Alexandra isn't Moslem."

"Are there many Palestinians here in Beirut?" she asked.

"There are some, but not too many."

"I will try to find some of my countrymen while I'm here," she said.

"There are many Americans here," he offered.

"I meant Palestinians."

"You are an American. Better you should find your American countrymen here in Beirut."

"I don't understand."

"Not very many people have the good fortune to be born in our part of the world and to be Americans too."

"What do you have against Palestinians?"

"I have nothing against Palestinians. But it is hard enough trying to keep what you Americans call Humpty Dumpty together. That's what Lebanon is. We are a Humpty Dumpty nation, a nation of tribes and families put together most recently by the French—and which is waiting for its great fall. And when the Humpty Dumpty that is Lebanon has its great fall, I'm afraid nothing and nobody will ever put it back together."

"What has that do to with Palestine?" Alexandra asked.

"If this Arab-Israeli conflict isn't settled, sooner or later it will spill over into our tiny, weak, corrupt nation, and that will be the end of Lebanon."

"Don't you think Arabs and Israelis can live in peace in Palestine?"

"Arabs and Christians are living in relative peace here in Beirut," he replied.

"Do you think it will last?"

"Today it will last. We'll have to see about tomorrow," he answered.

"That's not very encouraging."

"You want encouragement? I'll take you to a Chinese restaurant, and you can read fortune cookies. What we have here is not the perfect union, but it works."

"So what do you think holds it all together?" Alexandra asked.

"In a word?"

She smiled. "OK. In a word."

"Money, Alexandra…money. Money is the glue that holds Lebanon together."

"It can't be that simple," she said, frowning as she looked out the window at the reflection of the sun shimmering on the inviting blue water of the Mediterranean.

"But it can, and it is. That's the problem. As long as no one rocks the boat, our common greed will keep us from destroying each other. But let the politics and the fanaticism of the region sweep through here so that everyone begins choosing sides, and that will be the end of Lebanon."

"But it will sweep through here sooner or later, won't it?" she asked.

"Who knows?" He shrugged. "Maybe it will and maybe it won't. Until then, Beirut is as close to paradise as any place on earth."

"Perhaps Beirut can escape the winds of change," she said.

"Have you ever heard of the yellow winds, Alexandra?"

"No. What are the yellow winds?"

"They are the winds every Bedouin fears. They are the winds that suffocate and destroy everything. Not all winds bring fresh air."

"What has that to do with Palestine?" she asked.

"Look, we are passing through Ras Beirut. See those apartments there to the east?" He pointed to a cluster of old, tired three- and four-story buildings crowded together along several blocks of twisting, narrow streets. "Living in there, you will find Sunni and Shiite Muslims; Greek Orthodox, Maronite, and other Christian sects; and Druze, Kurds, and even Jews. They compete, trade with one another, and even visit each other for weddings, birthdays, deaths, and other special occasions. They're both friends and neighbors, and they'll remain that way until these winds we speak of start to blow through here."

"And then what will happen?"

"And then everyone will have to declare themselves. You watch how quickly those winds suffocate something as fragile as friendship."

Alexandra's thoughts shifted to Noah. "I understand," she said softly.

The taxi owner turned and looked over his shoulder at Alexandra. "To the north is Ain al-Mraissi," he said, pointing ahead through the windshield. "It's really a very lovely area, very picturesque. And a little farther on, along the coast, you have to visit the Avenue de Paris—quite beautiful, Alexandra. The university is up ahead, just in front of us."

Noticing that Alexandra was making notes on a pad, he asked, "What is this, 'Meet the Press'?"

"Well, sort of. I work for the *Washington Evening Star*. I'm a correspondent as well as the assistant to the Beirut bureau chief."

"Mother in heaven," he whispered. "I'm being interviewed by the press!"

"Does that bother you?"

"Only if you spell my name wrong."

"Is there strong support for the Palestinians here in Lebanon?" she asked.

"It depends who you ask," he replied.

"Suppose I ask you."

"Well, what is the definition of support? Is it support for an Arab state in Palestine? The Arabs rejected that in nineteen forty-seven when Jews were willing to accept partition. Is it support for the destruction of Israel? The Israelis demonstrated that that won't be so easy to achieve when they took the entire Sinai in a couple of days last year."

"What do you think the Palestinians want?"

"It depends which Palestinian you ask. That's the real problem, Alexandra. No one is uniting the Palestinians around a common goal."

"What about Nasser?"

"Nasser." Mitre shrugged. "What about Nasser? He's the most charismatic Arab of this century. Millions of Arabs will follow him anywhere, but Ben-Gurion is the man that has to be convinced. The rhetoric frightens me, Alexandra. Israel isn't going to go away, and all we'll do is lose valuable time ranting and raving about driving her into the sea."

As they entered the university's grounds, Alexandra settled back and concentrated on the Mediterranean architecture of the campus.

"I guess we're here," she said. "How much do I owe you, Mr. Mitre?"

"Journalists ride free," he answered with a grin.

"Oh, I can't let you do that," Alexandra protested.

"It's done. Just remember to spell my name right—M-i-t-r-e," he said as he jumped from the car and pulled open Alexandra's door. The hot, humid atmosphere immediately sucked the cool, air-conditioned air from the Mercedes.

Several students were gathered on a nearby walkway, engaged in animated discussion, when Alexandra stepped from the taxi. Their attention soon shifted to the attractive American standing on the side-walk and stretching her back while squinting against the brilliance of the midday sun hanging high in the blue sky over Beirut.

Noticing their eyes on her, Alexandra smiled at the group of students and, with some hesitation, raised her hand to wave as her eyes met theirs. The three men wore American-style jeans and casual short-sleeved shirts, while the four girls in the group wore Parisian designer ensembles.

"This is the administration building," George Mitre said, nodding his head at the building in front of them. "They'll sign you in and give you your dormitory assignment. I'll wait here with your luggage and take you to your room when you're through."

***

As soon as Alexandra slipped the key into the lock, her roommate pulled open the door.

"Hi!" said the young woman. "I've been waiting for you all day!"

"I guess you're Monifa," Alexandra said, regaining her balance. "They gave me your name when I registered and said I would probably find you here."

Alexandra liked her roommate immediately. Monifa Bayoumi had a warm, full smile; dark, smooth skin; and eyes that sparkled. She was approximately Alexandra's height, and her straight black hair, which just brushed the tops of her shoulders, was pulled back and held in place by two red barrettes. Alexandra took note of the matching red shade of her recently manicured fingernails. Monifa was slender but shapely. The crisp, sleeveless white dress she wore was cinched snugly to her waist by a narrow gold belt, and she had on gold sandals fashioned from the same material used for her belt.

"Call me Moni. I'm from Egypt, but my English friends christened me Moni at school," she said with a broad, enthusiastic grin.

"Moni, this is my friend, Mr. Mitre. He brought me here from the airport," Alexandra said, introducing her new roommate to the taxi owner.

George Mitre exchanged some words in Arabic with the young coed, then set Alexandra's luggage down in the middle of the room and turned to leave.

"I think you're in good hands, Alexandra," he said.

The two girls spent most of the afternoon getting acquainted. After Alexandra unpacked and put away her things, she and Moni walked across the campus to the bookstore, where they purchased the texts they would need for their classes starting the next week. The university, perched midway up a knoll that ambled from the coast on into the hills to the east of the city, provided a breathtaking view of Ras Beirut and the Mediterranean shoreline. The two girls strolled around the campus, and by the time they got back to their small room, they felt as though they had known each other a long time.

Monifa, Alexandra had discovered, was from a diplomatic family and had traveled extensively in Europe and, for a short time, had lived in London. Like most Arabs from families with means, she was fascinated with America and Americans. So, she was deliriously happy to have been matched with a roommate who was both Arab and so thoroughly American.

When the two young women returned to their room, Alexandra found a note that had been slipped under the door. She immediately recognized the logo of the *Evening Star* on the envelope and guessed the message was from the *Star*'s bureau chief in Beirut, David Ellis.

"It's from my boss," she told Moni after checking the signature.

> Alexandra:
> Meet me at the Saint Georges at 4:00 this PM
> We have work to do, girl!
> Ellis

"Oh my God!" Alexandra said excitedly. "He wants to meet me this afternoon."

"You really are a journalist?" Moni asked in wonder.

"Yes, I really am," Alexandra said. "I'm going to run down to the administration building and try to call Ellis. Maybe he can pick me up. I'll be back shortly."

Alexandra returned to the room a few minutes later, bursting with excitement. The fatigue that had begun to dog her only a short time earlier seemed to have vanished.

"David Ellis is coming here to pick me up. We're going to the Saint Georges Hotel to talk." She began combing her hair.

"Why doesn't he just talk with you here?" Moni asked.

"He says the campus is drier than a bucket of talcum powder. I think he likes a little liquid refreshment in the afternoon."

"Not bad. You've been here two hours, and already you're having cocktails at the Saint Georges."

"Mr. Ellis says it's where the members of the working press hang out," she said excitedly. "He said he'd introduce me to the vipers. He said the Saint Georges would have to do until I graduated to the Phoenicia."

Apparently that's where the really big-name journalists go, especially if they're covering oil and Aramco." A touch of lipstick, and she was off.

"Have a good time," Moni called after her.

***

In front of the administration building, Ellis pulled up to the curb in his small, red, bullet-shaped Renault and pushed open the door on the passenger side for Alexandra.

"Well, ain't you a sight for sore eyes," he said, extending his hand to her.

"I beg your pardon?" she replied with a broad smile as she shook hands with him.

"What I mean, Alexandra, is that you're the prettiest thing those sore-eyed vipers at the Saint Georges will have seen for a long time."

David Ellis was a well-known figure in Beirut, especially in the bar at the Saint Georges. He was as reliable as they came when he was sober, but his desire, or need, for the solace he found in alcohol had cost him the edge he once had, and the greatness that had been within reach was now, he knew, beyond his grasp.

Alexandra studied him carefully as he drove them away from the university. Ellis was a tall, trim, imposing man. He appeared well dressed but at the same time disheveled. The side pocket of his light-blue seersucker suit was stuffed with folded papers, and a standard business-size envelope protruded from his inside pocket under the fold of his lapel. His gray, wavy hair still had a few streaks of auburn but had been thinned by the passage of time. His face was liberally freckled, as much from his boyhood summers on the streets of the Bronx, she later learned, as from the years spent strolling along the shores of the Mediterranean and exploring the vast and beautiful reaches of the Bekaa Valley. The purplish-red capillaries that streaked down onto his cheeks from his generous nose confirmed Alexandra's suspicions that lemonade was not his favorite drink.

As Ellis had predicted, Alexandra did not go unnoticed when she and Ellis made their way to a table at the Saint Georges. Many of the men did not like the idea of women in the bar at all, let alone a female as young as Alexandra. But David Ellis could get away with almost anything, and no one was about to make an issue of it.

"Our office is just around the corner," Ellis said as they settled into a booth along the sidewall of the bar, "but it's small as hell, so we'll meet here a few times a week to talk."

"How will I file my stories?"

"You can give them to me, and I'll have our office manager and Girl Friday telex them, or you can come by the office and telex them yourself."

"Who's 'our Girl Friday'?" she asked.

"Elva Hines. She used to teach at the university, but now she works for me. She keeps me out of trouble and files all my stories. She's a spinster who I haven't seen smile since she came to work for me, but she's a great no-nonsense worker."

"Well, I can't believe I'm here. I don't know where to begin," Alexandra said. "What do you want me to do first?"

"You can begin by leaving all the Middle East and Lebanese intrigue to me. Your beat is the university, Alexandra. No one has really covered that enclave before."

"Is there anything worth covering there?" Alexandra asked, making no effort to hide her disappointment.

"Well, it'll be your job to find out, young lady," he said, leaning forward on his elbows to emphasize his point. "The future leaders of the Arab world just happen to be your classmates, Alexandra. The place is a hotbed of Arab nationalism, and I think tomorrow's ideas and movements are incubating right there on that campus while we're sitting here trying to figure out what you should do."

Alexandra nodded. A waiter came to take their order; after a moment's hesitation, she ordered a glass of wine.

"Young lady, you're sitting on top of the breeding ground of the biggest stories of this generation. Only problem is, nobody knows who the players are going to be yet, and I'm not sure we'd recognize a germinating story if we tripped over it."

"What do you want me to do?"

"I think you should start doing a series of features on the more interesting kids you meet at the university."

"How am I supposed to know who tomorrow's leaders are?"

"Well, that's the difference between being a reporter and just being a pretty typist, isn't it?" he said. "These kids won't be walking around with 'future leader' tattooed on their foreheads. Your job will be to poke around, pay attention, and use your intuition. If you're half as good as Markazie seems to think you are, I have a feeling your nose will lead you to the right people. Then, once you think you've found them, you need to stick with them. It's not enough that you make your readers aware of the presence of these future leaders; you have to make Mr. and Mrs. Middle America understand what it is that drives these people. Right now the Arabs are just a big mystery to most Americans. I want you to personalize and humanize them. Then, maybe ten or fifteen years from now, we'll look back and tally up the score."

"Tally up the score?" she asked, beginning to understand Ellis's expectations of her.

"Yeah…we'll see how many of tomorrow's leaders you wrote about. Meanwhile, try to develop some features about what interests the kids you go to school with. History and time will take care of the rest."

They chatted for about an hour while Alexandra nursed her wine and watched nervously as Ellis tossed down one Canadian Club and water after another. She soon found herself more preoccupied with the hazards of the ten-minute drive back to her room than with the challenge of the next four years at the university.

***

Alexandra was thankful that Moni wasn't there when she returned to her room. Exhaustion was beginning to overpower her, and there was something she wanted do to before crashing for the night.

Quickly, she fed paper into her portable Underwood and began her
first dispatch from Beirut.

MONIFA: IT MEANS "I AM LUCKY"
By Alexandra Salaman

*Beirut, Lebanon, September 4—Monifa is a beautiful
girl, and her name exudes optimism. It means "I am
lucky."*

*Monifa Bayoumi is one of 2,800 students at the
Phoenicia University at Beirut. She is my roommate and
the first classmate I met upon my arrival here as a student.
Monifa is a daughter of Egypt. Her family name literally
means "of the sea." She is a classic Arabian beauty, full of
life; her eyes smile as dramatically as her full and expres-
sive lips, and she exudes warmth and friendship.*

*Most Americans know nothing of Monifa. She
and millions like her are an enigma to us. Yet, it is the
Monifas of the Middle East who are the only hope we
have of bridging the enormous chasm that exists between
East and West.*

*Not all eyes and lips smile in this part of the world,
and there are those whose warmth has been chilled by
politics and who have despaired of ever experiencing
friendship.*

*A strong wind has begun to blow in this part of the
world. It is called Arab nationalism. To understand
Arab nationalism, we must understand the Arab nation,
and we do not. We see the Arab as a warrior who has
fought against European ideals, against the Christian
Crusaders, against the French and the British, and now
against the Jews in Palestine.*

Americans are steeped in European history and culture and largely ignorant of the rest of the world. We observe the struggle against the French, and we know there are so many just and decent Frenchmen; and we observe the struggle against the English, and we know there are so many just and decent Englishmen; and we observe the struggle against the Israelis, and we know there are so many just and decent Israelis. We know all of that, but in our knowledge we forget about all the just and decent Arabs.

Who are they? They are shepherds and citrus growers. They are peasants and traders, architects, teachers, and doctors.

They revere their land and their families and their God.

To the West, "Arab" is synonymous with mystery, fear, and turmoil. In our knowledge, we forget Monifa.

Alexandra sat back in her chair and carefully reread the first few paragraphs of her first feature. Satisfied, she folded her arms over her typewriter and rested her head in the crook of her elbow. Her eyes fluttered shut, and she surrendered completely to exhaustion.

CHAPTER
TWENTY-THREE

Following Ellis's directive to connect with "tomorrow's leaders" among her classmates proved easier than Alexandra had thought. When she related her conversation with Ellis to Moni the next morning, her roommate's response was swift and certain: "You must speak with Ali Abdul Shoukri."

Now the two girls sat in the cafeteria, sipping Cokes and waiting for Shoukri to join them.

"I asked him to meet us at noon," Moni said, glancing at her watch; it was a minute before the hour. "He seemed quite intrigued to meet you when I told him you were a journalist from America. He spent some time at a school somewhere in America. I think some religious group arranged for him to study in America for a while."

"You make me sound so exciting, Moni." Alexandra smiled warmly at her roommate. "I hope while you were telling him what an important journalist from America I am, you managed to slip in the fact that I'm also just a lowly freshman here at the university."

"That she did," said a voice behind Alexandra. "But she failed to mention what a beautiful lowly freshman you are at that."

"Ali!" Moni's smiling gaze was directed over Alexandra's right shoulder. Alexandra turned in her seat and looked up into the smiling face of Ali Abdul Shoukri.

"May I join you?" said Shoukri, leaning down and kissing Moni lightly on the cheek as she gestured him into an empty chair. "I hope I'm not late?"

"No, you're right on time," said Moni. "Let me introduce you to my roommate, Alexandra Salaman. Alexandra, may I present the 'Voice of Palestine'—Ali Abdul Shoukri, future leader."

Ali gave a small chuckle at Moni's grandiose description and reached across the table to shake Alexandra's extended hand.

"I like to think I'm a present leader as well," he said. "But all of me—past, present, future—is entirely happy to meet you, Alexandra."

"The pleasure is mine," said Alexandra, quite aware of Ali's firm and lingering grip. His warm smile and large, dark eyes seemed both welcoming and mysteriously foreboding.

"Moni tells me you're a journalist," Ali said, gazing intently at Alexandra. "What will you write?"

"What I see and what I hear," she replied.

"Then you must be neither blind nor deaf."

"What do you mean?" she asked, intrigued by his sudden seriousness.

"Only that you must keep not only an open eye and open ear but an open mind and an open heart as well. Moni tells me you were born in Jaffa—is that correct?"

Alexandra nodded. "Yes. We had a small citrus grove. We were forced to leave when I was just a child."

Ali's face was grave as he nodded his understanding of an all-too-familiar story. "It is important that you understand, Alexandra, that nothing is as it was when you left. Do you understand that?"

Alexandra stared at him for a moment. She wasn't sure that she did quite grasp what he was trying to tell her, but she found herself nodding all the same. "I…I think I do," she finally managed to respond. Something about his intense gaze and the solemnity of his words made her uneasy, not completely sure of her own mind. He seemed a contratiction. Genuinely warm and friendly one moment, yet eerily cold and distant the next.

They chatted a short while longer, Ali asking more questions than Alexandra did. It wasn't until Moni discreetly cleared her throat that Alexandra realized a silence had fallen over the table while she and Ali simply gazed at each other.

"We should probably start thinking about getting to our next class," Moni said and began gathering her things. Alexandra quickly glanced at her watch and was shocked to find that over half an hour had passed since Ali joined them, not the few minutes Alexandra had thought.

"Oh, you're right!" she said, somehow both relieved and sorry to end her encounter with Shoukri. She busied herself gathering her things, aware of Ali's eyes constantly on her. As she rose from her seat, he rose as well.

"Well, I really appreciate you meeting with me like this, Ali," she said, extending her hand to him once again. He took her hand firmly in both of his and smiled once more. Alexandra hadn't realized how tall he was until they both stood and she had to tilt her head back slightly to look into his eyes.

"The pleasure, as you say, is all mine," said Ali.

***

Alexandra's second meeting with Ellis was not quite as pleasant as the first. As they sat in the Saint Georges bar, Alexandra regaled Ellis with a vivid description of her brief introduction to the dashing and mysterious Ali Abdul Shoukri. She described him as someone who could have been sent from central casting, and she expressed hope that she and Ali might eventually have a chance to get to know each other better. Ellis listened carefully and silently as Alexandra talked about Shoukri. She could tell by his tone of voice when he'd ordered their drinks that something was troubling him. She waited until he had taken the first drink from his tumbler before she pushed the matter further.

"You don't seem as pleased as I thought you'd be," she ventured tentatively. "Is something bothering you?"

"What bothers me," Ellis replied, "is that you're letting a schoolgirl flirtation interfere with your work."

"What are you talking about?" Alexandra felt her face flush. "I barely know Ali—I only just met him—and I certainly wasn't flirting with him. And nothing has interfered with my work at all. I finished my first story the night I arrived, and I intend to have a story every week."

"What the hell do you think this is out here—Feature Writing 101?" Ellis said. "Your job is not to write a story once a week, like some homework assignment. Your job is to ferret out stories and features of substance, stories that give our readers a look into this part of the world they can't get anywhere else. Ike made us players in the Middle East when he intervened in the Suez crisis last year. Americans don't know diddly squat about this part of the world, and we're here to educate them."

"So why are you jumping down my throat? I can write the kind of stories and features you want."

"That's what I was told when Markazie leaned on me to take you on. And I thought the Monifa story was fine, Alexandra. But that's the easy stuff. Features about school in the Middle East won't cut it for long."

"What are you saying?"

"I think you're wasting a dynamite source. Something's brewing here in Beirut, especially at the university. The whole place is in a state of ferment with this Arab nationalism business, and it sounds to me like this Shoukri fellow could be right in the middle of it. Someone like me would never, in a million years, be able to pick his brains, but he falls right at your feet. Suddenly, we—maybe—have something every Western paper would love to have: direct access to one of the new young Turks. But what happens? Our journalist flutters her eyelashes and says, 'Oh, gee, I hope we get to know each other better someday.'

That's great, Alexandra, just great!" He was making no effort to hide his anger. "Maybe if you play your cards right, he'll ask you to the prom. Gosh, wouldn't that make a swell story?"

Alexandra fought to control her composure. His rebuke stung, and for a moment her voice failed her.

"I just didn't want to rush things," she finally said.

"Hey, I got news for you, young lady," he replied, leaning forward to emphasize the point. "Events in this part of the world aren't going to be put on hold to give you time to play hard to get. Goddamn it, this isn't *True Confessions* you're working for! Your job isn't to get a date for Friday night. Your job is to find and report the story. This Shoukri character has 'source' written all over him. And a journalist, a real journalist, doesn't let her heart—or whatever part of your anatomy it is that's kicking into overdrive right now—get in the way of aggressively pursuing that source. You're either a pro, or you're not. If you are, start acting like one. If you're not, I heard they need a towel girl at the pool over at the Phoenicia. Maybe you're better suited to do that."

Alexandra pursed her lips to keep from crying. She was enraged, both at herself and at Ellis, but she chose not to respond, not yet.

"So, what's it going to be, young lady?"

"I'm a pro, damn it!" she answered in an angry whisper.

"Yeah? Then go prove it," he said, drilling her with his stare.

Alexandra stared back furiously for a moment before getting to her feet. "You're right about one thing, Mr. Ellis," she said, leaning forward on the table.

"Yeah, what's that?" he replied.

"You wouldn't stand a chance with Shoukri. He wouldn't give you the time of day."

Ellis's hard expression melted into a soft smile as he watched Alexandra storm from the bar.

***

Alexandra spotted Shoukri the next morning while on her way to her first class. He was standing in front of a classroom building, engaged in animated conversation with two other men whom Alexandra assumed were also Palestinians. As soon as he saw her walking toward him, he stopped in midsentence and smiled warmly.

"Good morning!" she said brightly. Standing in the sunlight, Ali seemed even more handsome than Alexandra had remembered.

"I was hoping we might have a chance to talk again," she said.

"I can't think of anything I'd like more," he said. "The student union? Four o'clock?"

"Four o'clock," she said. She smiled and then after a moment's hesitation, turned and continued on her way to class. Sensing Shoukri's eyes following her, Alexandra smiled to herself and concentrated on a strong and steady stride.

"Whew!" one of Shoukri's companions murmured as soon as Alexandra was safely out of earshot. "Where did you find that beauty, Shoukri?"

"That's an American beauty," Shoukri replied, grinning broadly.

"She's a friend?"

"Not quite yet, but she will be," Ali said. "One day she will be much more than a friend; she will be mine."

"Sure, and someday Palestine will be yours too, right, Shoukri?" His friend laughed.

The smile on Shoukri's face slowly faded, and his eyes hardened into an icy stare. "Do you doubt, for a moment, that we will, one day, have Palestine?" he asked, his tone light but slightly menacing.

His companions knew the moment for levity had passed. No one was prepared to antagonize Shoukri when his mood changed so suddenly and he became so cold and humorless.

"Relax, my friend. We all know Palestine will one day be ours again."

Shoukri's face softened just as quickly as it had hardened, and his smile grew warm again. "Yes, Palestine will be ours," he agreed, "and Alexandra will be mine."

***

They found a corner table at the student union where they could talk. Ali was momentarily too distracted by the beautiful American from Jaffa to focus on the conversation. He took note of the way her long, wavy hair framed her face and of her green eyes that seemed so fresh and exciting. Her olive Mediterranean complexion belonged more to the land of the Fertile Crescent than to the mongrelized shores of America, he thought. She was home now. Surely she saw that.

Still finding herself flustered in Ali's presence, but with Ellis's admonitions ringing in her ears, Alexandra was determined to get right down to business.

"Moni referred to you as 'the voice of Palestine,'" she said, her pen poised over an open notebook to jot down anything Ali might say. "From the way I've heard others speak of you here on campus, I think she's right, or at least partly right. I think there must be many voices being raised in Palestine, and you articulate some of the sentiments being expressed here."

"There may be other sentiments being expressed, but there can only be one truth," he answered.

"And you speak the one and only truth?"

"Well, there are many truths in the world, certainly. But about Palestine? Yes, I speak the one and only truth."

"And that is?"

"And that is that Palestine must be restored to the Palestinians."

"Do you reject ancient history entirely?"

"Historians write ancient history. It's interesting, but irrelevant. You see, Alexandra, it is the warriors who write current history."

"And you intend to write current history?"

"The current history of Palestine will involve millions of authors."

"You mean millions of warriors?"

"You could view us that way, yes. Or you could more accurately see us as millions of liberators."

"I would like to meet some of them."

"Are you, Alexandra, not one of 'them'?"

Alexandra, taken aback by his question, realized she had no ready answer. Instead she simply replied, "I would like to meet some of those you work with in your liberation efforts."

"Do you want to expose them?"

"I want to help the rest of the world understand them," she replied.

"I tell you, there are millions of us all over the Middle East."

"I'm sure that's true, but I can't be all over the Middle East. I'm here in Lebanon. Can you help me meet important Palestinians here in Lebanon?"

"We'll have to see," he said, his intense gaze throwing her off balance.

"What will we have to see?" she asked, breaking his gaze by looking down and staring sightlessly at the scribbles in her notebook.

"Where your heart lies?"

At this, she glanced sharply up at him again. *You're either a pro, or you're not.* Ellis's stinging rebuke still echoed in her head. "My heart, Ali, lies with my profession."

"Not with your people?"

"I want there to be no misunderstanding about this," she said firmly. "I am here as a journalist as well as a student. I want to help my readers understand today's Palestinian students who are going to be tomorrow's Palestinian leaders."

"So you feel totally detached from the struggle?"

"Regardless of how I may feel, I have to write from a detached position. They're not paying me to advocate anything. I can express your passion, but not my own passion."

"Do you have no passion for Palestine?" he asked, his eyes riveted to hers.

Alexandra considered his question. She hadn't arranged to meet Shoukri for him to interview her. "Yes, of course I do," she finally answered softly.

"Then we see eye to eye," he replied.

"We'll have to see," she said, echoing his words back to him. "I have a feeling, Ali, that there is one profound difference in our viewpoints: I don't believe that violence is ever the best way to solve anything."

He smiled, admiring her candor and amused by her obvious naïveté in such matters. "So, you'd liberate Palestine with kindness then, is that it?"

"What I want is peace."

"Peace with servitude? That isn't a solution, Alexandra, that's simply surrender."

"Peace with justice," she replied without wavering.

"That's called liberation, Alexandra."

At an impasse, they just looked intently into each other's eyes for a moment.

Then Alexandra broke the silence. "Listen, Ali, my purpose is not to try to influence you. My job is to help our readers understand you."

Shoukri nodded. "I see. So what can I do to help you?"

"I want to understand what is going on and who the players are."

"You realize that once you understand what is going on and who, as you say, 'the players are,' you will no longer merely be a detached journalist. You'll be with us, Alexandra. You will, inevitably, share our passion."

"I'm a journalist, Ali. I'll maintain my integrity."

"You were a Palestinian long before you were a journalist, Alexandra. I believe you'll find that your integrity as a Palestinian will overshadow everything in your life."

She searched his eyes as she contemplated what he had said. She saw both affection and conviction and something else she couldn't quite fathom.

"*Everything*, Alexandra."

She nodded, but did not reply.

"If you are sure you want to know what is happening, I will help you. Just don't curse me later."

"I am sure, Ali."

"I hope so, Alexandra," he said. "I hope so."

***

During the next few months, Alexandra carefully balanced her time between her courses in journalism and language and her work for the *Evening Star*. Whatever free time she had, she usually spent at the student union, where a raucous debate on Middle Eastern politics always seemed to be raging. Alexandra rarely accompanied her fellow students into Beirut for dinner or entertainment, given the pricey tabs at nearly every popular nightspot. Though she and Ali had gone out on several casual dates, Alexandra felt as if he was biding his time, testing her for something, though she wasn't sure what. What she did know, though, was the more she was with him, the more she wanted to know about him and yet, inexplicably, the more elusive he became.

Then one evening, Shoukri invited Alexandra to go with him to a private room at a coffeehouse in Ras Beirut, just a short distance from the Saint Georges Hotel. Four other young men were waiting when she and Shoukri arrived. Ali introduced Omar Samir as his closest friend and confidant. Alexandra thought Omar's smile was insincere, and she detected a touch of contempt in his eyes. She recognized Mohammad Kareen as one of the men with whom Shoukri had been talking on campus. Like Samir, he seemed pensive and humorless. The hard and almost hostile stare with which he contemplated Alexandra revealed an intensely suspicious nature and a demeanor poisoned by bitterness. Abu Mansour and Daoud Nasser, both in their early twenties, were Palestinians from Hebron. Like Ali, both were uncommonly handsome, and their greetings were warm and friendly.

"Shoukri tells me you are a journalist," Samir said as he poured her a cup of strong black Arabian coffee.

"I write for the *Washington Evening Star*," she replied.

"What do you write?" Nasser asked.

"I'm a feature writer. I write what the paper likes to call human-interest stories. My boss wants me to write about interesting students at the university, especially Palestinians."

Alexandra took note of the way Samir's eyes darted to Mohammad Kareen and then to Shoukri.

"What is so interesting about Palestinian students? Our classes are the same as the others," Samir said.

"My paper is not interested in your classes, Omar. They're interested in your aspirations and your vision of the future."

"Ah, I see. You want us to bare our souls for your readers," he replied, somewhat cynically.

"We Palestinians are a mystery to most Americans," she said. "I want to introduce America to Palestinian thought."

"What would you like to know?" Daoud asked.

"I intend to know you, Daoud. I intend to know all of you and to introduce America to you and to the soul of Palestine," she said.

"That's a big responsibility, being the soul of Palestine," Daoud replied. "We're just five students here in Beirut. Maybe there are better candidates to be the soul, as you say, of Palestine."

Feeling as though she was heading toward a dead end, Alexandra changed her approach slightly. "I'm told that Ali is considered the student voice of the Palestinian people," she said. "Does he speak for all of you?"

Daoud and Abu exchanged glances before answering. Alexandra noted the momentary hesitation.

"We all speak from one heart," Omar Samir answered. "Ali is the most articulate, but he expresses what is in all our hearts."

From there the conversation seemed to flow a bit easier. In answer to Alexandra's questions, the young men assured her they were ready to die for Palestine and that there were millions like them ready to liberate their country.

"Of course you intend to write about many more subjects than the five of us?" Samir said.

"Yes, of course."

"We will cooperate with you, Alexandra," Samir said. "We will share whatever we can with you so you can write about the liberation movement, a movement that has already begun. But first you must give us certain assurances."

"What assurances do you need?"

"We must have the right to review and approve whatever it is you write before it is submitted to your paper, and we must know the date anything you have written about us will appear in the paper."

"I'm sorry, Omar," said Alexandra, shaking her head slowly. "That's out of the question. I can't give you any such assurances."

"Then I'm afraid we have nothing to say," he answered with the smugness of a poker player who had just called an opponent's hand.

Alexandra shrugged. "With or without the five of you, I intend to write about Palestine," she replied. "My paper would fire me if I submitted my work to you for approval. It would be the same whether I was interviewing you or the president of the university or the president of the United States."

"What about informing us of the dates on which your stories about us would appear?"

"I have no way of knowing. It's not as if I'm there in the newsroom where I can ask," she said. "They'll appear when they appear."

"Look, Alexandra, this is important," Shoukri said, the first words he had spoken since he had introduced Alexandra to the others. "We all have friends or family back in Palestine. It would mean a great deal to us to be able to get word to them so they can try to get a copy of the paper that carries these stories. American papers are hard to come by there, but they can be obtained if we can provide our people with the right dates."

Alexandra considered Shoukri's request. "I'm sorry, I hadn't really thought of it in those terms," she answered. "It's going to be a lot of bother, but maybe it can be done. If you're all willing to provide me with the kind of information I need, the least I can do is try to provide you with the dates."

"Then it's agreed?" Samir asked.

"Only the dates, Omar. There will be no review and no approval of anything I write. Understood?"

"Understood," he said, nodding reluctantly.

***

Alexandra returned to her room too stimulated by her meeting with the five Palestinians to even think about sleep. She told Moni about the conversation she'd had. It was not merely the information she would now have access to that excited her, but also the knowledge that she had indirectly become involved in an emerging liberation movement. Alexandra found herself attracted to the mystery and, she admitted to herself, to whatever danger Shoukri and his companions were flirting with. But her last thought before finally drifting off to sleep was not of the liberation movement, but of Shoukri's dark eyes gazing intently at her, as though reading her very soul.

***

Across campus, the four young Palestinians looked expectantly toward Ali Abdul Shoukri, standing at the head of their table.

"Brothers," he said, "I believe we have found our messenger."

"To the messenger!" Abu Mansour and Daoud Nasser proclaimed, holding their fists high above their heads.

"To Palestine!" Shoukri exclaimed in a strong, firm voice, a triumphant smile lighting his face.

CHAPTER TWENTY-FOUR

Samira and Sharif waited anxiously for Alexandra's letters, which arrived each week, usually with the Monday morning mail. At first Alexandra wrote mostly about her classes, providing vivid descriptions of her professors. In each letter she would include some detail about a part of Beirut or the surrounding countryside. While she frequently wrote about Monifa, Alexandra decided not to write about Shoukri or the other Palestinians she had met. Her growing fascination with Ali was still too new and uncertain to share with her family. Besides, she hadn't yet decided what approach she was going to take with the articles she planned to write about Shoukri and his friends.

Alexandra's Monifa feature appeared in the Sunday *Star* about three weeks after she had arrived at school. Samira and Sharif had never known greater pride than when they opened the *Star* that Sunday morning and saw Alexandra's byline from Beirut.

Noah received a clipping of Alexandra's first feature from Beirut the week it was published. It arrived in a letter from his father. "Imagine, our Alexandra—a *Star* correspondent!" Hy had written.

Noah read and reread the column several times. At first he felt only excitement at seeing Alexandra's byline from Beirut. Then he was filled with sadness. Alexandra was on the other side of the planet now, very much at home in a world he didn't understand and one he found threatening. The distance between them was measured in more than miles, and it widened with each passing day.

Noah and Karen spent most of their free time together, and although they made no formal plans about their future, they both assumed they would marry after graduation. So far removed from physical proximity to Alexandra, Noah felt less burdened by his dual loyalties to the two women. Loving Karen was uncomplicated and fun. Contemplating the future with her did not bring on the anxiety that had so often accompanied his thoughts of Alexandra. Everything about Noah and Karen seemed perfect. They were an attractive couple whose lives pulsated with the exhilaration of youth

Noah's life at Stanford, in many respects, mirrored his life with Karen. He found his studies, especially economics and finance, stimulating and challenging. Grades of A seemed to come as easily to Noah in college as they had in high school, although it seemed almost no one got mediocre or poor grades at Stanford. He was well liked by his classmates, particularly those who comprised his dining club, a veritable institution at Stanford. Noah did not, however, pursue much social life beyond his relationship with Karen. They were a familiar sight together, meeting in front of MemChu as they did every morning before lunch and after classes each afternoon. By the time the Thanksgiving break rolled around, everyone considered Noah and Karen to be one of Stanford's more serious couples, and no one was surprised to learn that Noah was spending the holiday in Highland Park with the Rothschild family.

Yet, no matter how full his thoughts were of Karen, there loomed, not very deep in the shadows of his mind, his fantasies of Alexandra. Noah savored the time he was alone with his thoughts and could summon her to his consciousness. He would picture her in his mind, always serene and lovely and smiling. He would have a few moments of contentment, and then reality would crowd his thoughts and the joy would vanish.

***

Alexandra's first year in Lebanon seemed to fly by. She and Monifa roomed together throughout the year and occasionally dated some of their male classmates, though Moni had far more free time for socializing than Alexandra had. Between her schoolwork and her determination to please Ellis and Markazie, Alexandra found little time for building new friendships, and she relied mostly on Moni for companionship. She spent some part of every day at the *Star*'s Beirut bureau, and by the end of the spring semester, she was routinely filing a report or feature every week—far more than either Markazie or Ellis had expected of her.

She also continued to maintain her contacts with the political activists on campus and made a point of keeping lines of communication open with Shoukri and his friends. Though she felt an attraction to Ali, he, for reasons she didn't fully understand, maintained a careful distance between them, a fact that both relieved and frustrated her.

It was with both anticipation and anxiety that Alexandra returned home after the first year. She knew her reunion with Noah would be different this time. Their correspondence had diminished as the school year progressed, and Noah seemed more a fond memory than a longing. They hugged and kissed when he came to the Salaman home to greet her, but their subsequent conversations were too proper, too safe.

When she and Noah and Yusuf were able to, they spent hours talking about their lives, their plans, and the experiences they'd had. They talked about everything and about nothing.

Noah and Yusuf worked long days that summer, helping their parents build Milk & Honey. There were more acquisitions to be made, stores to be converted, and plans to be honed. Alexandra, meanwhile, was a minor celebrity among the interns at the *Star*. She was proof of what an intern could become.

***

Summer for Omar Samir and Ali Abdul Shoukri was consumed with planning and more planning. They sat hunched over the small desk in Shoukri's room, studying the map spread out under the glare of a metal gooseneck lamp. The Mediterranean coastline of Lebanon and Israel had been traced over with thick black ink, and the name of every coastal city and village from Tripoli to Gaza was neatly underscored. Samir saw that Shoukri had circled the villages of Nahariya and Akko. Twelve miles to the east of Nahariya, the Arab town of Tarshiha was also circled. Directly under Tarshiha, Shoukri had written the name Maalot. Before and after Maalot, a Star of David had been drawn in black ink.

Samir noticed the angry strokes with which Shoukri had scratched through the name Israel and had printed the name Palestine.

"If it were only so easy," he mused.

"It will be done," Shoukri answered.

"So what have we here, my friend?" Samir squinted at the map through the blue smoke wafting from the cigarette that dangled from his lips.

"The Jews have created a new settlement next to Tarshiha. They call it Maalot. Their settlement will be integrated with the municipal government of Tarshiha. Tarshiha is a small community, so the Jews will be able to elect all the officials."

"So?"

"So Maalot-Tarshiha is, on a small scale, what is happening to all of Palestine. Soon Tarshiha will become the Arab slum of Maalot. The Zionists will try to use the new Maalot-Tarshiha as proof that Arabs and Jews can live and work together. We will prove that Maalot is a cancer in the side of Tarshiha, just as Israel is a cancer in the side of Palestine."

"Go on."

"We will...visit Tarshiha next summer. We can cross into Syria and make our way to Kuneitra on the Golan. Then, when the time is right, we'll go on to Tarshiha and prepare for our next assignment. Meanwhile, I've found a place where we can hide arms and explosives on the coast between Nahariya and Acre. The Jews have renamed Acre and now call it Akko, but there are still many Arabs there."

"Will they help us?" Samir asked.

"We have friends there. We'll get the help we need," Shoukri replied. "All we have to do is put the equipment and material ashore at a designated point on the coast. Our friends will pick up our little deliveries and keep everything secure until the time is right."

"So between this summer and next, we smuggle what we need down the coast, and these friends of yours will conceal everything for us."

Shoukri nodded.

"And our messenger will let our friends know whenever a drop is to be made?"

"Exactly."

Samir rubbed the stubble on his face as he considered Shoukri's plan. "Our messenger is the weak link," he finally said.

"She's perfect," Shoukri answered.

"I don't know," Samir said. "She has no loyalty to our cause. We don't even know if she has any sympathy for her own people."

"So much the better," Shoukri said, a cold smile turning up one corner of his mouth. "She suspects nothing. We can use the little stories she writes to send our messages to our brothers in Acre, and she'll never know the difference."

"She would curse your name if she knew."

"Someday she will know and she will thank me," Shoukri replied with absolute certainty.

"I wouldn't count on it, my friend."

"Trust me."

"You I trust, Shoukri. It is the girl I don't trust."

"As long as she knows nothing of our plans, there is no harm done."

"Correct, Shoukri. But, if she should learn of our plans or figure out what we are up to…" Samir didn't finish. He didn't have to. He just shook his head as one does in the face of inevitable tragedy.

Shoukri stared at Omar Samir for several moments. "I would never allow the mission to be compromised," he finally said.

***

The summer passed quickly, and as Labor Day neared, Noah and Alexandra prepared to return to their separate worlds. They had spent the entire summer in close proximity and yet had never been more distant. Alexandra had no idea how Ali might have spent the time between semesters, but she found herself surprisingly anxious to get back to Beirut to find out. Karen, who'd spent the summer in Europe on a Stanford Summer Abroad program, would soon be back in Palo Alto, where Noah would eagerly await her return.

CHAPTER TWENTY-FIVE

When school resumed in the fall, Shoukri waited impatiently for his first opportunity to see Alexandra again. He finally spotted her at the coffee machine in the student union. She was alone.

"Welcome back, Alexandra!" he said, smiling as he approached her. "I brought you a present."

"Hello, Ali!" Alexandra responded, surprised at how pleased she was to see him. "Can I buy you a cup of coffee?" she asked.

"I would love a cup."

"So, what's this about a present?" she asked, as they made their way to an empty table.

"I brought you the *Voice of Palestine*," he answered.

"Yes, I can see that," she grinned, looking him up and down. "But shouldn't you be gift-wrapped or something?"

"No, I mean the real *Voice of Palestine*," he said, tossing a magazine down on to the tabletop.

Alexandra looked at the magazine for a moment or two before reaching down to pick it up.

"Where did you get this, Ali?" she asked, thumbing through the publication.

"I subscribe to it," he answered, excitement in his voice. "It's published in Cairo and sent to Palestinians throughout the world."

"Who publishes it?"

"It's a student magazine published at King Fuad the First University. I want you to have it. I'm going to give you my copy after I read it each month. You want to know what is happening among the Palestinian students? Then you must read *Voice of Palestine*."

"Is it a university publication?"

"No, it's published by the Union of Palestinian Students. Mohammed Yasser Arafat got permission from the authorities to publish the magazine when he was student chairman. Now Palestinians read it everywhere. It's passed on from one student to another, so even those that cannot afford to subscribe will, sooner or later, get a copy. It's not sophisticated like your *Life* magazine, but it instills pride in every Palestinian student who reads it."

"Tell me why," she said.

"Everyone wants to destroy the identity of the Palestinian. The Jews want the world to believe there is no Palestinian People, and so do most of the Arab governments. But the *Voice of Palestine* reminds us that there is. It gives us hope, Alexandra."

"You don't believe the Arab nations are solidly behind your struggle?"

"Do you think they'll raise a finger to take on the Israelis after the beating they took last year? The Israelis took the entire Sinai and Gaza as though there were no Egyptian army at all."

"So where does that leave you and your friends, Ali?"

"It leaves us in charge of our own destiny. We know that we, and we alone, will have to take responsibility for liberating Palestine."

"You can't be serious," Alexandra replied.

"Oh, I'm serious, Alexandra," he answered without hesitation. "I assure you I'm serious."

"But if the entire Egyptian army couldn't stop the Israelis, how in the world do you expect to defeat them?"

"By building a movement. Nothing can stop an idea whose time has come, Alexandra. That's as basic as the law of gravity."

"You think it's that simple?"

Shoukri nodded, slowly and deliberately and with absolute conviction.

"Ali, don't you see that the Israelis feel exactly the same way? They believe the movement that resulted in the establishment of Israel has been one of the greatest miracles in all of history. They believe that no people have ever been more faithful to a dream or struggled harder and against greater odds than they have in reestablishing the state of Israel."

"You're comparing Zionism with our movement?" he asked, spitting out the word like a bitter herb.

"I am telling you how three million Israelis feel," she answered.

"The battle does not always go to the army with the most troops, Alexandra. Did not your own adopted country free itself from tyranny with only a handful of men? Men willing to die rather than remain enslaved?"

"Now you're Patrick Henry? A moment ago you compared your movement to the law of gravity."

"It is just as certain," he said.

"Well, you seem to like metaphors, Ali. What about the law that tells us what happens when two objects of equal mass collide at equal force?"

"So, what about it?" He shrugged.

"You know damn well 'what about it.' There's an opposite and equal reaction. They repel one another, but one never overpowers the other."

"Then we'll have to make sure that when the collision occurs, the two forces are not of equal mass and equal force, won't we?"

"Your movement could bring great misery to the Palestinian people."

"Alexandra, you were in America so long you don't even realize how much misery there is among your own people. And it's not our movement that is the cause of their misery."

"Ali, please." Her voice took on a pleading tone. "This kind of thinking can only lead our people to destruction and despair."

"Alexandra, your fears are too late," he said, his voice growing gentle, as though trying to cushion the blow while explaining an unpleasant truth to a small child. "Palestine has already been destroyed, and our people are in despair."

A heavy silence fell between them for a few moments. Then Alexandra rose and began gathering her books.

"I have to go," she said quietly. "I have a nine o'clock class."

Ali also rose and placed a gentle hand on Alexandra's arm, bending to look into her downturned face. He saw that her eyes were clouded with tears.

"I didn't come to argue with you," he said, putting his arms around her reassuringly. "I only wanted to give you the magazine."

Alexandra rested a moment in his embrace, fighting to maintain her composure. She wasn't quite sure what upset her. The disagreement with Ali? The futility of his struggle? Her fears for him and for the Palestinian people? She glanced up at his face and saw pleading in his eyes.

"Maybe I started the argument," she said sympathetically and, he thought, tenderly.

She pulled hastily away from him and forced a smile. "Thanks for the magazine."

***

Shoukri and his friends were waiting for the right moment to use Alexandra. Their colleagues in Acre had already been alerted that a shipment of small arms and explosives would be put ashore sometime during November. They had been told to wait until a feature appeared in the *Washington Evening Star* about certain young Palestinians studying in Beirut. The articles would be under the byline of Alexandra Salaman. Four shipments would be dispatched during the school year. The first shipment would be on the way after the first appearance of Shoukri's name, the second after Omar Samir's name appeared, and the others after Abu Mansour's and Daoud Nasser's names. It was that simple. Once Shoukri was interviewed, the rest would only agree to be the subject of a story when an arms shipment was ready to be dispatched. Alexandra was to become an unwitting accomplice to sabotage and, before it was over, perhaps murder.

CHAPTER
TWENTY-SIX

Despite what Alexandra felt to be a growing trust between them, she was rather puzzled that Ali had so far been unwilling to be interviewed for one of her *Washington Star* reports. Normally he took every possible opportunity to discuss the struggle for Palestinian liberation with an almost evangelical zeal. Even so, Alexandra had no trouble filing her stories each week. The other students were always cooperative, and Beirut was a treasure trove of material for her features.

Alexandra also wasn't sure what to make of her growing feelings for Ali. As she began to accept his obsession with Palestine, she also began to understand him better. She could never condone the violence he espoused or the hatred that seemed a theology to him. But she could understand its genesis and both admired and feared Ali's unwavering devotion to the cause of Palestine. No less important was her growing physical attraction to Ali. He was tall and slim, with a perpetually rumpled look that made Alexandra want to smooth his hair whenever she saw him. There was a hunger in his gaze that she found strangely seductive. She was unnerved by Ali and by the fantasies he invoked, but when her thoughts wandered to such fantasies, it was Noah's face she saw before her. "Alexandra we're in love. People in love stay together," Noah had said to her. Had it really been such a short time ago that she and Noah were inseparable? It seemed like another lifetime now.

***

Shoukri waited for a beautiful spring day to ask Alexandra to accompany him on a drive into the Bekaa Valley. He had borrowed a car from Samir, he said, and wanted to show her one of the most beautiful places in all of the Middle East. She suppressed the urge to laugh when he proposed a picnic. Alexandra could think of nothing more out of character for Ali Abdul Shoukri, the voice of Palestine, than relaxing at a picnic. But Palestine did not appear to be what was on Ali's mind that Sunday afternoon. He seemed more relaxed than he had ever been with Alexandra. She wondered what, or who, was responsible for his apparent newfound contentment. She hoped it was his proximity to her that now soothed his restless soul.

Shoukri pulled Samir's '49 Chevy off to the side of the road and pointed to the East. "Over those hills lies Syria and Damascus," he said. "This was a burgeoning trade route even before the Indians found their way to America. There, to the south, lies what was once Babylon. Civilization began somewhere around here. And it's ours. Do you know what I mean? This is our part of the world."

"I know." She smiled, finding herself sharing his pride.

"I love this place."

"What is it that you love about it?"

"The noise goes away."

"What noise?"

"The noise in my head," he answered. "Do you think I'm mad?"

"No, Ali, I think you're passionate about what you want for your people. Perhaps that can be seen as a sort of madness. I think I understand your passion for Palestine, but sometimes it frightens me."

"Sometimes it frightens me too, Alexandra."

"You're the most driven person I've ever known," she said.

He nodded. "I know. It's always been like that with me."

"Are your parents as intense as you are?" she asked.

"I don't remember my parents. My mother died bringing me into the world. My father was killed by the Israelis during the war in 1948."

Ali's father, a farm laborer, had left the boy with his own father and fled at the outbreak of the so-called Israeli war of liberation to join the invading Egyptian army, Ali told her. He was killed attacking a bunker at Yad Mordechai, a kibbutz not twenty kilometers from his home. Shoukri had not been grief stricken upon hearing of his father's death, or at least he did not reveal it. Instead, he was consumed with frustration and resentment that his father had been killed not by enemy soldiers, but instead by farmers defending their kibbutz, and so had been denied the glory of martyrdom. Ali had continued living with his grandfather until the old man's death five years later.

Alexandra listened with rapt attention as Ali told her of his childhood.

"Do you have any fond memories of your boyhood?" she asked.

He thought for a moment and then looked away. When he turned back to her, she saw tears in his eyes. She had never thought him capable of such emotion.

"Ali," she whispered compassionately.

"I have no fond memories," he answered softly. "I don't think I had a boyhood."

"But how did you manage?" she asked. "You're here at the university. You must have gone to school."

It was true that Ali had gotten enough formal education as a child to learn to read, and he'd taught himself passable English by sneaking into movies and sitting through hour after hour of American feature films. But it wasn't until he was nearly a teenager that he was offered a visa to study in the United States by a minister of the Dutch Reformed Church.

Reverend Ezra Dykstra loved the Holy Land with a passion, and his annual mission to that tormented corner of the world was to recruit young men and women for the freshman class of the New Holland Preparatory Academy in New Holland, Michigan. In Ali Shoukri, Dykstra saw the ideal candidate for the academy. The boy tested well and had a workable command of English. What was more important,

Ali Shoukri was penniless. New Holland would represent absolute salvation for the pensive youngster from Gaza. The poor ones were the best candidates, Dykstra thought. They worked the hardest and were the most appreciative; they would never forget who had saved them.

Reverend Dykstra had arranged for Ali and five other Palestinian teenagers to travel on Egyptian passports, and he had personally prepared the papers necessary to obtain a student visa from the State Department. New Holland Prep, nestled in the lush green Michigan countryside halfway between Kalamazoo and Grand Rapids, was a fully accredited liberal arts school with a strong emphasis on Christian ethics and values.

Ali Abdul Shoukri took full advantage of the opportunities afforded him during his stay in the United States. He devoured all the newspapers, books, and magazines he could find and developed a command of the English language that impressed his teachers. He was a brilliant student whose work was nearly always flawless. While his teachers assumed that Ali was spending all of his spare time on homework assignments, in truth they were often completed in the hallways during the ten-minute break between classes. The rest of his free time was usually spent in the New Holland Public Library, where Ali created his own educational curriculum, stretching and challenging his mind in ways his teachers never imagined.

After graduation, Ali returned to Gaza, where he drifted from job to job. He barely earned enough for food and rent and for a small furnished room over a butcher shop, where the smell of rotting flesh constantly permeated the air.

Ali's life would change when he read a note slipped under his door one day that asked him to meet Reverend Dykstra at a nearby café. The New Holland Preparatory Academy seemed not only in another country but also in another life altogether. His first response was to toss the note away without further thought. But curiosity got the better of him, and he found himself that afternoon sitting down to coffee with the reverend.

"Why are you in Gaza?" Ali asked him. "You said you had something important to discuss with me."

"Ali, listen to me very carefully," the reverend said, excitement evident in his voice. "I believe I can help you obtain a scholarship to the Phoenicia University at Beirut. You have heard of the university there?"

"Of course. Everyone has heard of it. But how can you do this for me?" Ali asked, puzzled.

"I have known Dr. Haddad, the director of admissions there, for years. He wrote to me about a new program they are beginning. They want to offer scholarships to the children of Palestinians. Mostly, they are looking for Palestinians who are no longer living in the Middle East, but I believe I can arrange to have you included under this program. Ali, it would be a miracle for you. It would change your entire life," Dykstra said with great enthusiasm.

Ali sat staring silently at Reverend Dykstra's beaming face. Never, even for a moment, had Ali Abdul Shoukri given a thought to going to college.

"Ali, without a university education, you will spend your best years leaning against some wall with your hands in your pockets, waiting for some Israeli to offer you a few hours' work picking oranges. This is an opportunity of a lifetime. We have an expression in America. It says opportunity only knocks once. You'll never have another opportunity like this—never!"

"Why are you doing this?" Ali asked. "Why me?"

"Frankly, I can think of no one for whom such a program could possibly do more good than you."

"I'm not sure I understand," Ali replied.

"Let me be more direct then. Ali, you are hopelessly poor, horribly isolated, and, I know, incredibly bright. In fact, in the entire history of New Holland Preparatory Academy, there has never been a student who showed such outstanding academic promise as you did. You can do something for yourself if you go on with your education, Ali. And maybe you can also do something for your people."

Ali remained silent, his mind trying to process this unexpected turn of events.

"Ali, what shall I tell Dr. Haddad?" Reverend Dykstra asked, growing slightly impatient with Ali's lack of response. "Shall I urge him to extend the invitation to you?"

Finally Ali looked into Reverend Dykstra's eyes and smiled. "Tell Dr. Haddad that Ali Abdul Shoukri will come," he answered. "Yes, I will come."

Reverend Dykstra held Ali's gaze for a moment, and then his lined and weathered face broke into a broad grin. "Good! Then it's done!"

Ali reached out and took Reverend Dykstra's hand into his. "I am indebted to you," he said sincerely.

"You can now fight for your dignity," Reverend Dykstra said.

"I shall fight for the dignity of Palestine," Ali replied, a sparkle in his eyes.

***

When Ali had finished recounting his meeting with Reverend Dykstra and his vow to use his education to fight for his people, Alexandra asked, "So, you are pursuing this opportunity not for yourself but to make yourself useful to the cause?"

"I suppose." He shrugged. "What does it matter? Individuals live and die, Alexandra. In the overall scheme of things they—we—are unimportant. Only the cause matters. Only the movement matters. Individual men and women are but grains of sand on the face of the earth. They are minuscule and insignificant stars in the heavens."

"No, Ali. Your causes and movements only exist to serve the just interests of men and women. Without compassion for people, the movements are sterile and meaningless."

"I am not without compassion, Alexandra. But I'm also realistic. No war can be won if the comfort of people is placed above the welfare of the cause they are fighting for. Or do you imagine that all the just interests of men and women, as you put it, have always been won without some injustices? There are still people who are homeless because their homes were reduced to rubble in the course of the recent fight for 'just interests.' But these people are displaced in a land free of the tyranny of their would-be oppressors. Do you think they would be happier as slaves in the comfort of their own homes? Nothing is gained without some sacrifice."

"And you, Ali?" Alexandra said. "What are you willing to sacrifice?"

"Everything," Ali answered without hesitation.

"Oh, Ali," Alexandra said, burying her face in her hands, "don't you see? War and violence aren't going to benefit the Palestinians' cause. They will destroy it. Palestinians and Israelis will, sooner or later, have to learn to live together, not try to destroy one another."

Shoukri thought for a moment before responding. Then he looked into her eyes and smiled. "Tell me, Alexandra, what is the difference between passion and anger?"

"There is nothing virtuous about misdirected passion, Ali. It can be as destructive as wild and unrestrained anger. You may think the cause or the movement is so important that anything done in its name is justified. But in the end, no good can come of it."

Much to Alexandra's frustration, Ali's smile simply widened at her words. He then took her hand in his, turning it over and tracing the lines on her palm.

"Ah, a long life, I see," he teased, "full of happy people and pretty thoughts." He bent and placed a tender kiss on her palm, a gesture that sent a shiver through Alexandra's body. It was not an unpleasant feeling.

"I will not argue with you, Alexandra. Not today," Ali said, placing Alexandra's hand gently on her lap, as though it were made of the most delicate porcelain. "I will allow your naïve view of the world to be the final word on the subject, at least for now. I brought you here to have a pleasant afternoon, not another debate."

"That's…that's fine with me," Alexandra stammered. Ali had once again left her feeling off balance, unsure of her own thoughts and feelings.

"Good!" he said, slapping his hands on his thighs as though to punctuate the end of the discussion. "Now, I think I'm ready to let you interview me for one of your stories."

"Just like that?" she said, taken aback by the abrupt change of topic.

He smiled. "Just like that."

"You've put me off for a whole year, and now you just announce that you're ready to grant me an interview? Maybe I'm not ready to do the interview."

"Of course you're ready. You have been asking me about it for weeks."

"So why all of the sudden are you so ready?" she asked curiously.

"Some friends in Gaza are going to be in Cairo for the next few weeks. They will be able to obtain a copy of the *Evening Star* there. I would like the story about me to appear when my friends can easily obtain a copy of the paper."

Alexandra considered his response and despite a nagging suspicion that there was more to it than he was divulging, decided to accept his explanation.

"OK, we'll do it!" she said.

As Shoukri and Alexandra made their way to the top of a knoll that afforded them a magnificent view of the Bekaa Valley, a small trawler steamed out of Beirut harbor and headed south, hugging the rugged shoreline of Lebanon.

Alexandra watched Shoukri smooth the blanket he had spread out on the ground for their picnic and then sit down on it.

"Come," he said, reaching up to her. "Let's have something to eat."

As Alexandra took his hand, she thought for an instant of Noah reaching out to her as he used to do when they would climb to their rock high above Pierce Mill in Rock Creek Park. *Noah would die,* she thought. *He would simply die.*

They spent the entire afternoon on the hillside overlooking the Bekaa Valley. Shoukri had brought a variety of cheeses and two loaves of French bread. The Chablis he had refrigerated the night before had lost its chill by the time he poured Alexandra's first glass. It was, nonetheless, refreshing and relaxing.

After they had eaten, Ali lay back on the blanket, hands clasped behind his head.

"Someday I will take you to the ruins of Anjar," he said. "It's beautifully preserved and not very far from here. It was built by the Umayyads ages ago. Someday I'll show you every square mile of the Bekaa."

Realizing that Shoukri would probably never be more willing to talk than he was at that moment, Alexandra reached into her handbag and took out her note pad.

Shoukri spoke again about his childhood in the streets of Gaza and of his determination to return there someday as one of the men who would help set it free. The unseasonably warm breezes gliding effortlessly through the Bekaa that afternoon, and the soothing influence of the wine they shared subdued the tensions that had arisen during their earlier conversation. By the time the interview concluded, the sun had set over the western hills of the valley.

Shoukri gently pulled Alexandra to her feet. He held her for a moment and then took her into his arms. Alexandra offered no resistance. She reached up, as she had so often longed to do, and tenderly smoothed his unruly hair. When Ali gently touched his lips to hers, Alexandra found herself surprisingly receptive to his advance. Ali's hands slid under her blouse. She shivered at the feel of his touch on the bare flesh of her back.

"Ali, please," she whispered, pushing herself gently away and turning her back to him as she fought to regain her composure.

"What is it, Alexandra?" Ali said, putting his hands on her shoulders.

"Reality, Ali," she answered sadly, not turning, afraid of what she would do if she looked at his face at that moment.

"We are not friends?"

"Yes, we are friends," she said. "But let's be content with friendship for now."

"I love you, Alexandra," Ali said. "I've loved you from the moment I met you."

"Oh, Ali, no," Alexandra cried, turning now to face him. "Please don't speak of love, not to me, not now! I'm just passing through your life right now. Before long I'll be returning to a world that will always be alien to you. There is no place for you in that world and no place for me in yours."

"But this is your world, Alexandra!" he said, grasping her shoulders tightly and looking deep into her troubled eyes. "This is where you belong! These are your people! My struggle is your struggle. We share in common everything that matters."

"No, Ali," she said firmly. "We were born in the same region of the world, that's all. Of course I have feelings for you...but those feelings are nothing compared to all that separates us."

"We have a great deal in common," he said.

"Wasn't it you who told me to be realistic?" she replied. "Yes, we have feelings for each other, but it's too soon to be speaking of love."

He bent to kiss her again, but she turned her head away.

"Please, Ali, no. I just can't. Not now. Not yet."

"I'll wait until you are ready," he replied.

"I don't know that I'll ever be ready," she said. "We'll have to see."

"What is there to see?"

"I need to see who you really are, and you must see who I really am. We may not like what we see."

"I've seen all I have to see," he said.

"You've seen very little, Ali, and I've seen even less."

"Then," he said, "we shall indeed have to see."

This time when he bent to place a soft kiss on her lips, Alexandra didn't resist. They stood clinging to each other for another moment, Alexandra's eyes gazing over Ali's shoulder at the full moon that had just begun to emerge over the ruins of Baalbek—the same moon that hung over the clock tower at Howard University and Memorial Church at Stanford University.

***

While Ali Abdul Shoukri and Alexandra Salaman sped through the hills of the Bekaa Valley on their way back to Beirut, Omar Samir peered into the darkness at the lights of Sidon from the trawler slowly making ts way south toward the ancient city of Tyre.

CHAPTER
TWENTY-SEVEN

Moustafa Ahmed, a young Palestinian from the West Bank town of Jenin, drove the '48 Plymouth, its trunk filled with explosives, from the outskirts of Damascus to the Lebanese town of Nabatiyeh, where a wooden case of Russian semiautomatic assault weapons was loaded onto the floor of the car and covered with a blanket. Less than an hour after leaving Nabatiyeh, Ahmed eased the automobile to a stop behind a rock formation just north of the coastal city of Tyre. There he waited until a rubber dinghy came ashore to carry off the cargo he had brought from Damascus. He had no idea exactly where the arms and explosives were to be taken and had been instructed not to ask. He watched as everything was loaded onto the dinghy and rowed out to the trawler anchored about fifty yards off the coast. Then Ahmed sat in the car and watched until the boat vanished into the darkness as it continued down the coast toward Israel.

Some hours later, another young Palestinian worked quickly to lower the cache of arms and explosives into a dry well on a small and long-abandoned farm about halfway between the cities of Nahariya and Akko. He had no time to spare if he was to be back on the trawler and in Lebanese waters before the first light of dawn reached the coastline.

The beginning of a lethal arsenal was now in place for use the following summer against the new Israeli town of Maalot. In the adjacent town of Tarshiha, a small group of accomplices would wait for word that the cargo had been delivered. Then they would retrieve the shipment from the abandoned well and take it to a safe house in Tarshiha. Word of its arrival would come in the form of a column about Ali Abdul Shoukri in a Sunday edition of the *Washington Evening Star*. Each week, an Arab taxi driver picked up copies of the Sunday *Star* at the King David Hotel in Jerusalem and delivered them to George Saleh, a young lawyer in Tarshiha. He and his companions were to wait until Alexandra's interview appeared before venturing to the well near Akko.

The night after her outing with Shoukri, Alexandra mailed a copy of the *Voice of Palestine* to Yusuf at Yale. She wrote that she thought he would find the magazine interesting and was anxious to get his reaction to the publication. Then she sat down at her Underwood and began to type.

THE ANATOMY OF A WARRIOR
By Alexandra Salaman

Beirut, May 5—Ali Abdul Shoukri is a young man with a mission. He is a young man at war with history.

When the state of Israel was formed by the United Nations ten years ago, nobody bothered to ask Ali Abdul Shoukri how he felt about it. In fact, nobody bothered to ask any of the Palestinians who had lived and worked on the land how they felt. Shoukri was just a child then. But now he, and thousands of young Palestinians just like him, intend to challenge history by writing a few chapters of history themselves. They are very serious about their mission—deadly serious.

They intend to do what every Arab army has failed to do. They intend to succeed where their fathers have failed. They intend, quite literally, to liberate Palestine.

Ali Abdul Shoukri, unlike many Palestinian refugees, has no fond memories of the good old days. For Ali Abdul Shoukri, life has been cruel from the moment of his birth—the day his mother died. History made an orphan of Shoukri before he was ten years old. His father was killed attacking an Israeli kibbutz less than twelve miles from his house in Gaza. After his father's death, the streets of Gaza became Shoukri's home. He was taught by deprivation and nourished by hatred. Like all young people, he craved recognition, but no one cared what he thought and no one listened when he spoke. In time, violence emerged as the only antidote to the chronic frustration that had begun to poison his soul.

Ali Abdul Shoukri has no family. He has few friends and, by his own reckoning, millions of enemies. Yet he speaks of liberation with absolute conviction. The ultimate triumph of his cause is, he believes, a certainty.

American values are alien to the Shoukris of the world. We place individualism at the center of the American universe. To us, there is little in life more precious than the individual. In the world of Ali Abdul Shoukri, the cause, the movement, is at the center of the universe. He knows men will die in their quest to alter the course of history. He knows he may die in the service of his cause.

To Ali Abdul Shoukri, the death of the individual is of no importance if it serves the cause to which he and his comrades have consecrated themselves.

We Americans see the violence, but we are blind to its genesis. We hear the hateful rhetoric, but we were deaf to the cries of anguish that preceded it. We marvel at the achievements of the victors, but we ignore the plight of the vanquished. Ali Abdul Shoukri has lived among the vanquished all his life, and he stands ready to vanquish in return. We Americans will, eventually, vilify him and fear him and perhaps even fight him. But if we do not learn to understand him, we will create millions just like him. Ali Abdul Shoukri and his compatriots believe their idea is just, and, as he reminded me, there is nothing so powerful as an idea whose time has come.

We Americans do not have to agree with the Shoukris of the world, but we do have to understand them. They are going to write a lot of history. And while we cannot predict whose cause history will bless and whose cause history will curse, we know we have not seen history's final chapter in this part of the world. There are no final chapters in history.

History may not always reward the just or the mighty, but history always punishes the ignorant.

***

Alexandra's Shoukri interview appeared in the *Star* on the third Sunday in November. The column at first dumbfounded the Greenspans, who always searched the *Star*'s pages for Alexandra's byline. As the words sank in, their shock turned to hurt and then to anger. "How could this be?" Hy agonized aloud over and over again to no one in particular.

If the Greenspans were angered and hurt by the column, Sharif and Samira Salaman were terrified by the words they read. They understood the danger inherent in Arab fanaticism and the risk to which Alexandra was exposing herself.

Yusuf, too, found the column to be particularly troubling in light of the magazine Alexandra had sent him. He again picked up the *Voice of Palestine* and thumbed through it. Slowly he turned the pages and skimmed story after story written "about Palestinians, by Palestinians." The *Voice of Palestine* was, according to one article, reaching out to young Palestinians throughout the world, even to those in America. Yusuf assumed his sister was being intensely recruited by some extremist liberation movement with which Ali Shoukri was involved, and given the tone of Alexandra's piece for the *Star*, Yusuf feared that Shoukri had succeeded in winning Alexandra, perhaps in more than just political matters.

***

George Saleh sat in the small office in the rear of his home in Tarshiha and reread Alexandra's column. His heart raced as he stared at the name Ali Abdul Shoukri in print right there in front of him. It was all beginning to work. There was a plan and a movement, and it was all working. Fellow Palestinians he didn't even know had succeeded in hiding arms and explosives, and they had secretly communicated with him through the pages of one of the world's leading newspapers.

The struggle has really begun, he thought. He focused once again on Shoukri's name. It was like a battle cry calling Palestinians everywhere to the great confrontation about to take place.

George Saleh carefully folded the newspaper and tucked it under his arm. He opened the front door of the modest but comfortable cinder-block house and stepped out into the brisk autumn air. Within an hour, he had visited four other homes and at each one had handed the Sunday *Star* to a young man who had also waited patiently for Alexandra's column to appear. As each one read the column, which Saleh had circled in ink, his eyes, wide with excitement, darted to Saleh, who in turn merely smiled and nodded.

By 2:00 a.m. the entire consignment of munitions had been moved from the well near Akko to Saleh's home in Tarshiha. There the contraband was carefully placed in shallow trenches that had been dug under the floorboards of his family home.

Who is Ali Abdul Shoukri? Saleh asked himself as he worked. And who is Alexandra Salaman?

***

George Saleh was not the only one in Israel whose curiosity was aroused regarding the person of Alexandra Salaman.

Amos Ben-Chaiyim—whose forebears had immigrated to Jerusalem from Vilna, Lithuania, eleven years before Patrick Henry shouted his preference for death over servitude in Richmond, Virginia—rushed past the reception desk of the King David Hotel and hurried down the corridor to the main dining room. He stood at the entrance for a moment until he spotted the thin, balding Binyamin Bar-Levy seated in the far corner of the room, sipping tea. Amos grinned when he saw that Bar-Levy was the only man in the crowded dining room wearing a coat and tie. Bar-Levy's appearance made him seem more like a college professor or British bureaucrat than the intelligence expert he was. His exploits had become legendary within the halls of the Mossad during its brief but impressive history.

The two men were a striking study in contrast as the much younger Amos took his place across the table from Binyamin Bar-Levy.

"Ah, good morning, Amos," Bar-Levy said, reaching out to shake his young colleague's hand. "All is well?"

"Is all ever well?" Amos answered with a broad grin.

Amos Ben-Chaiyim had worked with the Mossad for two years, and he loved it. A striking figure, over six feet tall, Amos was a young man with strong and handsome features that commanded attention. His eyes were dark, almost black, and his gaze was direct. His thick, wavy black hair, always in need of a trim, brushed the top of his shirt collar. His high cheekbones and broad but straight nose reminded Bar-Levy of the Cossacks who roamed the back country of rural Russia, not the scholars of Vilna from whom his young friend was actually descended.

"So, who is this columnist who appears out of the blue promoting sympathy for those who have chosen the path of violence?" Bar-Levy asked as he smeared his favorite apricot preserve on a wedge of toast.

"She seems harmless enough. As far as our people in Washington can determine, Alexandra Salaman is apparently a Palestinian-American who is now studying at the Phoenicia University at Beirut. She began working at the *Evening Star* while she was in high school, and they made her a special correspondent when she left to go to Beirut. She has often written about students at the university there.

"That's all?"

"Not quite. There's an interesting twist to the story. I asked our people to send me everything they could find that she has written at the *Star.*"

"And…?" Bar-Levy's eyebrows arched slightly in anticipation.

Amos smiled, knowing that Bar-Levy always rose to the bait of intrigue like a bee attracted to honey.

"Her first byline at the *Star* was titled 'The Heirs of Eden.' I have it here." He reached into his jacket pocket for the clipping. "It's a story about her family and their friendship with a Jewish family. Alexandra Salaman apparently is, or was, in love with a Jewish boy, and though the families were friends, there was always this Arab-Jewish problem. It's really a very touching story," Amos said, handing the old news clipping to Bar-Levy.

"And now she's extolling the virtues of violence and terror," Bar-Levy answered, somewhat impatiently.

"I wouldn't put it quite that way," Amos said. "All she wrote was that we are breeding a violent generation among the Arabs."

"It's the same thing, Amos. Believe me, the last thing we need is sympathy in the West for Palestinian troublemakers."

"Well, there is sympathy for the refugees already. There was certainly sympathy for our people when we were refugees."

"But we didn't remain refugees very long, did we?" he retorted. "The Arab countries have made it policy to make the Palestinian refugees a permanent part of the landscape here in the Middle East. They rejected the UN partition plan that would have given the Palestinians a state of their own—a plan we accepted. Their rejection created a refugee problem that they deliberately perpetuate." He tossed the clipping back to Amos without reading it. "It makes me sick!"

Amos nodded absently, unimpressed by Bar-Levy's outburst. "Come on, Binyamin, there's plenty of blame to go around, and you know it. The Salaman girl's first article is quite lovely, and you should read it. By the way, here's her picture." He handed Bar-Levy the clipping that announced Alexandra's appointment to the *Star*'s Beirut bureau. "She's from Jaffa."

Bar-Levy winced. "Jaffa, of all places," he whispered. His expression softened as he studied the photograph of Alexandra.

"Not our finest hour?" Amos replied, a touch of sarcasm in his voice.

"War is never equitable, my young friend." Bar-Levy sighed almost apologetically. "Perhaps, in some cases, we were overzealous."

"As in Jaffa?"

"Jaffa, Haifa…what difference does it make? When there's war, you don't ask too many questions."

"I know. I was in Gaza last year, remember?"

Bar-Levy looked into the young eyes staring at him from across the table, eyes he knew had seen war and suffering and death. "Sorry," he replied softly. "You, I needn't lecture."

"So, what do you want me to do?"

"Amos, the *Star* is an important newspaper in the capital of America. This student correspondent, Alexandra Salaman, is cutting her reporter's teeth on the Israeli-Palestinian issue. Right now she's not important, but she has a long career in front of her, and she could give us a lot of grief in the future. I want to know everything we can learn about the Salaman family. Who is her father and who is her mother? What did they do in Jaffa, and what were the circumstances of their departure?"

"Anything else?"

"Yes, while you're at it, find out who in the hell Ali Abdul Shoukri is."

CHAPTER
TWENTY-EIGHT

Early in January, an interview between Alexandra and Omar Samir, the newly elected president of the Union of Palestinian Students at the university in Beirut, appeared in the Sunday *Star*. George Saleh underscored the name, and within hours a second shipment of small arms and explosives was picked up at the abandoned well near Akko and hidden in the safe house in Tarshiha.

Shoukri and Samir were now beyond rhetoric and plotting. They were engaged in an enterprise that if discovered by the Lebanese, would mean expulsion and if discovered by the Israelis, would probably mean death.

In Tarshiha, George Saleh and his compatriots stood ready to begin their campaign. The scheme was almost perfect—almost, but not quite. It had never occurred to either Shoukri or Samir that they or Alexandra would become objects of curiosity by anyone within the Mossad.

Two days later, when a messenger delivered a file from Interpol, Amos learned that Ali Abdul Shoukri had a history, albeit one Amos had seen a hundred times before. Amos studied the grainy seven-year-old photograph of Shoukri clipped to the top of the file. *Just a kid*, he thought as he read the file, which contained the usual petty acts of violence one might expect from someone of Shoukri's background, but with one important difference: while most young men would leave such behavior behind with adolescence, Shoukri exhibited the tenacity that Amos considered the hallmark of a terrorist in the making.

Amos reported his findings to Bar-Levy over breakfast the following morning. Bar-Levy listened with intense interest.

"So Shoukri was educated in the States, as was this Salaman girl," Bar-Levy said when Amos had finished his report. "More than a coincidence?"

"I'm not so sure," Amos replied. "The Salaman family settled in the States a thousand miles from where Shoukri was attending the mission school, and there's nothing to suggest any contact between the two during Shoukri's time there. And Alexandra was recruited to the University in Beirut with a scholarship reserved for Palestinians. It's perfectly logical that Shoukri wound up there the same way and they just happened to meet."

"In any event, this Shoukri character seems to have considerable capacity for violence," Bar-Levy said. "Miss Salaman doesn't appear to be very concerned about the company she keeps."

"I doubt she knows just how violent he can be," Amos said.

"Of that I am certain," Bar-Levy answered as he poured himself a cup of tea.

"You have more information on Shoukri?"

"I think so."

"Go on." Amos leaned forward on his elbows. "What are you talking about?"

"Two summers ago an IDF patrol intercepted a group of armed Palestinians crossing into Israel from the Sinai. They said they were making their way to their homes in Gaza. When questioned about what they were doing in Egypt, they divulged that they had been training with other Palestinians for action against us."

"Fedayeen?"

"Yes. Our boys made them identify everyone with whom they trained. They identified both Shoukri and this Samir character—you know, the one our friend interviewed in her last column."

"The newly elected head of the Union of Palestinian Students."

"Right. They both trained a full summer as fedayeen."

"You're right," said Amos. "Great company she's keeping."

"There's more."

"I'm almost afraid to ask, but go on."

"According to the Palestinians we intercepted, Shoukri and Samir were heading north through Jordan on their way back to Lebanon. They traveled along the Jordanian side of the Negev up past Masada."

"And…?"

"Their path would have put them in the vicinity of Ein Geddi at an interesting point in time."

"The Abarbanel murder!" Amos exclaimed. "The bastards killed Dov Abarbanel."

"You have a good memory."

It wasn't a time Amos was likely to forget. The murder had occurred at the western edge of the Dead Sea, about twenty-five kilometers east of Hebron and not more than one and a half kilometers from the small Israeli community of Ein Gedi. Ein Gedi, due north of the ancient mountain fortress of Masada, lies at the very tip of the portion of the northeastern Negev that protrudes like an arrowhead into the underbelly of the West Bank of the Jordan.

Dov Abarbanel had been driving through the area, researching his doctoral thesis on the Roman siege of Masada, retracing the steps the Romans must have taken as they marched on the zealots who chose to die as martyrs in the land of David rather than live as slaves in the land of Caesar. Abarbanel had been alone. He brought with him only his notebook, a ballpoint pen, and the Soviet-made Kalashnikov machine gun that lay on the floor of his jeep. But the gun had been useless against his unseen attackers. The young Israeli never even heard the loud crack of a weapon before the burning-hot projectile severed his spinal cord and shattered his jaw, killing him instantly.

"Binyamin, Dov Abarbanel was my friend," Amos said, the painful memory adding urgency to his voice. "He and I were classmates at the university, and we served in the army together. I was at Dov's funeral. I'm very familiar with the case. A seven-point-six-two-millimeter steel-core cartridge, probably fired from a Kalashnikov, severed his spine. What were the Palestinians we intercepted carrying?"

Bar-Levy sighed. "Kalashnikovs. With a supply of seven-point-six-two steel-core cartridges."

"Unbelievable!" Amos whispered.

They again speculated about how and why Alexandra and Shoukri met in Beirut.

"In any case," Amos said, "we'd have to conclude that Alexandra's sympathies are with the Palestinians."

"Well, the Palestinian issue is certainly one she would be expected to cover for the *Star*, and she won't find any Israelis to interview at the university in Beirut."

"There's nothing we can do about that," Amos replied.

"Oh, I'm not so sure," Bar-Levy answered.

Amos recognized the sparkle in Bar-Levy's eyes that always signaled a bold idea about to be divulged. "Something tells me I don't want to hear what's coming next," he said.

"Listen, Amos. We have a very serious situation here. Something is brewing in Beirut, and the sooner we find out what it is, the better. The campus has been a hotbed of anti-Israeli fervor ever since the Suez crisis. Now we have confirmed fedayeen involved in campus politics, and maybe even a murderer. To make matters worse, we have an American journalist taking up with these killers. The damage her stories can do back in the States is really troubling."

"So?"

"So, I think you should get up to Beirut. We have friends among the Maronites who will provide cover for you."

"And my mission?"

"Twofold. First, I want you to find a way to establish contact with Alexandra Salaman. We have to determine what she knows about

Shoukri and Samir. Let's also determine how much she hates us and just how much of a shill she is for the Palestinians."

"And second?"

"Let's try to confirm what we think we know about Shoukri and Samir."

"And if we can place them on the road to Masada at the time of the ambush of Dov Abarbanel?"

"Kill them," Bar-Levy answered curtly.

Amos nodded. "What do we do about Alexandra Salaman if we find her to be in league with the Palestinians?"

"Find a way to make the fedayeen believe she's only posing as an Arab sympathizer, but…"

"They'll kill her," Amos replied, startled.

"Well, then, that will be the end of it, won't it?"

***

By the middle of April, three shipments of munitions had been delivered to Akko and concealed in the abandoned well. The weapons and explosives had been systematically and quietly transferred to safe houses in Tarshiha. The first phase of the mission was almost complete. Everything would soon be in place. The coming summer would be a time of action, a time of new beginnings. And although the Mossad had developed an impressive dossier on Ali Abdul Shoukri and Alexandra Salaman, neither Amos Ben-Chaiyim nor Binyamin Bar-Levy had even an inkling of the bloodbath being prepared.

That all changed when Moustafa Ahmed stopped to pick up a hitchhiker. Ahmed was crossing into Lebanon to deliver the fourth and final consignment of munitions to the mysterious but familiar trawler that periodically appeared off the coast of Nabatiyeh. Ahmed knew his compatriots would probably kill him for so serious a breach of security if they ever found out, but he quickly rationalized the harmlessness of offering a fellow Arab the hospitality of his automobile. The boredom and monotony of the drive from Damascus had all but driven him to despair. Besides, he reasoned, to ignore a traveler in need of assistance would be contrary to the teachings of Islam.

Akif Said settled into the seat next to Moustafa, smiling appreciatively. He, too, was bored and tired and anxious to get home to Nabatiyeh. He had been working near the Syrian border since early morning and looked forward to a good meal and a long night's sleep.

Akif Said was not much older than Moustafa, who had sized up his passenger as soon as he got in the car and decided he liked him. There was an alert sparkle to Akif's eyes, and his agile mind seemed rarely at rest. He had a leathery, tanned complexion; a thick, unkempt head of hair; and a disarming manner. He chattered away entertainingly.

Akif Said was, however, an observer. His job seemed easy but was fraught with danger. He observed traffic crossing into Lebanon from Syria. He made note of foot traffic and vehicular traffic. He observed the type and number of vehicles rumbling westward from Syria and studied whatever might be particularly interesting about the passengers or cargoes. He was especially mindful of unfamiliar men traveling in groups and of shipments in which the goods being transported appeared to be concealed. Open trucks with cargo areas covered with tightly tied canvas were always suspicious and the object of special attention. Akif Said reported his weekly findings to a trader who came through Nabatiyeh about twice a month. Within twenty-four hours of when Said delivered his report, his information, along with that of numerous other observers, was filed with the Mossad in Jerusalem.

Akif Said shook hands with Moustafa, praising his generosity while committing his face to memory. He would also remember the '48 Plymouth with the rear springs that groaned under the weight in the trunk. By the time they reached Nabatiyeh, Moustafa had revealed that he was working as a volunteer for the liberation of Palestine. Akif praised his benefactor's generosity and courage and offered prayers for the success of his good work. Moustafa refused Akif's offer of coffee in Nabatiyeh, explaining that he had to meet a boat on the coast to transfer the provisions he had brought from Damascus.

Akif embraced Moustafa and wished him Godspeed before getting out of the car. Then, standing in the dirt road, he waved as the Plymouth drove off, his eyes fixed on the heavily laden trunk.

***

Binyamin Bar-Levy looked grim when Amos met him in the noisy dining room at the King David Hotel.

"Doesn't look as if you're enjoying your breakfast," Amos said, glancing at the cold toast and full cup of tea.

"It's hard to enjoy anything these days," Bar-Levy replied. "Amos, we've got major trouble brewing, and it looks as though this Alexandra Salaman and her friends are right in the middle of it. I think you should go to Beirut immediately."

"Give me the details."

"We don't know the details. In fact, we know damn little. But we do know we're sitting on a powder keg. Something big is cooking, Amos. I'm positive."

"Tell me what we do know."

"Last Monday, one of our operatives in Lebanon warned us that he suspected a shipment of arms had been sent by boat from Nabatiyeh south toward Israel. We immediately alerted our people, and sure enough, they intercepted a trawler on the coast near Akko. There was a brief firefight in which the crew of the trawler perished. When our people boarded the boat, they found enough arms and explosives to ravage a pretty large village."

"Too bad the crew was killed," Amos replied. "They could have answered a lot of questions we can only guess at."

"Amos, we think this was just one of several shipments that have been made."

"You mentioned the Salaman girl."

"Our people found four copies of the *Washington Star* on board the trawler. We scoured the papers, and each one carried one of the Salaman girl's stories."

"Go on," Amos murmured.

"It gets better, or perhaps I should say worse," Bar-Levy replied.

"Amos, someone had circled the name of the person she had written about in each story. The first name circled was that of this Shoukri character. Then the name of Omar Samir was circled in a subsequent column she wrote."

"I remember both stories," Amos said.

"Then she wrote about another student named Abu Mansour. His name was also circled. Her last column featured someone called Daoud Nasser."

"Also circled?"

Bar-Levy nodded ominously.

"What do you make of it?"

"If we assume there's some connection between the *Washington Evening Star*, Alexandra Salaman's columns, and the arms shipment, we have to conclude that there have been at least three other shipments."

"One for each column," Amos replied.

"Exactly. Amos, if there have been three other shipments as large as the one we intercepted, we're talking about enough firepower to wage a small war."

"And you think Alexandra Salaman is using her column to signal accomplices here in Israel whenever a shipment has been dispatched?"

"Do you have any better explanation?"

"Do you think Akko is the target?"

"Who knows," Bar-Levy answered with a shrug. "We don't know shit about what's happening, except that a bad storm seems to be brewing. That young lady could have a lot of blood on her hands, Amos."

"We're not sure she's part of this conspiracy."

"What the hell do you think she's up to?"

"Oh, I think her columns are being used to signal something all right. I'm just not positive she knows as much as you think she does," Amos said. "As long as these fedayeen know with some certainty what is going to appear in her columns, they can use that information to signal others without her ever knowing what they're up to."

"Why in hell are you defending her?"

"I'm not defending her. But I don't want to see Israel embarrassed either. I smell a hit coming, and before we start taking out Americans, we'd better know what we're doing."

"Amos, if these people are plotting a massacre, and that's what I think we're dealing with here, they have to be destroyed before one innocent Israeli is cut down. Understood?"

"Understood," Amos answered.

"I figure at least three shipments are already on the ground in or near some Israeli village. That means carnage unless we stop it."

"I understand," Amos said.

"So, get up there and find out whatever you can. Meanwhile, we'll see what we can learn from our people in Akko. And when the time comes, Amos, I have to know that you're prepared to take them out."

"I said I understood, Binyamin," Amos answered sharply.

"All of them, Amos!"

***

Amos Ben-Chaiyim enjoyed relative freedom to roam the campus in Beirut. Traveling as an engineer with a Greek passport bearing the name Amos Andropolis, he made contact with a sympathetic Maronite family. Gabriel Gamlish, who was himself a student at the university, accompanied him to the campus each day. Amos spoke Arabic fluently, and given the many dialects heard on campus, there was little to distinguish him from many of the foreign students. He spent most of his time in the library or the student union, observing and listening. While he was not surprised at the fervor with which the students embraced the Nasser vision of Arab unity, he was not prepared for the depth of hatred for Israel he found there.

Amos had read through Alexandra's file once more before he'd left for Beirut. He was convinced she was being used and doubted she had any idea of the danger she was in. If, in fact, he found she was involved in a conspiracy to attack an Israeli community, it could cost her her life. He knew he would have to look her in the eye and talk with her to make that judgment.

Gabriel pointed out Alexandra in the student union the first morning Amos accompanied him to the university.

"She's a beauty," Amos said under his breath.

"She seems to spend a lot of time with some of the real militants here," Gabriel reminded him.

By the end of the week, Amos had familiarized himself with Alexandra's schedule and was waiting for an opportunity to make contact with her.

***

Alexandra smiled ever so slightly as she glanced over her shoulder and saw that the man sitting at the next table was watching her, just as he had the day before. He returned her smile before he averted his eyes. Alexandra stood and walked resolutely toward him.

"Excuse me, but do I know you?" she asked in Arabic.

"Not exactly," he replied in English.

"You speak English?"

Amos nodded.

"How did you know I spoke English?"

"I've read some of your columns in the *Washington Star*. I admire your writing."

"Why didn't you just come over and tell me?"

"I didn't want to intrude," he answered.

"Don't you consider staring at someone an intrusion?"

"Only if you get caught." He smiled mischievously and rose to his feet, extending his hand to her. "Alexandra, my name is Amos Andropolis. I'm very pleased to meet you."

Alexandra paused for a moment before taking his hand. Her face softened into a warm smile. "I'm pleased to meet you too, Amos Andropolis," she said, taking his hand.

"Please, can you join me for coffee?"

"Just for a minute," she replied. "I have a class at ten."

***

Alexandra watched as Amos moved through the line with her coffee. He was older and certainly more mature than most of the students, which she found appealing.

"Are you a student here?" she asked when he returned with the coffee.

"No, I'm an engineer from Athens. I'm visiting a family here in Beirut, and I often meet their son here. He's a student. Maybe you know him. His name is Gabriel Gamlish."

"No, the name's not familiar," she replied.

"Are you from Washington?"

"Originally from Jaffa, but we've lived in Washington for more than a dozen years."

"And already a journalist?"

"So what do you admire about my writing?" she asked to change the course of the conversation.

"You make me think," he answered. "I like that."

"Thank you. That's probably the greatest compliment a writer could ever hear."

"How in the world did someone so young ever get a job as a correspondent with a major newspaper like the *Washington Star*?"

She explained how she began working at the *Star* as an intern and how her father applied for her scholarship in Beirut.

"Are you Greek?" Alexandra asked, again changing the subject.

"A little Greek, a little Arab, a little Lithuanian, and, it's rumored, even a Jew somewhere in my ancestry," he answered as nonchalantly as possible. "And how about you? A Palestinian blue blood through and through?"

"No, not really. My grandfather on my mother's side was English, and my grandmother was Egyptian," she replied.

Amos decided to not to push any further and simply nodded his understanding.

"Which of my columns did you read?" she asked.

Amos looked into her eyes and was momentarily tempted to say all of them, even "The Heirs of Eden." Instead he said, "Several. I especially remember 'The Anatomy of a Warrior.' Is there really a guy named…?"

"Shoukri?" she said. "Yes, there's a Shoukri. In fact, he's a student here."

"Ah, someone you met since arriving in Beirut?" Amos asked.

"Why, yes," she said, slightly puzzled. His question had struck her as a bit odd. "You may have noticed there aren't a great number of students from Washington, DC, here."

"Yes, of course," he grinned. He knew he had played that one badly, and he was anxious to put the conversation back on safe ground. "It must have been difficult leaving your family and putting yourself among strangers in a strange land."

"Yes, it was difficult leaving my family," she said, choosing her words carefully. "But I don't feel like a stranger here. The Middle East is the land of my birth, and these are my people. In many ways you could say that I left home in order to come home."

Amos nodded his understanding, hoping Alexandra was innocent in the matter he had come to investigate.

"Look, I have to go. I'm going to be late," said Alexandra, breaking the silence.

"I'm sorry," said Amos. "I didn't mean to keep you so long."

"Not at all," she said, standing to leave. "It was nice meeting you, Amos."

"Alexandra, can we meet again? Maybe for lunch one afternoon, or even dinner?"

She looked into his eyes again before responding.

He returned her gaze anxiously. "I'd really love to see you again," he added softly.

"Um, I…ah…could grab a quick bite this evening," she replied, both pleased and flustered by his last statement. "My last class is at four."

"Great! I'll meet you at the main gate," he said.

"All right. Main gate at five fifteen?" There was a touch of excitement in her voice.

"Five fifteen, then," Amos answered, surprised at the excitement in his own voice.

CHAPTER
TWENTY-NINE

Amos waved as soon as he spotted Alexandra making her way through the congestion on the walkway leading to the main gate of the campus.

"Hi! Hope you're hungry," he said, reaching out and gently squeezing her arm.

"Starved," she replied with a smile. "I skipped lunch today."

"I thought we'd walk down toward the waterfront. There are some really good cafés down toward Pigeon Grottoes. Is that OK?"

"Sounds great," she answered. "I know a great Italian place near the lighthouse just off of Rue Ardati."

"Rue Ardati it is then."

They made their way toward the Mediterranean, and Alexandra pulled her jacket close to protect herself from the increasingly cool winds and the first mists of drizzle blowing in off the water. Amos looked down at her as she turned her face toward his shoulder in search of a barrier from the cold air. Putting one arm around her shoulder, he unbuttoned his raincoat and extended it out in front of her, providing a shield against the approaching storm.

"Just our luck," he said.

"Unseasonably cold," she replied, although she was not at all sorry that the weather had forced such close contact with the handsome Amos Andropolis.

The café was small and drab except for the bright red-and-white-checkered cloths that draped the tables. Lively music, which sounded more Greek than Italian, could be heard through the cheap speakers built into the ceiling. Along the walls, empty wine bottles with collars of hardened wax drippings were suspended by coarse hemp. Makeshift candlesticks consisting of a single wine bottle just like the ones hanging along the walls stood like sentries at the center of each table.

They dined on pasta with meat sauce and shared a loaf of hot Italian bread. Alexandra declined the Chianti Amos offered and instead ordered espresso. Amos waited until they were nearly through with their meal before changing the subject from small talk about life in Washington to the more relevant matter that was the focus of his interest.

"So, I guess it must be difficult for you to maintain a professional distance from the people you write about," he said as casually as possible.

"No, not really," Alexandra said. "My job is to simply report what my subjects do and say. My personal feelings or opinions can't enter into it."

"But, if I recall the column you did on this…ah…what's his name? The 'Voice of Palestine'?"

"Shoukri," Alexandra replied. "Ali Abdul Shoukri."

"Yeah, Shoukri. Weren't you kind of sympathetic to him in your 'Anatomy of a Warrior' column?"

"I really don't think so. I just wrote there was a reason why Shoukri was so hostile and that the world was breeding tens of thousands just like him."

"Do you think he's dangerous?"

"Why are you so interested in Shoukri?" she asked.

"I'm not particularly interested in him," he lied. "But I'm interested as hell in your notion that we're breeding tens of thousands of hostile young men just like him. I mean, what's that going to do to the Middle East?"

"Maybe destroy it," she answered somberly.

"Are you serious?"

Alexandra nodded. "Damn right I'm serious. Shoukri and his friends are committed to nothing less than the destruction of Israel."

"How do you feel about that?" he asked, trying not to seem overly concerned about what happened to Israel.

"I think more Palestinians will die than anyone else, and I can't imagine Israel is ever going to go away. I'm afraid there'll be absolute carnage. A lot of innocent people on all sides are going to be hurt."

"And this Shoukri fellow sees things differently?"

"He's absolutely certain that the Palestinians will ultimately prevail," she said.

"But there must be voices of reason among the Palestinians, as well as revolutionaries like this Shoukri fellow. You did a column about another student who had just been elected president of some Palestinian student organization. What about him?"

"You mean Omar Samir? He's president of the Union of Palestinian Students."

"Yes, he's the one. How does he feel about all of this?"

"He and Shoukri are two peas in a pod," she replied. "And, Amos, that's the point. The emerging leadership among these students is comprised of idealistic militants who intend to get their land back."

"And where does Alexandra Salaman stand in all of this?"

"You know, you'd make a great reporter," she answered.

"Why do you say that?" he replied with a laugh.

"Do you realize you talk in questions? This entire conversation has been an interrogation."

"I'm sorry, Alexandra. I didn't mean to offend you. It's just that I find all of this so damn fascinating."

"Oh, you haven't offended me at all. In fact, I find it flattering. I really meant what I said. You'd be a fine reporter. You have an inquisitive mind."

"Thanks. I'll remember that if I'm ever out of work."

"Tell me about your work. What kind of an engineer are you?"

"Civil. I design roads and bridges. I even worked on a dam," he lied with studied ease.

"Really? Where?"

"I worked on a proposal for a dam in Egypt," he replied, recalling recent stories about the huge hydroelectric project that had dominated the news out of Egypt lately.

"Aswan?" she asked enthusiastically

"Yes, but it was just a proposal. It doesn't look as though my firm will get any of the work."

"What part of the proposal did you work on?" she asked.

"I ran various assumptions on power generation. The power requirements will dictate the size of the project," he answered as though he knew what he was talking about.

"I would have thought they would have used electrical engineers for that."

"Well, what I was doing was pretty basic stuff. Had we gotten the green light to develop a more detailed proposal, we would have called in the electrical guys," he replied.

"Maybe that's why you didn't get the job," she said with a smile.

He laughed. "Yeah, you could be right about that."

"Do you travel a lot?"

"It's what I enjoy most about what I do."

"Where do you travel?" she asked.

"Mostly in Greece, although my work also takes me to Italy and Belgium. Every once in a while I get an assignment in France."

"Ever been to Israel?"

"Several times, but never on business. I've vacationed there."

Alexandra nodded. "I'd like to go back someday."

"I wouldn't tell that to too many of your classmates."

"No, I don't. The anti-Israel feelings are running pretty high here, especially among the Palestinians."

Amos, pleased with what he had learned so far, decided not to push any further that night. Instead, he directed their conversation to safer topics, asking her about the influence of television journalists such as Edward R. Murrow and Eric Sevareid.

Although the winds had subsided considerably, the air was cold and damp against their faces as they stepped onto the sidewalk outside the café. Amos instinctively put his arm around Alexandra's shoulder. She smiled up at him and put her arm around his waist as they strolled back toward the campus.

At the main gate, they made their way past a group of students smoking and talking under a lamplight. Alexandra was surprised to see Shoukri and Daoud Nasser.

"Good evening, Ali. Hi, Daoud," she said. "I'd like you both to meet a friend of mine from Athens, Amos Andropolis."

"Good to meet you," Amos said, grinning enthusiastically. He reached out and firmly shook hands with each as Alexandra introduced them.

"Nice meeting you," Daoud responded, while Shoukri simply smiled impassively at Amos when he was introduced.

"Friendly guy," Amos said under his breath as he and Alexandra continued on their way to her dormitory.

"Ali has been terribly preoccupied the past few days," Alexandra said, feeling oddly guilty at Ali having seen her in the company of another man, yet, at the same time, equally anxious for Amos to think well of Ali. "I don't know what his problem is, but he's just not been himself lately."

Amos knew what was gnawing at Shoukri. The fourth shipment of arms he had sent south was now in Israeli hands. Shoukri could only guess at whether there were survivors who were also in Israeli hands.

He had to know the Israelis were onto something, but he had no way of knowing how much they knew.

"Maybe he learned he flunked his last round of exams," Amos said, joking.

"That's not likely," said Alexandra. "Ali is one of the most intelligent people I've ever met. I'm afraid it may be something far less trivial than his studies that has him so on edge."

"Then you have some idea what has him so upset?"

"No..." She hesitated as Ali's words came back to her: *If you are sure you want to know what is happening, I will help you. Just don't curse me later.* The memory sent a shudder through her body. "I don't know," she concluded, "and I don't think I want to know."

"Now, that doesn't sound at all like the inquisitive Alexandra Salaman I have come to admire so much."

"There's such a thing as knowing too much, Amos. With Ali, there are some lines I have no desire to cross."

"Are you afraid of him?"

"Of Ali? No. But I am afraid of some of his beliefs, which is not quite the same thing."

"Has he ever harmed you?"

"No, I don't believe he would ever harm me, unless..."

"Unless?"

Alexandra considered for a moment, choosing her next words carefully. "Let me just say that absolute conviction combined with consuming passion can be pretty dangerous. Ali has this really deep conviction that Israel must be destroyed, and he has a real passion to see his land restored to his people. His conviction and his passion may well destroy him. In fact," she added softly, "it might destroy us all."

"You're being very cryptic."

"And you're being very inquisitive."

"Sorry, but you sort of dangled something that would tease anyone's curiosity."

"Look, I don't see any reason that you should concern yourself with Shoukri and his friends in any way. No good can come of it."

"And you consider my asking these questions to be dangerous?" he asked as though incredulous.

"No, I consider my answering them to be dangerous," she replied.

"Touché." Amos knew it was time to let the subject drop—for now. "Will I see you again?" he asked as they arrived at the entrance to Alexandra's dorm. "I'll be around for several more days. Why don't we meet at the cafeteria where we met this morning? We can make arrangements for lunch or dinner then."

"Great! I really had a wonderful evening, Amos," she said, then reached up and kissed him on the cheek.

"Me too, Alexandra," he replied.

***

Deep in thought, Amos Ben-Chaiyim walked back toward the main gate of the campus, his hands thrust in his pockets and his shoulders hunched against the cold. *She'd curse my eyes if she knew*, he thought. Amos quickly dismissed his self-recriminations and began to concentrate on what he had learned from Alexandra. He was certain she was not willingly involved in Shoukri's clandestine activity. For that he was relieved. On the other hand, he knew of no way to obtain the missing pieces of information about what Shoukri and his fellow collaborators were up to other than through Alexandra.

Amos walked briskly through the main gate and headed along Avenue de Paris toward the harbor and the densely populated neighborhood where the Gamlish family lived. When he reached Rue Dar al-Mrayssé, he heard the sound of footsteps about fifty feet behind him. He alternated his pace, first slowing down and then speeding up, and listened with a trained ear for the sound of whoever was following in the shadows. There was only one person behind him, one person who slowed down when he slowed down and sped up whenever Amos quickened his pace. Amos continued along Rue Dar al-Mrayssé to where it doglegged into Rue Minet al-Hosm. Then, when he reached

Rue Phoenicie, he stopped and lit a cigarette. The footsteps following behind abruptly halted. Amos turned, almost casually, and looked down the long street behind him. It was empty.

Whoever was following him was an amateur, probably more intent on learning where he was going than on attacking him. A professional would have simply continued on his way and walked nonchalantly by. A professional would have known that disappearing into the shadows would be the most suspicious move one could make, a dead giveaway.

Amos stood on the corner smoking his cigarette for several minutes. Then he walked unhurriedly to the harbor and stopped at the first bar along the way. He ordered a bottle of beer and asked the bartender to call a taxi for him. Twenty minutes later he left the bar and had the taxi driver take him to the Phoenicia Hotel. From there he took another taxi, which delivered him near the Gamlish home fifteen minutes later.

It took Daoud Nasser nearly forty minutes to make his way back to the campus after losing Amos at the harbor bar.

Gabriel's father, Michel Gamlish, Amos's Maronite host in Beirut, had a message for Amos from Bar-Levy. He was to convey to Amos that time was of the essence. Bar-Levy had reasoned that the conspirators, fearing their plans were in jeopardy, would accelerate their timing and launch their attack. Amos had to get answers back to Jerusalem without further delay.

***

Shoukri sat in the cafeteria the next morning, deep in thought about the conversation he'd had with Daoud Nasser the previous night. Shoukri had had Nasser go over Amos's movements the night before several times. Daoud had explained that there was nothing suspicious about the Greek engineer's behavior; Nasser had simply lost him at the bar when he decided to take a taxi. There was just no way to follow him from the harbor area.

Still, Shoukri was uneasy about a stranger showing up so soon after the Israeli interception of their arms off the coast of Akko. They still didn't know whether any of the trawler's crew had fallen into Israeli hands or whether anything on board would tie the munitions to Shoukri and his comrades in Beirut. And was it really just bad luck that the stranger who suddenly showed up in the company of Alexandra could not be followed to his destination the night before? Were they dealing with a professional sent by Israel to destroy their mission and, perhaps, destroy them as well? And if this Amos was really a professional sent by the Israelis, where did that leave Alexandra, Ali wondered, as he sat drinking his coffee and waiting for her to join him.

***

Amos stood in the hallway leading to the cafeteria and casually surveyed the crowded room. It was a habit he'd developed when he first entered the intelligence service. It gave him more time to consider options and adjust his thinking to the circumstances at hand. He spotted Shoukri almost immediately. The Arab from Gaza had positioned himself in a corner of the room with his back to the wall. For a moment Amos wondered whether Shoukri was always that cautious or whether his anxiety had been heightened by Amos's arrival on the scene.

Amos knelt down as though retying his shoelaces and checked the position of the gun—a Parabellum Tokagypt variant of the Soviet Tokarev TT-33—he had strapped to his calf. All of his trousers were slightly flared above the cuff to give him ready access to the Hungarian-crafted pistol. Amos preferred the Tokagypt because it was smaller than all comparable weapons except for the Soviet Makarov, and its muzzle velocity of 1,378 feet per second was second only to the Spanish .357 Magnum and the Czech M52. The Tokagypt was, however, considerably lighter than either of these alternatives. Its 9-millimeter cartridge made it a remarkably powerful weapon for its size, and Amos knew its accuracy at long range provided an edge that could be the difference between life and death.

Amos watched Alexandra enter the cafeteria with Monifa. His eyes darted to Shoukri, who sat at his table impassively sipping his coffee and observing the two women. Ali made no effort to join them.

Amos walked into the cafeteria and went straight to the table where Alexandra and Monifa were seated.

"May I join you?" he asked.

"Amos, good morning!" Alexandra replied. "Your ears should be burning. I was just talking about you. I'd like you to meet my room-mate, Monifa Bayoumi. Monifa, this is Amos Andropolis."

"Monifa…hello," Amos said, reaching out to shake the Egyptian's hand.

For the next fifteen minutes, the three of them engaged in convivial small talk. Then Monifa glanced down at her watch, signaling that they would soon have to leave to make their first class. Amos reached out and placed his hand on Alexandra's forearm.

"Alexandra, there's something I want to talk to you about," he said.

"That sounds like my cue to leave," Monifa said, getting to her feet. "It was nice meeting you, Amos."

"I really should go too, Amos," Alexandra responded. "I don't want to be late."

"When can we meet?"

"I can join you here in an hour," she replied.

"No, that won't work for me. How about lunch at the café on Rue Ardati?"

"That'll be great. See you there between twelve fifteen and twelve thirty."

"Ciao," he said, smiling.

"Bye, Amos. See you later," Alexandra called over her shoulder as she rushed to catch up with Monifa.

Amos remained at the table after the women had gone, collecting his thoughts for several minutes. Jerusalem was pushing him faster than he wanted to move. He knew that by now all the communities in the vicinity of Akko would have been placed on heightened alert in an effort to cut off any attack before it took too great a toll. But security would be marginal at best unless they knew where the attack was to take place. Without that information, many innocents would die.

They would die at the hands of the man he knew was seated not forty feet behind him. Amos wanted to turn and study Shoukri, to take the measure of the man who was planning the murder of his countrymen, the man who had probably cut down his friend on the Ein Geddi road to Masada, as well.

"Andropolis, isn't it?"

The voice was neither menacing nor friendly. It was cool, just as Shoukri had been when they had met the night before. Amos turned casually, taking care not to show too much interest in who had called him.

"I am Ali Abdul Shoukri. We met last night. May I?" he asked, nodding toward the seat opposite Amos.

"Yes, of course," Amos replied, inviting Shoukri to join him. "You were at the gate when Alexandra and I returned to the campus last night."

"That's right." Ali's lips were curved into a smile, though his eyes remained deadly serious. "Alexandra said you were from Athens?"

Amos nodded without speaking.

"Are you a journalist too?"

"No, I'm an engineer," Amos replied, pleased that Alexandra had not spoken with Shoukri since their return to the campus the night before. "Where's your home?" he asked.

"Gaza," Shoukri answered—almost defiantly, Amos thought.

Again, Amos merely nodded.

"What brings you to Beirut?" Shoukri asked.

Doesn't beat around the bush, Amos thought. "I'm visiting friends."

"Are they on the faculty here?"

"No. I come over and use the library. That's why I'm on campus so often."

"Don't they have libraries in Athens?"

"Sure, they have libraries in Athens, and when I'm home I visit them pretty regularly. And when I travel I frequent the major libraries wherever I am."

"How long will you be staying in Beirut?"

"Oh, probably just a few more days. How long will you be staying in Beirut?" Amos asked, having decided he didn't want to answer any more questions.

"Until school is out," Shoukri answered.

"Then what will you do?"

"Oh, I don't know." Ali smiled coolly again. "Travel?"

"Where to?"

"I guess we must all see where the winds take us, yes?"

"You must have been delighted when the breeze blew Alexandra your way," Amos said.

"Yes, of course," Ali replied. "I guess it just proves that the wind carries us all home eventually."

Before Amos could reply, Ali changed the subject. "By the way," he said, too casually, "I'm curious: what kind of engineering do you do?"

Amos thought for a moment before responding. This is the son-of-a-bitch that killed my friend, he reminded himself.

"I build bridges," he answered. "Are you interested in building bridges?"

"Not at all," Shoukri replied without hesitation, adding slyly, "Are you?"

Amos returned Ali's cold smile. *What did Ali know about him*? "Well," he replied, "it is, as they say, a living."

Then, following Ali's own example, Amos shifted the subject abruptly. "Alexandra's a gifted writer," he offered. "I think she has a brilliant future."

"We are fortunate to have her here writing about Palestinians," Shoukri said.

"Do you think her writing has been helpful to your cause?"

Shoukri considered his response to Amos's question. "She is our *Sahafi*, our *Kutub*."

"Your journalist…your writer."

"Yes, exactly. And her most important words have not yet been put on paper."

An uneasy silence fell between them as Amos and Ali assessed each other across the table—Amos silently probing, Ali unflinching.

"Well, I have to go," Amos finally said, standing to leave.

"I'm sure we'll meet again," Shoukri replied without offering his hand to Amos.

"Yes, I'm sure we will," Amos agreed. "As you said, we must all see where the winds take us."

"Yes," Shoukri said, rising to his feet, "they do have a tendency to shift in the most unexpected directions." With that he turned and walked away.

***

When Alexandra walked through the café door that afternoon, her face was radiant—as much from the damp frost in the air as from the excitement of another date with Amos.

He stood to greet her, saddened by the knowledge that their brief relationship was probably about to end.

"Glad you could make it, Alexandra."

"Glad you asked me."

After they were seated, Amos decided the best thing to do was simply dispense with pretense. "Alexandra, I was followed last night when I left you," he began. "Someone followed me from the university."

"Oh my God," she whispered. "Who would do such a thing?"

"I don't know," he said, studying her face carefully. "Who do you think would want to have me followed?"

Alexandra stared back at him for a moment. Her eyes widened with understanding. "You think it was Ali, don't you?" she said, a hint of agony in her voice.

"No, I don't think so," Amos answered. "I think Shoukri would have done it right."

"Whatever are you talking about?" she asked, confused by his remark.

"Whoever was following me was a bungler, a rank amateur. I think it was some kid who was told to find out where I was staying in Beirut."

"Amos, how would you know an amateur from a professional, and why would anyone care where you were staying?"

"Listen to me, Alexandra. I wish I had time to prepare you for what I am going to tell you, but I don't. I'm about to break every rule in the book because we've run out of time and something horrible is going to happen if I don't stop it from happening."

"What are you talking about, Amos? You're not making any sense at all."

"Alexandra, the reason I know the difference between an amateur and a professional is because I am a professional, and the reason someone cares where I am staying is that they're expecting me."

"You're a professional? A professional what, Amos? I don't know what you are talking about."

"Alexandra, my name is not Andropolis. I'm not from Athens, and I'm not an engineer."

Alexandra sat back in her chair and slowly took in what Amos was saying. The sound of her own heartbeat reverberated in her ears. She sucked in a deep breath as the truth began to dawn on her. "You're an Israeli!" she gasped. "You're here to spy!"

"I'm here to try to stop a massacre, Alexandra."

"I know nothing of such things! How dare you involve me in your dirty business!"

"You're not listening to me, Alexandra. My 'dirty business,' as you call it, is to stop dozens, maybe hundreds of innocent people from being massacred. Remember the innocent victims you spoke of yesterday? Well, their date with destiny is here, and whether you know it or not, you are involved. In fact, you've been the key to the entire filthy operation."

"You're mad!"

"I wish I were, but I'm not. It's your friends who are mad, Alexandra, the ones you plead for the world to understand."

"Who the hell are you?" she demanded angrily.

"Who I am is unimportant right now. Let's just say I'm someone trying to avert a great human disaster."

"I won't be any part of this. You have the nerve to try to recruit me! What makes you think I would have any sympathy for what you are trying to do?"

"Listen to me carefully, Alexandra. Shoukri and his friends are using you in a plot to commit mass murder. They have betrayed you and your newspaper."

"That's a lie! They've never asked me to do anything. You're wrong, Mister...whoever you are."

"It's still Amos, Alexandra. Amos Ben-Chaiyim," he said reaching out and taking her hand in his.

"You son of bitch!" she snapped, wrenching her hand away from his. "You are an Israeli spy!"

Amos noted that she was expressing her fury in angry but hushed tones. She was balancing her anger with an effort to avoid exposing him to anyone else in the café.

"Why don't you stop worrying for a minute about who and what I am and try listening to what I am saying? You, Alexandra Salaman, are being used in a plot to commit mass murder. Aren't you even curious?"

"I don't believe that for a minute. I've done nothing that could even be remotely construed as being part of such a plot. I won't let you entice me into helping you by listening to your lies."

"You were the messenger, Alexandra. You've been the means by which the conspirators alerted those who are to do the killing that their weapons have been delivered. They've used your columns to do that," Amos said.

"That's impossible. They knew nothing about what I was going to write—nothing!"

"Want to bet?"

"What are you saying?"

"I'm saying that they knew when you were going to write about Ali Abdul Shoukri, when you were going to write about Omar Samir and Abu Mansour and Daoud Nasser. They alerted their compatriots to watch your columns for these names because their appearance was a signal that arms had been concealed in some predetermined place. Now, you tell me, Alexandra, did they or did they not ask you to tell them the exact dates the columns about each of them would appear?"

Alexandra was momentarily dumb struck by Amos's question. "They said they needed to know the dates so they could tell their family and friends to buy the right issue of the paper," she finally answered.

"That's bullshit, Alexandra. They needed to know the dates so that killers would know when to pick up their arms."

"How do you know this?" she asked, the anger gone from her voice.

"We intercepted the trawler carrying their last arms shipment off the coast of Akko. Alexandra, there was enough weaponry to fight a small war. Know what else we found? We found four copies of the *Washington Evening Star* on the trawler. Each copy carried your column about one of the men I mentioned. Their names were circled."

"What did the crew say?"

"They were all killed."

An involuntary groan escaped Alexandra's lips. "I think I'm going to be sick," she whispered.

"This isn't the time to get sick, Alexandra. If they succeed with their mission, that'll be the time to get sick."

"How can you be sure these students were involved in the plot? Maybe they're being used the same way you say I was being used. Maybe someone else they told about my columns is using the information to send messages. Isn't that possible?"

Amos nodded. "It's possible, but highly improbable. We've confirmed that Shoukri and Samir spent a summer training as fedayeen. Fedayeen train for one purpose, Alexandra—to kill Israelis. In fact, we believe those two were responsible for the murder of a young Israeli a few summers ago."

"I can't believe that!" she replied, stunned.

"Can't you? You, yourself, have called Shoukri violent."

"But murder..."

"Shoukri's no hero. Don't make him into one. He's a killer who shot down a brilliant young student, a friend of mine, on the road to Masada. He's planning to kill again. That's his mission in life, to kill."

"What about this friend you say he killed?"

"It happened on the road from Ein Geddi, Alexandra. Dov. His name was Dov Abarbanel," Amos said.

"I can't believe Shoukri did that," she said.

"Then ask him."

"If he killed Dov Abarbanel?"

"No. He'd probably kill you if he thought you knew that. Just ask him if he'd kill for Palestine. I think you know the answer to that."

"Amos, don't ask me to help you!" she said, clenching her napkin in her fist. "I'm a Palestinian. Your people took our home and forced us off our land. Haven't we sacrificed enough? Please, just leave me alone!"

"We have to know where the attack is going to take place, Alexandra. We have to know who the local assassins are."

"What will happen to them?"

"Their homes will be destroyed, and they'll be jailed if they're caught or killed if they fight," he said impassively.

Alexandra lowered her head into her hand, and Amos saw tears fall through her fingers.

"For whom are you crying, Alexandra? The victims or the assassins?"

"Damn you, Amos...whatever your name is!" She wiped frantically at her eyes with the crumpled napkin.

"Ben-Chaiyim, Alexandra. It means 'son of life.'"

"I'm crying for me and for the lunacy that makes some people victims and some people assassins. You think all the Palestinians who are prepared to fight for their land are assassins and thugs, but I don't hear anyone saying that about the Jews who fought and killed for the very same land. My family had lived in Palestine for generations," she protested.

"As has mine," he answered. "We purchased land late in the eighteenth century. The land was sparsely populated. There were few Jews or Arabs or Turks, for that matter. My family had a legitimate claim to the land, as did yours. But those who followed on both sides didn't or wouldn't or couldn't learn to share. So you tell me, Alexandra, who's to blame?"

"Don't talk to me about blame. I'm sick of talking about blame. No matter what I do or don't do, good and decent people are going to die. I won't let you make good people of the Israelis and bad people of the Palestinians."

"Do you have any idea what a seven-point-six-two steel-core cartridge does when it rips into human flesh at short range? It nearly decapitated Dov Abarbanel."

"Please, Amos. Don't do this to me. Do your people use weapons that are less devastating?"

"There are approximately sixty Kalashnikovs and an equal number of nasty Makarov pistols hidden in some Israeli town. They're going to be aimed at civilians—old men, women, and kids, Alexandra, lots of kids. You want to debate right and wrong, justice and injustice, good and bad? Fine! But we'll have to do it some other time. Those friends of yours have everything they need in place to destroy dozens, maybe hundreds of lives. And do you know why they're going to do it? To make a statement, Alexandra. It will be their way of saying, 'Look world, we're here!'"

"What is it you want of me?"

"I need to know where they are going to attack and, if possible, when."

"How do you expect me to get such information?"

"You are close to the people planning the attack. Just listen carefully. Keep your eyes open. Maybe you'll learn something. Maybe you'll stop a massacre."

"Maybe I'll cause one," she whispered.

"Alexandra, no one will die needlessly."

"Don't lie to me, Amos. The Palestinians involved in this desperate act will die for their desperation."

"I'm only interested in saving lives," he replied. "If we can stop this attack from taking place, no one will die. There may be deportations or prison, but there won't be any killing. I can promise you that."

"I doubt that I will be able to help."

"Listen, if you come upon any information you think might be important, bring it here. There'll be a gray van parked out front. You just come in, and someone will follow a minute or two later. And, Alexandra, if you need help, if you need to get away from here yourself, the van will remain for a week following any action we take. I'm keeping it here to provide assistance to you if it's needed."

"Don't do me any favors, Amos. I hate what is happening. I hate what I'm doing, and I hate you for involving me in this business."

"And do you hate the people whose lives you may be saving? Do you hate them too?"

Alexandra stared at him for what seemed an eternity. Then, without speaking another word, she got up and walked out of the café.

CHAPTER THIRTY

Alexandra had never known the kind of fear she experienced that afternoon. She decided to cut her classes and spend the time collecting her thoughts. She went to her room and told Monifa, who was just leaving for her two o'clock class, that she had a headache and was going to nap for an hour or so.

Stretched out on her bed, hands at her side, she stared at the ceiling, pondering what to do next. Alexandra knew Amos was right. Ali was quite capable of the ambush Amos had ascribed to him. "And you, Ali?" she had asked him. "What are you willing to sacrifice?" Even as she remembered the warmth of Ali's embrace that day, the tenderness of his kisses, Alexandra could also hear the absolute certainty with which he had answered, "Everything." Despite her desperate desire to believe otherwise, she knew in her heart that Ali would let nothing stand in the way of his obsession. Nothing…and no one.

Alexandra spent the balance of the afternoon considering and eliminating various tactics that might reveal what Shoukri and the others were planning. If what Amos had told her was true, she was dealing with a trained terrorist, a killer who would be alert to almost any subterfuge. She knew Ali was too intelligent and cautious to divulge anything about his mission through casual conversation. Finally, she began to focus on the one device, the one skill she had that provided some chance of matching wits with Shoukri. She decided to try to arrange another interview with him.

***

Alexandra found Shoukri and Daoud in the dining hall. They had just finished dinner and were talking over coffee when she approached them.

"Am I glad I found you, Ali," she said, all but ignoring Daoud.

"If you're glad you found me, then I'm glad too," he said with a smile.

"Ali, I need a column. I owe the paper one this week, and I don't have anything for them. If I don't file something by the end of the day tomorrow, it would be like not showing up for work. My boss will really be upset with me. Will you help?"

"What do you want me to do?"

"Let me interview you again."

"About what?"

"I haven't the vaguest idea. We'll have to see what gels as we go along."

"But you've already done an interview with Ali," Daoud said. "It may be confusing if you do another column about him."

Alexandra saw that Daoud was looking anxiously at Ali. She knew he was concerned that their conspirators in Israel might interpret any column about Ali as a signal. Daoud probably feared it would cause Palestinian accomplices to think Ali was dispatching another shipment to replace the one that had been intercepted.

"No one will be confused, Daoud," Alexandra said, fighting to keep her voice casual, her tone even. "Ali and I will think of a completely different angle. It's done all the time."

"I don't think you should do anything that might confuse people, Ali," Daoud said, making no effort to hide the urgency in his voice.

"When will the column run?" Ali asked.

"Well, they haven't run my last feature yet, so I would say it will be at least two weeks. It's just that I don't get paid unless I turn one in."

"You see," Shoukri said with a grin, "no one will be confused."

Alexandra interpreted Ali's response to Daoud to mean that the attack would occur in less than two weeks.

"Ali, why participate in unnecessary interviews?" Daoud replied.

"Daoud, I thought you were my friend," Alexandra said with a smile.

"I am your friend. I just don't want to see Ali look foolish."

"I would never make him look foolish. You know that."

Frustrated by Ali's apparent decision to go ahead, Daoud shook his head. "It serves no purpose."

"Daoud, how can you say that, after I told you I need the material?" Alexandra replied.

"I meant no offense, Alexandra. You wouldn't understand what I am talking about. It's a private matter between Ali and me."

"Enough, Daoud!" Ali interrupted. "No harm can come of this. If we can help Alexandra, we will help her." Turning to Alexandra, he asked, ""When would you like to do this interview?"

"Now," she replied. "Could we do it now?"

"We will do it now," he answered. "But the dining hall will be closing in a few minutes. Let's go to the library." Alexandra could tell Daoud was upset as she and Ali rose to leave.

Alexandra tried to remain calm as they walked across campus. Ali seemed the most relaxed he had been at any time during the last week. She knew he would never have agreed to such an interview with anyone else, and that his rage would know no limit if he had even an inkling of what she was up to. Alexandra was about to betray Shoukri, just as he had betrayed her. She had no desire to help the Israelis. The aspirations of the Palestinian people had been a preoccupation since she had arrived in Beirut, and giving expression to their cause had been the mission of her reporting. Through her, millions of Americans could learn of the misfortune that had descended upon the Palestinian people. But if the death of innocents was to be the magnet that attracted attention to the cause of the Palestinians, she wanted no part of it.

Shoukri and Alexandra found a table in the corner of the library's central reading room and took seats in front of a huge, ornate window composed of decorative panels of stained and mirrored glass. Behind

Ali's right shoulder she could see her own face reflected back at her. She was relieved to see that she did not look as tense as she felt. She pulled a note pad from her coat pocket and gave Ali what she hoped was a carefree smile.

"Ready?" she asked, as she pulled the top off her pen.

"Ready," he replied, smiling softly.

"Ali, will you ever return to Palestine?"

"Yes, when it is free," he answered without hesitation. "When we Palestinians have taken it back"

"Are you serious?"

"You know I am."

"But how will you do what you say no Arab army can do?"

"It will take time, but we have an advantage over the other Arab countries."

"And what is that?" Alexandra asked.

"We are there. We are throughout the countryside. We don't have to penetrate the borders of Palestine because we live within the borders of Palestine. We will use guerrilla tactics. We must be patient. We must arm, and we must give hope to our people. Then, when the time is right, Palestine will fall into our hands like fruit from a tree."

"And how will you give hope to the people of Palestine?"

For the first time since the interview began, Shoukri paused before responding. He stared hard into Alexandra's eyes for a moment, and then his expression softened into a smile.

"We will make the Israelis afraid to walk their streets and afraid to go to bed at night."

"And that will give hope to the Palestinian people?"

"Yes, that will give hope…and courage…and pride to our people."

"And there are plans to do that?"

"There are plans to do that."

Alexandra could not believe the candor with which he was responding to her questions. For the first time, she found herself at a loss for questions. He had divulged so much. Dare she ask when?

Where? She knew that pushing too far, too fast could bring the interview to an abrupt end.

"Ali, what are you saying?" she asked, carefully laying down her pen to signal that she would take no notes of what he revealed. Again Shoukri searched her eyes before responding. Then he reached into the inside pocket of his corduroy jacket and removed a folded piece of paper. Alexandra could see it was a map and assumed it was of Israel, but she couldn't tell for sure.

"Someday this will be an historical document, Alexandra. *This*," he said, shaking the folded paper for emphasis, "is the beginning."

Reflected in the mirrored panel behind Shoukri, she saw the writing on the back of the folded map he held in front of her.

"May I quote you?" she asked as calmly as possible.

"You may quote me," he answered. "This is the beginning!"

Alexandra picked up her pen and wrote as though she were recording his dramatic statement. Instead she wrote on her notebook page what she saw reflected in the mirror: tolaam-ahihsrat. Then, after turning the page as nonchalantly as possible, she continued.

"You would kill for Palestine?"

"I would kill for Palestine," he answered, with a smile so cynical that she had little doubt he had killed Amos's friend on the road from Ein Geddi.

"Oh, Ali, do you know what you are saying?" she asked, tears welling up in her eyes.

"I know what I am saying, and I know what I am doing, Alexandra."

"What? What, Ali? What are you saying? What are you doing?" she cried.

"I am saying I will do anything to free my land. I am proud to be the warrior you wrote about."

"You will die, Ali. Others will die, and nothing will be accomplished."

"Then you tell me what to do, Alexandra. Are you prepared to be the one to decree that Palestine is no more? That Palestine is forever gone, like Troy and Babylon? Tell me how to return Palestine to the Palestinians without spilling blood. You tell me how to do that, Alexandra."

"When you kill innocent people in the name of Palestine, you kill a part of Palestine too. You will leave nothing but a legacy of misery and broken people. You say this is the beginning," she said, gently laying a hand over Ali's still holding the map, "but where does it end?"

"It doesn't," he said, pulling his hand away from hers and replacing the map carefully in his pocket. "Not until Palestine is once again restored to the Palestinians."

***

It wasn't until she returned to her room and held the page up to the mirror that Alexandra understood what was about to take place. There, the bold strokes she'd duplicated from her mirrored view of Ali's own notes were reflected back to her: TARSHIHA-MAALOT.

***

Alexandra's heart raced as she hurried along Rue Alfred Naccache. Her senses were numbed by embattled emotions. She was driven by what she believed was right, having abandoned all efforts to make sense of it. She was both a savior and a traitor. Her sympathies and, she believed, her loyalties were with the Palestinian people. Yet she was conspiring with the Israelis. At that moment, she longed to be home with Sharif and Samira and her brother, Yusuf. She felt only loathing for Amos Ben-Chaiyim and Ali Abdul Shoukri and the circumstances that imposed such choices on her.

She turned the corner and saw the gray van parked in front of the café, just as Amos had said it would be. Walking at a firm and steady pace, she approached the café entrance without so much as a glance at the van. She was shown to a table, where she ordered a cup of espresso. Then she lowered her head into her hand and tried to collect her thoughts while she waited. Several minutes later, Amos entered the café and greeted her as though they were meeting for a routine date.

"Hi, Alexandra, glad you could make it," he said, smiling affection-ately. "Sorry I'm late."

"Are you?" she asked, genuinely confused by his nonchalant manner.

"I waited to make sure you weren't being followed," he whispered as he leaned down to kiss her on the cheek.

"Please!" she whispered, drawing away from him.

"What have you learned?" he asked, turning serious, as he sat down next to her.

"When and where," she replied, lifting her eyes to meet his.

"Where?" he asked, his voice more demanding than inquiring.

"I have what you want. You must give me what I want," she replied.

"Alexandra, this is no time for games," he said menacingly.

"Good, then I'll get directly to the point. I want your personal guarantee that no harm will come to Shoukri or the others here in Beirut and that you will not harm their accomplices in Israel except in self-defense."

"You're bargaining with the lives of defenseless civilians?"

"No, you are," she replied. "I mean this, Amos. I will not be involved in any plot that targets these people."

"They are killers, Alexandra."

"Then they will be killed someday—I have no doubt about that, and I don't think they do either. But my hand will not kill them. I can't live with that."

"I can't believe you feel any need to protect the likes of Shoukri," Amos replied.

"You were going to kill him, weren't you?"

Amos thought for a moment before responding. "Yes," he said. "My instructions are to kill them all."

"You lied to me. You said no harm would come to them."

"Yes! Yes! I lied to you, Alexandra," he answered, angry and impatient. "These friends of yours are about to kill any number of innocent people. And when they are through with this attack, they will begin planning their next. How many women or children would have to die before you came to regret the demand you are making of me?"

"One, Amos, just one," she whispered, agony in her voice.

"They will kill dozens, maybe hundreds, if they are not cut down."

"Then it will be your job to cut them down, but not with my help."

"Why are you bargaining for them, Alexandra? We both know what they are."

"Yes, we both know what they are, but I know why they are what they are," she said. "They are desperate, Amos, and desperate people do desperate, terrible things."

"They are monsters!"

"They were not born monsters. Who and what made them monsters, Amos?"

He did not respond to her question. Instead, he looked at her, contemplating what she had asked. Then he reached out and placed his hand on her arm. The anger she had seen in his eyes only moments earlier was gone.

"They will not be harmed," he said softly.

"Tarshiha-Maalot," she whispered.

"Maalot," he repeated. "Of course!"

"I know of Tarshiha," said Alexandra. Though she had not been there, she had heard of the Arab town in the north of Israel, not far from the Lebanese border and the coastal city of Akko. "But I don't know Maalot."

"It is a new Jewish community right alongside the Arab town of Tarshiha. They share a common city council. It is an example of Arabs and Jews living side by side in peace."

"Anathema to Ali Abdul Shoukri," she said, shaking her head. "When is the attack to take place?"

"Sometime during the next two weeks."

"You are certain?"

"As certain as I can be," she answered and then told him about Daoud's reaction.

"Alexandra, I know you are angry and probably wish you had never laid eyes on me. But, in spite of what you may think, I am not your enemy. God only knows when, or if, your people and my people will ever reconcile their differences. But that's still my dream. I'll fight to defend my country and to protect its people, but my dream is for the people of this land to live in peace with one another."

Alexandra looked at him sadly and nodded. "I believe you," she said softly. "And I know that if you hadn't found me, innocent people would have been slaughtered. But the Shoukris of the Middle East are no more than symptoms of the real problem. Israel seems determined to fight the symptoms while ignoring the problem. It's a therapy that will ultimately fail, Amos. The symptoms will only increase."

"Alexandra, return to Israel with me. You can continue your studies in Jerusalem or Tel Aviv or even Jaffa for that matter. You will be safer there."

"I can't. I would be seen as a traitor, and I am not a traitor. My sympathies are with the Palestinians, Amos. I belong here, with them."

"You will be in danger here. If Shoukri learns of the help you have given us, you will be seen as a traitor whether you stay or leave."

"Then there's no difference, is there?" she asked.

"Of course there's a difference," he said. "No harm will come to you in Israel."

"I believe I'll be safe in Beirut," she answered with all the confidence she could muster.

"If you insist," said Amos, exasperated by her stubborn refusal to face reality. "But remember, the van will remain for a week after we act in Maalot."

"I'll remember, but don't take any unnecessary chances. The danger will be greater for you than for me."

"We can take care of ourselves, Alexandra. We have to remain in the area to protect friends we have here. We'll stay until we're sure they are safe."

"I'd better go," she said. "I have your word that you will try to stop the trouble before it begins so that no one will be hurt unnecessarily?"

"You have my word. Now, give me your word that you'll come to the van if you even suspect you might be in danger."

"I intend to stay here, Amos," she said, rising to leave. "I hope we meet under different circumstances someday."

"You've not seen the last of me, Alexandra," he replied, smiling warmly.

"*Inshallah*," she answered with a smile touched with sadness.

"Yes, 'if God wills it,'" he said. "*Shalom*, Alexandra."

"*Salaam alaikum*, Amos," she replied as she turned and walked from the café.

***

Amos kept his promise to Alexandra. Seventy-two hours after he passed the words "Tarshiha-Maalot" to Binyamin Bar-Levy, he received word confirming that the conspirators had been apprehended in Tarshiha and that three separate arms caches had been recovered from their homes. Once Bar-Levy knew that the new city of Maalot was to be the target, he informed the Shin Bet, Israel's hard-nosed domestic security agency, which had been on alert ever since the plot had been uncovered. Shin Bet agents immediately picked up George Saleh, a known agitator in Tarshiha, and as he was being interrogated, another Shin Bet team searched Saleh's house and quickly found the arms from the first shipment. Fearful that her house was about to be demolished, Saleh's mother led the Shin Bet to the other conspirators and the arms they had hidden away. Within forty-eight hours of when Shin Bet had been informed that the target was to be Maalot, the conspiracy had been broken and the weapons confiscated.

Bar-Levy was livid when Amos informed him that sparing Shoukri and his colleagues was the price he had agreed to pay for the information. But he accepted Amos's judgment in the matter.

That might have been the end of the entire affair had events not conspired, once again, to draw Alexandra into the currents of intrigue. Five days after the arrest by the Shin Bet of the Tarshiha conspirators, the story broke in the *Jerusalem Times*. Whether the leak sprang from Shin Bet or Mossad was never determined, nor did anyone know whether the leak had been intentional or inadvertent. Alexandra learned of the story from an anonymous telephone call. A stranger's voice reported that she had been the subject of a story in the *Jerusalem Times* that morning that connected her with the foiled plot in Maalot.

"The van remains at your disposal," the caller said before abruptly hanging up.

Alexandra was frantic. She knew the *Star* would get the story and would fire her in a minute if they thought she had used her position, and their pages, to send messages to assassins in Israel. Her parents would, of course, be beside themselves when the story broke in the States, and her standing at the university was certain to be terminated if the school believed she had been involved in an international scandal. Alexandra didn't know if she was a fugitive or, for that matter, whether her name had even been used in the story. Her uncertainty ended abruptly with the sound of angry pounding on her door.

"Alexandra! Alexandra, open this goddamned door!" David Ellis bellowed.

"David, please, it's not what you think!" she protested feebly, anticipating the reason for his anger as she pulled open the door.

"Have you seen this?" he yelled, holding a telex of the *Jerusalem Times* article in front of her face. "Answer me, have you seen this!" he yelled again.

"No, I haven't seen it, but I heard about it," she replied, hastily pulling him into the room and closing the door behind him.

"You've compromised me, and because of you, I've compromised my paper. We've broken every rule in the book. The Lebanese would be totally justified in closing down the bureau. We gave you an opportunity people would kill for, and you turn around and play these kinds of games? You've screwed the paper, Alexandra. You've screwed me, and you've screwed Markazie. This is a fucking disgrace! How in God's name could you have done this to us?"

"How dare you accuse me of disgracing you or the paper without hearing…without even asking for my side of the story! How dare you do that!" she yelled back at him.

"Did you or did you not use the paper to send messages?" he demanded, his voice now low and menacing.

"Yes. I mean, no! I mean…the people who did this used my column to send messages. I didn't know what they were up to. The paper was used, I was used, the bureau was used, but I had no more idea what was happening than you did. Do you really believe for a minute that I would, or could, ever do something like that? Do you really believe that?"

"What I really believe, Alexandra, is that your career is quite likely over, and perhaps mine as well. There is no way the paper can continue to have you reporting from this bureau. A journalist's credibility is essential. And your credibility, Alexandra, has been destroyed." He turned and opened the door, then turned back to her. "And if these people you say used you think that you betrayed them, your career won't be the only casualty in this situation."

Alexandra stood in the open doorway watching Ellis, looking bent and defeated, walk away from her without another word. It was only when she turned to go back into the room that she noticed the piece of newspaper on the floor that had been pushed beneath her door before Ellis had confronted her.

"Oh my God," Alexandra moaned, as she recognized the article from the English edition of the *Jerusalem Times*, across which had been scrawled the words "SO NOW WE KNOW." Alexandra's mind immediately flashed back to that day in the Bekaa Valley with Shoukri. "I must see who you really are, and you must see who I really am," she had said to him.

"So now we know," she whispered to herself. Shoukri knew, and he had risked coming here to make sure Alexandra knew it.

"Alexandra, are you all right?" It was Monifa, startled to return and find Alexandra standing in the open doorway, as pale and still as a marble statue, the newspaper clutched in her hand.

The sound of Monifa's voice helped bring Alexandra out of her shocked state, and she moved weakly across the room, sinking down onto the edge of the bed and putting her head in her hands.

"Alexandra, what's going on?" Monifa asked, anxiously rushing into the room.

"Please, Moni, not now," Alexandra said wearily.

Monifa sat down next to Alexandra and put her arm around her roommate's shoulder. "I'm here, whenever you want to talk about it," she said in a soft voice.

"Thanks," Alexandra whispered.

As Monifa held her roommate and tried to comfort her, her eyes fell to the newspaper article still clutched in Alexandra's hand. Alexandra didn't resist when Moni gently tugged the paper from her grasp. She gave a sharp, involuntary gasp as she read the message scrawled across the article. Then, with one arm still around Alexandra's shoulder, she began to read.

WASHINGTON STAR REPORTER INVOLVED IN MAALOT CONSPIRACY

Jerusalem, May 5—The Jerusalem Times learned today that a reporter in the Beirut bureau of the Washington Evening Star had been alerting Arab conspirators in Tarshiha to the delivery of the arms that were to be used in a planned massacre of Israelis in the adjoining community of Maalot.

Usually reliable sources said Alexandra Salaman of the Star's Beirut bureau used names of individuals she interviewed at the Phoenicia University at Beirut, where she is also a student, to tip off assassins in Tarshiha that weapons had been delivered to an abandoned well near the coastal city of Akko.

Authorities said the firepower that had been shipped into Israel for the assault was awesome and that civilian casualties would have been extremely high had agents of Shin Bet and Mossad not successfully broken the back of the conspiracy when they did.

Sources attributed the discovery of the plot to an unknown source that tipped off the Mossad, which had been following Salaman's columns with interest ever since she began reporting from Beirut. The breakthrough in the case came a short time ago when the Israeli navy intercepted a trawler carrying arms from Lebanon. Back copies of the Star were found onboard on which someone had circled the names of subjects interviewed in Salaman's columns. The Mossad guessed, correctly, that the names were some kind of code used to tip off conspirators that arms were being delivered. It is not known how the Mossad learned that Maalot was to be the target of the assault as the entire crew of the trawler was killed during the interception at sea.

The government of Israel declined to say whether it had yet lodged a formal protest with the United States State Department.

"My God, Alexandra, is this true?" Monifa asked as she skimmed the article once again.

Alexandra lifted her head and took the paper from Monifa and began to read the story.

"Jesus," she whispered, as her eyes darted back and forth from line to line. "Sweet Jesus! What have they done?"

"Alexandra, is it true?"

"Is what true, Moni?"

"Was there going to be a massacre? Were you sending messages through your column?"

"Yes, there was going to be a massacre. No, I was not sending messages through my column," Alexandra answered, her voice burdened by exhaustion.

"I don't understand."

"Shoukri and his wonderful friends were using me and my column to send the messages. I had no idea they were doing it."

"The Israelis think you were part of a massacre plot? My God, Alexandra, they'll come after you!"

"They know I wasn't part of the Maalot conspiracy. The story is just plain lousy journalism."

"What are you saying? How would *you* know what *they* know?"

"Moni, please, not now. Don't ask a lot of questions I can't answer."

"You can't answer, or won't?"

Alexandra looked at her roommate while she considered her response.

"Alexandra," Moni persisted, "is this story true? Were you in contact with the Israelis? Is that what this"—she pointed to the message scrawled across the newspaper—"is all about?"

Alexandra had grown to love Monifa, but she could not truthfully reply to her questions, and she was too tired and emotionally drained to think of a plausible subterfuge.

"Alexandra, you are telling me a lot by your silence. I don't know what you're involved with, but if Shoukri thinks you're involved with the Israelis, he'll kill you."

"No one is going to kill me."

"Shoukri and some of the others you've interviewed—they were the conspirators planning the massacre?"

"You're asking questions you don't want to know the answers to, Moni."

"Shoukri has to be one of the conspirators the Israelis say you were working with."

Alexandra shrugged noncommittally.

"Alexandra, you have to get out of here right now! Obviously Shoukri suspects something terrible, and if you can't do a better job of convincing him that you haven't been in contact with the Israelis than you've done of convincing me, he'll think you were the one who divulged that Maalot was their target. Someone had to have told the Israelis."

Alexandra clutched her head even more tightly, rocking back and forth ever so slightly in her roommate's protective embrace.

"Alexandra, please get out of here," Monifa pleaded. "Shoukri will come after you as soon as he's able. He was already this close," she said, shaking the newspaper article for emphasis. "Alexandra, he'll kill you."

"I can't just leave. Where am I to go?"

"Go to your boss. Go to the American Embassy. Go anywhere!"

"I may be a fugitive, for all I know."

"The Israelis will have to make it right with your government, won't they?"

"What?"

"Can't you get the Israelis to tell your government that you're innocent? Isn't there some way you can reach them?"

The van remains at your disposal, the voice on the phone had said.

"Moni, stay here," Alexandra said, springing to her feet. "If anyone comes looking for me, tell them I'll be back shortly."

"Where are you going?"

"I love you, Moni," Alexandra said, hugging her roommate.

"Where are you going?" Monifa repeated as Alexandra ran from the room.

***

Alexandra walked, unrushed, through the campus to the main gate, anxious to avoid attracting any unnecessary attention. Then, as soon as she reached Rue Alfred Naccache and was reasonably certain no one was following her, she began to run toward Rue Ardati. Gasping for breath, she rounded the corner not far from the Italian café and, horrified, stopped dead in her tracks.

The street was empty. There were no cars, and there was no van on Rue Ardati between where she stood and where the street curved out of view about a block beyond the café. Alexandra, too winded to run, rushed as fast as she could toward the spot where the van had been parked. Panicked, she turned and hurried into the café. When she reached for the door, it swung open and Amos pulled her inside.

"Amos!"

"Shh, calm down," he said. "There are guests dining in the back of the restaurant."

"I thought I was going to die when I saw the van was gone," she whispered frantically.

"We pulled it off the street shortly after calling you. We were worried that security would be heightened in the area around the university because of the reference to you and the school."

"I don't know what to do!" she said, making no effort to hide the fear in her voice.

"Alexandra, listen to me. You have to leave here. Shoukri and Samir disappeared before we could seize them. By now they know you betrayed them. Until they're found, you are in terrible danger, whether you want to believe it or not."

"I know," she replied, seeing again the words she was sure Ali had scrawled across the *Jerusalem Times* article before shoving it under her door: SO NOW WE KNOW.

"I'm terrified, Amos."

"Good! That's the smartest instinct you could have right now."

"What should I do?" she asked.

"We're going to leave from here. I'll call for the van," he said, pulling a small walkie-talkie from his jacket pocket. "It's waiting about two miles from here."

"But I have to get my clothes…I have to let the university know what is happening."

"Nothing will happen to you as long as you are with me. You can buy more clothes in Israel, and we can figure out a way to deal with your education later. Right now we have to get you away from here."

"You believe it's that serious?"

"Alexandra, any time now, the campus is going to be electrified by the news of the foiled massacre, if it's not already. You've been identified as a key player in the affair. Everyone will assume that somebody assisted us. Sooner or later, Shoukri and his gang will need to make an example of someone."

"I want to go home," she said softly.

"Then we'll get you home. We owe you that and a lot more. We'll square things with the *Evening Star* and with the American authorities. Meanwhile, we've made arrangements for you to stay with a Palestinian family in Jerusalem. We thought you would be more comfortable that way."

"OK," she said softly.

"Alexandra, we'd like you to talk with some of our counterespionage people. They have a lot of questions about Shoukri and Samir."

"I won't do that, Amos!" she cried. "Please don't ask me to do that. I'd rather stay here and take my chances with Shoukri than become an informer."

"You feel that way even though you know you are in danger because of Shoukri?"

"I have no doubt he would kill me or anyone he thought of as the friend of his enemy, but I know what has made him what he is. He and thousands like him are the garbage that was left over after the politicians carved up this region. Well, they're determined not to be garbage any more."

"They're going to kill again, Alexandra, or at least they're going to try."

"Then it will be your job to stop them. After all, someone in Jerusalem put me in danger!"

"Is that your final word on the matter?"

"Are you making my cooperation a condition for getting me out of here?"

At that moment, Amos felt more passionate about Alexandra Salaman, a Palestinian from Jaffa, than he had ever felt toward any woman.

"No," he said in a whisper. "There are no conditions. You will come out with us. And if you had remained behind and I thought you were in danger, I would have come back for you."

"Why?" she asked, moved by his response.

He wanted to say *because I've fallen in love with you*, but instead he simply took her hand.

"Because I would never let anything happen to you," he finally answered.

CHAPTER
THIRTY-ONE

Franklin Markazie called Sharif and Samira as soon as the Maalot story broke in the United States. Initial coverage of the affair was spectacular and corresponded to the *Jerusalem Times* version, but Markazie knew right away that there was more to the story.

"There is no way that daughter of yours was mixed up in this thing," he told the Salamans. "I know Alexandra, and I'm sure she didn't use the paper to send messages to assassins. That's sheer bunk, Mr. Salaman. We'll get the full story, and I'm sure we'll have it quickly. I'll call you as soon as I hear anything more."

Within hours, David Ellis confirmed that Alexandra swore she had been duped and had no knowledge of the way her columns were being used by Shoukri and the others. Markazie passed along Ellis's news and assured Sharif and Samira that the *Star* would give prominent coverage to the information exonerating Alexandra. Sharif immediately called Yusuf and then relayed the latest news to the Greenspans.

The week had been an emotional roller coaster for the Salaman family. But their confidence in their daughter had never wavered, and now they knew the allegations of her involvement in the horrible business in Maalot were false. Yet, when the phone rang later that same day, Samira lifted the receiver with dread.

"Mrs. Salaman?"

"Yes?"

"It's Franklin Markazie again."

"What has happened?" Samira asked stoically.

"Well, we're not sure anything has happened, and I probably shouldn't be calling and alarming you like this, but I thought you should know..."

"Yes?"

"Alexandra is apparently missing."

"Oh my God!" Samira's hand flew to her chest as though to restrain her wildly beating heart.

"Now it may not be anything at all," Markazie rushed to reassure her. "But she left her room yesterday afternoon and told her roommate that she would be right back, and, well, she never returned."

"Oh my God!" Samira whispered again. The agony in her voice tore at Markazie's own heart.

"Listen, Mrs. Salaman," he said, anxious to say anything to relieve her suffering. "This is just a hunch, but I think she's all right. Her roommate..."

"Monifa."

"Yes, that's it, Monifa. She says she urged Alexandra to get away from the university because one of the Palestinians involved in this Maalot business had threatened her. Monifa says this guy thought Alexandra tipped off the Israelis that a massacre was being planned."

"But you said Alexandra told her she would be returning to the room."

"Monifa said she had urged Alexandra to get away from the campus, and she did, though she said to tell anyone who came looking for her that she would be right back."

"Isn't that the same thing?"

"You'd think so, except for one thing. Alexandra hugged her room-mate before she left and said 'I love you' to her. Monifa says she knew then that Alexandra wasn't coming back."

"Did she leave her clothes?"

"Yes, she did. She left everything. But keep in mind, this all happened over twenty-four hours ago when everything was still very confusing. You can imagine how upset Alexandra must have been when she learned of the article in the *Jerusalem Times*."

"Thank you for calling, Mr. Markazie. I'm sure you're right and Alexandra is fine. If so, I think I'll probably hear from her before you do. I'll call you as soon as we have any news."

"Let's hope the next news is good, Mrs. Salaman."

"*Inshallah*," she whispered. "If God wills it."

***

The following days were hell for the Salaman family. Yusuf returned home as soon as he heard that his sister was missing. Esther Greenspan rushed to be with Sharif and Samira while they waited for word from the Middle East, and Hy called Noah to tell him what they had heard.

Karen made it a point to stay close to Noah, and she watched, somewhat painfully, as he agonized over Alexandra's uncertain fate.

Then, nearly four days after the Salamans had learned that Alexandra was missing, Samira heard her voice through the static of a transoceanic telephone call.

"Mom, I'm OK," Alexandra's voice announced as soon as Samira answered the phone.

"Alexandra! It's Alexandra!" Samira cried, choked with emotion. "Where are you?" she yelled into the phone.

"I've just arrived in Jerusalem," Alexandra said. "I'm at the King David Hotel right now, but I'll be staying with a Palestinian family in an Arab neighborhood in Jerusalem."

"Thank God you're safe. We've been worried sick."

"I know. I'm sorry all of this happened. I know how horrible it must have been for you."

"What are you doing in Israel?" Samira asked, glancing confusedly toward Sharif and Yusuf.

"Mom, it's too long and too complicated a story to go into on the telephone. I had to get out of Beirut, and an Israeli I met at the university brought me here. Let it go at that until you receive a letter I've written to you. It will explain everything."

"You met an Israeli in Beirut?"

"Mom, I can't go into it now."

"But you're all right?"

"I'm fine. I've already been offered a job writing for an Arabic newspaper, and I think the authorities are working out something with Hebrew University concerning my degree. I'll be able to explain more later."

"When are you coming home?"

"I'm not sure. I want to stay nearby until things are cleared up about my degree. Meanwhile, there's a lot I want to do here. I'm planning to go to Jaffa."

"Alexandra, you're not in any difficulty? You're free to leave whenever you want?"

"Mom, I'm fine, and, yes, I'm free to leave."

"The news was terrible."

"I know."

"Were you...? I mean, did you...do..."

"Mom, I didn't do anything wrong. Please don't worry, and don't pay any attention to the *Jerusalem Times* story. It's wrong. All wrong."

"I know. Mr. Markazie told us how you were being used. The *Star* has already run a story saying that the *Jerusalem Times* article was wrong."

"Mom, call Mr. Markazie and tell him I'm safe. Tell him I'll call him in the next twenty-four hours."

"Maybe he'll have a job for you in Jerusalem," Samira said.

"I want to take the job with the Arab newspaper. Maybe the *Star* will carry what I write—you know, like a syndicated column."

"I'm sure Mr. Markazie will do whatever he can."

"Is everyone OK?"

"They are now that they know you're safe," Samira answered. "Do you need anything, Alexandra?"

"I don't have any clothes here. Can you wire me some money so I can buy what I need?"

"Yes, yes, of course."

They spoke for several more minutes, Samira passing the phone to Yusuf and Sharif before hanging up.

***

At Alexandra's insistence, the only correction that ran in the *Jerusalem Times* was a brief squib reporting that earlier coverage linking a journalist in Beirut with the foiled plot in Maalot was a mistake. "We regret the error," was the extent of the *Times* apology. There would be no coverage casting her in the role of a hero or even commenting on the part she had played in preventing a disaster at Maalot.

CHAPTER
THIRTY-TWO

Emile Abu Awad and his wife, Leila, greeted Alexandra warmly and welcomed her to their small but meticulously appointed home near the edge of Beit Safafa. Alexandra judged them to be about the same age as her parents. They were both well-educated, professional people. Emile was tall and trim and dressed, Alexandra thought, like a lawyer or an accountant. His ample oval-shaped face seemed too large for his thin frame, but his eyes were alert and bright and radiated warmth when he smiled. Alexandra was pleasantly surprised to learn that he was a professor of Middle Eastern history at Hebrew University. His wife was the lawyer.

Leila Awad was an attractive woman, diminutive but well proportioned. Her short dark hair was stylishly swept back, accentuating high cheekbones, and a slight touch of makeup gave her a distinctly Western appearance. Alexandra was impressed when she learned that Leila practiced law in Israel and that most of her clients were Arabs with civil rights grievances against the state.

The Awads served a special and generous meal to celebrate her arrival. Alexandra realized most of it had to have been prepared the night before, since both of the Awads worked. The three of them dined on roast lamb served with small bowls of pilaf, yogurt, *markook*—thin, crepe-like bread—and vegetables. It was an unrushed and relaxed evening, punctuated by convivial conversation that steered clear of any subject the Awads thought might make Alexandra uncomfortable.

"Something has been on my mind," Alexandra finally said during a brief lull in the conversation.

"I would think there are many somethings on your mind after what you have been through, Alexandra," Emile said with a warm smile. "What is the first something you want to discuss?"

"Please understand, I mean no disrespect, and I don't want to appear ungrateful."

"Understood," Leila replied softly, inviting Alexandra's question.

"Why you?"

"I beg your pardon?"

"Why did the Israelis select you to be my hosts here?"

"They didn't select us," Emile said. "Amos Ben-Chaiyim asked us if we would have you stay here. We know Amos, and we knew his parents as well."

"Why did you agree to have me?"

"Because there is nothing we would not do for Amos," Leila replied and then smiled at the look of confusion on Alexandra's face. "That surprises you?"

"Yes, I guess it does," Alexandra answered.

"Alexandra, like you and your parents, Emile and I were born in Jaffa and lived there until we moved to Beit Safafa three years ago. During the fighting in nineteen forty-seven and forty-eight, things got very ugly in the neighborhood where we lived with Emile's parents. Most of the Arab families in our area were terrified and fled to escape the fighting. There were instances where entire neighborhoods were abandoned. It was a horrible time."

"Go on," Alexandra said, leaning forward to catch every word.

"Well, an army patrol came by our house and told us we would have to leave. They said we lived in a strategically sensitive area. But Emile's father wouldn't hear of it. He said if we left we would have no home to come back to. He begged the officer in charge to leave us alone, but it was useless. We were told to vacate the house within the hour."

"What happened?" Alexandra asked anxiously.

"A crowd had begun to gather in front of the Awads' house, and many of the people urged the soldiers to evict us. Then an older man in orthodox dress came forward and told the young officer to stop. He said he had no right to harass us."

"That was Amos's father?"

"Yes, it was. Anyway, the officer repeated that we lived in an area strategic to the defense of Tel Aviv and that it had to be cleared of Arabs. The old Jew responded that our family was no threat to Tel Aviv and that surely the army had more important things to do. The officer said we had to leave and that we would have an opportunity to make a compensation claim once the fighting was over."

"We were evicted from our property in Jaffa, too," Alexandra said.

"I know, Alexandra, I know," Leila answered.

"Please, go on. What happened?"

"Amos's father turned to Emile's father and said, 'Sell me your home.' The two men stared at each other for several minutes without speaking. Then Emile's father said, 'We have nowhere to go.' The old man said, 'You will live with us until the fighting ends. Then I will sell your house back to you for what I pay for it.'"

"And your father agreed to do that?" Alexandra asked incredulously, turning to Emile.

Emile nodded, tears in his eyes. "My father agreed. He believed a man's eyes are a window to his soul. He looked into Amos's father's eyes and liked what he saw."

"And your father actually sold his house to a total stranger?"

"Yes, it took all of Amos's father's savings to satisfy the authorities that it was a legitimate sale."

"And when the fighting was over, Amos's father sold the house back to your father?"

Emile nodded. "For what he had paid for the house, just as he said he would."

"Amos told me his family's dream had always been that Arabs and Jews would live together in peace in this land," Alexandra recalled.

"There were many who once shared that dream," Leila said.

"Will it ever happen?"

"If you asked me *could* it ever happen, I would answer yes," Leila replied. "*Will* it ever happen? That's a much more complicated question, Alexandra."

"Do you have much contact with the Jews here in Israel?"

"More than most Arabs," Leila answered. "Emile works at Hebrew University where most of the faculty is Jewish, as are most of the students, and while my clients are mostly Arabs, I represent them before judges and administrators who are mostly Jewish."

"And it all works?"

"Surprisingly well," Emile replied.

"Are there many Arab students at Hebrew University?"

"Quite a few," he answered.

"Do they tend to stick together?"

"For the most part, yes. There is not much friction between the Arabs and Jews, but it's rare that you see any really close friendships between them."

"It was the same way in Beirut. There were some Jewish students at the university, but they didn't mingle very much with the Arab students."

"Speaking of the university in Beirut, I think we will be able to work something out."

"I'll get my degree?" Alexandra asked.

"We've approached the administration at Hebrew University to see if they would be willing to honor all the credits you've completed in Beirut," Leila explained. "If they were willing to do that, you could get a degree from Hebrew University once you've completed your last two years there. You could enroll in the fall and graduate in June of sixty-one."

"Do you think they would do that?"

"Ordinarily, no. Transfer students usually need comparable credits. However, I think they're receptive to accommodating you as a special case. They were very sympathetic to the predicament you're in, given the circumstances that brought you here."

"That's certainly worth thinking about," Alexandra agreed.

"It's a lifesaver of an opportunity, Alexandra," said Emile. "If they agree to do it, you'll be salvaging virtually all of your education in Beirut."

"I don't think my father will like the idea of my living in Israel or getting my degree here. It's not exactly what he had in mind."

"I can understand how he might feel, but you know, you are much closer to your roots here than you were even in Beirut. You're living with Arabs here, you're working for an Arab newspaper, and you would be less than an hour from your birthplace."

It did not take Alexandra long to warm up to the idea of finishing her schooling in Israel. She waited until the university had made a final decision before telling her parents what she wanted to do.

***

Alexandra's call came the same morning Sharif and Samira received the letter she had promised, explaining as much of the Maalot affair as she dared. Alexandra ended her letter with:

I have mixed feelings about being in Israel, but I have been very well treated. The authorities here seem sensitive to my heritage, and, at the same time, appreciate my help regarding the terror plot.

Please kiss Yusuf for me and let the Greenspans know I am all right. Also, send news about Milk & Honey. How many stores are in the chain now, and how are

they doing? I haven't heard from Noah for a long time.
I hope he is well. Tell him I send my regards.

Love,

Alexandra

Sharif and Samira had just begun to discuss the letter when Alexandra's call came through from Israel. They were in no frame of mind to argue with her when she called to plead for permission to finish her degree at Hebrew University.

∗∗∗

Amos headed south from Tel Aviv for the final leg of the drive to Jaffa. He had called Alexandra to see how she was doing with the Awads and volunteered to drive her to Jaffa when she told him she was going to try to find the old Salaman family citrus grove. They drove along the Mediterranean coast and turned inland as the tower of the Franciscan monastery on the north side of the city came into view. Amos slowed down as they reached the center of the city and stopped opposite the old clock tower.

"Recognize anything?" he asked.

"Vaguely," she replied. "Everything seems older and smaller and more crowded than I remember."

"Well, the city is older." He smiled. "And you were a little girl, so I guess things would have seemed taller than they do now. You have a lot more to compare all this to than you did the last time you set eyes on these structures. Come to think of it, these probably were the tallest buildings you had ever seen then."

"My father says the day we left here was the saddest day of his life."

"Do you think he'd be happy to know you came back?"

"I think it will be bittersweet, but, yes, I think it will thrill him to know that a Salaman has stepped foot on the soil again."

They drove east, away from the harbor, and climbed an incline that took them past several groves with trees heavily laden with plump oranges ready for harvesting. Then Amos steered the car onto a dirt road and, after a few minutes, slowed down as they came abreast of a white stone wall about shoulder high. He pulled to a stop opposite a wrought-iron gate.

"Welcome home," he said.

Alexandra looked at the walled compound and then turned her eyes to Amos.

"I don't understand," she answered.

"This is, or was, the Salaman citrus grove," Amos responded.

Suddenly, Ali's words during their first meeting came back to Alexandra. *It is important that you understand, Alexandra, that nothing is as it was when you left.* She shook her head to rid it of the unwelcome memory, then turned to Amos. "I don't recognize anything."

"Don't worry, you will," he said, opening his door. "Come with me."

"What is this place?" she asked.

"It was an orphanage for a short while. It was built in the late forties for the children who arrived here after the war without parents. Now it's just a school."

Amos opened the gate and accompanied Alexandra onto the grounds of the school, which had been vacated for the summer. He watched as she moved along a path that ran parallel to the front of the one-story building, looking for some familiar perspective.

"It's all so strange," she said sadly. "I can't believe I ever lived here."

Amos nodded. "Come," he said, taking her by the hand and leading her around to the back of the building. They walked along a wooded path that led toward higher ground for several minutes. Then, as they reached the top of a knoll, he took her to a clearing where they could see down to the Mediterranean.

"Look familiar?"

Alexandra stood transfixed, gazing down at the blue expanse. She did not speak as her eyes feasted on the picturesque seascape that had soothed the Salaman soul for so many years.

"Yes!" she cried. "I do remember! Isn't it beautiful?"

"As it has always been," he replied.

"I'm so glad I came."

"There's more, Alexandra," he said, leading her to a clearing between the only two orange trees that still stood on the property.

She walked with him into the center of the clearing, where he pointed to a marble plaque on the ground. Alexandra looked at Amos and then back down at the plaque. She moved closer and knelt down to read the words engraved on the smooth white stone. There, in both Arabic and Hebrew was inscribed:

HERE LIES IBRAHIM SALAMAN LAID TO REST ON THE LAND HE LOVED REMEMBERED BY HIS LOVING FAMILY 1865 – 1940

"How lovely," she whispered, greatly moved at the sight of her grandfather's grave.

"The children who were first brought here installed this plaque when they graduated."

"Why would they do that?"

"This land had become their salvation. Some of the people from Jaffa who worked here told them the land had belonged to your family and that you lost it as a result of the war. These were all kids who had no idea where their own parents were buried, and, I was told, they were all very moved when they learned that your grandfather's grave was all that was left of the Salaman presence here. I imagine it was their way of showing respect and, I suppose, their appreciation. The orange trees were actually replanted here as a symbol of what the land had been."

"I think my father would be pleased," she said.

"I hope so. He's entitled to feel bitterness and resentment about what happened here. But the kids, at least, obviously did what they thought was right."

Amos put his arm around her shoulder to lead her back toward the car. As they walked away from the hillside and Ibrahim's grave, he gently and affectionately tightened his hold on her.

She reached up and took Amos's hand in hers, giving it a gentle squeeze. "Thank you for bringing me here," she said.

"Anything else you'd like to see while we're here?"

She thought for a moment as they walked. "Yes, I'd like to see where the Awads lived, where your father saved their home."

"Ah, you've heard about that," he said, smiling.

"It's a wonderful story."

"It was not a big deal to my father. It was simply the right thing to do. That's the way he conducted his life. His decisions were always easy. He did what he believed was right."

"He was a very courageous man," she said.

"He was simply a good man, Alexandra."

"Sometimes that takes courage."

"Yes, I suppose you're right."

"Were your parents and the Awads close friends after the Awads moved back to Jaffa?" she asked.

"Well, there was real affection, yes. I think, mostly, they had tremendous respect for my father."

"When did he die?"

"Five years ago. My mother died less than a year later."

"Leila says she and Emile would do anything you asked of them."

"You know, that kind of talk always embarrassed my father, and it embarrasses me too. He believed it was a *mitzvah*, an honor, to be able to really help someone. His reward was just to have been there to help the Awads and to make a difference in their lives."

"Arab honor requires that such a deed, such a mitzvah, as you say, never be forgotten."

"You know, my father died brokenhearted because of the deterioration of the relationship between Arabs and Jews. He believed the Arabs and Jews of Palestine had more in common than any other peoples in this region. The idea of Arabs and Jews working and living side by side in harmony was the cornerstone of his vision. He saw it all go up in smoke."

CHAPTER THIRTY-THREE

Karen could not have picked a worse time to urge Noah that they get married right after graduation. Even if Alexandra hadn't been on everyone's mind after the Maalot affair, Noah would have wanted to wait until his work and career had a chance to take shape. But Karen saw that only Alexandra could have caused his hesitancy, and it was simply more than Karen could handle. She had watched Noah agonize over Alexandra's safety, and on more than one occasion during their junior year, she had found herself wondering whether Noah's mind would ever really be free of the Arab girl from Jaffa.

"You still love her, don't you?" she asked, as they strolled across the grassy mall in front of Stanford's Memorial Church.

"I love you, Karen," Noah answered wearily. "I intend to marry you. What more do you want me to say?"

"That you no longer love Alexandra, damn it! This isn't a game, Noah. We're talking lifelong commitment here."

"Listen, Karen," Noah said. They stopped walking, and he turned to face her. "You can make this as complicated as you want, but what purpose will it serve?"

Karen angrily wiped away the tears that began spilling down her cheeks as he spoke.

"Alexandra's not my girlfriend—you are," Noah continued, taking her by the shoulders and giving her a gentle squeeze. "But I can't and won't try to erase her from my memory. She was a very important part of my life, and probably always will be. If you can't live with that, I'm sorry. I really am."

"I don't think I should spend my life wondering whether my man is thinking about an old flame."

"I don't think you should do that either."

"I think getting married next summer would put all of that behind us."

"Karen, give me a little time to get on my feet after we graduate. That's all I'm asking."

"Has it ever occurred to you that maybe I could help? That we could get started together, like most couples do?"

"We can do all of that. Come to Washington. Let's have fun while I get started. I just don't want to begin a marriage and start a career at the same time. I'm not exactly asking you to stay away and wait for my call."

"Do you want to know what really nags at me, Noah?"

"You mean there's something else?"

Wrapped in her anger, Karen ignored Noah's weak attempt at levity. "I know damn well that if Alexandra came home tomorrow and told you she wanted to marry you, you'd do it, and you'd do it like that," she said, snapping her fingers.

Noah was stung by her words, not only because they were said with such bitterness but also because he suspected they were true.

"That's...ridiculous," he said unconvincingly.

"Look, my parents have offered to take me to Europe as a graduation gift," she said, though showing no enthusiasm for the trip. "I think I'm going to accept."

"That's great!" said Noah enthusiastically. "What a fabulous thing to look forward to."

"Damn! You're hopeless!" she said and turned abruptly and stormed away from him.

"What the hell's wrong?" he called after her.

"Not a damn thing!" she yelled back. "I was just hoping for something else."

"Karen, we can get married in a year or two. Is that so bad?" he asked, picking up his pace to catch up to her.

"And maybe I won't be interested in a year or two," she snapped.

"You're being childish."

"How dare you call me childish!" She stopped in her tracks. "You, who are totally incapable of shaking off some goddamned childhood romance, dare to call me childish!"

"You're jealous over nothing."

"That's a lot of bull!"

"This isn't about, Alexandra. It's about me, Karen."

"Then to hell with you—to hell with both of you!" she yelled over her shoulder as she stormed away.

***

Graduation was not a particularly joyous event for Noah. He picked at his meal as he ate dinner with his parents the night before commencement. At breakfast the next morning, the Rothschilds and Greenspans made small talk about business. The silence between Karen and Noah was painful for the two of them and uncomfortable for everyone else.

Noah was relieved to finally be on his way home. Stanford was now a part of his past, and as for Karen, well, he was pretty sure her summer in Europe with her parents would, in time, assuage her anger..

Noah didn't hear from Karen until just before Labor Day. He had learned from another classmate who was also traveling in Europe that Karen had been spending a lot of time with a law student she'd met in Rome. But Karen said nothing about that when she called to tell him she'd gotten a job in Illinois Congressman John Kluzynski's office on Capitol Hill; Kluzynski was chairman of the House Public Works Committee and a friend of Paul Rothschild's. The conversation was cordial, even conciliatory, Noah thought. Not quite a conversation between lovers, but for the moment, Noah was prepared to settle for friendship.

Noah's reunion with Yusuf after graduation was, as always, enjoyable. They had succeeded in cultivating a friendship that could be picked up where it had left off, even though long periods of time had elapsed. Yusuf had found a job in Baltimore, and Noah drove to meet his old friend for dinner at Hausner's, one of the city's most popular and famous old restaurants.

They were enjoying their Maryland crab cake dinners, and Yusuf had just finished telling Noah about his new job with a Baltimore architect. He was making decent money and just waiting for the right girl to come along to help him spend it.

"And what do you hear from Alexandra?" Noah asked.

"She's fine...gave us all a hell of a scare last year, but she's been doing great ever since."

"What is she up to?" Noah asked

"She's working on a book about Arab art or something, and, of course, she'll graduate next year. I have to admit, the Israelis really came through for her."

"Well, she didn't do so badly for them either."

"She did what she felt she had to do, but they saved her college career. She'll get her degree from an internationally recognized university without losing any time or credits."

"Does she enjoy living over there?"

"Actually, I don't detect any resentment in her letters at all. I'm rather surprised."

"Yusuf, is she seeing anyone? I mean, she's finally living in a country with no shortage of Arab men to date."

Yusuf looked into his friend's eyes and smiled sympathetically. "Still hooked?"

"Karen thinks I am. It drives her crazy."

"I didn't ask Karen. I asked you."

"No...yeah...I don't know...I guess so."

"Not exactly unequivocal, Noah."

"Yusuf, I loved your sister, I love your sister, and I will always love your sister. What more can I say?"

"What about Karen? Do you love her?"

"Yes, I love her," he answered, nodding.

"Then you ought to marry her."

"We sort of broke up just before graduation."

"Not over Alexandra, I hope."

"Yes and no. Karen wanted to get married right after school. I wanted to wait until I get on my feet a little bit."

"So how does that involve Alexandra?"

"Karen thinks the reason I don't want to marry her right now is that I've still got Alexandra on my mind. She thinks I'm still hoping I can put things together with Alexandra when she returns to the States."

"Is she right?"

Noah took in a long, deep breath before answering. "I don't know," he finally responded. "Nothing's really changed, has it?"

"I guess a lot has changed, and nothing has changed," Yusuf replied.

"Yeah." Noah nodded, and then said, "Say, you never answered my question. Is she seeing anyone over there?"

"I don't think she's dating anyone. She sees a lot of a guy named Amos Ben-Chaiyim. He was mixed up in that mess she got involved in."

"Amos Ben-Chaiyim...not exactly an Arab name," Noah mused.

"Like I said, I don't think she's dating the guy or anything like that."

CHAPTER
THIRTY-FOUR

Milk & Honey had forty new convenience stores by the time the chain celebrated its fourth anniversary. By Noah's reckoning, the Greenspans and Salamans would saturate the market with the opening of another forty stores in Maryland and Virginia. In just two more years, the expansion of Milk & Honey in the Washington area would, essentially, be over.

Noah's negotiating skills drove the chain's acquisition program. For their part, Hy and Sharif had spent the years before Noah graduated integrating into a cohesive business the stores Noah had acquired during the summers. Hy showed little acumen for negotiating the acquisition of new businesses, so he concentrated on the retail operations. Sharif, who did possess a keen talent for negotiations, preferred to devote his energy to the considerable task of buying for the chain, rather than acquiring the businesses of other merchants.

Yusuf designed all of the early units while he was still in school, and those that followed were really improved variations of the original stores. By the time Yusuf graduated, the architectural contribution he was able to make to Milk & Honey had largely been completed. When he was offered a position with a medium-sized architectural firm in Baltimore, Yusuf eagerly accepted the job. A year later, a developer offered him a commission to design a major urban redevelopment project—the conversion of a large factory on the Baltimore waterfront to a residential building. Yusuf shared the vision of a handful of urban pioneers about the future of the decaying inner harbor and jumped at the chance to be in the vanguard of efforts some hoped would spur a major restoration.

While Noah's responsibilities directing the expansion of Milk & Honey could provide another two years of challenge, his attention was soon diverted by another opportunity he believed was beginning to emerge in the nation's capital. It had started after dinner with Karen at Duke Zeibert's, a favorite restaurant not too far from the Georgetown apartment she had leased. As Noah had predicted, their time apart seemed to dissipate whatever anger and frustration Karen had been feeling before graduation. She never mentioned the young man it was rumored she'd spent much of her time with during her travels, and Noah chose not to ask. Noah had been genuinely glad to see Karen upon her return to the States, and if their détente was to be built on words unspoken and questions unasked, Noah was happy to play along.

It was a warm and pleasant evening, so Noah and Karen decided to stroll along fashionable Connecticut Avenue to a theater just north of Dupont Circle. As they walked past the Mayflower Hotel, Karen mentioned how disruptive the construction of the new Metro, Washington's proposed subway, was going to be to the city.

"This entire area will be a construction zone, " she said.

"Do you really think this city will ever get the money to build a subway?" Noah asked as they crossed M Street.

"Well, the majority counsel at the House Public Works Committee says if the highway lobby is ever persuaded to cooperate with the rapid-rail lobby, there will be no way to stop it."

"I thought the highway people had already killed the project," Noah replied.

"They did, but only because they were concerned that money for highway construction would be cut. The retailers in downtown

HEIRS OF EDEN 357

Washington have formed a new organization called Downtown Progress. They say the subway is the only hope for the inner city. They
really intend to lobby for new subway legislation."

"They'll never beat the highway lobby," Noah said.

"My boss says they're going to form something called a Joint
Committee for Balanced Transportation."

"What the hell is that?"

"A compromise. They'll propose new legislation that will guarantee
an agreed-upon level of highway construction in return for a commitment to build the subway. Meanwhile, the construction trades that will
benefit from a public works project of this size, joining with the downtown retail community and the people who make all the trains and
stuff, will constitute a pretty formidable lobby in their own right."

"And your boss thinks the highway people will end their
opposition?"

"Yeah, he really does. He says if they think they have a chance of
losing, they'll compromise."

"Where's the subway going to run?"

"All over town and out into the Maryland and Virginia suburbs."

"Well, you're right. It will be disruptive as hell," Noah agreed.

"Can you imagine all our main streets being torn up to build
tunnels all over the city? I mean, a lot of older rinky-dink neighborhoods will be torn up too, but this thing is going to burrow all over
this town. It's supposed to run under Connecticut Avenue, F Street,
Wisconsin Avenue, Pennsylvania Avenue, out to Rockville in Maryland,
Alexandria in Virginia, the airport—I mean, all over the place."

"What did you say?" asked Noah, his walk slowing as his thoughts
began to race.

"I said it's going to go everywhere."

"No, I mean about tearing up old rinky-dink neighborhoods."

"There'll be dozens and dozens of stops along the different lines.
Can you imagine how many neighborhoods this thing will have to

snake its way under to get out to Rockville or all the way to Brentwood or Alexandra?"

Noah stopped walking and just stood for moment.

"Can I get a copy of those proposed routes?" he asked.

"Sure, it's all public record. I can get you a copy of the testimony in which the various routes were presented."

"Karen, will you remember to do that? I'd really like to see that testimony."

"Sure. I'll bring a copy home Monday evening. But why the sudden interest? Do you want to see whether the stops are near Milk & Honey stores?"

"I want to see those so-called rinky-dink neighborhoods," he said as they resumed walking.

"Why are you worried about rinky-dink neighborhoods when some of the prime real estate in this city is about to get torn to pieces?"

"Because I can't afford to buy prime real estate, but I can arrange to tie up property in those run-down neighborhoods you mentioned. They won't stay rinky-dink very long once that subway starts to run. You watch—you'll see shopping centers and condominiums cropping up all along those routes."

"I never thought of that," she said.

"Karen, you show me a map of the proposed subway, and I'll show you a map of tomorrow's prime real estate."

∗∗∗

Noah removed the transcript of the testimony from the envelope Karen had handed him and sat down on her couch to read it.

"Don't start reading that stuff now," she called from the bedroom, where she was changing out of her work suit. "We're going to have to rush if we want to get to the theater by curtain time."

"We'll leave whenever you're ready," he called back to her. "Besides, *The Ice Man Cometh* goes on forever. We could miss the first hour and still be numb by the time it's over."

"It's supposed to be great!" she responded.

He began to thumb through the document and stopped as soon as he came across the double-page spread of the proposed subway route map. His eyes traced the bold black lines that snaked their way from the center of the city out to the far-reaching suburbs in Maryland and Virginia. Then he traced the route back into the city, taking note of the dozens of neighborhoods in its path.

"Karen, do you have any idea who else has requested copies of this transcript?" he called out to her.

"I'm a step ahead of you, Mr. Tycoon," she called back. "I checked the request list before I left the office. There were a handful of requests by the transportation trade press, and a lobbyist for the Budd Company called for a copy."

"Who in hell is the Budd Company?"

"I think they manufacture passenger cars for trains and subways," she replied.

"Logical," he mused. "Anybody else?"

"Nope. Not as far as I know."

"Were the hearings well attended?"

"Mostly the trade press and lobbyist types," she answered as she walked hurriedly from her bedroom and kissed him on the cheek on her way to the door. "C'mon, we can talk on the way over to the Arena Stage."

***

During the performance Noah was mostly oblivious to the action on the stage. His thoughts kept returning to the subway map he had studied earlier in the evening.

"Enjoy the show?" Karen asked afterward as they drove toward Georgetown and Billy Martin's Carriage House, where they had reservations for a late dinner.

"Yeah, I thought it was great," he replied.

"Who did you think gave the strongest performance?"

"Huh?"

"I asked who you thought gave the strongest performance?"

"Larry. The guy who played Larry was really great."

"Noah, I love you, but you're full of shit," she said with a laugh.

"What's wrong, you didn't think the guy who played Larry was any good?"

"I thought he was terrific, but you wouldn't know if he even had any lines."

"What are you talking about?"

"Noah, your mind has been on the damn subway ever since I handed you that transcript."

He looked at her and smiled. "Sorry," he said. "You're absolutely right."

"Is it that important?"

"I think it might be. Especially if your boss is right about the chances of new legislation eventually passing."

"What are you going to do?"

"Ask some questions. I have to find out how they will finalize exactly where the subway stations will be located and where the main junctions or transfer points will be along the various lines."

"And you'll really start buying land near those future stations?"

"Unless I miss my guess, I think this is an opportunity of a lifetime. There absolutely will be second-rate neighborhoods that will soon become very important. Land values are going to increase dramatically."

"But you'll have to guess, right?"

"Right. I have to figure out exactly where the final locations will be. That property will soon be worth a lot more than it is now. Those subway stops will bring tremendous value to the surrounding land."

"So you're going to do it?"

"Karen, I haven't thought about anything else since we first discussed the subject."

"Where will you get the money?"

"I'm not sure yet. I could see if my folks and the Salamans were interested, or I could borrow the money myself. I could also option land and try to sell it before the option expires."

"I wish I could do something to help," she said.

"Maybe you can."

"I'm all ears."

"I need to understand the politics. You know, I need someone to explain to me who the players are, what the opposition is, and what the timetable will be for getting the job done."

"I'm your girl." She smiled and gave the back of his neck a playful squeeze.

"I never doubted it for a minute," he said, never taking his eyes off the road.

***

During the following month, Noah immersed himself in the city's subway project. He identified a dozen prospective sites that were particularly attractive because of the availability of surrounding undervalued land close to densely populated residential areas.

He had little difficulty convincing the loan officer of the Riggs National Bank, where Milk & Honey did all of its banking, to advance the money needed to begin optioning property around the targeted future Metro stations. Noah's reputation at Riggs was solid, and their regard for the convenience store business he'd helped develop couldn't have been stronger.

Time was soon to make a prophet of Noah. When the city's leading newspapers, many months later, published a map of the subway system that would soon be serving the nation's capital, Noah Greenspan held options on thousands of acres of land that was suddenly being sought by the area's leading developers. Almost overnight, Noah had become one of Washington's nouveau riche, establishing himself as something of a boy wonder in the city that had become Kennedy's Camelot.

***

Although Alexandra had never intended to remain in Israel, the pleasant weeks with Leila and Emile somehow flowed into months, then years, as she worked and continued her studies. The *Desert Song* offered her a daily column when she graduated, and Alexandra wrote to Sharif and Samira that she would work in Jerusalem through Christmas, and then probably return to the States. But by the time the year had ended, Alexandra had again decided to stay on for just a while longer. She flew to London to spend a week with Samira and Sharif; Alexandra had suggested London when Sharif said he wasn't prepared to return to Israel, or as he put it, to Palestine.

Alexandra loved her work and adored Leila and Emile. She also felt more and more drawn to the land of her birth. She loved the air she breathed, the sounds she heard, and the ancient landscape her eyes feasted on day after day. She was keenly aware of the irony of her stay in Israel. Her father, brooding over the loss of his home at the hands of the Israelis, had urged her to study in Lebanon, where she might reestablish a link to her roots. Instead, she had found her real roots and sanctuary in Israel.

After Alexandra had finished college, she and Amos spent part of almost every week together. There were times, of course, when his work would take him away for several days in a row. She learned not to ask about what he did at work. Like guide and tourist, they explored the countryside—she thrilled by her proximity to the landmarks of her heritage, and he thrilled by his proximity to her.

Amos had kept to himself the depth of his feelings for Alexandra. He understood only too well how strongly she identified with the Palestinians; he knew her heart was with the refugees who had lived for over a decade now in abject squalor in the camps and slums of neighboring Arab states. He savored his time with Alexandra and was unwilling to do or say anything that would chill the relationship they enjoyed.

Alexandra was, of course, not oblivious to how Amos felt about her. At times she agonized over her own feelings toward Amos and the extent to which he had become a part of her life. But she knew the pain caused by relationships that just could not be. It was pain she was determined never to experience again. So they pretended just to be friends with a common interest in the land of their birth. It was, however, a charade that faltered every time their eyes met, every time they touched, and every time they allowed themselves the luxury of fantasy unencumbered by the burden of history.

Perhaps the word *love* would have never crossed their lips had they not journeyed to Masada to look down on the plain where the mighty forces of Rome had once assembled to cast the ancient Hebrews from the land of Israel.

"Can you imagine the raw emotion of the Jews who stood here two thousand years ago to confront the Roman legions who had come to destroy them?" Amos asked as they scanned the horizon that spread before them.

"They chose to die here rather than to live as slaves in Rome," Alexandra said in quiet awe of the courage and determination required to stand strong against such fearsome forces.

"Masada is Israel," Amos said. "To understand the mentality of today's Israelis, one only has to understand the history of Masada."

"We have our Masadas too," she replied in a quiet, almost inaudible, voice. "The refugee camps are our Masadas. The Palestinians there have nowhere else to go."

Amos drew in a deep breath, his mood suddenly sagging. "I'm sorry, Alexandra. I wouldn't have brought you here if I had known it was going to upset you."

"Masada is no more upsetting to me than anything else in this land," she replied with a smile. "I'm developing a love-hate relationship with this country. I love the land because it is where my roots are. I know that will never change. But I also hate the land because modern history has denied me and my people any place here, and it has become the symbol of our banishment and our humiliation."

"And are you developing a love-hate relationship with me too?" he asked.

Alexandra looked up and smiled affectionately as she saw the agony in his eyes. "Emile's father once said a man's eyes are a window to his soul. Do you know when he said that?"

"No," Amos replied, shaking his head.

"He said that when he looked into your father's eyes and made the decision to sell him his home. I think your eyes are a window to your soul, and I could never hate you."

"Could you ever love me?" he asked in a whisper.

Alexandra was speechless for a moment, caught off guard by the very question she had asked herself dozens of times since she'd met Amos.

"Are you asking if I could love you or if I could commit my life to you?" she finally replied.

"I'll settle for either answer…for now."

"Amos, I can't do this to myself again. I've experienced one doomed relationship in my life, and I don't want to go through that again."

"Alexandra, this is not Washington, DC, and I am not a teenager named Noah Greenspan."

"What difference does that make?" she asked. "It is what you and Noah have in common that would cripple us."

"No, that needn't be true. That was then and there and him. This is now and here and me. You have as much a place here as I do; certainly more of a place than you have in America."

"Amos, how can you say that? My parents are there, and they can never return here. I am an American citizen. Here, I am a deportee, an exile."

"Here, you were a victim, Alexandra, but now this country is indebted to you. You will always be welcome here."

"This country is not indebted to me. I did nothing for Israel. I could not stand by and watch a massacre take place when I was in a position to prevent it. I wanted to save innocent lives, and I wanted to spare those misguided fools who believed the massacre they planned served the interests of Palestine.

"Alexandra, you're not a kid any more. There is no one to interfere with the judgments I make, and there shouldn't be anyone to interfere with your life either. I love you, damn it!"

"What do you want me to say?" she asked, looking up into his eyes, moved by his words.

"If you love me, Alexandra, tell me. That's all I ask."

For a brief moment, Alexandra saw Noah standing before her making the same plea, as he had so many times during those naïve and innocent years in Washington. Was it love she felt coursing through her body as they stood on the high ground of Masada looking down over the Dead Sea? And if so, for whom?

"I don't know," she finally whispered.

"Oh, you know all right, Alexandra," Amos said, his frustration evident in his voice. "You may not have the courage to deal with love— or me—but you do know how you feel."

"How I may feel and what I can do aren't necessarily compatible, Amos."

"Alexandra, you feel with your heart, you do with your head. I'm asking about your heart. I'm willing to deal with your head later."

"Do all Israelis see everything in metaphor?" she asked, smiling.

"No more than all Arabs," he replied.

"This is like standing and talking to Noah all over again," she said, shaking her head.

"I'm no starry-eyed boy with a crush on a Palestinian girl, Alexandra."

"Noah was never a starry-eyed boy, Amos. You and he speak the identical language, at least where I'm concerned."

"Maybe it was never realistic for the two of you to think about a life together in America."

"And it would be realistic for the two of us here in Israel?"

"More than any place on the face of this earth, this land *is* where you most belong."

"*Was*, Amos," she protested angrily. "This land *was* where I once belonged. We were banished, damn it!"

The cool breeze had strengthened, blowing Alexandra's hair wildly about her face as though whipped into frenzy by her anger. In her momentary fury, she was, Amos thought, the most beautiful woman he knew. He also knew the time for discussion was past. Abandoning the caution and restraint he had so carefully maintained when they were together, Amos reached out and pulled Alexandra into his embrace. Kissing her passionately, he lowered his grasp to her waist and, holding her tightly against his body, pulled her off her feet.

Alexandra, taken by surprise, struggled for a moment against his embrace. But her halfhearted protest only made Amos hold her that much tighter. Alexandra felt all her desire to resist evaporate. Throwing her arms around his shoulders, she responded hungrily to his kiss.

"Oh God, I love you," he whispered as he kissed her again.

"Amos, no!" she cried, reluctantly fighting to regain her composure. "Please, I can't handle this. Not now."

"What? What can't you handle? I love you. I admire you. I want you. What can't you handle?"

"We don't exist in a vacuum, Amos. Life is not as easy as 'I love you, I want you.'"

"So life isn't easy. Welcome to the world we live in, Alexandra. No, life isn't easy, but neither is it impossible. It's worth fighting for, damn it!"

"Please, Amos. Take me home. I need time to think."

"That's all I ask, Alexandra. Think. Take the time to think."

They spoke very little as they drove back toward Jerusalem. It wasn't an angry silence, only a shared weariness, each of them emotionally drained. She glanced at him and returned his smile when he took his eyes off the road long enough to look at her and reconfirm, without speaking, his affection for her. She looked away and closed her eyes as, once again, she saw for an instant Noah sitting there next to her.

***

When Alexandra returned home to Beit Safafa, Leila embraced her. "You have mail from home," she said, handing Alexandra an envelope.

Alexandra immediately recognized her mother's handwriting. She kicked off her shoes, laid back on her pillow, and tore open the envelope.

February 13, 1962

My Dearest Alexandra:

All is well here and we trust all is well with you. Milk & Honey continues to grow, and the Greenspans and the Salamans continue to prosper in the process. I only wish the rest of the world was doing as well. We read with interest and anxiety the news of unrest in Lebanon and Algeria, and, just yesterday, I saw that Syria is seeking aid from Russia. President Kennedy's recent announcement of aid for the government in Saigon concerns us all. Your father says Kennedy is picking up where the French left off in Indo-China and that no good can possibly come of it.

Everyone is suddenly interested in Arabs ever since Lawrence of Arabia came out last month. Is it playing in Jerusalem?

Yusuf is doing wonderful work in Baltimore. He says the inner harbor restoration will be one of the most exciting urban renewal projects in the country, and he is right in the middle of all the activity. He really believes he can make a name for himself in Baltimore, and he seems to love his work. Incidentally, Yusuf made the Baltimore newspapers because of a talk he gave about the plight of the Palestinian refugees. He also recently wrote a letter to the editor of the Baltimore Sun about the refugee problem. They published the letter, and we were surprised by all of the people who wrote in to object. Yusuf was never one to remain silent about the plight of our people. We hope none of this interferes with his career, but it wouldn't matter if it did. Not to Yusuf it wouldn't. We can all be very proud of Yusuf.

Noah is also doing well with his real estate business. He spends most of his time buying and selling land and has made quite a name for himself by acquiring so much property around the locations for the new subway stations. Your father says he showed real genius by moving so quickly and beating the speculators. We have all benefited from Noah's judgment.

Speaking of Noah, I guess I'll be the first to let you know that he and Karen are planning to marry. Esther Greenspan says they're going to get engaged soon. Karen is really a lovely girl, and we're all very happy for both of them. I know you'll receive this news with mixed but good feelings. You and I haven't discussed Noah for a long time, and so much has happened since you two were kids together. I feel things have worked out for the best, and I hope you feel that way too. I'm sure Noah would be thrilled to hear from you should you decide to drop him a note.

Well, that's all from here. We look forward to hearing from you soon.

Your loving parents.

Alexandra let the letter drop to her chest. She began to laugh and cry at the same time. She knew, of course, that the only news her mother was really conveying was about Noah and Karen. Everything else had simply been a kind distraction, intended to soften the blow.

CHAPTER
THIRTY-FIVE

Amos was always a little uneasy whenever Binyamin Bar-Levy summoned him to breakfast at the King David Hotel. It usually meant something important was about to happen. Binyamin always saved the tough ones for breakfast at the King David.

"Ah, Amos, my boy, good to see you. Tea?" Bar-Levy asked, holding up a white ceramic teapot.

"Yes, that would be fine," Amos replied, pushing the cup at his place setting toward Bar-Levy.

"I understand you've been seeing quite a bit of the Arab girl."

"Alexandra," Amos replied, lifting his eyes to meet Bar-Levy's. "Yes, I have. And I intend to see a lot more of her." His expression warned that Bar-Levy was getting into sensitive territory.

"Don't worry, Amos. I haven't summoned you here to lecture you about matters of the heart," Bar-Levy said. "Not yet, anyway."

"Not ever, Binyamin!"

"As you wish, Amos. I trust your judgment."

"Good."

"Of course she is an…"

"Don't say it, Binyamin. Don't start down that path with me, please."

"Amos, you should know that your friend may be in some danger," Bar-Levy said, looking over the top of his cup as he prepared to sip his tea.

"What are you talking about?" Amos replied anxiously.

"Shoukri has resurfaced."

"Do you know where he is?"

"We know where he *was*. Two weeks ago he was spotted by our people in Amman."

"What do you make of it?"

"I think the only reason he would have made his way to Jordon would be to cross into Israel somewhere closer to Jerusalem."

"Shit," Amos whispered bitterly.

"It may be nothing, but I thought you should know."

"Thanks, Binyamin. I really appreciate it."

"As I said, it may be nothing."

"It's something, and you know it."

"I don't think Shoukri can get to her easily here in Jerusalem," Bar-Levy said.

"He's a tenacious, murderous bastard, and he obviously knows she's here. He knows Alexandra betrayed him, and I'm sure by now he knows I helped. God only knows what he'll do if he discovers that Alexandra and I are seeing each other."

"Amos, just how much are the two of you seeing of one another?"

"I'm in love with her, Binyamin."

"I presume that means she's in love with you too."

"I don't know," Amos answered quietly.

"I hate to put such difficult questions to my intelligence people," Bar-Levy said sarcastically.

"There are complexities, Binyamin."

"How perceptive of you, Amos."

"Can we keep an eye on her?" Amos asked anxiously.

"Of course. We owe her a lot."

"She says we owe her nothing."

"We'll still keep an eye on her," Bar-Levy said, adding somewhat slyly, "I presume you'll do the same."

"What about Shoukri?" Amos said, ignoring his companion's last remark.

"Well, we both know he could cause trouble for Alexandra without coming here himself, but I wouldn't put anything past him."

"If he decides to move against her, I'm sure he'll do it himself," Amos said.

"Why do you say that?"

"Because it's his nature. He'd feel it was retribution that only he could inflict."

"So you agree there's a good chance that Shoukri may be plotting to murder Alexandra and perhaps you too. The big question is, what are you going to do about it? You've been warned; Alexandra hasn't."

Amos stared, almost contemptuously, at Binyamin Bar-Levy. He knew, of course, that Bar-Levy was right. Alexandra was in danger, and he knew he had no right to keep their suspicion about Shoukri from her.

"I'll tell her what we know," Amos said.

"You should tell her to go home to the US, Amos."

"Yes, I know," he answered softly.

***

Alexandra listened carefully as Amos related his conversation with Bar-Levy. He left little doubt that both he and Bar-Levy believed Shoukri's reappearance was a real threat.

"So, he knows I'm here," she said pensively, her unseeing gaze fixed on some distant point outside the window of Amos's apartment over-looking the old city.

Amos nodded. "Yes."

"I guess it was only a matter of time," she said wearily. "Shoukri probably thinks I was working for the Mossad all along. Do you think he will come after me?"

Amos thought for a moment before replying. His every instinct was to put her mind at ease, to assure her that she needn't worry. Instead, he said in a whisper, "Yes. Shoukri will come, or he will send someone."

Alexandra folded her arms in a lonely embrace as though comforting herself. "Shoukri will come himself."

"You could leave, Alexandra. You could return home."

She sighed. "No, I will not run from him. I'll leave on my terms when I'm good and ready."

"He was spared because of you," Amos said. "What a grotesque irony."

"You warned me that he was being spared only to kill again."

"Yes," Amos whispered.

"I guess I didn't realize I would be a target for so long," she said sadly.

"Alexandra, you won't be Shoukri's victim," Amos said vehemently. "So help me, he'll never hurt you! We'll see he doesn't get to you."

Alexandra looked at Amos for a moment and then knelt in front of him, resting her forearms on his thighs.

"It would make your life easier if I returned home, wouldn't it?" she asked softly, looking up into his eyes.

"It would make my life miserable, Alexandra," he said, cupping her upturned face gently in his hands. "I don't ever want you to leave."

"You can't spend all your time protecting me. What kind of a way is that to live?"

"Alexandra, I would protect you even if I didn't love you. You've earned that from all of us. But the fact is that I do love you. I love you more every day, and if you leave I'll spend my life worrying about you anyway."

"Amos, I don't know where I will settle. This land is an enigma to me, and I think it always will be. I don't know if I could ever make my home here, but I do know that I will never forget you."

"I don't want to be just a memory to you."

"Tell me, Amos, just what do you want. What do you expect of me?"

With that question hanging in the air, Amos took Alexandra in his arms and pulled her firmly but gently to her feet. A moment later, they were locked in a passionate embrace.

"What do I want?" he finally asked, putting his hands affectionately on the sides of her face. "You, Alexandra! You! I want to live by your side," he said, kissing her. "I want to make love to you. I want to spend my life with you. What do I expect of you? Only that you do what your heart tells you. What do you feel, Alexandra?"

She looked at him but said nothing.

"What do you feel, damn it!" he yelled as he took her by her shoulders. "Say what is in your heart!"

"I can't!" she cried.

"Because you don't love me?"

"Because I do love you," she answered, weeping. "And because I resent loving you."

"Oh, Alexandra, Alexandra," he whispered as he tried to kiss away her tears.

"Amos, you don't want to do this. There must be a thousand beautiful Israeli women with whom you could spend the rest of your days. Find one, Amos. You'll have a much happier life."

"I have found my beautiful woman, Alexandra. Losing her would make me miserable."

"No good will come of it," she whispered, surrendering more to his persistence than to his logic. "No good will come of it," she said as she clasped her hands behind his neck and reached up to kiss him.

Amos held her in his arms for several minutes, savoring the feel of her lips against his lips, her body firm against his. Alexandra felt her heart pounding in her chest as Amos gently sank to his knees, carefully pulling her down with him. Without a word passing between them, they helped each other shed their clothing, and a moment later they were lying naked, kissing, caressing, exploring one another. As each moment melted into the next, Alexandra and Amos cast aside their so carefully nurtured restraint and abandoned themselves to the ecstasy of the moment.

While Amos and Alexandra lay entwined in each other's arms in the aftermath of their lovemaking, their breathing still labored and hearts still pounding, Binyamin Bar-Levy, sitting in his office barely five miles away, picked up the phone on his desk.

"Trouble," the voice said.

"Speak," Bar-Levy replied.

"Shoukri has left Amman."

Bar-Levy listened to the studied silence as he ran his fingers nervously over his bald head. "Anything else?"

"Negative," the voice answered.

Bar-Levy, after a moment's consideration, disengaged the connection. Then he dialed Amos's number.

"Shoukri left Amman."

"Do we know where he's headed?" Amos asked.

"We know only that he left."

"I'll tell Alexandra," Amos said, preempting Binyamin's next question.

When he replaced the receiver, Amos turned and looked down at Alexandra, who had slipped on his shirt and was sitting up against a leather club chair.

"They think he's coming?" she asked, her eyes wide.

"No one knows exactly what he's up to, but he's apparently left Amman."

"He's coming," she said with chilling finality.

"Maybe you should go home, Alexandra. Maybe America is the only safe place for you."

"Is that really what you want me to do?"

"What I want you to do is be safe."

"I told you. I won't leave because of Shoukri."

"Then marry me," Amos said without warning.

"Do you ask everyone you're supposed to protect to marry you?" she asked, smiling for the first time since the call from Bar-Levy.

"Alexandra, this is no joking matter."

"No," she whispered, turning serious again.

"I've asked you to be my wife."

"I'm not ready to be anyone's wife, Amos."

"What does it take to be ready? You're twenty-four, you're incredibly bright, capable of making good judgments. Are you so undecided about how you feel about me?"

"I just made love to you. Do you think I would have given myself to you if I was undecided about how I felt about you?"

"Then tell me why you're not ready?"

She studied him carefully for a moment before responding. He was so much like Noah. She thought, *I love you, you love me—to hell with reality—let's get married.*

"Amos, yes, I do love you. But, no, I do not long to spend the rest of my life with you. Utopia is not available to us, Amos, and neither is peace of mind nor tranquility. I think that means we would be two people in love who were denied any real chance of being happy. I don't want that...not for me and not for my children."

"So, do you just turn off your feelings for me? Do you just one day say 'enough' and it's over?"

"I don't know," she whispered.

"I'm playing for keeps, Alexandra. You had better know that. I have no interest in a relationship that amounts to no more than an affair to be spent and discarded."

"You have a very graphic way of putting things, Amos Ben-Chaiyim. I have no intention of being 'spent and discarded.'"

"Then tell me, what do you intend?"

"Well, given Bar-Levy's call, how about just surviving?"

"You'd be safer living here with me," he said, a cold edge to his voice.

"I'm staying with Leila and Emile. Can the Israelis protect me in Beit Safafa?"

"You would be safer here."

"Can you protect me in Beit Safafa?" she asked again.

"We can protect you in Beit Safafa. Until we determine where Shoukri is, we'll have someone pick you up, take you to work, and bring you back home. You'll be with someone all the time."

"Are you angry with me?"

"No," he replied, "I just never dreamed we would spend the afternoon both making love and arguing."

"Then let's not argue," she said, holding her arms out to him.

***

Leila hugged Alexandra as soon as she returned home.

"Your day was a good one?" Leila asked.

"It was better than good and worse than bad," Alexandra answered.

Leila's smile quickly faded as she pondered Alexandra's strange response. "What is this 'better than good and worse than bad'?"

"Amos was the better-than-good part of the day."

"And the 'worse than bad'?"

"Shoukri. The Israelis say Shoukri seems to have resurfaced and might be coming after me."

"The Israelis won't let anything happen to you, Alexandra," Leila said reassuringly, but Alexandra noticed she'd gone slightly pale.

"That's what Amos said."

"He'd have to be mad to come here."

"You don't know Shoukri. If he were determined to reach me, he'd come."

Leila changed the subject. "Tell me about the better-than-good part."

"Amos and I were...together. He asked me to marry him."

"Oh my," Leila said, sitting down as though stunned by Alexandra's response.

"I told him I wasn't ready to even think about marriage. I also told him it would never work."

"And you call that 'better than good'?"

"Amos is better than good. He's really a wonderful human being."

"But forbidden. Is that it?"

Alexandra nodded. "Yes, something like that."

"Well," said Leila, deciding it was time to change subjects again, "I have a surprise too. Someone dropped off a back issue of the *Evening Star* for you."

"A back issue?"

"Yes, it was stuffed in the mailbox. I assume someone got hold of an old copy and thought you would like to have it."

"Where is it?" Alexandra asked nervously.

"I'll get it for you," Leila replied. "I left it in your room."

She returned a moment later, carrying the newspaper.

"Here," she said, handing it to Alexandra.

"Oh my God," Alexandra murmured as she unfolded the paper and held it up with shaking hands. "Oh my God."

"Alexandra, what is it?"

"He's here!" she gasped, opening the paper to the editorial page. "Look!"

Leila leaned closer to the paper to get a better look at the page Alexandra held out. It was a column with Alexandra's byline and photograph. "'Anatomy of a Warrior'…what does that mean?"

"It's a column I wrote about Shoukri," Alexandra said weakly. "He's here. He delivered this himself."

"Why would he do that?"

"To terrify me," Alexandra said with quiet resignation. "To let me know that he knows where I am and that he can reach me whenever he chooses to."

CHAPTER THIRTY-SIX

Alexandra and Amos watched the team from Shin Bet dust the newspaper and the mailbox for prints. Amos had rushed to Emile and Leila's home right after Alexandra's frantic call.

"He's here! Amos, Shoukri's here!" she had cried into the phone.

Now, her composure restored, Alexandra shook her head skeptically. "This is ridiculous," she said. "Shoukri won't care if they find his prints. He left the damn paper to let me know he's here."

"They know what they're doing, Alexandra," Amos explained. "They won't leave any stone unturned. Who knows who else may have handled that paper? They'll follow every lead, question every possible suspect or accomplice they can identify."

"I had convinced myself I was safe—until Leila held up that newspaper. Then my blood ran cold. How in the hell did he get into the country—into Jerusalem and then Beit Safafa—without being detected?"

"He probably came in through Jordan. Somehow he must have slipped in from East Jerusalem."

"Damn!" she whispered angrily.

"We can have you back in the United States in twenty-four hours, Alexandra. Maybe it's the most sensible thing to do."

"I won't run from him, Amos. I can't do that! Besides he'd hunt me down in America sooner or later, anyway. If there's to be a showdown with Shoukri, I'd rather it be here and now. With Israeli security, I have a chance. I'd never be the priority in America I am here. They might put out an alert for Ali for a month or two, and then I'd be on my own. Shoukri would just wait until they relaxed their guard."

"Alexandra, we won't relax our guard until we have him or until we know he's gone. You'll have Shin Bet watching wherever you go."

"Great," she murmured sarcastically.

"You'd be safer with me."

"Amos, we've been all through that."

"Leila and Emile would be safer too."

Alexandra's eyes darted to meet his. She didn't speak.

"It stands to reason, Alexandra. I can protect you better than they can. And don't forget—Beit Safafa is an Arab community. The neighbors aren't going to take well to Shin Bet hanging around all the time."

Alexandra lowered her head into her hand and closed her eyes. "Damn!" she said again.

***

Binyamin Bar-Levy ordered every possible precaution to protect Alexandra. He assigned someone to stay in close proximity to her around the clock and ordered his people to begin interviewing every contact they had among the Palestinians who might have heard anything at all about Shoukri. By the end of the first week after the old newspaper turned up at the Awad home, they still had no additional information about Shoukri's whereabouts or his intentions. All they had was the newspaper. They found only one identifiable fingerprint on the entire paper. It belonged to Shoukri, and it had been pressed down directly, deliberately, and ominously onto Alexandra's photo.

Amos told Alexandra they had found Shoukri's print on the paper. He decided, however, not to tell her where Shoukri had chosen to leave his mark.

During the week, Alexandra was the responsibility of Shin Bet. From sundown Friday until sunrise Monday, however, Bar-Levy agreed, reluctantly, that the protection of Alexandra Salaman would be left to Amos. This arrangement, Amos had argued, would provide him and Alexandra a modicum of privacy without sacrificing her security. Amos was, after all, as qualified as anyone to protect Alexandra and far more motivated than any other security agent in the world.

After five weeks, though, Bar-Levy began to speculate that perhaps Shoukri had not ventured into Israel at all. There had been no trace of him, nor had any of the Palestinians who regularly provided reliable information heard anything about him. Maybe, just maybe, Bar-Levy speculated, Shoukri had had the paper smuggled into Israel and delivered to Beit Safafa by someone else.

Amos was furious at the notion that security might be relaxed one iota. The government had committed to protecting Alexandra, and that meant around-the-clock, high-alert security until further notice. Bar-Levy assured Amos he had no intention of suspending the security detail, but Amos knew that apathy would begin to numb the sharp edge of alert minds as soon as people began whispering that a warrior who existed only in an old newspaper was stalking Alexandra.

***

The weather had become unseasonably warm. On the Sunday before Passover, Amos asked Alexandra if she would like to drive down the coast to Jaffa and then on to Ashkelon for lunch. He was anxious to get her away from the tensions the city had evoked ever since Shoukri had announced himself. Alexandra had been sharing Amos's apartment with him for six weeks, and the only real peace of mind she experienced was when they were together.

As they drove south along the coast Amos reached over and squeezed her knee affectionately.

"Relaxed?"

"I was until you asked," she replied, placing her hand gently over his.

"How's work going?" he asked to change the subject.

"I really enjoy what I do. Here I am in Israel writing for an Arab newspaper."

"Nothing unusual about that," Amos replied.

"Maybe not unusual, but you have to admit it's pretty ironic. I mean, me winding up here writing for an Arab newspaper."

"What are you working on?"

"A story about an Arab family that has lived in Jerusalem since before the Crusades."

"Nothing unusual about that, either."

"This is an incredible land," she said.

"It's where you belong, Alexandra."

"Yeah, me and my bodyguard living happily ever after."

"What do you want me to tell you, Alexandra?"

"Oh, I don't know, Amos. Tell me this is all just a nightmare. Tell me I can go on living my life without having to look over my shoulder all the time. Tell me when this is all going to end."

"It would have ended a long time ago in Beirut if you hadn't intervened to save the bastard."

"Do you think killing Shoukri would have made a difference? Don't you think there are others just as radical as Shoukri? At least with Shoukri we know who we're dealing with."

Had Amos at that moment looked into his rear-view mirror, he would have observed the second car behind him pull over to side of the road as soon as the car directly behind Amos pulled out to pass. Then he would have known that someone trying to remain undetected was following him. But Amos was relaxed and didn't notice.

"Hungry?" he asked as they passed through Ashod.

Alexandra nodded. "Famished."

"We'll be in Ashkelon in a few minutes. Can you wait?"

"Sure," she replied, lying back against the top of the seat and closing her eyes.

"Tired?"

"I'll be fine. I just want to rest my eyes."

When Amos glanced over at her a few moments later, she had drifted off into a light sleep. He was still love struck by her beauty. Her lips were parted ever so slightly. He watched the faint rise and fall of her breasts as she breathed and the way a few strands of hair that ran down her forehead and the side of her face to the corner of her mouth seemed to shimmer with each breath she took. Carefully, he eased the car to a halt on the side of the road and turned off the ignition. He sat there just watching her for a few minutes while she slept, paying no attention to the passing cars or the one that pulled off the road again about seventy yards behind them. Amos yearned to lean over and kiss her lightly on the lips, but decided not to disturb her. He had watched her sleep many times in the young light of a new dawn after long and unhurried nights of lovemaking, and he still found the sight of her in such vulnerable repose as alluring as ever. His love for her was overwhelming.

Alexandra awoke to see Amos looking at her.

"I guess I dozed off," she said, brushing back the few strands of hair that fell across her face. "How long were you watching me?"

"For just a few tantalizing moments."

"You sound like a voyeur."

"You've turned me into one."

"Do you enjoy watching sleeping women?" she teased.

"Only one," he replied, leaning over to kiss her.

As he did, he dropped out of view of the gun sight trained on his head from the automobile parked on the side of the road behind them. In that car, Shoukri whispered, "Drift closer," and lifted his head from the gun sight. The driver nodded and released the hand brake.

Amos lingered a moment longer after kissing Alexandra to nip playfully at her ear lobe. She tightened her embrace and kissed him again, teasing him this time with her tongue.

Amos pulled away from her and smiled.

"Let's have lunch on the beach," he whispered.

"Sounds great," she replied.

As he straightened up, he suddenly caught sight of the automobile gliding to a stop behind them.

"Get down!" he yelled, just as a single round exploded from the barrel of the high-powered rifle.

Then everything flashed before Alexandra in slow motion. The bullet crashed through the rear window, grazing the side of Amos's skull just above his right temple. Her blood-curdling scream filled the air as Amos collapsed on the seat beside her. She didn't hear the squeal of rubber spinning against asphalt as the car behind them came to a screeching halt.

"Out!" Shoukri yelled. He pulled the car door open and yanked her from the car.

"Amos!" she screamed reaching out to the motionless body sprawled on the seat of the car. "Amos!" she screamed again, but Shoukri pulled her to the waiting car and pushed her through the rear door and onto the floor.

She thrashed and kicked as Shoukri pulled a chloroform-soaked hood over her head, but Alexandra was too shocked to fight effectively. Within moments she plunged headfirst into a gaping void, enveloped by darkness and the echo of her own terrified screams.

**

Shoukri hid Alexandra in a cave-like rock formation on the coast just a few miles from Beit Lahiya, near the border with the Gaza Strip. He waited until nightfall to take her out to sea in a small rowboat rigged with an outboard motor. They traveled along the coast until they reached the outskirts of Gaza, where they went ashore and were met by comrades who had trained with Shoukri in Egypt. A few minutes before midnight, they arrived at an abandoned farmhouse not two miles from the place where Shoukri was born.

Alexandra, still partially drugged and thoroughly exhausted, lay crumpled on the floor of the farm's abandoned barn, no longer unconscious but too groggy to fully comprehend what had happened.

It was late morning before she fully awoke. Nearly twenty-four hours had elapsed since the attack on the road near Ashkelon.

Her eyelids fluttered, and when she finally opened them, Shoukri came into focus, squatting down next to her. At the sight of him, Alexandra squeezed her eyes shut as if to force the grogginess from her head.

"I made you some coffee," Shoukri said, holding a steaming cup near her mouth.

She glared at him. "You bastard!" she whispered and propped herself up on her elbows.

"Now is that any way to greet an old friend?" Ali smiled coolly at her. "Someone for whom you feel such…what was the word you used? Ah! Such tenderness."

"That was before I knew you used me, Ali. How could you? Whispering words of love in my ear one moment, and all the while using me for your own ends with no regard to how it would affect my life!"

"As we've discussed in the past, Alexandra, sacrifices must be made."

"And is Amos one of those sacrifices too?" she asked, her defiant tone faltering with the memory of Amos lying motionless on the front seat of the car.

"The Greek engineer?" he said and smiled sarcastically.

"Where is he?" she demanded.

"According to the radio, he's alive and well. I merely cut a new part in his hair. Lucky man, your Amos. I intended to kill him, and I thought I had. He's a real bleeder."

"He's alive?"

"For now."

Alexandra closed her eyes against the tears that now flowed for the first time since the ambush.

"What do you want of me?" she finally asked.

Shoukri looked down at her for several moments before answering.

"Leave us!" he shouted over his shoulder. Several men Alexandra hadn't known were there emerged from the shadows and left the barn. One of the figures separated from the departing group and emerged from the darkness. Alexandra saw it was Omar Samir, Ali's friend, Ali's accomplice, from the university.

"This is madness, Ali," Samir hissed, glaring down at Alexandra with such obvious and intense hatred that Alexandra's blood turned to ice. "There was no reason to endanger the entire operation by bringing her here, just because you—"

"Enough!" Shoukri shouted. "As long as I am in charge of this operation, you will do as you are told." Both men continued to look down at Alexandra, Ali with seeming affection that Alexandra knew better than to trust, Samir with utter contempt. The look in each man's eyes filled Alexandra with equal dread.

"Fine, Ali, have it your way," Omar replied, making no effort to hide his anger. "But this 'operation,' as you call it, might have a better chance of success if you were to run it with your head and not your—"

Ali once again cut Samir off. "And I say this operation would still have a perfectly fine chance of success if it were run with one less person, Omar."

Shoukri neither raised his voice nor looked in Samir's direction as he spoke, but Alexandra saw that Samir's tough demeanor quickly faded with Shoukri's thinly veiled threat.

"Now, I suggest you go check on the others," Ali continued, still gazing down at Alexandra with a slight smile on his lips, "before I begin to reevaluate what—and who—is truly necessary to our purposes."

Samir gave Alexandra one final look that telegraphed his utter contempt for her presence, but he made no further verbal protest before turning and storming out of the barn.

As soon as they were alone, Ali rose and extended his hand to her. Pointedly ignoring his offer of assistance, Alexandra struggled to her feet.

"You're a very stubborn woman, Alexandra."

"I want nothing from you, Shoukri," she replied, trying to maintain her balance.

"Really?"

"Really."

"How about the right to live another day?"

"You harm me, and you'll never get out of Israel alive."

"We're not in Israel."

"What?" Alexandra cried out incredulously.

"I said we're not in Israel. We're in Gaza, Alexandra. Israel will provoke a war with Egypt if she tries to look for you here. Why would Israel risk an international incident for you?"

Alexandra tried to hide the despair she felt upon learning she was no longer in Israel.

"I'm afraid I'm not being a very gracious host," Ali said with the same cool smile curling one side of his mouth. "Come—clean yourself up and eat something. You're a mess, Alexandra."

"I have no intention of eating with you, Ali, and if I'm a mess, you made me that way. You'll have to get used to it."

For a moment Shoukri said nothing. His eyes took on a sudden chilling intensity, and fear washed over her anew. He came toward her, and as he advanced Alexandra retreated until her back was against the wall and Ali's face only inches from her own.

"You listen to me, my love," he said between clenched teeth. "Do you think this is some game I'm playing here? Do you think this is another pleasant day's outing where you can tease and lie and bend me to your will? Is that what you think?"

"Ali, I never..." Alexandra began, her mind flashing back to Ali's tender embrace the day he had told her he loved her. It was hard to imagine the gentle man from that day being the same menacing person who had shot Amos and was now holding her captive.

Before she could continue, Ali turned away from her and walked toward the door. "There's a well in the corner," he said, pointing to the side. "I want you cleaned up when I return."

***

Binyamin Bar-Levy sat at the side of the hospital bed and watched Amos struggle to awaken from the night's sedative-induced sleep. He had regained consciousness in the emergency room at Ashkelon's only hospital late in the afternoon after the attack. It was nearly midnight before he was able to recall anything at all of the previous twenty-four hours. Then, as his memory began to emerge from the numbing pain, he became frantic. He knew Shoukri had Alexandra. At midnight, the doctors had ordered a strong sedative to calm him. Now, as he awakened, it was nearly noon, and the ambush and kidnapping were nearly twenty-four hours old.

"Well, my young friend, you're very lucky to be alive," Bar-Levy said.

"Have…they…found…Alexandra?" Amos asked, his voice still heavy from the concussion and the sedative.

"No," Bar-Levy answered, making no effort to hide the defeat in his voice.

"God, I fucked up," Amos said.

"We all fucked up, Amos. I was positive the newspaper was little more than a practical joke."

"If anything happens to her, I'll kill myself," he murmured in agony.

"No, Amos, you'll not kill yourself. You'll kill her assassin, or you'll help us kill him."

"She trusted me, Binyamin," Amos cried. "She said she always felt safe when she was with me."

"What happened, Amos?"

"I don't know. We had pulled over to the side of the road. I remember noticing a car pulling up behind us. That's all I remember."

"There was a trace of lipstick on your lips."

"I kissed Alexandra. She had fallen asleep and we were just sitting there. When she awoke I leaned over and kissed her."

"Can you remember anything at all about the car that pulled up behind you?"

"It happened so fast. I remember yelling 'get down' to Alexandra…
and that's all."

"Why did you yell 'get down'?"

"I sensed danger as soon as that car pulled up behind us."

"What kind of car was it?"

"I don't know."

"Was it a convertible?"

"Yes, I think so.."

"Are you sure?"

"Yes, I remember. It was a convertible. I'm sure."

"How did he fire if he was behind you? Did he get out of the car?"

"No."

"Was there no windshield in the car?"

Amos tried to concentrate. "There was a windshield. I remember
seeing the reflection of the sun on the windshield."

"So he had to stand in order to fire"

"I'm telling you there was a windshield. I have no recollection of a
gun being fired."

"You're very lucky, Amos. I'm sure he was aiming to blow your
head off. "

"It feels like he did."

"At least it feels."

"Binyamin, I'm not sure, but I think the car was white."

"Why do you think that? Can you picture it?"

"No, I really can't, but somehow white or light seems more right
than a dark car. I definitely don't picture a dark car behind us."

"Well, it's a start. We'll look for an abandoned light-colored car."

"Where do you think he took her?" Amos asked.

"Somewhere nearby. Maybe even Gaza."

Startled, Amos looked up at the older man. "How could he cross
into Gaza?"

"It would be difficult, especially with a reluctant prisoner. Unless…"

"Unless what?" Amos asked, his mouth suddenly dry with rising dread of the answer he'd already discerned for himself.

"Unless he entered by sea," Bar-Levy said, confirming Amos's own conclusion.

"In broad daylight?"

"Perhaps last night."

"Gaza," Amos said in a dejected whisper. "Shoukri's from Gaza. He'd have contacts there, and he must know the area like the back of his hand. Do we have operatives there?"

"We have operatives everywhere, Amos. You know that. They are working. We'll find her."

"You think she's alive?"

"Right now?"

"Yes."

"Yes, I think she's alive. He kidnapped her for a reason."

"Do you think he intends to kill her?"

"I don't know why he kidnapped her, Amos. Maybe he wants to trade her for some of our prisoners. He may think we won't move against him as long as Alexandra's alive. Maybe he thinks she effective-ly checkmates our ability to sweep in on him, assuming we determine where he is."

"Do you think we'll find her alive?"

"That's impossible to know for sure."

"I didn't ask you if you knew for sure. I asked you if you *think* we'll find her alive."

Once again Bar-Levy looked at Amos without speaking.

"Do you?" Amos asked urgently.

"No, Amos, I don't," he answered softly.

***

Within hours, Shin Bet agents had located the car. A chloroform-soaked sack found on the floor confirmed that they had the right vehicle. From the abandoned car's location, they presumed that Shoukri had made his way by sea into the Gaza Strip. Maps identifying every known residence, farm, and commercial building were quickly assembled, and seasoned minds began assessing where, along the coast, Shoukri would most likely have gone.

***

Alexandra had never before experienced such terror. But she was sure now that Ali Abdul Shoukri would not hesitate to kill her. Alexandra knew Ali believed she had turned her back on Palestine when she turned her back on him. "I love you, Alexandra," he had whispered to her that day in the Bekaa Valley. And she, in turn, had betrayed him. She knew that would be the way Ali saw things. How would he now act out his revenge for that betrayal?

Alexandra's empathy for Palestine had not diminished, but neither was she conditioned by the kind of misery that molded the likes of Ali Abdul Shoukri. She was incapable of hating anyone because they had descended from Sarah and not Hagar. She and Shoukri were no longer of the same world, and though she understood him, she knew he was incapable of understanding her—and *that*, she believed, could cost her her life. Alexandra was sure she was about to die, to be executed, in a barn in Gaza. She thought of all those she would never see again—her parents, Yusuf, Amos, Noah.

"How are you feeling?" Shoukri asked as he walked into the barn. "Are you ready to talk?"

"What is there to talk about, Ali?" she asked without rising from the stool on which she sat.

He came over to her and reached a hand toward her face. Alexandra angrily turned away from his touch.

"Alexandra," he said quietly. "I have no desire to hurt you." He once again reached toward her and gently smoothed her hair away from her face.

Again Alexandra's mind raced back to that day in the Bekaa Valley when she had made a similar tender gesture toward him.

"Do you think this is some kind of game I'm playing here?"

"Really?" she replied with more courage than she actually felt. "I thought you intended to kill me."

"I didn't say I wouldn't kill you. I said I had no desire to hurt you. There's a big difference."

Alexandra tried valiantly to control the tremble in her hands and voice. "Why did you hunt me down like this, after all this time?" she managed to say, more calmly than she felt. "It's been over three years."

"You're right. Anyone who betrayed the cause the way you did should have been dead long ago. You have been kept alive by my good graces, Alexandra, and nothing more."

"Am I supposed to thank you?" she asked, her fear giving way to incredulity. "Ali, I never betrayed you. But you! You lied to me. You used me and caused a great deal of pain to me and…to others."

"And this Jew you seem to care so much about, the phony Greek architect, did he not lie to you, use you, and cause you a great deal of pain, too?"

Alexandra was silent for a moment. As always, Ali had a way of confounding her thoughts like no one else she'd ever met. He was right, of course. Amos, too, had used her to his own ends. "Yes, Ali," Alexandra said quietly. "Amos did do all those things, it's true. But Amos was desperately trying to save lives. You were planning to destroy innocent lives."

"But you're wrong!" Ali said, fire in his eyes. "Individual lives may have been sacrificed, it's true. But those lives would have been lost in the greater effort to redeem an entire people. The part you played, Alexandra, it was vital to that cause—vital. Can't you see that?"

"What I see, Ali," Alexandra said wearily, "is that I was an unwitting pawn in your game. It didn't matter whether I was for or against your cause. I was never given a chance to make that choice. You made it for me."

"I'm giving you that chance now, Alexandra. That's why you're here."

The shadows in the barn grew deeper as the sun slowly descended toward the horizon. Ali reached up and lit a rusty lantern hanging from a low beam. The firelight gave an eerie intimacy to the drafty barn.

"Where are the others?" she asked.

"They've gone ahead," he said. "I told them I—we—would join them later with the supplies."

"Gone ahead where? Supplies for what? Ali, what are you planning to do?"

"I see you're still every bit the journalist," he replied, smiling at her inquisitiveness. "We're merely continuing the work we started while you and I were at the university. Thanks to your friend Amos and his accomplices, it's taken far longer to rebuild our resources, as we've been forced to do all our work in even greater secrecy. But the movement is as alive as it ever was, Alexandra. And I want you to be a part of it. I'm giving you the chance to redeem yourself."

"Redeem myself? Ali, I don't need redemption."

"I'm offering you salvation, Alexandra."

Walking over to Alexandra, Shoukri reached down, gently took her by the shoulders, and pulled her from the stool.

"Even though you betrayed us—betrayed me, Alexandra—I still love you."

"Oh, Ali, you can't be serious!" Alexandra cried, genuinely shocked. Then she felt a sudden surge of panic as she saw how her words stung him. "Ali, I'm sorry, but…"

"But what? You once told me that you had feelings for me, did you not?"

"Yes, but…"

"And you said that we would need to wait until we each saw the other clearly."

"Yes, I did, but…"

"Things could not be any more clear than they are now, Alexandra. So I think we've waited long enough, don't you?"

Omar Samir's aborted protest suddenly came back to her. *There was no reason to endanger the entire operation by bringing her here, just because you—just because he*—just because Ali…And suddenly she understood. She wasn't there because she had betrayed Ali's cause; she was there because she had broken his heart.

***

The Shin Bet agents had quietly slipped ashore at the point where the first cluster of farm dwellings appeared on their maps. Their arrival had coincided with the departure of Ali's compatriots. The defiant Arabs, taken into custody and their weapons seized, denied any knowledge of anyone named Ali Abdul Shoukri. Nor, they claimed, had they ever heard the name Alexandra Salaman. But a quick search of their pockets produced maps that revealed the exact location of the farm where, it turned out, she had been taken. Now, in the gathering dusk, the agents silently surrounded the barn where Shoukri was holding Alexandra. Their orders had been clear: save the girl, and make sure Shoukri did not escape alive.

***

"Alexandra, Palestine is our land, it is our destiny. We can be happy here, together."

Alexandra struggled for the words with which to reason with Ali. Despite her growing desperation, Alexandra knew she had to buy herself whatever time she could.

"Ali, listen," she finally said. "I'm really exhausted. Couldn't we talk about this in the morning, when we've both had a chance to rest and clear our heads?"

A shiver coursed through Alexandra as she saw the look of compassion on Ali's face. How could it be, she wondered, that any man could look on her with such tenderness yet be capable of killing her at any moment.

He came and placed an arm around Alexandra's shoulders. She fought the urge to shrink from his touch.

"I know this has been a trying time for you." He spoke as though he'd had nothing at all to do with her ordeal, and she wasn't about to do anything to change his newly found tenderness. "Let us go to the house, and we'll have something to eat. Then we'll sleep. We have a long journey in front of us in the morning." He smiled at Alexandra as though sharing with her the excitement of a long-anticipated adventure.

Alexandra allowed herself to be guided to the barn door. Shoukri opened the door and, with a smile and a small theatrical bow, gestured for Alexandra to precede him.

As soon as she stepped through the doorway, she was grabbed by strong arms and thrown violently to the ground. Confused, she struggled to free herself from the unknown assailant. In the split second before the gunfire began, her eyes met Ali's and she heard him cry out, "Alexandra!"

Alexandra's screams filled the night as Ali Abdul Shoukri was cut down in a hail of gunfire.

CHAPTER
THIRTY-SEVEN

Binyamin Bar-Levy held onto Amos's arm as he helped him walk from the side door of the hospital to the waiting car. The moonlit sky and soothing warmth of the spring air seemed in sharp contrast to the awful reality of the day.

"God, I feel so empty, so awful," Amos said, his voice barely above a whisper.

"You've had quite a shock, Amos."

"Life just turned upside down from one instant to the next. In one split second, I lost everything."

"So far, we don't know if you've lost anything at all," Bar-Levy said, as he opened the rear door of the Mercedes sedan for Amos. "You're alive, damn it. Maybe Alexandra is alive as well."

"Christ, the bastard took her from me! In broad daylight he stalked me and took her. He must have been stalking me all the way from Jerusalem."

"We broke a rule, Amos," Bar-Levy said, sliding in next to Amos. "We allowed someone with an emotional attachment to a subject to become personally involved with the case. I would have never allowed that had I really believed that Shoukri was still a threat."

"An emotional attachment to a subject?" Amos repeated sarcastically. "Is that what I am, someone with an emotional attachment to a subject? Is that what Alexandra is—a subject?"

"I think you know what I mean," Bar-Levy answered patiently. "And I'm not the person you're angry with."

"Yeah, I know," Amos answered. "I've never loved anyone the way I love Alexandra."

"Enough, Amos! Stop feeling sorry for yourself. If you want to know the truth, I think you botched it. A few professional glances in your rear-view mirror should have alerted you that something was wrong, but you were too busy thinking about Alexandra to even notice that you were being followed. And yes, damn it, I botched it too. I knew we were compromising Alexandra by leaving her in your care."

"Oh God, I love her," Amos said, breaking down for the first time since the ambush.

"Don't give up hope, Amos," Bar-Levy said, putting his arm around his young colleague in an uncharacteristic display of affection. "Don't give up hope."

The call came on the car phone just as the driver headed the sedan north, the opposite direction Amos and Alexandra had been driving forty-eight hours earlier.

"It's for you, Chief," the driver said over his shoulder.

"Bar-Levy here," he answered, picking up the phone in the rear compartment.

Amos's heart quickened as he watched Bar-Levy concentrating on whatever the caller was telling him. Dread radiated through his body. He glanced instinctively at his watch to note the exact time the call came through. Bar-Levy lowered the phone against his shoulder and turned to Amos.

"It's over," he said. "She's safe. We have her."

Amos brought his hands to his face and wept.

"Shoukri is dead," Bar-Levy said, hanging up the phone.

"She's all right?" Amos asked, regaining his composure.

"A bit roughed up, but she's all right," Bar-Levy answered.

***

Amos and Alexandra returned to Amos's apartment in Jerusalem to once again savor life and one another. For several days and nights, it seemed that neither could satiate the other. Nothing came between them during those first days after her rescue. Alexandra was happiest when she was with Amos, when they were together in his apartment. Life would be so pleasant, she thought, if each person's universe extended only to the space shared with loved ones, or to those imaginary oases of tranquility where one could, from time to time, escape long enough for the tensions and anxieties of life to subside.

Despite her sense of well-being when she was with Amos, Alexandra couldn't erase from her mind the sight of Ali's face looking down at her as the bullets hit him. He had been, at that moment, neither friend nor foe, guilty nor innocent, hated nor loved. He had been a force in her life, both threatening and moving, and was now a fatality of the very violence he espoused so fervently. Ali's face haunted her dreams and still filled her with dread. Happiness came only when Amos was at her side, and she knew that couldn't last.

One evening a week after their ordeal, Amos was gazing down on Alexandra when he sensed that Alexandra was troubled. She was sitting on the floor, deep in thought, with her back against the wall. She could have been posing for a portrait, he thought, her arms embracing her legs, pulling them tightly against her chest, her chin resting on her knees.

"Are you all right?" he asked.

"I'm fine," she answered after a disconcerting pause.

"Something's bothering you. Are you worried that you haven't heard the last of Shoukri's pals?"

"No. I was there because of Ali, not because of them. They resented my presence. I think I'm the last person they want anything to do with."

"Then what is it?" he asked again.

"It's nothing really," she said with a sigh.

"Maybe I can help, Alexandra."

When she turned to him, he saw the tears in her eyes.

"Alexandra, please. What is it?"

"I just feel I have to resume my life. My book is finished. My newspaper work is fine but…"

"Are you unhappy with me?"

"Amos, no one could be unhappy with you."

"Then, what is there about your life that's making you sad?"

"There is no context to my life, Amos. My work…you…this land… nothing makes sense. I don't feel I have a place here."

Amos now found himself deep in a conversation he had known was coming but had dreaded for weeks.

"Some things take time, Alexandra. Things will only get better with us."

"Yes," she mused. "With us things would get better; I would only learn to love you more. But my life, Amos…that I'm not so sure of."

"Alexandra, this country will grow on you. You must see that already. What do you feel when you're not rushed and just strolling on the streets, when you observe life surging all around you in Israel?

"Resentment," she answered without hesitation.

Amos closed his eyes, sorry he had asked the question.

"Amos, I'm sorry, but that's our curse. Things happen and will continue to happen in this country that will either please or infuriate me or you. And what pleases me may infuriate you, and what pleases you may infuriate me."

"Every couple has disagreements from time to time. It needn't be the end of the world."

"I'm not talking about mere disagreements, Amos. I'm talking about belonging, about knowing who I am and feeling good about who I am."

"You're not being reasonable, Alexandra. We would both have to compromise, but if we made the effort, things could work out. I know they could."

"You're missing the point, Amos. I know I could bend and twist and find a niche in which I could survive here. You call it compromise. Sure, I could compromise, but..."

"But what?"

"But I don't want to compromise on this. It's not like deciding to wear a different dress, you know. We're talking about compromising who I am and how I feel. We're talking about a compromise that may haunt me for the rest of my life."

"And maybe, just maybe, you'd come to have positive feelings about this land, Alexandra. Its history will always be relevant to you, as well as to me. We're both bound to this land. Historically, the current conflict between the Arabs and Jews is no more than a moment in time. We both can find common ties to the land which unite us."

"The current conflict, as you call it, encompasses all my lifetime and my father's lifetime. It will probably encompass my children's lifetime and their children's as well. Historically, it may just be a moment in time, but it's the moment in which our entire world exists."

"You could be happy here, Alexandra," he protested. "I know you could."

"But think of what it would take for me to be happy here. Think of what I would have to be turning my back on to be happy here, Amos. Someday, it would all catch up to me. Maybe it would be when my parents refused to come visit me because it would be too painful for them. Maybe it would be when I watched some Arab laborer pulling weeds for an Israeli homeowner, or when I read of some misguided Arab like Shoukri getting shot trying to sneak into Israel from Gaza. Maybe that's when I would be repulsed by my own happiness."

Amos felt his resolve sag as Alexandra countered whatever logic he could muster. He had created his own private world with Alexandra and had been prepared to defend it against any outside assault, but now Alexandra herself was battering it. What he didn't want to admit was that perhaps her vision peered into the future with greater clarity than did his own.

"Can I declare a truce in this engagement?" he asked, holding up his hands as though to fend her off. "This battle isn't going well, and I'd rather regroup my forces than surrender."

Alexandra got to her feet and smiled.

"Truce," she said, holding out her arms to him.

"Don't ever leave," he whispered into her hair as he embraced her as tightly as he dared.

Alexandra looked off into space over his shoulder and then closed her eyes. Truce," she murmured.

"Truce," he whispered, again pulling her off her feet. Amos walked across the room with her literally hanging in his embrace and eased her down onto the top of his desk. They desperately fumbled at their clothes, and then Alexandra pulled her legs up around his hips. They kissed and embraced feverishly as he entered her.

It was at moments like this, when they existed for no one but each other, that they could almost believe their love could shelter them from any earthly threat. Then, as they hung on to one another, spent and exhausted, Alexandra opened her eyes and searched the room for something, anything, that was hers, something, anything, that told her she belonged. What she saw instead was the bright moon shining through the window, illuminating the path home.

***

The truce held for the next two weeks. For a while, Alexandra's contentment when she and Amos were together was sufficient to steel her against the doubt she battled during those hours when they were apart. There was nothing, and, she believed, there could be nothing she could bond with in this land other than Amos. He had argued that was enough. But Alexandra couldn't suppress the unrelenting longing that had begun to assert itself day after day—the longing for home. Images of Sharif and Samira and Yusuf were frequent visitors from the recesses of her mind. She coveted those moments and welcomed them. More unnerving, however, was the growing frequency with which she found herself reminiscing about the years in Washington when Noah was her constant companion. Her recollections were of Noah as a boy and Noah as a young man who went away to Stanford. Her consuming curiosity, however, was about Noah the adult, Noah the man she did not know.

***

Just before midnight on the last day of May, the announcement came on the radio that the Israelis had hanged Adolph Eichmann.

Alexandra and Amos had spent the evening in the apartment. She had been anxious to finish a series she was writing about Algerian independence, which everyone seemed to think would be an accomplished fact by midsummer. The *Desert Song* had devoted extensive coverage to the fighting in Algeria, and Alexandra, whose writing was enjoying a growing readership among Israeli Arabs and more than a few Jews, had written several articles on the issue. Her theme was the demise of colonialism, and more than one pair of eyebrows had been raised within Israel's security circles at Alexandra's repeated admonishments that all of the Middle East would remain in turmoil until the last vestiges of European colonialism had been eradicated from the region. Even Bar-Levy had called Amos in to see if he could prevail on Alexandra to tone it down a bit.

"Good riddance," Amos murmured upon hearing the terse radio announcement of Eichmann's execution.

"Where will they bury him?" Alexandra wondered aloud.

"They won't. I understand they're going to cremate the bastard and scatter his ashes over the Mediterranean from an airplane."

"To deny the lunatic fringe a grave to worship?"

"Something like that."

"Smart thinking on someone's part," she replied. "It closes the chapter on Eichmann with finality."

"Oh, I doubt it will ever really be closed," Amos said. "There will be other similar trials as more Nazi war criminals are hunted down. The Eichmann affair must have been terrifying to the others who are in hiding."

"You like that, don't you?"

"You're damn right I do. Don't you?"

"I certainly have no sympathy for war criminals who may still be in hiding, but I question whether Israel is the country that should be bringing them to justice."

"What are you talking about?" he asked impatiently.

"They didn't break any of the laws of Israel. There was no Israel when the crimes were committed."

"So who should try them—Germany?"

Alexandra looked at Amos for a moment as she contemplated his question. "Yes, now that you mention it," she finally answered, "Germany would be a more appropriate prosecutor than Israel."

"You have to be kidding."

"No, not at all. German and other European Jews were victims at the time. Not Israelis. Poland would be appropriate, or France or Hungary or certainly Russia, but not Israel, not in a strict legal sense, anyway."

"Come on, Alexandra," he replied sharply. "Don't give me this *not in a strict legal sense* bullshit. Nationhood is irrelevant. People were victimized and had a right to demand justice. Today those people are Israelis, so Israel brought him to justice. What's wrong with that?"

"Amos, when we Palestinians have tried to redress our grievances, leaders of Israel have said there was never a country called Palestine and, consequently, there is no Palestinian people. Doesn't that logic fly in the face of what you're telling me?"

Amos tried not to show his anger. He believed she had used an issue about which he and every other Israeli had strong, passionate feelings to score a few points in her never-ending debate over Palestine.

"Don't twist what I'm saying, Alexandra. Israel has achieved nationhood and the power to stand tall among any nation on the face of the earth, and that confers certain rights. One of those rights is to enact laws and to enforce those laws. Eichmann was tried under Israeli law, and he was executed under Israeli law. It's that simple."

"God is on the side of the nation with the strongest artillery," she said with irony.

"You're damn right!" he replied, too quickly. Then a moment later he asked, "Who the hell said that?"

"Napoleon," she responded, her expression unchanged.

***

Alexandra's discomfort living in Israel increased with each passing day. Her attention was focused more on what she wasn't than on what she was. She felt alien as she watched Arabs going about their business on the streets of Jerusalem or Jaffa, and she was bothered by the lower standard of living of the Arabs with whom she worked. While Israel's Arabs enjoyed a far more democratic life in Israel than did the Arabs of any other country in the Middle East, they were still second-class citizens in their own land. She longed for the United States with all its contradictions and freedoms. So by the time her father's letter arrived, Alexandra already knew it was time to return home.

Amos watched as Alexandra opened and then read the letter.

June 15, 1962

Dear Alexandra:

We hope this letter finds you well and happy. Everything is good here in America. I have thought for a long time now about what I am about to write. I have hesitated to write these words, but now I believe the time has come to say what is on my mind. Alexandra, we want you to come home. We know better than to demand that you return. You are a woman now, and your mother and I admire and respect your independence, and all that you have become, and all that you have accomplished. We respect you too much to demand anything at all of you. But we both long to hold you and to see you again, and we feel you will understand if we ask that you return. It is a request driven by our love and nothing else.

It is ironic that I who urged, if not demanded, that you go to the Middle East to study and live, now pray for your return. Ironic, because I only wanted you to be near the land of your birth, and now that you are actually in your homeland, I worry more than ever that we will lose you.

I want to see you make your home with us here in America. Once we were Palestinians. Fate turned us into Americans. That's what is so different about America. She allows all newcomers to become Americans. Other countries accept immigrants, but they never really become Frenchmen or Englishmen or Egyptians or Kuwaitis. Only in America do the newcomers truly become Americans. You became an American like the rest of us. I don't want to see you become anything else. You've been away so long now. Your mother and I miss you terribly and we feel we belong together. We have written many times how much we miss you, but have never begged you to return. We wanted you to finish your education, of course. And then, after we learned of your special friendship with Amos, we were reluctant to interfere in your personal life. We wanted to give you the room you needed to make your own decisions. We still feel that way, but we hope you feel your place is with your family. We hope we haven't waited too long to let you know how we feel about this. Your mother and I are not getting any younger.

When we think of all that you have been through, our longing for you just grows stronger. If you share that longing, then please come home to us.

We await word of your return.

Inshallah,

Your loving mother and father

Amos knew, even before she lifted her tear-filled eyes, that Alexandra had finally made up her mind.

"Everything all right?" he asked softly.

Alexandra simply nodded, too gripped by emotion to try to speak.

"Something they wrote has upset you."

"Yes," she whispered.

"What is it, Alexandra?"

"They want me to come home."

His heart ached as he saw the tears run down her cheeks. He knew there were no more words to be summoned to his cause. He understood he was losing her.

"And you?" he asked sympathetically.

"I know they're right," she answered, lifting her eyes to meet his.

Amos nodded and smiled to reassure her that he understood.

That night, as they held one another and kissed and embraced, they felt and tasted each other's tears. It was a night of tender lovemaking, of giving and taking, and of unspoken farewells.

CHAPTER
THIRTY-EIGHT

Noah stood at the corner windows of his Maine Avenue waterfront office and gazed at the construction cranes to the east. They rose from the demolished remains of what had been one of Washington's notorious slums, barely a stone's throw from the nation's Capitol. To the south lay Haines Point, the small peninsula that jutted out into the Potomac from the edge of the city, and beyond the Point, Washington National Airport. His eyes followed an Eastern Airlines Electra as it lazily made its way down the Potomac toward Alexandria and then turned, as he knew it would, to double back and lumber down to a landing at the south end of the airport's main runway.

Noah loved the view from his tenth-floor office. He often stood there, mesmerized by the placid waters of the Potomac. He could see, on the other side of Haines Point, several crew teams from Georgetown University slicing through the water on a practice run. So mesmerized was Noah by their distant, rhythmic efforts that he was oblivious to the door opening behind him.

"Thinking or plotting?" Karen asked, leaning into his office from behind the half-opened door.

Noah turned and smiled as she moved quickly to his side and wrapped her arms around his neck.

"Well, don't you look gorgeous!" he responded as she stepped back to show him the new crisp, white, sleeveless jumpsuit she was wearing.

"You like?" she asked, turning like a model.

He answered with a grin.

"Is this what you do for a living these days, just stand here looking at the view?"

"Isn't it beautiful?" he asked, putting his arm around her waist and pulling her to his side.

"You really love this town, don't you?"

"I can't imagine there's a more beautiful urban view in the entire nation than what we are looking at right now," he said.

"The view isn't too shabby to the west, either," she replied, turning to the window on the right wall of his office, which framed the top half of the Washington Monument.

"Sometimes I feel so exhilarated by everything that's happening, I think I'm going to burst," he said.

"Like what?"

"Like how well my folks and the Salamans are doing with their business and how well things have gone for me ever since the land sales...and us," he quickly added as he saw the smile start to fade from her face.

"I'm glad you were able to squeeze me in," she said, jabbing him in the ribs playfully.

"Fortunes are going to be made here, Karen," he said, ignoring her remark.

"You have that same look on your face you had when I first told you about the plans for the Metro," she replied. "What's this year's vision?"

"See the area to the east of here?" he asked, pointing down Maine Avenue.

"Yeah, looks like a war zone."

"Well, it's all scheduled to be redeveloped."

"So?"

"So, soon people will be moving back into the city. They've spent the last fifteen years running uptown and out to the suburbs."

"Like your folks and the Salamans."

"Exactly. But that former slum is going to turn into a boom town," he said, tilting his head toward the construction cranes to the east.

"Are you planning to buy some more land to sell?"

"No, this time I want to develop something myself."

"Well, you certainly made a lot of money selling land to others who wanted to develop something. Why take on the added risk of development?"

"Because I don't want to just be a land speculator. I want to leave my own mark on this city. I want to build something really special."

"Like what?"

"I'm not sure. Yusuf is doing such exciting work over in Baltimore. He says that eventually they hope to redevelop the entire harbor area, like the stuff they're doing in San Francisco."

"And you want to do something like that here in Washington?"

"Yeah, I think so."

"What would you do? I mean where could you do something so grandiose?"

"I don't know," he shrugged. "I just started thinking about it."

"You're incredible, Noah Greenspan."

"And what makes me so incredible?"

"You're incredible because you are going to do it. I know you, Noah. You just stood here and decided to redevelop a chunk of Washington, and you're going to do it. I know you're going to do it."

"What do you think?"

"I think it's exciting as hell," she said throwing her arms around him once again. "I think I'm going to be married to a brilliant guy."

"It doesn't frighten you?" he asked, pulling her off her feet with his embrace.

"No," she whispered, tilting her face up to kiss him. "Why should it frighten me? Developers make a lot of money," she added in a sultry voice before she kissed him.

"Developers also lose money," he murmured and kissed her on the side of her neck.

"You gonna lose money, Noah?" she asked in a whisper, her interest in the conversation quickly waning.

"Nah," he replied, playfully nibbling at her neck.

"Noah! You leave a mark, and so help me I'll kill you!" she said pulling away from him.

"'Highland Park Girl Kills Washington Developer,'" he said and laughed, easing her back to the floor.

"Please tell me you didn't leave a mark." She extended her neck for his inspection.

"No, I didn't leave a mark, but I'd like to," he teased.

"Noah, you're hopeless."

"But not hapless," he said, tightening his embrace.

"Definitely not hapless," she replied softly as he brought his lips down on hers once again.

***

By June, Noah had optioned property and completed preliminary land-use plans for Potomac Centre, which he thought could be one of the boldest real estate ventures in the city's history. Noah observed, to his amazement, that property along the Potomac and Anacostia Rivers in the southeast portions of the city had for years been viewed as undesirable, marginal land and, as such, was grossly undervalued. He wasted no time moving to assemble and option land along a stretch of Potomac River frontage from east of Fort McNair and the National War College, all the way to the intersection with the Anacostia River, and then on toward the old Navy Yard in southeast Washington.

Noah's plans called for a mixture of luxury high-rise residential development, a square mile of townhouses, an office complex, three hotels, a major regional shopping park, and a large marina. In addition to a major chain supermarket in the center of the shopping park, Noah also provided for two Milk & Honey convenience stores, one at each end of Potomac Centre.

***

Karen was deliriously happy to be engaged. Noah, while less enthusiastic about the seemingly endless planning for the perfect wedding Karen envisioned, felt they were pretty much the perfect couple. Their lovemaking had become wonderfully satisfying, except for those nagging instances at the height of his ecstasy when visions of Alexandra would abruptly intrude into his consciousness.

Karen kept her apartment but used it less and less, preferring to stay with Noah in the townhouse he had purchased at Tiber Island, a new upscale redevelopment project only a few minutes' walk from his Maine Avenue office.

Noah's Potomac Centre project attracted constant publicity. Articles about the young visionary from LeDroit Park began appearing in all of the city's daily papers. By Labor Day, features had also run in the *Boston Globe*, *Chicago Tribune*, and *Los Angeles Times*. Noah enjoyed the excitement surrounding Potomac Centre, but was becoming increasingly uncomfortable with all the publicity it engendered. So far, all he had done was tie up the land and complete preliminary land-use plans, but people were talking about Potomac Centre as though its grand opening was just around the corner.

By fall, Noah had hired a young land-use specialist, Daniel Weingard, newly graduated from Catholic University, to begin laying out more detailed plans for the project. And he soon persuaded Karen to quit her job on the Hill and come work for him as project coordinator for Potomac Centre.

Noah knew it was time to begin thinking about choosing an architect for the project. Architecture was not a field in which he had any particular expertise, although he felt he had a better-than-average appreciation of aesthetic quality. He had toyed briefly with the idea of retaining the firm where Yusuf worked, but ultimately decided against involving them. He knew the firm was relatively small and probably overworked in Baltimore. And then there was the matter of Yusuf's growing profile as an advocate for Palestinian rights. Noah avoided engaging Yusuf in debate on those rare occasions when they were together, but he'd caught himself suppressing feelings of resentment more than once when he read of various lectures Yusuf had given. At this point in their lives, Noah believed his friendship with Yusuf was well served by the distance that separated them and the relative rarity of their contact with each other.

While Noah's confidence in the future of his project couldn't have been stronger, his vision for Potomac Centre was still incomplete. Without the added vision of a good architect, Noah's plans still lacked detail and aesthetic conviction, and this weakness began to haunt him. So the call from Edward Scallion, founder and publisher of the *Urban Architect*, came at an opportune time.

The articulate, self-assured publisher kept the conversation brief and to the point. He had an idea for Potomac Centre and wanted to meet with Noah. They arranged to meet at Hogates the following day at noon.

***

"Hello, Mr. Greenspan, I've saved the corner table for you, as you requested," the hostess said as she greeted Noah.

"Thank you, Martha," Noah replied. "I'm expecting a guest any moment. Will you just send him over to the table whenever he arrives?"

"Mr. Scallion is already here, Mr. Greenspan. He's…um…warming up," she replied, tilting her head toward the bar.

"Really?" He turned toward the bar.

"Yes. He arrived about a half hour ago. Shall I bring him to the table?"

"No, no. I'll get him," Noah replied. "Thanks, Martha."

Noah walked into the dimly lighted lounge, where he spotted the lone customer at the end of the bar. "Mr. Scallion?"

"Ah! The boy wonder, himself!" the man said and got to his feet to greet Noah.

"Hi, I'm really pleased to meet you," Noah replied, studying Scallion as he shook hands with him. Edward Scallion was slightly taller than Noah and about thirty years older. He was trim and well dressed in a light-blue cotton-cord suit and crisply starched buttoned-down white shirt, festooned with a dark-blue, white-striped tie.

Could have been sent from central casting, Noah thought. Scallion had steel-gray eyes and thinning faded-blond hair. His complexion was fair, tinged with bluish-red capillaries across his nose and cheeks. Despite the two empty martini glasses on the bar in front of him, Scallion seemed stone sober and steady on his feet.

"Come on, our table is ready," Noah said pleasantly, leading the way into the dining room.

"So, you're the new L'Enfant everyone is talking about?"

"I'm flattered," Noah replied.

"Don't you consider yourself in the same class as L'Enfant?"

"Hardly," Noah replied, "but I do think we've got an exciting concept."

"But no architecture," Scallion said tauntingly.

"I beg your pardon?"

"You've got no architecture."

Noah squirmed slightly as his mind raced for an appropriate response to the gratuitous and, he thought, impudent remark.

Edward Scallion scrutinized Noah carefully. Then he smiled. "Relax, Greenspan. It's not like I accused you of cheating on your wife. All I said was that you have no architecture for Potomac Centre."

"What makes you so sure?"

"By now everyone would be talking about which architect had the job. You haven't even produced any advanced renderings yet—at least none have run in the press. I've really checked all the press on Potomac Centre—lots of ink, lots of aerial maps, but no renderings."

"So?"

"So, I want to help you, that's all."

"How can you help?"

"Well, first…am I right? My hunch is that you haven't even selected an architect yet. Am I right?"

Noah paused for a moment to consider whether he should divulge anything at all to Edward Scallion, whom he had only known for ten minutes. "Why are we having this conversation, Mr. Scallion? Are you here to recommend an architect?"

"Yes and no."

"Look, I'm sure we're both busy," Noah said, a look of impatience crossing his face.

"I'm going to find you the perfect architect, Mr. Greenspan."

"You're going to find the perfect architect? What…is he hiding somewhere?"

"What I'm going to do, if you agree, is establish an architectural competition for Potomac Centre. What I want to do is deliver to you proposals from the nation's, maybe the world's, most prominent architects."

Noah sat back in his chair and stared at Scallion. "You're serious, aren't you?"

"Damn right, I'm serious. What do you think, I'd put my magazine to work for you just for the fun of it?"

"You're going to use the *Urban Architect* to promote an architectural competition for Potomac Centre?"

"What is there, a goddamned echo in this place?"

"Why would you do that?"

"Because you need the best architect in the country for your project."

"That still doesn't explain why you would do that."

Now it was Scallion's turn to sit back to contemplate Noah. "Because I need the best project in the country for my magazine," he finally said.

"I beg your pardon?"

"A lot of people are talking about Potomac Centre, Mr. Greenspan. It's considered the boldest urban project in the country. We haven't seen this kind of private inner-city investment in years."

"And?"

"And, I want people to turn to *Urban Architect* as the authority on it. When Potomac Centre comes up in conversation, I want people to say, 'Oh, yeah, that's the project *Urban Architect* has been covering.'"

"Why?"

"Because my magazine hasn't excited anyone for a long time, Mr. Greenspan."

"I see," Noah said sympathetically.

"No, you don't see, Mr. Greenspan."

"Call me Noah, please."

"I founded *Urban Architect*, Noah, and for years it was the best damned book of its kind in the country. We had a great niche."

"Urban development? Public works architecture? That sort of thing?"

"Exclusively."

"What happened?"

"The field began to get crowded. We suddenly had to fight for every dollar of advertising revenue and every new subscription."

"But you were the guy with the established magazine. I would think you'd have been able to hold your own."

"You'd think so. I don't know, maybe the competition was younger, hungrier, more creative, more energetic…"

"More sober?" Noah asked softly and sympathetically.

"Yeah, that too," Scallion replied without hesitation.

"So, tell me what you have in mind."

"OK, Noah, here's the pitch," Scallion said, somewhat excitedly. "First, we run a cover feature on the entire project. We do aerial photography, highlighting the area to be developed. The way I see the piece shaping up, the feature is subdivided into sections under headings like Residential High Rise, Townhouses, Hotels, Office

Buildings, Commercial, Marina, and so on. Then we announce an international competition to select one architect to design one of the nation's most exciting urban-development projects. All the rules, all the land-use specifications will be available in the *Urban Architect*. Each month we'll run updates and any modifications to the land-use plan that are made."

"And who judges the proposals?"

"You do. The only thing is that the public announcement of your selection is made in the *Urban Architect*."

"What do I know about judging architectural competition?"

"You know what you like and what you don't like. Besides, I've judged architectural competitions. I'll give you all the help you need."

"Why couldn't I just select a top-flight architect and accomplish the same thing?"

"You could. I mean, that's what everybody else does."

"But?"

"But, you'd never get the interest I'll generate through *Urban Architect*. You'll have architects crawling out of the woodwork, Noah, and you'll get surprises too, because architects you don't even know exist will submit entries."

"And everyone who wants to follow the project will follow what we're doing in the *Urban Architect*."

"That's what's in it for me."

"Are you an alcoholic, Edward?"

"What the hell would you ask a question like that for?" Scallion snapped angrily, blindsided by Noah's abrupt shift in topics.

"Because this project is too important for me to rely on anyone who's apt to let me down," Noah answered, his eyes holding fast to Scallion's glassy stare.

"Yeah. I'm a fucking alcoholic," he finally replied, making no effort to hide the self-disgust in his voice.

"Good. Had you lied about that, that would have been the end of it."

"What are you telling me?"

"Can you go without drinking for the duration of this project, until an architect is selected?"

"You're damn right I can. I've done it before."

"Good. Let's say we'll talk at five o'clock every afternoon, Edward. If you don't take my call or if you sound fat in the tongue when I call, I'll impose a total embargo against *Urban Architect* on news about Potomac Centre. Agreed?"

"Agreed!"

"OK. I like your idea," Noah said, reaching out to shake Edward's hand. "Find me an architect."

"You'll never regret this, Noah," Scallion said, his voice shaking with emotion. "So help me, you'll never regret this."

The waitress asked if she could bring them a drink before lunch.

"Never touch the stuff," Scallion answered.

***

The *Urban Architect* ran the cover story Edward Scallion had promised two months after their meeting at Hogates. It was just as Scallion had said it would be. The cover was a full-page aerial photograph showing the dogleg riverbank where the Anacostia empties into the Potomac. Most of the frontage between Fort McNair and the Washington Navy Yard was shown in a yellow tint. Across the top of the cover, in bold print appeared the heading "POTOMAC CENTRE: AN ARCHITECT'S DREAM."

"Noah! Can you believe it?" Karen asked as she burst into Noah's office excitedly, holding up the magazine for him to see. "We're on the cover of the *Urban Architect*!"

He looked up from his desk and smiled at her. Karen was every bit as excited as he was about Potomac Centre.

"Well, *Life* magazine it ain't," he said with a smile.

"No. But it's a hell of a lot more important to you than *Life* magazine."

"What's it say?"

"Only that you've electrified Washington with your grand vision."

"It says that?"

"Well, almost," she replied. "They've announced the contest."

***

Edward Scallion had delivered everything he'd promised, and he kept on delivering. Month after month the *Urban Architect* kept up a steady drumbeat about Potomac Centre. Scallion began his coverage with what he called ramp-up stories about plans for the project. Architects, city planners, engineers, and urban politicians all over the country were soon talking about Potomac Centre. It became everyone's favorite proof that there was hope for America's decaying urban centers. Interest in the architectural competition quickly transcended the trade press as newspapers and general-interest magazines began to focus on the multimillion-dollar architectural sweepstakes that Noah and Edward Scallion had unleashed.

Karen was besieged with requests for appointments from financiers, advertising agencies, property management firms, equipment suppliers, construction contractors, even agents who wanted to promote Noah as a speaker. Several literary agents called to urge Noah to write a book or authorize them to have a book ghosted for him. They all envisioned a work on the salvation of America's cities. Noah's workday was soon consumed by demands on his time that he simply could not accommodate.

Every afternoon at five thirty, Edward Scallion arrived at Noah's office for a two-hour review of architectural entries. Scallion had been right. Plans began arriving from all over the United States. Several entries from the United Kingdom, the Netherlands, and West Germany found their way to Noah's office, along with several from Japan.

Soon Noah and Scallion found themselves regularly working late into the night in an effort to keep up with the deluge of Potomac Centre drawings flooding Noah's office. Each architect had been instructed by the *Urban Architect* to submit his or her entry in two separate parts. A numbered envelope was bound into the magazine, along with an official mailing label that bore a matching number. The label was to be used for the mailing tube in which each architectural firm would send its conceptual drawings, identified only by a number that corresponded to the number on the label and the envelope. The envelope, with its matching number, was to contain documentation to identify the architect submitting the entry. Securely sealed, the envelope would be included in the tube with the renderings. Upon receipt, the drawings to be considered would be separated from the envelope with the identifying documentation and each filed separately by number. This procedure, Scallion said, would assure that he and Noah would not know whose work they were judging. They would open the numbered envelope identifying the contestant only after they had judged the corresponding entry.

Not surprisingly, calls from all over the world soon tied up the phone lines as architects began pressing for information about the progress of the contest. When would a winner be announced? Were they still in the running? Would finalists have an opportunity to make verbal presentations?

The effort most of the competing architects had committed to Potomac Centre was breathtaking, and Noah was determined to carefully review each and every entry. And while the project would, eventually, benefit from the thousands of speculative man-hours devoted to its design, the contest soon began to take an unanticipated toll on the development schedule Noah had planned. As the schedule slipped, the working capital Noah had provided to bridge the gap between the project's planning phase and the cash flow from early leases began to run dry. Soon, Noah found himself drawing on personal investments to bolster the liquidity of the Potomac Centre project.

Noah's enthusiasm gave way to anxiety. He couldn't remember the last time he had really worried about anything, but now he was worried. He knew Potomac Centre could catapult him into nation-wide prominence—or drop him onto the waste heap of also-rans and has-beens, failed entrepreneurs whose skill and judgment had been inadequate to sustain their dreams and visions.

His anxiety prompted a phone call to Scallion. "Edward, we have to wrap up this contest," Noah said as soon as he got on the line. "I'm getting squeezed to death, and I can't start leasing anything until I have architectural renderings of the project and rough floor plans to show people."

"Everything in its time, Noah. We've set a deadline. We can't begin rushing things now."

"Why can't we just announce that we've found a winner and be done with it?"

"Come on, Noah. You know we can't do that. There are probably dozens of architects who have been working against our deadline. You stop the contest now, and you'll get billed or sued for the time they've expended in good faith and in accordance with the rules we laid out for them. If I were a contestant, I'd sue you myself if you ended this contest one day ahead of schedule."

"I know, I know," Noah sighed. "How many more entries do we have to look at tonight?"

"Three." Scallion answered.

"Three! We'll be here all night," Noah moaned.

"If we're lucky."

"Jesus, Edward, what have we created here anyway?"

"The most successful damn architectural competition in history. That's what we've created here."

"Touché, Edward. See you tonight."

"See you tonight, Noah."

"Edward!" Noah called out just as Scallion was about to hang up.

"Yes, Noah?"

"Thanks. You've been fantastic."

Edward Scallion paused momentarily, too moved to respond.

"Don't thank me, Noah. You've saved more than my magazine. I won't ever forget that."

CHAPTER
THIRTY-NINE

"Barb, get Ed Scallion for me, will you?"

It took only a moment for Noah's secretary to buzz him back with the call.

"Scallion here."

"Ed, it's Noah. Got a minute?"

"I haven't had a spare minute since I met you, Noah, but I'll deny myself the precious time I do have. What's up?"

"I just finished talking with Myron Abrahams at Capital City Bank. He's pressing me to start paying principal on a monthly basis beginning in the fourth quarter."

"Can you manage it?"

"For a while, but I wasn't planning to make any principal payments until the second year. That's the deal I made with the bank."

"Why are they squeezing?"

"He says he's heard that Potomac Centre is falling behind schedule. I told him we're doing fine, and he said he wasn't the least bit worried…"

"But?"

"But the loan committee would feel better if we were paying something on the principal."

"So, what can I do to help?"

"We've got to make a decision on the architecture. We have to get the concept out into the market so we can start preleasing. I have to start generating some cash flow, Ed."

"I got four new sets of plans in today."

"Damn it, Ed, the competition closed last Friday."

"These entries were postmarked on time. We can't very well tell these guys that they missed the deadline, can we? After all, there are thousands of man-hours of work in these damn renderings, Noah."

"We've got plenty we could go with now."

"Which one do you really love, Noah?"

"I don't love any of them, but that doesn't mean we can't go with any of them."

"Look you've reviewed sixty sets of drawings so far; another four won't kill you."

"Are you bringing them with you tonight?"

"Why should this night be different from all other nights?"

Noah laughed. "One Seder and you're dangerous."

"I haven't had so much as a taste of wine since. Can you imagine? When I dream of wine now, it tastes like grape pop."

"I'm sure that would make Mr. Manichewitz very happy."

"Hey, I don't mean to sound ungrateful. It was wonderful being with you guys in your parents' home, Noah. I really loved it."

"They enjoyed having you, Ed. We'll do it again next year. Meanwhile, we have an architect to find. What time do you think you'll get here tonight?"

"How's seven?"

"Six would be better."

"See you at seven, Noah."

***

Scallion arrived a few minutes before seven. Balancing himself on one foot, he pushed open the door to Noah's office with the other. Noah looked up to see the publisher ease the door shut with his rump, his hands too occupied with the four mailing tubes to negotiate the doorknob. Karen, who was standing behind Noah studying renderings from Japan spread out on his desk, burst out laughing as Scallion just let the plans fall to the floor.

"Well, shit, I got them here, didn't I?" Ed said, trying not to step on the tubes.

"Oh, if only the architects who labored so hard to produce those plans could see how carefully they were delivered to the judge's office," Karen said, laughing as she moved around Noah's desk to help Scallion gather up the tubes.

"Let's go over to the conference table," Noah said. "Do we have anything here, Ed?"

"Beats me. I haven't looked at any of them yet."

"I think I really like the stuff from Japan."

"That's been my nightmare," Scallion replied. "Here we have dozens of top American architects competing for a commission on the shores of the Potomac, and you select a Japanese firm."

"I didn't say I selected anyone, I just said I really liked Nakamora's work."

"I know, I know," said Scallion. "Nakamora is world class. No doubt about it."

"Fenner, Wald, and Nolan produced some pretty impressive stuff too," Karen said. "Their work has a really strong federalist theme. The buildings remind me of the governor's mansion at Williamsburg."

"F, W, and N would get my vote at this point," Scallion agreed.

"I like their work," Noah interjected, "but I don't hear bells and whistles when I look at their drawings."

"We're not building a railroad crossing, Noah," Scallion quipped.

"You know what I mean, Ed."

"Look, a massive federalist project in Washington, DC, isn't apt to make bells and whistles go off. I wouldn't worry about the bells and whistles. I'd concentrate on whether it works and whether it's appropriate for Potomac Centre. You want preleases? Then I wouldn't get too avant-garde."

"Probably good advice," Noah conceded. "Let's take another look at Fenner, Wald, and Nolan's entry."

"I'll get the drawings," Karen said. "They're in the file room; be back in a sec."

"Don't sell the F, W, and N idea short, Noah. It's damn good stuff and probably perfect for Washington."

"I'm not negative on the federalist look. I mean how could anybody be negative on federalist in Washington?"

"But?"

"But it's been done before."

"Very funny."

"No, I mean it. Federalist architecture is great if you're looking backward. Why can't we have something that looks forward into our future, something that would stop people in their tracks? You know, something that elicits a 'wow!' when people first see it."

"You're back to bells and whistles."

"Isn't every developer?"

"Probably not. Half of those wows would be from people who loved it, and half would be from people who hated it. This is America's most historical city, Noah. People have a sense of propriety about their architecture."

"Whatever happened to virtuosity?" Noah asked.

"Ask your bankers whether they want virtuosity or popularity."

"Here's Fenner, Wald, and Nolan's vision of Potomac Centre," Karen said, unrolling the plans across the table.

"Damned imposing architecture," Scallion opined.

"Damned boring architecture," Noah murmured under his breath. "This could have been designed two hundred years ago."

"That's the idea, Noah," said Scallion. "Great architecture is ageless."

"I don't call this ageless; I call it old."

"Listen, you guys, if you can't agree on F, W, and N, why not go with Nakamora?" Karen said.

"Karen, you're going to drive me to drink," Scallion moaned.

"Why, are you xenophobic?" she asked.

"No, I'm an alcoholic who is desperately trying to win new friends in the American architectural community. You know how many subscribers I have in Japan?"

"You're hopeless, Scallion," said Noah.

"Let's look at the new stuff," Karen interrupted. "I'm getting the feeling we won't be happy with either the federalist design or the entry from Japan."

"Here's number sixty-one," Scallion said, opening the first tube.

"Do we know who it's from?" Noah asked.

"No, I never open the envelope with the registration forms until we've reacted to the concept."

"No one's going to accuse Edward Scallion of playing politics," Karen said.

"Ha! Don't I wish? You can bet your sweet you-know-what we'll be accused of playing politics, but we'll know the truth, won't we?"

"Hmm, interesting," Noah murmured, as Edward smoothed out the renderings on the table."

"Not bad," Edward agreed. "Not bad at all. Kind of New England waterfront."

"Don't you think it looks a little too resorty?" Karen asked. "It's what I would expect to see in Rehoboth or maybe Ocean City."

"Have you been to Nantucket or anywhere else out on the Cape? This is real Americana."

"No, Ed, I've never been to Boston," she answered.

"I don't think of Washington as being that particular slice of Americana. I don't think we should have a Boston look. We should have a Washington look or a totally new look." she continued.

"Karen's right, Ed. It's not Washington."

"Don't you want to look at more of the detail?"

"No. If the concept isn't right, why bother? Noah answered.

"Number sixty-two," Scallion sighed, making no effort to hide his pique.

"Negative," Noah said as soon as the new set of plans was rolled out. "It's more federalist junk."

"For chrissake, Noah, it's not junk. At least look at the stuff!"

"If we're going to go federalist, we'll go with Fenner, Wald, and Nolan. If we've decided not to do federalist, why waste the time looking?"

"Damn it, we're not picking out handkerchiefs here. Some poor son-of-a-bitch has spent a few hundred hours humoring you, and you dismiss his work with the back of your hand like you were Caesar."

"Hey, Ed, settle down, will you. I'm tired, it's late, and we don't have time to look at concepts we've already rejected just because it was time-consuming to produce them."

"You're showing no respect for the artistry behind these entries. It really pisses me off."

"Come on you guys," Karen intervened. "We're almost there. Let's not become unglued this late in the game."

"I'm sorry, kids," Ed sighed. "I know we're on the homestretch now. I guess the tension's really getting to me."

"You that nervous about who's going to win?" Noah asked.

"Maybe I'm nervous because the whole process is winding down. You don't know what Potomac Centre has meant to me. It's been the most positive thing in my life. I guess I'm afraid to see it end."

"Listen, Ed, our relationship isn't going to end when this project is over. When I need architectural consultation, you're going to be my man. You've been a key part of Potomac Centre. I'm never going to forget that."

Ed smiled and nodded. "Thanks, Noah," he said haltingly, softly. "I don't have to tell you what you guys mean to me."

"Number sixty-three," Noah replied, smiling.

"Uh, right. Number sixty-three it is," Scallion said, pulling the next entry from the tube. "I like the feel of this one," he announced, holding the rolled-up drawings in his hands as though attempting to determine their weight.

"Da, dah!" Karen intoned in imitation of blaring trumpets as Scallion unrolled the drawings along the length of the conference table. There was breathless silence. In full color and unusually meticulous detail, a work of anonymous brilliance radiated seductively from the drawings lying before them.

"Jesus Christ! Will you look at this stuff?" Scallion said, bending over the drawings to scrutinize the entry.

"Now that's what I call architecture," Noah murmured.

"Talk about looking into the future," Karen agreed.

"Look at these elevations!" Scallion slowly turned from one drawing to the next.

"This is exciting!" Noah said under his breath.

"This is what I call Potomac Centre," Karen responded, moving to Noah's side and squeezing his hand.

They spent most of the rest of the evening poring over drawings of an outrageously contemporary Potomac Centre: strong, bold, clean, and uncomplicated lines, incorporating almost perfect symmetry.

"Not a goddamned frill on the whole schematic," Scallion said with admiration. "Every line looks and is structurally functional."

"Yet it makes a strong statement," Karen said. "Look at this view of the main boulevard running along the shoreline. The buildings look so…I don't know…proud, I guess."

"He's using an aluminum encasement over the superstructure, anodized to an absolutely black finish," Scallion said. "The only contrast comes from the aluminum window frames."

"They look like stainless steel," Karen said.

"That's how they would be anodized, Karen—to look like stainless."

"I like the height variations," Noah interrupted. "He's calling for clusters of twelve-story buildings, which is as high as we can go in this crazy town, offset by clusters of these six-story complexes."

"Son of a bitch knows his city planning," Scallion said. "It all hangs together in perfect harmony."

"There's nothing like it in Washington—that's for sure," Karen commented enthusiastically.

"No, there isn't. You'd have to go to Chicago to see anything like this. This stuff is right out of the Illinois Institute of Technology brand of architecture."

"You think you know the architect, Ed?" Noah asked.

"I've got a hunch. This is pure Mies 'less-is-more' van der Rohe. It's either him or someone marching to van der Rohe's drumbeat."

"Well, whoever it is sure knows what he's doing."

"You bet your ass he does, Noah. This is from a biggy, someone at the top of his career with the balls to be adventuresome. Ah, sorry, Karen. Didn't mean to offend you."

"Maybe it's a woman's work," she quipped.

"Well, if it is, she's got balls," Ed replied.

"Chauvinist!"

"OK, you guys, let's not worry about anatomy right now. Ed, who do you think designed this stuff?"

"I think it had to be van der Rohe himself or maybe some shop like a Skidmore, Owings, and Merrill. Noah, you're running in tall cotton here. This is the big leagues."

"So, do we have a winner?" Karen asked, her voice cracking with excitement.

"I think we've got it!" Noah responded, feigning a Rex Harrison English accent.

"By George, we've got it!" Scallion sang out.

"We've got the best plan in the land," Karen chimed in with a passable imitation of Julie Andrews doing Eliza Doolittle.

"In the land…in the land…we've got the best plan in the land!" they all sang out together, intoxicated and giddy from their accomplishment.

"Oh, Christ, this is exciting." Noah laughed, sweeping Karen off her feet.

"Let's see if Ed hit the nail on the head," she said as Noah spun around, holding her tightly in his arms.

"You've all gone daft," Scallion replied, shaking his head.

"C'mon. Let's see who it is."

"OK, here goes," Scallion said, ripping open the registration envelope. "Number sixty-three is…"

"Da dah!" Karen blared again.

"What the hell…?"

Noah and Karen looked at one another quizzically as the smile faded from Scallion's face.

"What is it, Ed?"

"I never heard of the guy. From the letterhead, it looks like it's from a one-man shop. Some guy named Yusuf Salaman did all this stuff."

"What?" Noah whispered in shock.

"Yusuf Salaman!" Karen repeated in disbelief.

"You know him, Noah? There's a note to you clipped to the registration."

"Let me see." Noah snatched the note from Scallion.

"What's it say, Noah?" Karen asked.

Dear Noah:

I hope you like my vision for Potomac Centre. I quit my job to devote full time to this. If it's off the mark— no problem. If it's what you're looking for, let's make some history. Love to Karen,

Yusuf

That was it. A brief note from an old friend attached to a world-class entry.

"Who the fuck is Yusuf Salaman?" Ed Scallion asked as he lowered himself into one of the conference-room chairs.

"He's an old friend," said Noah, still stunned. "He was my best friend when we were kids growing up."

"He's a contemporary of yours?" Scallion asked incredulously.

Noah nodded. "Same age."

"What kind of name is Yusuf Salaman? Is he a Jewish friend?"

Noah laughed. "No, Yusuf is an American Arab who came from Palestine."

"Oh shit! You've got to be kidding."

"No, I'm not kidding. Yusuf was born in Jaffa." Noah glanced over at Karen in time to see her lower her head into her hands.

"Hey, c'mon guys," Noah said. "What's the big deal?"

"What's the big deal?" repeated Scallion, incredulous. "I'll tell you what the big deal is, Noah. We're back to the starting block".

"What the hell are you talking about? Do we have a winning design or don't we?"

"First of all," Scallion replied, "a one-man shop can't handle a job of this magnitude."

"Bullshit! He can job out all the mechanical and electrical and plumbing and anything else he has to sub out, or he can hire draftsmen as he sees fit. All he has to do is oversee the execution of the concept. That's what we're buying."

"Second of all," Scallion continued, ignoring Noah's angry retort, "you bring in an unknown, inexperienced, one-man band to do this, and you'll relegate the most exciting job in the country to bush-league status."

"Listen to me, goddamn it…"

"Third, your financiers are going to scream their heads off. You'll deflate their balloons real quick with a stunt like this."

"Stunt! You accuse me of wanting to pull off a stunt! You're the one who wants to screw the winner!"

"Fourth," Scallion pressed on, "every architect in the country is going to be royally pissed. You put the best in the profession through a rigorous competition and then give the job to a nobody who, just coincidentally, happens to be your old pal. How did you put it? Your best friend?"

"You know damn well I had no idea the best entry was Yusuf's until you opened that registration."

"Fifth, you're going to make Potomac Centre a pariah among many of the prospective Jewish tenants. They'll call this the Arab project."

"Ed, that is absurd! You can't be serious."

"And sixth, if it matters, you'll make the *Urban Architect* a laughing stock. My credibility will be zero, absolutely zero in the profession. I'll be lower than whale's shit in a hole in the bottom of the ocean."

"Because I awarded the job to the architect who submitted the best of the proposals?" Noah asked incredulously.

"Because you ruined your project, because you turned a winner into a loser, because you wasted a lot of people's valuable time in the process, you jerk!"

"Noah…" Karen interrupted in a soft, calm, reasoned voice.

"Yeah?" he replied, thankful for her intercession.

"Please don't do this," she pleaded. "I know Yusuf is your friend, but don't turn your back on all these proposals by awarding the project to him. You should select an architect whose name will be electrifying. People are going to ask, 'Who is Yusuf Salaman?' Is that what you want for Potomac Centre?"

"Yes, damn it! Let them ask," said Noah, stung by her lack of support. "I'll tell them Yusuf Salaman is the brilliant architect who blew away the competition. I think that will be exciting as hell to most people."

"To most people, but not to the ones who really count, Noah," Scallion answered.

"Ed, you know damn well I had no idea Yusuf was submitting an entry, and you know I wouldn't have given him one iota of special consideration just because we were boyhood friends."

"What difference does it make if I believe you, Noah? That doesn't make this Salaman character any more acceptable."

"'Acceptable'? What was our criteria for acceptable? He won, damn it! There is no way I'm going to award this project to a runner-up just because Yusuf is an Arab and an unknown."

"There are plenty of architects who could give you van der Rohe if that's the look you want," Scallion argued.

"But none of them have, Ed. That's the point!"

"But they could."

"What are you suggesting?"

"I'm just pointing out that if someone knew that's what you liked, that's what they would give you. You could have one of the nation's most prominent architects give you van der Rohe. You could have van der Rohe and all the prestige that would go along with a firm like, say, Fenner, Wald, and Nolan."

"Jesus Christ, I can't believe I'm hearing this! What would we say to F, W, and N? We didn't like your federalist look, but we liked another architect's van der Rohe approach. Steal the other guy's idea, and we'll give you the job. Is that what you're suggesting?"

"I'm just saying it's an alternative, that's all."

"It's not an alternative! It's reprehensible. You have the nerve to lecture to me about all the work these people put into their submissions and how I wasn't being respectful of their artistry when I wanted to rush the process, and then you urge me to pull a stunt like this!"

"Listen to me, Noah," Scallion said, a note of urgency in his voice. "I admire your loyalty, your sense of fairness, and all that shit, but the fact is that you have every right to consider the contestant's experience and his depth—you know, his financial strength."

"Yusuf Salaman won this competition hands-down," Noah insisted. "There's no way I'm going to deny him the commission."

"You know, you told me that when you needed architectural help, I would be your man," Scallion said, a deep flush creeping over his face. "You said you'd never forget what I had meant to this project. Well, let me tell you something, Noah Greenspan. You need help right now. Do you know what I've devoted to this project? I put Potomac Centre on the map, Noah. I've made it *the* development project. Every architect in the country knows about Potomac Centre because of the *Urban Architect*. I didn't ask you for anything other then the opportunity to help make this a great success. All I stood to gain from all the months of work and all the space I gave you was the renewal of credibility and respect for the magazine."

"And I gave you that opportunity."

"You dangled it in front of me, but now you're yanking it away. I'll wind up with nothing except my identification with the year's biggest architectural fiasco. You know what you're doing, Noah? You're snatching defeat from the jaws of victory. This project is going to be scorned by the major firms that labored to win your commission. They won't give the *Urban Architect* the sweat off their balls when this gets out, and they won't give me the time of day. I wind up with nothing, Noah. Absolutely nothing!"

"Ed, I'm sorry you feel that way. I think you're dead wrong, but I never suggested that you'd have veto power over my decision."

"I never asked for it. I was confident that your judgment was my guarantee of success. I bet on a boy scout when I thought I was betting on a businessman."

"All the crap about not looking at the registration forms until we had made a judgment about the submission: that's all it was—crap?" Noah snapped.

"It served its purpose. The identity of the contestant never influenced your judgment. I don't think it's fair to call it crap."

"As long as I select someone who's a member of the club, is that it?"

"There's no club."

"Then stop trying to create one," Noah shouted, slamming his hand down on the tabletop with a fury that shocked both Karen and Ed.

"Noah, please," Karen implored.

"Please what?" he snapped. "What is it you want from me? What would make you happy? That I reject Yusuf because it would be the smart political thing do to?"

"You make it all sound so black and white," she replied.

"Isn't it?"

"Ed doesn't think so. He has a lot more experience in these things than you do. There can be a lot of things taken into consideration, just like he said."

"Look, let's not kid one another," Noah said. "There's only one problem here."

"But, Noah, there *is* a problem," Karen went on. "Why would you knowingly select an architect who is totally unknown when you have the world's best fighting for the opportunity to do this project?"

"Because Yusuf Salaman fought them all, and he won. Why is that so hard to understand?"

"May I make a suggestion?" Scallion asked.

"Yeah, sure," Noah replied wearily.

"Well, there is one more entry we haven't even looked at yet. Why are we at each other's throats when the competition isn't even over?"

Noah looked at the remaining tube Scallion had put on one of the chairs at the far end of the conference table. Karen and Scallion exchanged hopeful glances as they waited anxiously for Noah to react.

"Well, let's open it," Noah said.

"Right!" Scallion replied, as he hurried to the end of the table and picked up the tube. "Number sixty-four," he called out, smiling nervously.

When Scallion opened the remaining tube and carefully unrolled its contents, Noah resisted, unsuccessfully, the urge to laugh. Yet another federalist proposal was spread out on the conference table. The silence seemed to suck the energy from Karen and Scallion. They just stood staring down at the drawings as if they were cheap prints displayed alongside the work of a master.

"Well?" Noah asked, arching his eyebrows in anticipation of their capitulation.

"I vote for Fenner, Wald, and Nolan," Scallion whispered.

"You what?"

"I vote for F, W, and N," Scallion repeated nervously.

"Since when was this a committee?" Noah asked.

"You know what I mean. It's just a figure of speech. It's a way of stating an opinion."

"OK, OK," Noah answered, holding up his hands as though to forestall any further explanation.

"It's…it's what I've been saying," Scallion continued, his voice faltering. He looked nervously toward Karen for a moment and then back at Noah. "It's how I gave my opinion on how the competition was going."

"Oh, Ed," Karen whispered. "No."

"You offered an opinion?" Noah said with growing comprehension. "You offered a fucking opinion on how the competition was going?"

Scallion's head jerked erratically as he nodded his response.

"To whom?" Noah shouted. "To whom did you give an opinion? Who the hell had the audacity to ask?"

"Fenner, Wald, and Nolan," Scallion replied in a barely audible voice.

"They called and asked how the competition was going?" Noah asked, incredulous.

"Not exactly."

"Not exactly? What the hell is that supposed to mean?"

"They called to discuss advertising in the *Urban Architect*. They called to discuss a monthly schedule."

"And?"

"And they casually asked how the Potomac Centre project was going."

"How the *project* was going?"

"How the competition was going," Scallion answered quickly.

"And that's when you offered your opinion?"

"Yes, I told them they'd have my vote if it were up to me."

"Jesus Christ! I can't believe I'm hearing this!"

"Ed, how could you?" Karen asked.

"Look, when they called, we all thought F, W, and N had the strongest entry. It was just an opinion."

"It's been your opinion for a long time, hasn't it, Ed?" Noah asked.

"Yes, practically since it was submitted."

"Ever since they dangled an advertising schedule in front of you— that's what you mean to say, isn't it, Ed?"

"That's not fair, Noah," Scallion retorted. "I didn't sell my vote."

"You don't *have* a vote, goddamn it! You don't have a vote to sell, Scallion."

"Noah, please," Karen pleaded.

"Don't 'Noah, please' me Karen! I've been betrayed, Potomac Centre's been betrayed. We've all been betrayed by a goddamned coward trying to feather his own nest."

"Noah, are you crazy?" Karen said, her own voice rising. "Have you gone mad?"

"You're asking me if I've gone mad? I'm the only sane person here."

"I never betrayed you, Noah," Scallion said as he walked toward the door.

"Ed, come back," Karen cried. "He didn't mean what he said."

"I never betrayed you," Scallion repeated, his voice quivering with emotion, as he walked through the door, bowed by the burden of Noah's assault.

Karen turned back to Noah. "Oh, Noah, what have you done?"

"What have *I* done?"

"Do you really think Ed Scallion tried to compromise Potomac Centre? He may have run off at the mouth a little bit. Maybe he tried to make himself a little more important, a little bigger than he is, a little bigger than he's been in a long time. But he didn't sell you or this damned project out."

"He was wrong, Karen," Noah replied, but the anger was gone from his voice.

"So what? So he was wrong. Is that a capital offense?"

Noah stared at her without speaking for a moment. Then he closed his eyes to think, just as she had done only a few minutes earlier. "Go get him, Karen. Make him come back."

"Go get him? Where am I supposed to find him?"

"Look across the street at Hogates. It's the closest bar. That's where he and I first met. Get to him before he does something terrible, Karen."

"Do you think I could keep him from whatever he's about to do? He worships you, Noah. You cut him down, not me."

They stood staring at each other for several moments before Noah bolted from the room.

***

Noah rushed into the dimly lighted lounge but stopped in his tracks as soon as he spotted Scallion. Ed was standing at the end of the bar, contemplating the tumbler full of vodka in front of him. He lifted his head proudly as Noah moved toward him. Then he lifted the drink and held it just a few inches from his lips.

"The only reliable and predictable friend I have," he murmured.

"Ed, don't..."

"To think I almost gave this up for you and that lousy project."

"You did give it up, Ed. Not for me, or for Potomac Centre. You gave it up for Ed Scallion and the *Urban Architect*. You're this close to achieving everything you wanted to accomplish." Noah held up his thumb and forefinger for emphasis. "Are you going to blow it because of my temper tantrum?"

"What I did was wrong, Noah. I know that. I ran off at the mouth because the giants were coming to me. For a brief minute, I felt like I was on top again. But I never compromised you or the project. I'd have never done that, Noah."

"I know, I know," Noah answered in a whisper. "Put down the glass, Ed. Come on back to the office with me. We need you."

"I still think Fenner, Wald, and Nolan is the way to go, Noah."

"I know you do, Ed. But we're going to go with Yusuf Salaman, and I'm counting on you to make him the best known and most exciting young architect in the country."

Scallion paused a moment, and then suddenly, life seemed to sparkle in his eyes again. "Can I drink to the lucky bastard?" Scallion asked, holding his glass up as though he was about to offer a toast.

"Is that what you want to do?"

"More than anything," Scallion answered with a grin.

"Your choice, Ed."

"I kept my word. The contest is over."

"Yes, it is."

"It shouldn't make any difference to you now."

"No, it shouldn't. But it does."

"You don't need me anymore."

"Probably not."

"So?"

"So?"

"What difference does it make to you if I have a drink?"

"You do that, and your life will never be quite the same, and neither will mine. Nor will Karen's. You're going to screw up a lot of people with that drink, Ed."

Ed held the drink for several additional seconds. "What's that Arab kid's name again?"

"Yusuf. Yusuf Salaman," Noah replied with a smile.

"Here's to you, Yusuf!" Scallion said as he raised his drink. Then, without warning, he smiled and tossed the contents of the glass over his shoulder.

"C'mon, Greenspan. We got work to do," he said, going to Noah and putting his arm around the younger man's shoulder.

"I think you might want to put Yusuf's picture on the cover of the *Urban Architect*," Noah said as they walked from the bar.

"I think I might," Scallion replied. "I think I just might."

CHAPTER FORTY

Noah knew Karen was still unhappy with his decision when she finally left the office that night. At eleven o'clock, Scallion offered to drive Karen to her apartment. She glanced at Noah, hoping he'd insist on taking her home.

"Karen, do you mind if Ed takes you home tonight? I'd really like to spend some more time with these drawings."

"No," she lied, "I don't mind."

"You sure?"

"Yes, I'm quite sure!" she answered, a little too abruptly.

"Because if it's a problem…"

"I said I didn't mind!"

"OK, OK. I'll see you in the morning," he replied, leaning forward to kiss her good night.

"Good night, Noah," she said, offering her cheek coolly.

"Karen?"

She turned on her heels and hurried from his office, but not before Noah saw the tears in her eyes.

"Thanks, Ed," he called out to Scallion, who had already walked from the room. He ran his hand through his hair and down the back of his neck to assuage the tension. "Shit!" he murmured under his breath.

But when he walked back to the conference table and glanced down once again at Yusuf's drawings sprawled across the entire length, his mood quickly improved. He imagined the completed Potomac Centre, constructed to Yusuf's architectural specifications.

"All right!" he shouted, slamming his fist into the palm of his hand. "All right!"

He hurried over to his desk, reached for the address book he kept on his credenza, then dialed a number. He waited anxiously for Yusuf to pick up the phone in Baltimore.

"Salaman here," the familiar voice finally answered.

"Yusuf?"

"Himself."

"Yusuf, it's Noah."

"Hey! How are you, Noah?" Yusuf answered.

"I'm great, Yusuf. How about you? Hey, I got your note."

"Yeah?"

Noah tried to picture Yusuf's expression during the long silence he let hang there like a radio transmission that had gone dead.

"So?" Yusuf finally asked.

"So, how about making some history with me?" Noah answered.

"Are you kidding me?"

"Would I kid you about this?"

"You like my work?"

"Yusuf, it's brilliant. I love it."

"I heard there were dozens of entries."

"From all over the world. You ran circles around them all."

"Ah, you're prejudiced."

"Bullshit! I love you, but I couldn't have given you one ounce of advantage over any of the others in a competition like this. Yusuf, I'm telling you, we had no idea whose entries we were looking at. We flipped over your proposal. I nearly passed out when we opened the registration and saw who had won."

"This is unbelievable, Noah, really unbelievable."

"We can't announce anything for another two weeks. That's the advertised date that the winner will be revealed."

"Does that mean it's not final?"

"It means it's not official, but it's final. The competition is closed."

"Did the other judges agree?"

"I'm the only judge."

"Did the others agree?"

"You mean Scallion?"

"Yes, and Karen."

"They thought the plans were fantastic the minute they saw them," Noah answered, trying to circumnavigate Yusuf's question.

"What did they say when they realized whose work it was?"

"Who the hell remembers what they said. They thought the work was brilliant. That's all that matters."

Yusuf paused to consider Noah's response. "Something you're not telling me?"

"Nothing that matters," Noah answered, smiling at Yusuf's perceptiveness.

"How do you think the news will be received?" Yusuf asked.

"Who gives a shit? What I care about is Potomac Centre, Yusuf, and you've produced architecture that will make this project the most exciting urban development in the whole damn country."

"You've got balls, Noah."

"That's funny. That's what Ed Scallion said about you for proposing Mace-van-der-something-type of architecture for Potomac Centre."

"It's Mies, Noah, not Mace. Mies van der Rohe. He's the architect who influenced me."

"Right! That's the guy."

"You know I quit my job to work on the proposal?"

"Yeah, it was in your note. I'm awfully glad you did. I was hesitant to call you this late, but I figured it was worth waking you up for."

"You didn't wake me. I was just sitting here with an old friend of yours. We've been talking all night."

"No kidding."

"Yeah. Here, I'll let you say hello."

Noah tried to remember which of their mutual friends was living in Baltimore, but he drew a blank.

"Hi, Noah."

The voice on the phone sent his head reeling, his heart racing.

"Alexandra? Alexandra, is that you?"

"Yes, it's me, Mr. Tycoon. How are you?"

"My God, am I glad to hear your voice!"

"It's wonderful to hear your voice too."

"When did you get in?"

"This evening. I'm spending the night here with Yusuf."

"Oh, Alexandra," he said, "I can't tell you how happy I am that you're home. How long will you be here? I mean, are you staying?"

"I'm here for keeps. They've offered me a job at the *Star*. I start next week."

"God!" he whispered, his voice cracking with emotion. "When will I see you?"

"I'll be in Washington tomorrow afternoon. I'd like to see you… and Karen, of course."

Karen. Yes, well, he'd think about that later. Noah squeezed his eyes shut as though that would block the words on the tip of his tongue, the words he didn't dare utter. Christ, how he wanted to say it…to say, *I love you, Alexandra.*

"Noah, are you there?"

"Yes, yes, I'm here. I was just collecting my thoughts. So help me, if it weren't so late, I'd drive to Baltimore to see you."

"I'll call you when I get to Washington."

"I can't wait to see you, Alexandra."

"Same here. Bye, Noah."

Noah sucked in a deep breath as his shaking hand replaced the receiver.

Jesus Christ, I'm a wreck, he thought. *She's back in my life for three minutes, and I'm a goddamned wreck.*

***

Noah lay staring at the ceiling of his bedroom most of the night. Old memories floated endlessly and effortlessly through his mind.

Recollection soon gave way to fantasy as he tried to imagine just how much Alexandra might have changed since he had last seen her.

It was four thirty when he finally got out of bed and walked into the kitchen to find something cold to drink. The refrigerator was empty except for a six-pack of beer. Frustrated, he pushed the door shut and started to make his way back to the bedroom. When he saw the bright moonlight streaming into the apartment, he slid open the door and stepped onto the brick patio. He looked up at the full moon and smiled, recalling the pact he and Alexandra had made so long ago. There had never come a time when Noah could look at the moon without thinking of Alexandra, and now she was here again.

**

Noah went to work the next morning charged with anticipation. For the first time in nearly a year, something other than Potomac Centre dominated his thinking. Soon he would hear Alexandra's voice again. Soon he would see her, and he was as nervous as a teenager on the eve of his first date.

Karen was standing by the door to her office when he arrived at work. How complicated his life had become overnight.

"Hi, Karen," he said with a smile as soon as he entered the room. "Was Ed OK when he took you home last night?"

"Oh, he's fine. Whatever you said to him at Hogates proved to be the perfect medicine."

"It was a close call," he replied, kissing her on the cheek. "Another minute and he'd have been in the sauce. I don't think I'd ever be able to forgive myself if I thought I had driven him to drink."

"Good, then you won't want to drive me to drink, either," she answered with a coy smile.

"That would be different," he said with a laugh. "You can hold your liquor better than Scallion."

"Seriously, Noah, can we talk?"

"Since when can't we talk? Come on in," he said, holding the door to his office open for her.

"I spoke with my father last night. He was calling to say hi just as I came in."

"Everything well with your folks?" He was pretty sure she'd rushed home to call her father for advice.

"Yeah, they're great. He asked about you and the project and was thrilled when I told him the competition was finally over."

"Did you tell him about Yusuf?"

"Yes, I did. He said you have real guts."

"Well, at least my courage is being described in terms of higher anatomy."

"That's what I told him too. He said he'd have told you that you have real balls, but he could only bring himself to tell me you had real guts."

Noah laughed.

"Noah, he did say something I thought you should know."

"And that is?"

"Can I pour you some coffee?"

"Thanks," he said, leaning back against the edge of the conference table.

"Daddy knows David Wald."

"Who's David Wald?"

"David Wald of Fenner, Wald, and Nolan," she replied, handing him a cup of black French-blend coffee.

"Oh, *that* David Wald. So, your dad thinks I should give the commission to F, W, and N."

"Daddy wouldn't ever push himself into your business that way. You know that."

"But he does think F, W, and N should get the work, right?"

"Well, he said David Wald belongs to our temple in Highland Park. He said he's the salt of the earth and that he headed up the Israel Bond Drive in the northern suburbs of Chicago."

"Small world," Noah said with growing irritation.

"Daddy says David Wald told him you were brilliant."

"I'm flattered."

"He said all the young architects in the firm want to work on Potomac Centre. Mr. Wald told Daddy the firm wants the Potomac Centre job more than any project in the country. Isn't that incredible, Noah?"

Noah nodded, pausing to sip his coffee. "Incredible," he agreed. "It's the job Yusuf Salaman wants more than any other project in the country, too. He even quit his job to work on his proposal. It's the best proposal we received, and that's why he's getting the commission." Noah spoke calmly, evenly, and with finality, then took another sip of coffee.

"I have to hand it to you, Noah. You have a way of using language like a knife. You cut off discussion just by the way you express yourself."

"Karen, I didn't say anything to cut you off," he objected. "This was resolved last night. There's nothing to cut off because there's nothing left to debate."

"Then you'd better tell me to shut up because I'm going to debate your lousy judgment until you do."

"I'm not going to tell you to shut up, but I wouldn't count on me changing my mind either."

"Noah, you have an architect like David Wald, whose firm is one of the most respected in the country, eager to be of service to you."

"I'm really flattered, Karen. I really mean that, but that's no reason to award them a job when someone else's proposal was superior to theirs."

"'Superior' is totally subjective. Who's to say which proposal was superior?"

"I am! That's who's to say. Me!" he answered, less calmly and less evenly. "And, to keep the record straight, you and Scallion also declared Yusuf's work to be the superior proposal, until you realized who the winning architect was."

"Goddamn it, don't you dare accuse me of being motivated by prejudice!"

"Oh, come off it, Karen. What the hell else is this all about?"

"It's about doing what's best for Potomac Centre, that's what it's all about! David Wald is at the pinnacle. He's labored year after year for his firm and, yes, for Israel too. And I say that's good for Potomac Centre. How many of your commercial and residential tenants will be Jews, Noah? Fifteen percent? Twenty percent? How many of the customers you're counting on to come here to shop will be Jews? Twenty percent? Twenty-five percent? Tell me, Noah, how many will be Arabs? This has nothing to do with prejudice, but it has everything to do with common sense."

Noah placed his cup and saucer on the conference table with exaggerated care. He paused and slowly drew in a deep breath before responding. "That twisted logic won't cut it, Karen. I've seen it work its misery before. This project isn't going to be victimized by that same sick logic."

Karen stiffened her back, stung by his rebuke. "Damn you, Noah Greenspan," she said between teeth clenched in anger. "A man like David Wald claws his way to the top of a profession where there were few Jews a generation ago and opens the doors for thousands of others, and you—you! a fellow Jew!—you turn your back on him because you say he didn't quite measure up. You're upset with me because I would give an edge—an *edge*, goddamn it—to a David Wald over a Yusuf Salaman? How in the hell do you think we've made it to the twentieth century, Noah? We've looked out for one another when we could."

"Karen, I may be wrong, but I'd be willing to bet that if David Wald is half the man you say he is, he'd be horrified by what you're suggesting."

"Would you be willing to meet David Wald? I mean, wouldn't it be reasonable to interview the two finalists?"

"There aren't two finalists, Karen. There's a winner. It's Yusuf Salaman."

"You're going to ruin this project!" she cried in frustration. "You could guarantee the Potomac Centre's success, have one of the nation's leading architects identified with you, and help one of your own—all at the same time. Instead, you're going to achieve none of the above. Just what kind of decision do you think you're making, Noah?"

"The right decision, Karen. I thought you could understand that."

"Would you be so damn sanctimonious about reconsidering your decision if it was anyone else but Yusuf? OK, so we all liked his work—"

"We all loved his work," Noah corrected her.

"OK, we all loved his work. We loved it, but then we realized he was an architect who brought nothing to the project…"

"Except the winning proposal."

"We all realized that he was a one-man shop, an unknown, and, yes, someone who could alienate prospective tenants and prospective customers. Now I ask you, if it were anyone but Yusuf Salaman, would you stick to your initial decision this way?"

"I don't know. I hope so. I'd like to think so."

"I don't think you would, Noah. I think you're compromising for Yusuf's sake. I don't think you'd be doing this if it were anyone other than Yusuf, or if Yusuf was anyone other than Alexandra's brother."

As soon as the words were out of her mouth, Karen wished she could take them back. But too late, she instead stood firm and stared defiantly at Noah, her words seeming to hang visibly in the air between them.

"Karen," Noah said quietly, carefully, "let's leave Alexandra out of this."

"Touch a sensitive nerve, Noah?"

"Drop it, Karen."

"How can I drop it, Noah? Christ, what would happen to your judgment if she were here instead of halfway around the world?"

"My judgment is just fine," he replied, almost without thinking, "and she *is* here."

"What?" The word escaped as though knocked out of Karen's body by a physical blow.

"Alexandra's home, Karen. She arrived in Baltimore yesterday. I called Yusuf last night to tell him he had won, and she was there."

"You called Yusuf already?"

"Yes."

"And you spoke to Alexandra?"

"She was spending the night at her brother's. She was there. We spoke."

"Oh God," Karen whispered.

"Karen, don't get carried away. It's nothing for you to get upset about."

"That's what this is all about?" she said, dazed, addressing no one in particular.

"Karen, that's ridiculous."

"She's back? Yusuf is to be the architect, and Alexandra's back? Is that what you're telling me?"

Noah nodded. "Yes, I guess so. Yusuf is going to be the architect, and Alexandra is home. So what?"

"So, suddenly everything is different, that's what."

"Nothing's different."

"Noah, look me in the eye and tell me how you felt when you heard Alexandra's voice on the phone. Tell me you hung up and nothing was different."

"What do you want me to tell you—that I felt nothing? I can't do that. Alexandra was so much of my life for so long, Karen. Of course I felt something."

"What was it, Noah? What would you call what you felt?"

"Karen, please…"

"Who was on your mind last night, Noah? Who were you thinking about when you went to bed last night and when you woke up this morning?"

"I wasn't thinking about anyone," he answered, but he could not look at her as he spoke the words.

"I don't believe you," she said. "Goddamn it! I don't know if I want to go through life wondering who my husband is thinking about! How do you think it makes me feel, hearing that you still feel love for someone else? I could handle it when Alexandra was halfway around the world. It didn't make much difference then, but now…"

"It doesn't make any difference now, either!" he insisted. He looked into her eyes and saw that the anger was gone, replaced by only fear and pain.

"Maybe it makes a difference to me," she said softly, tears blurring her vision.

"OK, you want to know how I felt? It took my breath away when I heard her voice. Yes, I was up for hours last night reminiscing. But now you and I are together. We're planning to get married. I'm still planning to marry a girl named Karen Rothschild and not a girl named Alexandra Salaman. Isn't that what matters?"

"It's not that simple, Noah."

"I think it is that simple."

"No. No, it isn't. I'll always know you think about her. I'll just never know when. Maybe it will be when you're alone or whenever you've spent time with Yusuf, which will be all the time now, or maybe it will be when you and I are making love. Sometimes people meet people after they're married and life gets complicated this way, but I don't know if I want to begin a marriage when all this complication is already there. I don't know why anyone would do that."

"Karen, don't do this. Don't let this get out of hand."

"I'm going back to my apartment, Noah. I want to be alone for a while. I have some thinking to do."

"Karen…" he pleaded, reaching out to her.

"No!" She held up her hands to block his attempted embrace. "Just let me be…just leave me alone."

Noah stopped, his arms suspended in midair for a moment. Then he lowered them, aborting an embrace he was sure she craved and needed as much as he did. Shaking her head, tears streaking down her cheeks, Karen turned and walked out of his office.

Noah stood alone for several moments, his eyes closed as he tried to collect his thoughts. Then he walked into her office to find her, but the room was empty. Noah started for the door to go after Karen only to be diverted by the ringing of the phone.

"Greenspan," Noah answered curtly.

"Oh, Noah. Didn't expect you to answer the phone. It's Abrahams here at the bank."

"Oh, hi, Myron. My receptionist isn't in yet. What's up?"

"Nothing really. We have a loan committee meeting this morning, and I thought I would give our directors a little update. Anything new you'd like me to report?"

"Well, things are really going well. We've made a lot of progress."

"I understand the architectural competition has closed. Anything to announce?"

"Formal announcement will be made the first of the month..."

Noah paused, but the banker just seemed to hang on in anticipation of what was coming next.

"I mean nothing's official..."

"But you've made your selection?"

"You understand, nothing is official until the first of the month. We don't want word out on the street until we make an announcement in the magazine."

"Noah, I'm not calling from the street. I'm your banker. You do trust your banker, don't you?"

Noah wasn't sure he detected any humor in Abrahams's voice.

"Of course I trust my banker. I was just explaining why we haven't said anything yet."

"I really think it would be very helpful for our directors to know exactly where the project stands. This is no time to be coy. Potomac Centre is the largest commitment we have on our books."

"Of course, I understand. I'm not being coy. I have no problem sharing the decision with the bank. I just want everyone to know how important confidentiality is."

"Noah, we're bankers. Confidentiality is the hallmark of our business."

"OK, OK," Noah replied. "Well, as you can imagine, the competition was really intense. We had sixty-four entries from all over the world, including many of the leading architectural firms in the profession. We studied each entry, looking for strength of concept, suitability for the project, and best overall integrated design."

"And the winner is…?"

"We selected a brilliant young architect named Yusuf Salaman," Noah replied with all the enthusiasm he could muster.

"Great! Who's he with?"

"I beg your pardon?" Noah asked, cringing at his own response.

"Noah, you don't expect me to recognize individual architects, do you? Which firm is this fellow with?"

Oh shit, Noah thought. "He's his own firm. He's not with some big corporate architect."

"What's his name?" the banker asked again.

"Salaman. Yusuf Salaman."

"What's he done?" Abrahams asked, skepticism replacing the enthusiasm he'd expressed only moments earlier.

"He's done a lot of conceptual work on the Baltimore harbor area," Noah replied.

"Baltimore? What the hell is going on there?"

"Plenty. It's going to be one of the most exciting urban developments in the country."

"Noah, what buildings or developments can we tell our directors this architect has done? You know what I need. They'll want to feel the excitement of his other accomplishments."

"They'll feel the excitement of his vision for Potomac Centre. That's what we based our decision on. We didn't give any weight to past accomplishments. Who gives a damn about past accomplishments? Yusuf Salaman executed a brilliant plan for Potomac Centre. Tell your directors they'll be thrilled with the project they've helped make possible."

"Sure, sure. Don't get excited. Architectural selection is always one of the milestones in a project like this. Everyone always waits for word about the architect who's been selected. You know that."

"Well, we've got ourselves a brilliant architect."

"Had you ever heard of him before?"

Noah's mind raced as he tried to avoid the tortuous turn he knew the conversation had taken.

"Yes, I've heard of him. I mean, I've known him for a long time."

"Ah, good! That's encouraging. That's what I need. Go on."

Trapped, Noah thought. "What I mean is, I grew up with Yusuf Salaman." He knew his response sounded more like a confession than mere candor. "We were both from the same neighborhood."

"He grew up over by Griffith Stadium? Is that what you're telling me?"

"Yes, that's what I'm telling you. His folks had a grocery store down the street from our place."

"And you selected your friend from the neighborhood to do the architecture?"

"Myron, we selected the winning proposal in a blind competition. We had no way of knowing it was an old acquaintance until after we had appraised his entry."

Noah winced as he heard the heavy sigh on the other end of the line. "What's this fellow's name again?"

"Salaman. Yusuf Salaman."

"Yusuf? What kind of a name is Yusuf?"

"It's a first name," Noah answered sarcastically.

"Please. This is no time for humor."

"You want to ask me about Yusuf Salaman's architecture, fine. If you've got other things on your mind, you'll have to go elsewhere for information. Our only concern is architecture. Yusuf Salaman's designs were superior, his detail was exceptional, and his grasp of the project was light-years ahead of the competition. That should make your directors ecstatic."

"A smooth project that leases quickly without a lot of waves—that's what makes our directors ecstatic, Noah."

"Myron, I really have a full day ahead. Is there anything else I can help you with?" Noah asked.

"No. No, I suppose not. This has been, ah, interesting. I wish I could say it had been helpful."

Shit! Noah thought as he hung up the phone. *Shit*!

***

Noah sat alone at his corner table at Hogates, picking at a tuna salad. He had called Karen several times, but she either wasn't answering her phone or was not at her apartment. He decided he would run over to her place as soon as he left the office that afternoon.

When he returned to the office, Barb held up an envelope. "Karen left this for you," she said.

"She was here looking for me?"

"She came in and said she knew you'd be at lunch," his secretary said, handing him the envelope. "She asked me to give this to you."

Noah tore open the sealed flap and pulled Karen's note from the envelope as he walked into his office and closed the door. He sat down and leaned back in his chair and concentrated on the neat, familiar handwriting before him.

Dear Noah:

By the time you read these words, I'll be on my way home to Highland Park for a while. I think we both need some time and distance. I know I do.

You were right. You always have been very honest with me. You have told me several times that you'd probably always have strong feelings for Alexandra but that you loved me in a different kind of way. You said you knew I was more right for you than she was. I remember that, and I don't question your love for me. What I do question is whether I'm strong enough or confident enough to share you with anyone else. I don't know how else to say it, but I feel insecure every time I think of Alexandra. I think I always will. I don't know if I can handle that or whether I should even try. I'm so afraid I'll be miserable and that I'll make you miserable too. I think we're both stuck with some very difficult realities and we have some serious thinking to do. At least I do. I have to sort all this out. That's what I'm going to try to do for the next few days.

Regarding Potomac Centre, I feel as strongly as ever that you are making a terrible mistake. I'm sick over the whole thing. Not just because I disagree so strongly with you, but also because my enthusiasm for Potomac Centre seems to be a casualty of all the arguing. As I write this note, I feel like I really don't give a damn what happens to the project, and I can't tell you how sad that makes me.

I pray that a little time and distance will help everything get back on course with us.

I love you, Noah.

Karen

Noah folded the letter and slipped it into the top center drawer of his desk. He glanced at his watch and considered trying to get to the airport in time to keep her from boarding her plane for Chicago.

Barb!" he called.

"Yes, Noah," Barb answered, hurrying to the door of his office.

"How long ago did Karen come by?"

"About an hour and a half ago."

"Did you tell her I was over at Hogates?"

"She knew you were there. She said she had been sitting in a cab across the street waiting for you to go to lunch."

"Thanks," he said softly. "Find out when the last flight left for Chicago and when the next flight departs."

"She was booked on a two o'clock flight, Noah. She told me she had to hurry."

Noah glanced down at his watch. It was two-twenty.

"OK," he said with a feeble smile.

"Sorry, Noah."

"Yeah," he whispered, "me too."

CHAPTER
FORTY-ONE

Noah considered booking the first flight to Chicago in order to talk to Karen as soon as possible, but he quickly dropped the idea. Her assessment of their problems was, he decided, right on the mark. She had raised these questions before, and he could no more look her in the eye and tell her what she needed to hear now than he could when they'd argued about Alexandra at Stanford just before graduation. He was anxious to talk to Karen and hoped she would place the first call. He would call her if necessary, but not before he was ready to turn in for the evening. He wanted to give her as much time as possible to sort out her thinking that first night away.

It was nearly five o'clock when Barb stuck her head in to tell him he had a long-distance call.

Whew, he thought with a sigh, relieved that Karen had apparently decided to break the ice.

"I'm going," Barb said with a wave of her hand.

"See you in the morning," he replied, reaching for the phone.

But a man's voice was on the other end. "This is Mark Caztaneo. I'm the architecture reporter for the *New York Times.* How are you today?"

"Fine," Noah said, furious that Barb hadn't told him who had been holding.

"I just wanted to confirm information we had about your architectural selection for Potomac Centre."

"You what?"

"I'm confirming your choice of Yusuf Salaman—am I pronouncing the name right?—as the architect for Potomac Centre."

"The announcement is scheduled to be made on the first of the month," Noah protested.

"Well, once it's out, we have an obligation to our readers. All we need to know is whether or not it's accurate."

"Nothing is official until the selection is announced in the *Urban Architect.*"

"By the way, did I get the name right? The pronunciation, that is."

"What are you uncertain about?"

"Is it Salaman with an *a* or is it Solomon with an *o*?"

"It's Salaman with an *a*," Noah replied.

"So the information is accurate?"

Goddamn it, Noah thought, angry that he had let himself be manipulated by the reporter. "Look, Mr. Caztaneo, it would be very premature to have anything to say about this. The announcement belongs to the *Urban Architect!*"

"Mr. Greenspan, I think you should know that we're running a story about your bank's disappointment with your choice of Yusuf Salaman as the winning architect."

"Who said they were disappointed?"

"Sorry, I can't say. They spoke on background only, you know, not for attribution."

"Are you telling me the bank called to tell you they weren't happy?"

"Not exactly. We have our contacts with the bank. We keep in touch when we're interested in something on the agenda."

"You knock Potomac Centre, and so help me I'll sue you for libel."

"Mr. Greenspan, may I give you some very old but very sound advice?"

"I'm listening."

"Don't pick a fight with anyone who buys ink by the barrel."

"What?"

"Mr. Greenspan, your bank thinks your choice isn't worth, as John Nance Garner once said, 'a bucket full of warm piss.' I've spoken with a very reliable source at the bank who confirms that, and, I'm quoting, the bank is profoundly disappointed with the architectural selection for Potomac Centre."

"That's the bank's position?"

"No, their position is that they don't comment on such things."

"But someone told you they were disappointed?"

"Profoundly disappointed is the term we're using. Would you like to comment?"

"The winner won't be announced until the first of the month."

"Mr. Greenspan, you don't want to say that. I shouldn't be putting words in your mouth, but that's worse than saying nothing."

"What do you expect me to say?"

"I'd defend the hell out of my selection. What the hell do those bozos at the bank know about good architecture? I bet they haven't even seen the winner's submission."

"Goddamn it, you're right! They haven't seen the first drawing. What the hell are they profoundly disappointed about?"

"I don't know. You tell me."

The interview with the *New York Times* took nearly half an hour and left Noah exhausted. Controversy was the last thing he wanted, and it was certainly the last thing anyone at the bank should have wanted.

Noah called Myron Abrahams as soon as he finished talking to Caztaneo.

"This is Noah Greenspan, Myron. I'm profoundly disappointed in the bank," Noah said, choosing his words very carefully.

"What do you mean?"

"Some idiot of a banker told the *New York Times* that the bank was 'profoundly disappointed' in the selection of Yusuf Salaman as architect for Potomac Centre."

"That's unfortunate."

"Unfortunate! You call that unfortunate? I should have never given you the information about the architect. You assured me that—how did you put it?—oh, yes, 'Confidentiality is the hallmark of banking.' You are untrustworthy!"

"Surely you know the bank doesn't condone this. We have as big a vested interest in the success of Potomac Centre as you do, Noah."

"Someone on your loan committee has a big mouth, Myron, and I have to give real consideration as to whether Capital City is sophisticated enough for my business."

"Noah, a secretary could have leaked this."

"Secretaries don't express *profound disappointment*, Myron. You've got a director with a big mouth and an empty head."

"What do you want me to say?"

"I want the bank to apologize and to deny that the person who spoke to the *Times* was speaking for the entire loan committee."

"Well, we can certainly express regret that the confidentiality of the loan committee has been breached."

"I want the denial too!"

"I don't think we can do that, Noah."

"Why the hell not?"

"Because that's exactly how the committee felt, and the *Times* reporter obviously knows that. He'll make a fool of us and of you."

"The entire committee?"

"I'm afraid so. They think you've made a terrible choice, Noah. I was going to try to get you to change your mind, but now I'm afraid that's impossible. The public would think we were ganging up on Mr. Salaman."

"I guess you know you haven't made the job of preleasing the property any easier," Noah said.

"We didn't select the architect, Noah."

"What's that supposed to mean?"

"Your selection of Mr. Salaman is what's causing the controversy. It's unfortunate, but the *Times* is only reporting the controversy. If they hadn't gotten it from someone at the bank, they would have gotten it later from someone else. I'm afraid it's a controversy of your making, Noah. If you want to find someone to vent your spleen on, I suggest you look in the mirror."

"Good-bye, Myron," Noah said, hanging up abruptly. He took a deep breath and tried to calm his frayed nerves. He couldn't remember a more miserable day.

He sat at his desk for about fifteen minutes, head in hand, too numb to think. Then he reached over and picked up his phone again.

"Ed," he said as soon as he heard the familiar voice on the other end.

"Hi, Noah. I bet you're having a shitty day."

Noah smiled for the first time since his conversation with Karen early that morning. "You do get right to the point, don't you, Ed?"

"Why dick around?"

"The shit's about to hit the fan," Noah said.

"Yeah, I know. Caztaneo spoke to me right after he talked to you."

"Do we have a disaster on our hands?"

"Hell no. I don't think we've got a pimple on the ass of an elephant."

"You don't think the publicity is going to hurt?"

"Nah."

"Are you serious?"

"Listen, those bankers are going to look like a bunch of Neanderthals."

"They're going to be quoted as saying they're profoundly disappointed with our choice of architect."

"You're not surprised, are you?"

"I didn't expect to read about it in the *New York Times* two weeks before we announced," Noah said with more than a touch of bitterness. "What did you tell Caztaneo?"

"I told him if we left these things up to the bankers, the Centre would look like the Federal Reserve Building."

"You said that?"

"Yeah, and he's going to use it, too. Noah, I also told him I hadn't seen bolder or more innovative architecture since before the war."

"Ed, thanks. I don't know what to say."

"Hell, it's true. I never said the selection wasn't bold or innovative. I just said using Salaman was dumb."

"You know, Karen left…for a while."

"I know. She called me from the airport. If you let her get away, Noah, you get my vote for the dumbest primate ever to come down from the trees."

"Ed, anyone ever tell you that you speak with real clarity?"

"Don't sweat the *New York Times* piece, Noah. You'll look good. It's the bank that will look incompetent. It doesn't mean you're not going to have some problems—you are. But this will turn out to be your round."

"You really think so?"

"Yep, I really do."

Noah started to thank Scallion again when the other line began ringing. "Ed, I've got to go. The other phone's ringing, and I'm here alone."

He recognized Alexandra's voice immediately.

"You're here!" he said after they'd exchanged greetings. "Great! Where can we meet? How about Hogates? Thirty minutes?"

"Give me an hour," Alexandra said, laughing at his eagerness. "I'm having some delicious time with Mom and Dad, and I can't bear to break it off just yet—even for you."

Noah smiled at Alexandra's turn of phrase. How many times had she referred to him or to their time together as delicious? "We've waited this long, I guess an extra half hour won't matter," he said without conviction. If he could have willed her into the room that instant, it would not have been soon enough to see her again.

"Maybe you'd better wear a yellow carnation or something so I'll be sure to recognize you," she said.

"I'll wear a white *kaffiyeh* with a black *igal.*"

"Hah!" she laughed. "Noah of Arabia."

"Well, that was the general neighborhood of my original namesake."

"See you soon, Noah."

"Bye," he said as he hung up the phone and leaned back in his chair. *She's back*, he thought. *Alexandra's really back.*

At ten to six, Noah headed out the door, trying to keep himself from running to meet Alexandra. Had he waited just another minute or so, he would have heard the phone ring and received Karen's troubled call.

***

Alexandra stood watching Noah from the darkened lounge where he couldn't see her. She had arrived a few minutes early and gone into the lounge for a glass of water. As she headed back to the reception area, Noah walked in, and she stopped to study him for a moment. She smiled at the self-assured, successful young entrepreneur who glanced down at his watch. He turned to the mirror on the wall behind the receptionist's stand, adjusted his tie, and ran his fingers carefully through his hair just below the part. Then, through the mirror, he saw her standing there smiling at him. For a moment, he just froze, staring at her reflection.

"Hi, Noah," she said slowly and walked toward him.

Noah's mouth suddenly went dry, and for an instant he was a boy at McKinley Tech again.

"Alexandra," he whispered as he turned to face her. "My God, it's really you."

"Oh, Noah, I'm so happy to see you," she said, taking the final step into his embrace. For several moments they held on to each other, joyously hugging, half crying, afraid to let go.

"Let me look at you," he finally said, taking her by the shoulders and holding her at arm's length. She was even more beautiful than his last memory of her.

Noah asked the hostess for a corner table at the rear of the restaurant where they would enjoy some privacy. Alexandra reached over and squeezed his hand as they made their way to the table.

"I can't believe you're really here," he said as soon as they were seated. "I mean, I knew you'd be back someday, but I never expected..."

"Well, here I am," she said, adding after a slight pause, "It was time, Noah. It's been five years."

"There's so much to catch up on."

"Who's going to go first?" she asked. "I want to hear all about your life. Mom and Dad have filled me in on all your successes, but I want to hear the details from you."

"Well, I should let their version stand. It has to be more exciting than the truth."

"Hardly. Dad says you're the rising star here in Washington."

"Let's not talk about business just yet. We have all night for that."

"All night?" she said, raising one eyebrow suggestively.

"We're going to talk until one or the other of us passes out."

"Oh, I see," she replied with a coy smile. "I wasn't sure what you intended."

"Don't tempt me, Alexandra."

"Are you temptable?"

"I think maybe we'd better change the subject," he answered with a pained smile.

"OK," she replied. "So tell me, how's Karen?"

"Karen," Noah sighed. "Karen's home in Highland Park. We've had a little difficulty lately. It's kind of complicated."

"I'm sorry, Noah. I hate to think of you being unhappy. I hope it will all work out for the best."

He looked at her and smiled as he contemplated the subtle phrasing of her concern. "I think it will," he replied. "I'm not at all sure I'll like the way it works out, but I suspect it will be, as you say, for the best."

"Want to talk about it?"

"No, I don't think so. Not right now, anyway."

"Fair enough."

"What I mean is, I want to talk about you, right now. A girl I used to know just walked back into my life as a woman. I want all the blanks filled in."

"True confessions?"

"Whatever you want to talk about, I'm anxious to hear."

"Well, I'm probably the only college graduate who studied in Beirut and got her degree in Jerusalem. You heard about my run-in there with Ali Shoukri and the Tarshiha-Maalot affair? Yusuf has probably told you about Amos Ben-Chaiyim and me. Anyway, I began to need my family, my home. So I finished my book, quit my job, and told Amos good-bye." Alexandra had never told her family of her final encounter with Ali. It wasn't something she was ready to discuss with Noah either, not yet, not now.

"Four and a half years in one breath?"

"That's all it takes unless you want all the details."

"Every last one," he replied.

By one in the morning, they had covered a lot of territory, treading softly over some subjects, thoughtfully skipping others. They left the empty restaurant in silence, each contemplating what the other had revealed and wondering about the areas still too tender for retrospection.

"You know, Yusuf would never want to be the cause of so much friction and tension in your life," Alexandra said as they walked the few blocks to Noah's townhouse, where his car was parked.

"Of course, I know that," he replied. "Yusuf hasn't done anything but be a great architect and, I guess, a great friend too. That's the irony of it all."

"What are you going to do?"

"I intend to award the commission to Yusuf. How could I do anything else?"

"Fighting with the banks and this fellow..."

"Scallion."

"Yes, Scallion. Well, that's one thing. But fighting with Karen, that's something else."

"Yes, I really have the feeling she's on the verge of handing me an ultimatum over this business."

"Noah, she not going to let architecture come between the two of you."

"It's more complicated than that, Alexandra. It's not the architecture. It's the architect. It's my connection with the Salamans…and with you."

"She'll get over it."

"She may accommodate it, but she won't really get over it. You loom heavily in her psyche, Alexandra."

"Noah, don't take this the wrong way, but would you mind terribly if we didn't talk about Karen anymore tonight?" she asked, taking hold of his arm. "I don't know how many more times I'll have you to myself like this, and I don't want to spend the little time we have left before you drive me home talking about Karen and how much I upset her. I'm sorry I upset her, and I do understand why I upset her, but I don't want to deal with it right now. Is that terrible?"

"No, I should have never brought it up," he answered.

"Actually, I did," she said.

"Anyway, we're here," he said. "This is the Greenspan Palace." Noah gestured toward his townhouse with a sweep of his hand as they stopped in front of the redbrick Georgian building.

"Oh, I like the gaslights on either side of the door."

"They're old coach lanterns," he replied.

"Lovely," she murmured admiringly.

"Want to see the rest of the house before I drive you home?"

"You have etchings to show me, Noah?" she asked seductively.

"Yeah, they're called architectural renderings. The place is crawling with them."

"C'mon," she said with a laugh, "show me how Washington's finest live."

"Very modestly, I assure you," he answered and led her up the three steps to the front door.

As Noah walked her from room to room, Alexandra could not help but think of the dark and tired living quarters over the tiny grocery stores in the heart of the LeDroit Park ghetto where they had both grown up.

"We've come a long way," she mused, putting her arm casually around his shoulder as they started down the rear corridor toward his bedroom.

"Hmmm," she said playfully when they entered the room.

"It's cruel and unusual punishment to tease a vulnerable man," he said.

"How do you know I'm teasing?"

Noah looked at Alexandra curiously for a moment. Then, before he could respond, the ringing of the phone interrupted the charged silence.

"That has to be Karen," he said as he walked over to his desk to grab the phone. "Saved by the bell."

"Yes, saved by the bell," Alexandra whispered. "How lucky."

"Hi, Karen," he said as he lifted the phone.

"How did you know it was me?" she replied.

"I can tell your ring. You OK?"

"I'm fine...no, I'm not fine, I'm miserable. I don't know what I thought I was accomplishing by coming home."

"Well, maybe you did need some space. Besides, you haven't seen your folks for a while. I'm sure they're glad to have you home."

"Where in the world have you been? I've been calling all night. Were you with Ed?"

"Ah...no. Ed and I spoke on the phone before I left the office. There's going to be a story in the *New York Times* about Potomac Centre," he replied, trying to dodge her question.

"A positive story?"

"No, not exactly. The architecture reporter for the *Times* is quoting sources at the bank as saying the loan committee was profoundly disappointed with the selection of Yusuf Salaman."

"The *New York Times* is going to write that?"

"Probably tomorrow."

"Oh, my God, that's terrible!"

"Ed said it wouldn't be so bad. He's apparently going to be quoted as well—about bankers' taste."

"Aren't you worried?"

"I'm a little anxious about what the fallout will be from the press. We don't need any more aggravation right now."

"So, where've you been? You have a meeting or something?"

"Um...no. Alexandra called when she got home. We grabbed a bite and sort of got all caught up on things," he replied, shrugging at Alexandra.

Alexandra smiled sympathetically. She mouthed the words, *Want me to wait in the other room?* and pointed toward the door.

Noah shook his head.

"Grabbed a bite?" Karen said incredulously. "Noah, it's almost two a.m."

"Well, we had a lot of catching up to do. The time just flew by. You know how that can be. Before we knew it, it was one o'clock and they were closing up the place."

"I'm surprised you're home already. I mean it's not even two o'clock yet. You hardly had time for a good-night kiss."

"Come on, Karen. That's not necessary."

"I mean, Jesus Christ, Noah. I go home to get my head straight, and you're out with Alexandra before I get off the goddamned plane!"

"Karen, don't make something out of nothing, OK?"

"Is she with you now?"

"What?"

"Is Alexandra with you. Is she at your place?"

"Karen, please. This is nonsense. We stopped by to pick up my car. I was showing her the townhouse before I take her home, and the phone rang. Don't start something over nothing."

"And she's standing right there listening to us argue, isn't she?"

"Karen, I'm going to go now. It's late, and I have to get Alexandra home."

"I should have never left."

"Karen, please. We'll talk tomorrow."

"Yeah, we'll talk tomorrow," she answered, her voice the sound of sorrow and defeat.

"Whew!" he whispered as he hung up the phone.

"Sorry, Noah," Alexandra said. "I shouldn't have come in."

"Don't be foolish. Karen just jumped to all the wrong conclusions. We didn't do anything."

"Thank God," she replied with a wry smile.

***

It took Noah barely twenty minutes at that time of night to make the trip through Rock Creek Park up to Blagdon Avenue and to the Salaman house. They talked mostly about Alexandra and what she planned to do next.

"God, I feel like you never left," Noah said, pulling into the driveway of the ranch-style house the Salamans had purchased four years earlier.

As Alexandra turned to face Noah, he leaned over to kiss her on the cheek, and his lips brushed against the side of her face. Suddenly, she took his head in her hands and kissed him, passionately, on the lips. When they separated, he pulled back for a moment to look into her eyes.

"Sorry, pal, but I've been wanting to do that all night," she said.

Noah took her by the shoulders, pulled her back into his embrace, and kissed her frantically, squeezing her as tightly as he could.

"God, I'll never stop loving you," he finally said.

"Nor I you," she agreed breathlessly before he brought his lips down on hers again.

"What now?" she asked when they finally disengaged.

"I don't know. Has anything changed?"

"This isn't the time or place to try to answer that one, Noah. You sort things out with Karen first." She paused for a moment and quickly hugged him again. "Good night, Noah," she said, kissing him on the cheek. "Call me…soon."

"Good night, Alexandra," he replied and watched her hurry to the front door.

***

Noah spent another sleepless night thinking about Alexandra and how quickly things were spinning out of control with both his personal life and his business life. He finally dozed off around six thirty, only to be awakened by the ringing of the phone a half hour later.

"Hi, Karen," he answered, still half asleep.

"Sorry, wrong lover," Scallion replied.

"Ed, what the hell are you calling so early for?"

"I couldn't wait until I got to the office to see the *Times*. I ran out and got a copy over at Union Station."

"Oh shit. I forgot all about the *Times*. How bad did they do us?" he asked as he swung his legs over the side of the bed.

"Could have been worse. Want to hear it?"

"No, but go on anyway."

"Headline reads: Architect Selection Mires Potomac Centre in Controversy."

"Oh shit!"

"Relax, will you? It gets better."

"Go on."

"Washington, DC—One of the nation's largest and boldest urban development projects planned along the shoreline of the Potomac River may already be under water, according to sources at the Capital City National Bank, which is financing the mammoth residential-commercial undertaking.

"Sources say the bank's loan committee was unhappy with developer Noah Greenspan following his selection of an unknown architect who, coincidentally, also happens to be a boyhood friend. 'Many of the top names in architecture were competing for this commission, and we wind up with a virtual nobody' was the way one member of the bank's loan committee put it when pressed for a reaction by this reporter. Others at the bank expressed 'profound disappointment' and speculated that the selection of the unknown Yusuf Salaman as architect would seriously impair Mr. Greenspan's ability to sign up tenants for the project, which, in turn, could cause critical cash shortages a few months from now.

"'It was a bum decision…a poor choice,' said another source, who declined to be named. For his part, Mr. Greenspan is sticking with his choice of Mr. Salaman. "It was an absolutely blind competition," Mr. Greenspan said. "Yusuf Salaman won hands-down, and that's that."

"Mr. Greenspan's account of the competition was echoed by Edward Scallion, publisher of the *Urban Architect*, who has acted as architectural advisor for the project. 'Yusuf Salaman submitted a brilliant proposal and won the approval of the project's key officials. His identity was not revealed until after the selection was made. Mr. Greenspan made a tough but correct call, and I hope he sticks to his guns,' Mr. Scallion told the *Times*.

"When asked whether Mr. Greenspan, who is a relative newcomer to the rough-and-tumble world of real estate development, should have consulted with his bank before making a final choice, Mr. Scallion scoffed, 'Potomac Centre would look like the Federal Reserve Bank building if you left it to those Neanderthals.'

"Yusuf Salaman, a graduate of Yale University, has specialized in urban restoration projects in Baltimore. While virtually unknown nationally, his work is well regarded in Baltimore, where one colleague called Mr. Salaman an imaginative trailblazer. Bradley Chandler, president of Baltimore Downtown Progress, a business-supported organization devoted to rejuvenating the city's inner core, called the young architect 'brilliant.'

"'Potomac Centre deserves nothing less than the best. And that's what I attempted to do. I gave it my best,' the young architect said. Asked if he believed his prior friendship with Mr. Greenspan had helped, he answered, 'Noah Greenspan had no way of knowing which architect's work he was looking at until he unsealed the registration submission after his evaluation of the proposal. Besides, anyone who thinks Noah Greenspan would have shown preferential treatment just because I was an old friend doesn't know the man.'"

"You think that could have been worse?" Noah asked sarcastically when Scallion had finished.

"Damn right. They could have left my quote out."

"Right. Then my bankers would have never known they were Neanderthals."

"All bankers are Neanderthals, Noah."

"We've got no project without the bankers, Ed. Stop calling them Neanderthals."

"How about Cro-Magnon?"

"Very funny. We sure could have done without the line about possible critical cash shortages. It won't engender any confidence among prospective tenants."

"It's irrelevant…unless you miss a payment."

"Thanks, Ed. You're a paragon of reassurance."

"Keep me posted, Noah."

"Why? Are you expecting something to happen?"

"Well, now that your friend Mr. Salaman is public property, I suspect a lot of people are going to be sounding off."

"Like who?"

"Oh, I don't know…other architects, other competing projects, prospective tenants, and an assortment of people who wouldn't recognize a can of Shineola if they tripped on it but who will provide an opinion to anyone who asks."

"Ed, I'm glad we don't talk every morning. I'd have trouble getting out of bed."

"Call me if you need me, Noah."

"Thanks, Ed. I really appreciate your support with the *Times*."

Noah considered calling Karen but decided to wait until later that morning. His thoughts were filled with all the worst-case scenarios he could think of as he showered and dressed for work. For the first time since he'd started planning the Centre, Noah felt powerless. He was now dealing with events and circumstances over which he had no control but which he knew could bring down the project. But then there were images of Alexandra from the night before, which provided moments of exhilaration even as the dogs of despair hounded him.

As he worked at his tie that morning, he looked in the mirror and pictured Yusuf that first day at N. P. Gage. He could see him waving nervously through the chain-link fence. *Well, old buddy, Potomac Centre may sink or it may swim, but it's going to sink or swim with an architect named Salaman,* he thought as he pulled his tie into a tight knot.

CHAPTER
FORTY-TWO

"Noah, I've been holding your calls, but half the country has left messages for you," Barb said, leaning into his office and waving a fistful of pink message slips at him. He'd bought his own copy of the *Times* and had been sitting at his desk, reading it again, and wondering how so much could go wrong so quickly.

"Who called?" he asked.

"'Who hasn't?' might be an easier question to answer. So far you haven't heard from the president or the secretary of state."

"Well, maybe the phones have just been too busy for them to get through. So who has called?"

"Mostly press, some property-management types who say you'll need them, and several unidentifiables."

Noah reviewed the messages from the press with Ed Scallion over the phone before he returned the calls. There were several architectural journals to be called, and Scallion handicapped each one for Noah, providing whatever information he could about the writers he knew. Real estate writers from a half dozen daily papers, including the *Washington Post* and the *Star*, had called, and there were messages from the *Wall Street Journal* and *Forbes*.

Noah spent the entire day talking on the phone to reporters and columnists. Most were, he thought, like piranhas that had picked up the scent of blood in the water—his blood. They sensed the demise of a major development and jumped onto it. A few of the journalists were interested in the ethical question and seemed critical of the bank, but for the most part, Noah believed, he and Potomac Centre were in for a continued pounding.

His instincts were correct. Most of the press was buying into the perception that the Centre was, as one journalist put it, *dead meat.*

Yusuf waited until a couple of days after the *New York Times* article ran to call.

"It's the winner himself," Barb said as soon as Noah answered her buzz on the intercom.

"Yusuf!"

"Hi, Noah. I thought I'd wait a couple of days before I called. I kept hoping the press would get better."

"How you holding up?" Noah asked.

"I should be asking you that question."

"I've had better days."

"Yeah, me too."

"Hey, old man, you've become one of the best-known names in architecture," Noah said, trying to lighten up the conversation.

"Great. Yusuf Salaman, the architect who sank Potomac Centre."

"Bullshit! Nobody's going to sink Potomac Centre," Noah replied with a conviction he didn't really feel.

"Noah, you can walk away from my entry any time you want. So help me, there will be no hard feelings. It doesn't make any sense to jeopardize the project."

"Your vision is an integral part of the project, Yusuf. We're building the Centre together, and it's going to be your plan."

"Noah, listen to me. I'll never forget what you did. I don't mean selecting my submission; I mean not dropping me when the shit hit the fan. But I don't want the project hurt. It would be horrible to be known as the architect who killed a project, and it would be doubly horrible if it was your project I killed. Don't do anything foolish."

"I haven't," Noah replied, "and I have no intention of letting the project—our project—fail. I'll talk to you soon to set up a time to go over the plans together."

***

Noah threw his sport jacket across the counter of the bar as soon as he got home that night, loosened his tie, and reached for an old-fashioned glass. The phone rang just as the ice cubes landed in the tumbler.

"Noah?" It was Karen, sounding considerably more composed than when they'd last spoken. "How's it going?"

"Well, it's not exactly been the type of excitement I was looking for when we announced the winner," Noah replied.

"The stories have just been dreadful," she said sympathetically.

"Can you believe it? All because some prick at the bank had to run on at the mouth with the *New York Times*."

"Yeah," she answered, "it's terrible."

"Do I detect an *I told you so*?" he asked.

"Do you think I would do that?"

"Sorry. Guess I'm just a little sensitive these days."

"What are you going to do, Noah?"

"Right now, I expect to see it through. It's what's right for Noah Greenspan."

"Is it also what's right for Potomac Centre?" she asked.

"You sound like Yusuf Salaman. He pleaded with me not to do anything that would jeopardize the project. He said he didn't want that on his conscience."

"That's what I call a good friend. A very intelligent one too."

"Right on both scores," he replied.

"You know I love you."

"I love you too, Karen. But I hope what I decide to do about Potomac Centre doesn't become some kind of test."

"It's not a question of being a test. It's just that it's so frustrating to see you being so stubborn. It scares me, Noah. You're rejecting everyone's advice—mine, Ed's, the bank's, even Yusuf's. It doesn't make any sense at all. Yet, you plow on, full-steam ahead, just like the *Titanic*."

"I love your choice of metaphor."

"You know what I mean."

"Karen, I'm drained. I really don't want to talk about this right now. When the hell are you coming back?"

"When the hell are you going to ask me to come back?"

"I just did."

"No, you didn't. You asked when I was coming back, but you didn't ask me *to* come back. There's a difference."

"Jesus Christ, Karen," he said wearily. "What do you want from me?"

"I don't want anything from you," she replied coolly. "What do you want from me?"

"Hey, you're the one who left, remember?"

"Do you want me to come back, Noah?"

"You know damn well I do."

"I want to be with you too. You know that. So I guess that means I want to come back. But I have to tell you, there's a queasiness I get when I think of returning to Washington."

"What the hell's that supposed to mean?"

"It's just I get a little depressed when I think about it. I mean, I feel very secure here. I've spent a lot of time with my friends and with my family."

"So when did you, all of a sudden, get depressed about coming to Washington?"

"I think Alexandra's presence has really changed things for me."

"Karen, we've been all through that. Alexandra's back. And, yes, I'm glad she's back. But I still want to marry you. What else can I say?"

"How is she?"

"Actually, I haven't spoken to her since the night you left. She's busy with a new job at the *Star*, and, frankly, I think she doesn't want to be the cause of any problems between us. She knew how upset you were."

"I acted terribly the other night, but you can imagine how I felt when I realized you two were together."

"I know, I know. It was innocent enough..." Images flashed in his mind of Alexandra in his car, in his arms, their hungry, fevered embraces. "Are you temptable?" she had asked playfully. "But, uh, it was bound to be upsetting to you. I understood. I really did."

"I wish I could tell you it didn't matter—you know, Alexandra being back—but it really was like a punch in the belly. I want everything to be all right, Noah. You know that. But I'm really having a hard time over this. I guess I need some more time to think. Bear with me, won't you?"

"Take whatever time you need, Karen. I'm not going anywhere."

"I'll talk to you tomorrow then."

"I'll call you."

Noah hung up the phone and stood for a moment with his eyes closed.

Why in the hell am I telling her that Alexandra's presence here doesn't make any difference? Alexandra's the only bright spot in my life right now, he thought. He was, Noah finally admitted to himself, troubled at the prospect of Karen's return.

***

"Noah Greenspan?"

Noah assumed the man who greeted him in his reception room when he arrived at work the next morning was a reporter. The man didn't look like a businessman, and Noah knew he had no appointments that morning. He was certainly in no mood to talk to the press, especially when they showed up unannounced. But the man wasn't from the press, and after Noah nodded that he was indeed Noah Greenspan, it took the stranger no more than thirty seconds to finish his business.

***

"Barb!" Noah called angrily. "Barb!"

"Jesus, Noah, give a girl a break," Barb said as she walked into the reception room. "I just got here."

"Sorry," he sighed, exasperated. "Get Scallion for me."

"What's wrong?"

"I'm being sued, that's what's wrong."

"Sued? What's going on?" she called after him as he stormed into his office.

"I haven't the foggiest idea," he yelled back over his shoulder.

"Ed!" Noah shouted into the phone as soon as Barb signaled that Scallion was holding.

"Ah, the codefendant," Scallion answered.

"Codefendant! What the hell are you talking about?"

"Haven't you read the complaint yet?"

"No. I just opened the damn envelope."

"We're both being sued, Noah."

"What the hell's going on?" Noah asked incredulously.

"We've been hit with a very creative class-action suit, Noah. Some lawyer from Philadelphia claims he's representing all the architects who entered and lost the competition."

"What?!" Noah tried to keep from shouting. "That's ridiculous!"

"Actually, I'm not so sure. We'll need a lawyer to tell us that."

"What are they claiming, that they all should have won? How in the hell can all of the architects sue as a class?"

"As near as I can tell, they're not complaining that they didn't win. They're complaining that they never had a chance to win. They're saying the entire competition was rigged for your chum Salaman and that you and I ran a phony competition just to generate publicity."

"So what are they suing us for? The postage they used to mail us their drawings?"

"Noah, I don't want to upset you any more than you already are, but this doesn't look like a laughing matter to me."

"Ed, are you telling me you're taking this seriously?"

"Would you call two hundred and ten million dollars serious?"

The figure momentarily left Noah breathless. "How in the hell did they come up with a figure like that?" he finally managed.

"Well, it breaks down like this. They're saying the collective value of the proposals in terms of professional time was five million, eight hundred, and seventy-five thousand dollars. Actually, that sounds reasonable, considering that sixty-four firms or architects entered the competition."

"Go on."

"Then they're claiming another sixty-three million in what they're calling consequential damages. That's the work they could have secured had they not wasted their time on our phony competition. That only comes out to a million dollars for each entry. The competition ran for three months, and they're saying that each firm should have realized at least a million dollars in new billing if the same personnel they had assigned to their proposal teams for Potomac Centre had been free to work on legitimate business."

"That's absurd," Noah protested.

"I'm not so sure," Scallion replied. "They would have been working on something, and that work would have had value, even if it only entailed work on some other proposal."

"OK, so we're up to seventy million. Where does the two hundred and ten million come from?"

"Punitive damages. They're saying they are entitled to triple their actual and consequential damages as punishment for our conspiracy. Three times seventy million equals two hundred and ten million."

"We should tell them to go fuck themselves."

"Yeah—maybe while you're making out the check. Listen, Noah, I have a meeting with a lawyer from Higgens and Harper this afternoon at two o'clock. You want to come along?"

"You've called a lawyer already?"

"You know any reason why we should wait?"

"Ed, these bastards learn we've hired a lawyer, they'll think we're running scared."

"Noah, I am running scared. This is no nuisance lawsuit. My attorney says the lawyer who filed this suit is one of the big plaintiff's lawyers. The man wouldn't touch it if he didn't think he could win. Who do you think is going to believe it was just a coincidence that one of your closest friends won the competition? And, Noah, when I told Stanford Sherman—that's the lawyer I have the meeting with—that Yusuf Salaman's sister is an old flame of yours, he almost passed out. Know what he said?"

"How in the hell would I know what he said?"

"He asked how I ever got mixed up with a shmuck like you."

"And you want him to defend us?"

"Don't worry, I straightened him out. I told him that all of us selected Salaman's proposal but none of us knew whose work we were selecting."

"Did he believe you?"

"Beats the shit out of me. He just sort of whistled into the phone and said, 'This is the most bizarre thing I've ever heard.'"

"It *is* kind of bizarre, isn't it?" Noah replied, laughing.

"It's no laughing matter, Noah."

"So you keep saying. What time is our meeting?"

"Two, at Higgens and Harper. They're in a townhouse in Georgetown, on the northwest corner of Thirty-Fourth and Prospect."

"OK, I'll see you there at two."

As Noah hung up the phone, Barb yelled through the open door. "Noah, it's that *New York Times* reporter, Mr. Caztaneo, again. He says he wants your statement on the lawsuit."

"Oh shit!" Noah moaned. "How in the hell does he know about the suit already?"

"Greenspan," Noah said as soon as Barb had transferred the call.

"I see Saul Kronheim has you in the crosshairs, Mr. Greenspan," the *Times* architecture reporter said.

"Who in the hell is Saul Kronheim?"

"He's the lawyer who's suing you. Didn't you know that?"

"I thought the architects were suing me," Noah replied.

"Nah, it doesn't work that way. Theoretically, one or more architects are suing you on behalf of the class. The rest won't even know about the suit until they read about it in the newspapers. The way these things usually work, a lawyer like Kronheim recognizes an attractive case and arranges to find a client who belongs to the class he thinks is being damaged."

"And everyone in the class gets a piece of the action?"

"Once the class is certified by the court, they do—assuming they win."

"The whole class gets paid, even if they never saw fit to sue themselves?"

"Yep. That's the way it works, unless they opt out."

"Why would anybody opt out?"

"Usually because they're not satisfied with the settlement."

"You mean because they want more?"

"Something like that."

"You sound like you've heard of this Kronheim. Is he well known?"

"About as well known as the neighborhood pit bull. Most corporations settle as soon as they know he's the plaintiff's lawyer in one of these class actions."

"Why?"

"Because he's a master at concocting a case that nobody can afford to lose. Most defendants figure that even if there's only a ten percent chance of losing, they're not willing to play 'you bet your company' with those odds."

"Sounds like legal extortion, doesn't it?"

"Depends on whether you're guilty or innocent. If you're guilty, Kronheim has done a real public service. If you're innocent, you've got some tough decisions to make."

"Like whether or not I want to bet my company."

"Exactly."

"I think I can convince this Kronheim, and anyone else for that matter, that this was an absolutely straight competition."

"With all due respect, Mr. Greenspan, he won't give a shit."

"But why?"

"Because once he's decided there's enough to bring a case, he's perfectly willing to let the court decide the question of guilt or innocence."

"He'd force me to settle even if in his heart he believed I hadn't done anything wrong?"

"Mr. Greenspan, are you as naïve as you sound? The only thing a lawyer like Kronheim knows 'in his heart' is how to boost his own bottom line. Kronheim stands to pocket about twenty-five percent of what you settle for, or of the judgment if this goes to court."

"And if he loses the case?"

"He eats whatever it costs to bring the suit."

"I see. Well, Mr. Caztaneo, I certainly appreciate the short course."

"My pleasure. But that's not why I'm calling. I'm writing a story on the class-action suit, and I'd like your comment."

"You know this story is really going to hurt?"

"It's the suit that hurts, Mr. Greenspan, not the news coverage."

"This is a dishonest suit, devoid of merit."

"That's your comment?"

"Yes, that's all I have to say."

"OK. Thanks for the quote," Caztaneo said and hung up the phone.

***

Noah arrived at the law firm's redbrick townhouse offices at exactly two o'clock. Ed Scallion was sitting in the reception room reading an old copy of *Time* when Noah walked in.

"Isn't this a bitch?" Noah asked.

"Look, I don't know about you, but I don't have two hundred and ten million dollars," Ed replied, throwing the magazine down on the table next to him. "If these bastards win and I have to liquidate everything

I own, they'll still have about two hundred and nine million, nine hundred thousand to go."

"Maybe they just want to put us both under," Noah reasoned.

"Ah! The two conspirators," Stanford Sherman said with a grin as he burst through the door.

"Stan, this is Noah Greenspan," Scallion said.

"Noah, I've heard a great deal about you. Sorry we have to meet under these circumstances."

"Are we really going to have to go through a lawsuit?" Noah asked. "This is such unmitigated bullshit."

"I'm afraid we are, unless, of course, you decide to settle."

"There's nothing to settle."

"Well, then, the answer to your question is yes."

Sherman ushered Ed and Noah into his office and motioned them into comfortable upholstered chairs as he took his place in the high-backed leather swivel chair behind a massive mahogany desk. Noah judged Sherman to be about thirty-five, even though the man's black curly hair had begun to thin. He was just a bit shorter than Noah and quite a bit heavier.

Sherman was both sympathetic and frank in his discussion with Noah and Scallion and displayed a strong command of the legal issues involved in the class action. Noah liked how Sherman answered questions in a direct way. The attorney kept his eyes trained on Noah as they spoke. From time to time, Sherman would absently twist his thick, black mustache between his thumb and forefinger, which Noah found both humorous and distracting.

"So where do we go from here?" Noah asked after Sherman had walked them through the case the plaintiffs had crafted.

"We'll move for dismissal. We'll argue there's not a shred of evidence to support what the plaintiffs allege."

"What are the odds the judge will grant our motion for dismissal?"

"Fifty-fifty at best," Sherman answered.

"What's to stop us from countersuing for malicious prosecution?" Noah asked.

"My judgment," Sherman replied. "We'd have absolutely no chance of prevailing with such a suit."

"Why?"

"First of all, we do have some vulnerability here. It's bad enough that the winner of the competition just happens to be your friend. But there's also the problem of how you ran the competition."

"What are you talking about?"

"Noah, I'm afraid I fucked up real bad," Scallion answered in a pained voice.

"Jesus, what else could have gone wrong?"

"I didn't see any reason why we couldn't determine who submitted a proposal once we had all reacted to it," Scallion explained. "You know, once we agreed that we really liked or rejected a proposal, we opened the registration envelope to see who had submitted the entry."

"So?"

"So," said Sherman, resuming where Ed had left off, "the plaintiffs are asserting that none of the registration envelopes should have been opened until a winning submission was irrevocably selected. Then, and only then, should you have opened the corresponding registration envelope that identified the winning submission's architect. They're saying you violated the integrity of a blind competition by opening the registration envelopes prematurely."

"But Yusuf Salaman's submission was everyone's choice, and we didn't know it was his submission until we opened his registration envelope," Noah protested.

"According to who, Noah?" Sherman asked. "You, a defendant in this lawsuit? Ed, your codefendant? And, as I understand it, your fiancé? Hardly a panel of impartial eyewitnesses. I'm afraid the way it was handled leaves the contest open to second-guessing."

Noah stared at Sherman, the full weight of the situation slowly beginning to sink in.

"I knew better," Scallion said, shaking his head, "but who in the hell would have ever imagined that anything like this could have happened?"

"That's why blind competition means blind," Sherman said. "So you see," he continued, "on the surface, they've brought a perfectly reasonable case. They may be proven wrong, but we'd be hard-pressed to prove them malicious. All we'd do is infuriate Kronheim and make an eventual settlement that much harder."

"We don't plan to settle," Noah reminded him.

"You may feel differently once discovery has begun and you see how disruptive this suit can be. You'll also grow very tired of my bills, Noah. Right now, settlement may seem out of the question to you. Ninety days from now, you may feel very differently about the whole thing."

Scallion looked as if he were going to faint.

"Don't worry about the legal expenses, Ed," Noah said. "This should be my problem, not yours. I'll handle all of Mr. Sherman's bills."

"By the way," Sherman interjected, "refer any calls from the press to me."

"Oh, I'm glad you mentioned that. I spoke with the *New York Times* before coming over here."

"What did you tell them?" Sherman asked.

"I told them this was a dishonest suit, devoid of any merit."

"You called it a dishonest suit?"

"Yes, I did. Anything wrong with that?"

"You just called one of the most prominent lawyers in the country dishonest. He's representing his clients, with whom any reasonable man would, at first blush, sympathize. We want to try to disengage from this thing as painlessly as possible. We're not going to accomplish that by calling anyone names. It may make you feel better, but it only makes things harder for me and more expensive for you."

"What's the next step?" Noah asked, embarrassed by Sherman's rebuke mainly because he knew it was justified.

"I'll contact Kronheim in Philadelphia. I'll try to get a feel for what he's after."

"You have to convince him he's barking up the wrong tree," Noah insisted.

"I'll do all the obligatory objecting, Noah. But he's expecting that. It will roll off his back like water off a duck."

***

Noah decided to walk back to his office to steal an uninterrupted half hour to think. Potomac Centre seemed in shambles. Prospective tenants would probably start abandoning him; his bank was disgusted; the project had, overnight, become the bane of the architectural community; he was involved in litigation that could be his ruin; his fiancé found Washington too depressing; and even more depressing, Noah wasn't sure he was sorry she was gone.

Noah had always known that real estate development was an unforgiving business. One mistake could be a developer's undoing. But what had he done to deserve this free fall? What had been his mistake? Was it because the winner had turned out to be a friend? An unknown? An Arab? Barely a week ago Noah had been Washington's rising star. Now he found himself at the center of a scandal and the object of scorn.

"Damn it!" he protested aloud. "I've done nothing wrong, absolutely nothing!"

CHAPTER
FORTY-THREE

"Good morning, Noah," Barb said as soon as Noah walked through the door. "You've got company."

"Not again," he groaned.

"This is good company. She's in your office."

"Karen!" he called out as he rushed from the reception room into his office.

"Sorry, Noah, didn't mean to disappoint you," Alexandra said, her face flushed in reaction to his unexpected and misdirected greeting.

"Oh shit," he groaned again. "I can't do anything right these days."

"Perhaps I shouldn't have come."

"Don't be ridiculous. I couldn't be happier to see anyone. I'm just expecting Karen to come back anytime now, and I jumped to the conclusion that she was here when Barb said I had company."

"Has she decided to return to Washington?"

"I'm not sure. I don't know what she's going to do. It's great to see you," he added quickly, anxious to change the subject. "What's going on?"

"I saw the *Times* piece about the lawsuit, and I decided to run over here before work. I thought you'd need a friend."

"Thanks," he whispered.

"You're suffering more pain than is called for, Noah. Yusuf is sick at what they're doing to you."

"Alexandra, I've run this whole nightmare through my mind over and over again. So help me, if I had it all to do over again, I'd make the same decision. Yusuf won, goddamn it! He really won."

"But you've lost, or at least you're in danger of losing. If Yusuf winning means you losing, something's wrong."

"I haven't lost yet. Listen, this isn't about the integrity of the competition, it's about an unpopular outcome of a contest. It's about big losing to little. It's about power and politics and xenophobia and the whole goddamned Jewish-Arab madness. I'm not going to dance to their music, Alexandra, not if I have an ounce of fight left in me, I'm not."

Alexandra smiled warmly. "You haven't changed one bit," she said. "You're the same Noah Greenspan I've always known: the same impractical, idealistic, wonderful human being who wouldn't face reality then and who won't face reality now."

"You complaining?" he asked, returning her smile.

"No," she answered softly. "I appreciate you more now than I ever have. I just don't want you to be hurt, and neither does Yusuf."

"Abandoning Yusuf would hurt me more than losing Potomac Centre, Alexandra. These bastards can't do anything to me that I won't bounce back from."

"You might be able to bounce back, Noah, but if you go under and drag Yusuf with you, he may not be able to. He might be stigmatized as the architect who sank Potomac Centre."

"Did he express that concern to you?"

"No. Not him. He's as idealistic as you. He just doesn't want to be responsible for causing you to fail."

"Alexandra, he's not responsible. Selecting his proposal was my decision. Staying with it or abandoning it will be my decision. Yusuf will bear no responsibility for what happens to me because of those decisions."

"I hope not, for both of your sakes," she said with a soft smile, placing her hand tenderly on his cheek. "I'm glad I came by this morning. You know, I thought about you often during the years I was away. I always wondered what kind of man you'd become. I should have understood a long time ago what kind of man dwelled within the boy I knew."

"I like what I see too, Alexandra. I'm not the least bit surprised at who you've become. You're exactly the person I knew you'd be."

She smiled. "I really have to get to the paper," she said after a moment of awkward silence.

"Thanks for coming. I can't tell you how much I appreciate it."

"Love you," she said, brushing his cheek with a kiss as she moved toward the door.

"Love you too, Alexandra."

She paused at the door, turned to him, and smiled again tenderly. "There was one thing I was wrong about," she said.

"And what's that?"

"I was positive there would have been no hope for us. I always thought you were a dreamer whose dreams would be crushed by reality."

"And now you no longer think I'm a dreamer?"

"No. You're as much of a dreamer as you ever were. But now I realize that it takes dreamers like you to create new realities. I wish I had understood that a long time ago."

Noah stood staring at the empty door for several moments after Alexandra had gone. Fantasy momentarily teased his senses but was soon banished by the sound of the intercom.

Myron Abrahams was calling to tell Noah the bank was upset about the lawsuit. "There's real concern that this will be the final nail in the coffin of Potomac Centre." The telephone connection didn't filter out the aggravation in the banker's voice.

"There is no coffin, damn you, and the only carpenters trying to build one work at your bank," Noah replied angrily. "If you people hadn't run at the mouth the way you did with the *Times*, none of this would have happened."

"There's something else I wanted to ask you," Abrahams said, ignoring Noah's comments. "One of our directors here at the bank sent me a press clipping from the *Baltimore Sun*. It's a story about a Palestinian who gave some speech and said the Israelis have systematically trampled the rights of the Palestinians. That wouldn't be your Yusuf Salaman, would it?"

"I wouldn't call him *my* Yusuf Salaman, but if you're asking whether our architect is the Palestinian-American who has been speaking out on the problems in the Middle East, the answer is yes. He has very strong feelings on the subject. He and I have spent a lot of time over the years discussing the issue."

"You agree with him?"

"I didn't say that. I said we've spent a lot of time discussing the Middle East."

"But do you agree with him?"

"I fail to see how that's any of your business, Myron, or frankly, what in hell that has to do with Potomac Centre."

"Well, you're right, of course. It doesn't have anything, directly, to do with the Centre," Abrahams replied. "But I think you must have had your head up your ass to have selected an architect who schleps around as much baggage as your Mr. Salaman."

"You know what, Myron?" Noah replied. "You might be right. Then again, the location of my head isn't any more your problem than whatever baggage Yusuf Salaman may or may not be carrying around. The only thing you need to concern yourself with is the viability of the project your bank is financing. Potomac Centre is sound, Myron, and you know it."

"It was sound, and that's why we provided the initial financing. Whether it remains sound is open to question and, therefore, so is the issue of permanent financing for the project."

"What's that supposed to mean?"

"It means the bank will need a thorough review of the project before making final commitments for the permanent financing."

"I don't have time for this bullshit, Myron."

"I'd plan a full day if I were you, Noah. We'll want to review the marketing, prelease progress, where you are on the critical path, architecture, proformas, and legal problems—you know, all the basics. Let us know when you're ready."

"Right! You just sit by the phone until I call, Myron," Noah replied before slamming down the receiver.

***

Noah spent the next several days putting out brush fires fanned by the adverse press. He knew that those in Washington real estate circles who were presumed to know everything worth knowing now considered Potomac Centre destined for the scrap heap of failed ideas.

Alexandra called Noah each afternoon to offer whatever encouragement she could, and Yusuf kept in touch to remind him that he could pull the plug whenever he chose.

It had been nearly a week since Noah and Karen had spoken. Day after day he deferred the call he knew he should make to her, telling himself he was just giving her additional time to work through her conflicts. But the truth was that the call he had to make was just another problem complicating his life and one he was happy to put off addressing as long as possible.

It had now been over two weeks since the first *New York Times* story had reported the bank's disappointment over the selection of Yusuf Salaman. It seemed more like a year. Noah left for his office, anxious to hear from Stanford Sherman. He knew Sherman had had a late-afternoon meeting with Kronheim in Philadelphia the day before, and he was irritated that his attorney hadn't called him.

Sherman's message awaited Noah at the office. It was terse: "Meeting this afternoon at two. We have a bear hug." Noah knew "bear hug" was corporate lingo for the proverbial offer one can't refuse.

He called Sherman's office to see what the cryptic message meant, but the attorney's secretary said he wouldn't be in the office until just before the two o'clock meeting. A call to Scallion produced no additional information; Ed had received the identical message from Sherman and didn't have the foggiest idea what he was talking about.

Noah decided he had waited long enough for Karen to call, and he dialed her. But the Rothschilds' housekeeper said Karen had flown to Washington the night before. Noah sat staring at the phone, trying to make sense of what the woman had said. Why would Karen have returned to Washington without calling him? He reconstructed the last twelve hours in his mind to determine if he had, at any time, been unreachable, but he hadn't been. He called Karen's apartment, but no one answered. Then he called Karen's father at work, only to be told that Paul Rothschild was on his way to a convention in Toronto.

At one thirty Noah left for Georgetown and his meeting with Scallion and Sherman. He was preoccupied with Karen's whereabouts—he still hadn't heard from her—and hadn't given a lot of thought to the meeting with the lawyer.

Noah arrived promptly at two o'clock and was shown into a conference room, where Ed Scallion was already waiting. Ed was sitting across the table opposite the door and jumped up as soon as he saw Noah.

"Stan took the liberty of expanding this meeting a little bit," he said.

"What's that supposed to mean?"

"Good afternoon, gentlemen," Sherman said, hurrying into the conference room. "Noah, I believe you know Yusuf Salaman."

Noah was surprised to see Yusuf follow Sherman into the room.

"Hey, Noah. I hope this is all right," Yusuf said, extending his hand to his friend.

"Of course it's all right," Noah replied, taking Yusuf's outstretched hand and pulling him into an embrace. "How the hell are you?"

"I'm fine. It's you I'm worried about," he answered, returning Noah's hug.

"Stan, I presume you had something more than a reunion in mind when you called this meeting?" Noah said, turning to Sherman.

"Noah, what we're going to discuss obviously concerns Yusuf as much as it does you and Ed, so I took the liberty of asking him to join us. I hope you don't mind. I've just been briefing Yusuf here, and Ed and I did get to chat for a few minutes a little earlier today."

"So everyone's clued in but me, is that it?"

"Now don't get paranoid, Noah, it just worked out that way. I wasn't trying to line up support or anything like that."

"Support for what?"

"Kronheim's settlement offer."

"Stan, you know my position on settling."

"Goddamn it, Noah, you don't have a position until you've heard the offer."

"So tell me the offer."

"First, there's been another development we should consider. The judge has been selected for this case, and it ain't good. It's Maurice Golden."

"Who the hell is Maurice Golden?" Noah asked.

"He's one of the older, more conservative justices. He was also the Israel Bond Drive Man of the Year last year. This is the judge who is going to decide whether Yusuf Salaman keeps his commission."

"We're in deep shit," Scallion murmured.

"Can we ask for a new judge?" Noah asked.

"Sure, if you want your head handed to you in a basket."

"OK," Noah sighed. "So let's hear about your meeting with Kronheim."

"Kronheim laid out their whole case for me. I have to tell you, all things being equal, if I didn't know you guys, I'd rather be the plaintiffs' counsel on this one than the defendants' counsel," Sherman began. "Remember, Noah, in a civil case like this, all the plaintiffs need is a simple majority. It's not like a criminal case where the jury decision has to be unanimous."

"There was not a scintilla of impropriety in this competition, not a scintilla," Noah protested.

"I know that, I know that," Sherman said, raising his hands to ward off Noah's repeated protestations, "but we're probably not going to be able to get you on the jury, Noah. So let's talk about how all the rest of the world is going to view this case. They know your fathers are partners. Kronheim is going to dwell on that and the fact that Yusuf quit his job in Baltimore to work on the Potomac Centre proposal. He's going to ask why Yusuf would have done that if he hadn't had some assurance from you that he had an inside track. They're also going to put the renderings of the other competitors on display to focus on the unorthodox approach Yusuf took with his proposal."

"What's that have to do with anything?" Noah asked.

"It's a brilliant move," Sherman replied. "We'll object like hell, but if he finds a way to get that material in front of the jury, he'll have every one of those jurors asking themselves if they would have selected Yusuf's proposal. And you know what? Most of them wouldn't. A jury of inexperienced laymen would be certain to tilt toward more traditional architecture, especially in a city like Washington, DC."

"But what will that prove?"

"It won't prove a damn thing, but it will reinforce Kronheim's argument that the competition was rigged for Yusuf. He's going to mount a steady drumbeat challenging the odds of your old pal knocking off sixty-three of the world's leading architects in a straight competition. He'll put Yusuf on the stand and ask him about his experience with major urban projects like the Centre."

"Yusuf has been involved with some pretty creative stuff over in Baltimore," Noah countered.

"But nothing on the scale of Potomac Centre," Yusuf pointed out.

"All we have is truth on our side, is that it?" Noah asked sarcastically.

"Yes," said Sherman, "that's it, and in a case like this, it's almost irrelevant. Perception is what carries the day, Noah. I'm telling you the perception will be that something's fishy."

"So what did they offer to do, settle for only fifty million?"

"They offered to drop their demand for any monetary settlement at all. Kronheim said his clients would settle for a blue-ribbon jury selection of an architect for Potomac Centre. He said you and Ed could serve on the jury along with five others who would be above reproach. They would want the executive director of the Professional Society of American Architects to be on the jury, along with the editor of *Architectural World*, the chief architect of the Capitol here in Washington, someone designated by the city, and someone designated by the House District Committee, which has oversight over the district's budget. Every contestant would have a fair shot, including Yusuf. Kronheim stressed that if Yusuf won again, his clients would be the first to congratulate him."

"Noah, I think it's a fair compromise," Scallion said anxiously. "Potomac Centre would be out from under a cloud. We'd have a no-lose situation. I mean, no matter what, we'd have world-class architecture. We'd be off and running."

"Noah, I'd be willing to take my chances," Yusuf concurred. "I won once, I could win again."

"You know what I think, Sherman?" Noah said, unable to contain his anger any longer. "I think this is bullshit. This has nothing to do with the way the competition was conducted. These guys want you attorneys call another bite at the apple, that's all. This crap about dropping the lawsuit is extortion, and you know it."

"It's a suit they could win. It's my job to tell you that. Yes, it is extortion. But it's legal extortion. In my opinion, you'd have to be terminally stubborn or just plain stupid to turn down the offer they've made. I'm sorry to put it that way. I know you're not stupid, and stubborn is no reason to risk what you have at stake here. Kronheim is willing to settle for a normal fee instead of the contingency he would get if he won a class-action suit."

"Maybe he's not so sure he'll win," Noah replied.

"No, it's not that, Noah. He just happens to have clients who are more interested in getting another bite at the apple. That's all," Sherman answered.

"Noah, it's not like they're eliminating Yusuf from the competition," Scallion interrupted.

"The hell they're not!" Noah replied and turned to his silent friend. "Yusuf, are you a member of the Professional Society of American Architects?"

"Um…no, I'm not," he replied.

"OK, that's one vote against."

"Ed, you think the editor of *Architectural World* is going to vote for the guy the *Urban Architect* introduced to the world?"

"Well…he'd only have one vote."

"That's two votes against."

"Now, what are the odds of the chief architect of the Capitol voting for something as unorthodox as Yusuf's work?"

"Probably not very great," Ed agreed reluctantly.

"That's three votes against, and ditto for the representative of the city and of the House District Committee, which just happens to be one of the most conservative committees in Congress and is almost always antagonistic to the city. For chrissake, even if we were lucky enough to get the city's representative to vote with us, the guy from the House District Committee would vote against Yusuf just for spite. And let me ask you something, Ed. Are you going to vote for Yusuf if this so called blue-ribbon jury is impaneled?"

"Jesus, Noah, get off my back will you?" Scallion responded, his own temper rising. His eyes darted involuntarily to Yusuf.

"Got the picture, Yusuf?" Noah asked contemptuously.

"Noah, are you through?" Sherman asked calmly.

"Hell no, I'm not through. I've hardly begun."

"May I speak?"

"It's your conference room."

"Your bank called to ask about the status of the suit. I told them, of course, that I couldn't discuss the suit with them or anybody else…that you and Ed were my clients."

"Jesus Christ, they've got gall," Noah replied, making no effort to hide the disgust in his voice.

"I agree with you, but nonetheless, they did call. You know they're about to pull your permanent financing?"

"Yeah, they called to hassle me earlier today. They want a full-blown review of the project."

"They want to end their involvement in the project, Noah. That's what they want to do, and that's what they're going to do."

"Noah, you've got to bend a little," Scallion said.

"Mr. Scallion's right, Noah," Yusuf added. "This has gone far enough. Martyrdom is for more noble crusades."

"Listen, Noah, let me make a suggestion," Sherman interrupted. "If I go back and tell Kronheim no deal, I think Potomac Centre might be down the tubes. The project will be dead long before this litigation is resolved. You're losing your tenants, you're losing your financing, and you'll probably lose all of your net worth as well. It just doesn't make any sense. Let me tell Kronheim that you're considering his offer and that you'll have a decision by the end of the day Friday. That gives you forty-eight hours to think it over."

Noah stared angrily at the surface of the conference table for several moments without speaking.

"Goddamn it, Noah," Scallion said. "I'm a codefendant here. I've got a big piece of my hide riding on this project. I say we tell them we're considering their offer."

Noah looked up at Ed, the anger gone from his expression, and then he glanced at his friend. "You feel that way too, Yusuf?"

"Yeah, I do, Noah. They've got us by the short hairs. I think what Stan is proposing is best."

"OK, then," Noah said, rising to his feet. "You tell Mr. Kronheim we're considering his proposal."

"Good," the lawyer said, giving the conference table a satisfied thump with his hand. "I'll tell him that. You're doing the right thing, Noah. I know it stinks, but it's still the right thing to do."

Noah stood for a moment and looked at each of them, one after the other. As his eyes met Yusuf's, he wanted to tell him he was sorry he was being sacrificed so that Potomac Centre might survive. Instead, he turned and walked briskly from the room without uttering another word.

***

Alexandra knocked on the open door before entering Noah's office.

"Hi, Alexandra," he said, surprised by her unexpected appearance. "What are you doing here?"

"I always like to be where I think I may be needed," she answered.

"You know about Karen?"

"Yes, Barb told me. I tried to reach you earlier."

He nodded. "I know. I was walking around, trying to make sense of everything. I've been such a fool. I've been so damned unfair to Karen."

"I'm sure you can put it back together, Noah…if that's what you want to do. Karen will understand."

"She does understand, Alexandra. That's the problem."

"Is it the mess with the architecture?" Alexandra asked, though she knew the answer.

"Not really. It's so complicated. She's terribly hurt that I wouldn't budge, of course, that I wouldn't even consider her point of view. That got to her more than a difference of opinion over which architect should have been selected. She called my willingness to dismiss her concerns a real revelation to her."

"But there is nothing about this project that justifies her walking away from you. She must understand that."

"Potomac Centre is just the straw that broke the camel's back. I think Karen's real problem has been festering for as long as I've known her."

"Oh God, Noah, I'm not going to have this hung on me, am I?" she asked, dreading his response.

"No. I'm the one who's caused the problem. I've never been willing to let you go...not in my heart I haven't. I told Karen a long time ago that I would always feel love for you. I told her that I loved her and wanted to marry her, but that you were a very important part of my life and I would always have strong feelings for you. I told her that everything about our relationship was beautiful except, you know, the Arab-Jewish thing."

Momentarily speechless, Alexandra looked at him in wide-eyed amazement.

"Noah," she finally managed, "you actually told her all that?"

"There was no way I was ever going to lie about how I felt about you," he said a bit defensively. "We broke up over this before. But I thought we'd worked it out."

"Oh, Noah, you jerk," Alexandra whispered affectionately. "How could you expect Karen to accept that? She'd always have to guess whether it was she or me who occupied your thoughts at any given time. You can't expect any woman to live like that."

"So what was I supposed to do? Pretend you no longer mattered to me?"

"Probably."

"I couldn't do that. I wouldn't! It would mean denying the...the specialness of our relationship."

"Noah, there's a very thin line between having fond memories of a woman and longing for her. I don't think any wife could manage knowing that her husband longs for another woman."

"Hey, I never said I longed for you!" Noah protested.

"Ah," said Alexandra, her green eyes dancing with suppressed amusement. "I stand corrected."

"No, damn it!" Noah admitted with a sigh of frustration. "You stand absolutely correct. The fact is...I never stopped longing for you.

I never will, Alexandra. I finally came to accept your feeling that there would never be a place for us, but I never stopped loving you."

"And you still think you could marry another woman?"

He didn't speak. He just nodded.

"Oh, Noah," she whispered. "If that's really the way you feel, then go to her. Don't sacrifice a normal, wonderful life for what maybe could have been. You and Karen are now. You two are the present and the future. Don't confuse memory with reality."

"I'm not confusing anything with anything. I didn't leave Karen, she left me. I didn't want her to leave. I was ready to build a life with Karen, and I know it would have been a good life…for both of us. But…"

"But, you'd just maintain a little shrine in the cathedral of your heart for me, is that it?"

"I wouldn't put it that way, but if you're saying there would always be a place for you in my heart, well, that's right. There always has been, and there always will be."

Alexandra looked at him without speaking for a moment. Then her expression softened, and she smiled. "I know," she whispered. "You've never been far from my thoughts either. I guess I've known for a long time that it will always be that way."

"So now what?"

"So now you have to sort out your life, Noah. It's not fair, but you have to decide what you want, and you have to decide now. You can't be indecisive with Karen. She doesn't have that coming to her."

"That's a nice way of saying 'shit or get off the pot.'"

"I wouldn't have put it exactly that way."

"You didn't."

"I have to go, Noah," she said, kissing him affectionately on the cheek. "Good luck."

***

Noah knew Karen was waiting for him at his townhouse as soon as he saw that the living room lights were on. He took a deep breath and let himself in.

"Hi," he called out.

"I'm in here," she called back from the living room.

"Welcome home," he said, leaning down to kiss her on the cheek.

"I thought we should talk."

"Can I get you anything?" he asked.

"No, thank you." She smiled, disappointed that her return hadn't merited more than a kiss on the cheek. "How are things going?"

"Miserably," he said, fixing himself a drink at the bar, then returning to sit next to her on the couch.

"Isn't the project salvageable?"

"I didn't say the project was dead, I just said things were going miserably."

"Is there a difference?"

"Yes, there is. Sometimes things don't go smoothly, but that doesn't mean you cave in. It means you fight."

"Daddy can't believe you're doing this."

"Doing what?"

"Going to the mat over the controversy with Yusuf."

"Just thinks I should toss him to the sharks, is that it?"

"He just thinks you should save the project."

"I am going to save the project."

"And what about us? Are you going to save us too?"

"You're the one who left, remember?"

"Would you have stayed? Honestly, Noah, think about it. If the shoe were on the other foot, would you stay with me knowing that another man was constantly in my thoughts?"

"Karen, I've never deceived you—never. From the time we first met back at Stanford, you've known about Alexandra."

"I thought you would grow up. It's not normal to hang on to something like you cling to her."

"Is this why you came back, Karen? To rehash my relationship with Alexandra?"

She paused to consider his question. "Actually, no," she said. "I came back to try to talk sense into you. Daddy says your priorities are all screwed up. He says you're focusing on an ideal at the expense of a really great project. He thinks the project should come first."

"The project *is* coming first. Doesn't anyone understand that Yusuf is right for this project? Who knows what's right for this project better than I do?"

"Doesn't it mean anything to you that no one—absolutely no one—agrees with you?"

"No one has to agree with me. Who disagrees, anyway? A banker who wouldn't know a good architectural project from Levittown, a near-bankrupt publisher who doesn't want his subscribers or advertisers angry with him, a bunch of architects who lost in a fair and open competition, and a food broker from Highland Park."

"How dare you! Daddy has gone the extra mile for you, Noah. He adores you, and you know it!"

"I'm sorry, you're right. That was stupid. But the point I'm trying to make is the same. It's my project. It's my judgment, and it's my decision."

"How do your parents feel about what you're doing?"

"They trust my judgment."

"Yusuf's parents must worship you."

"They're afraid Yusuf will be blamed for hurting the project."

"And that doesn't worry you?"

"It all boils down to my judgment, Karen, and my judgment isn't going to hurt this project," he replied, a hard edge on his voice.

"You can be so fucking arrogant, Noah!"

"I'm sorry you see it that way. I don't think I'm being arrogant."

"What would you call it, then?"

"I don't know," he answered. "But I let other people's prejudices interfere with my life once before. I'm not going to let it happen again."

"Is that what this is all about?" she said, her voice now taking on a sharp edge.

"You're damn right that's what this is all about!" Noah snapped, suddenly getting to his feet, all his frustration reaching full boil. As soon as the words were out, he flung his drink at the wall with all his strength, shattering his own image in the mirrored glass over the bar.

Noah's sudden outburst stunned both of them. Silence filled the room for a moment, punctuated only by the sounds of liquid dripping from broken liquor bottles and shards of glass falling from the shattered mirror.

After what seemed an eternity, Karen rose slowly to her feet.

"Good luck, Noah," she said coolly, extending her hand to him.

"What's that supposed to mean?" he asked, turning to face her, his anger spent. He ignored her outstretched hand.

"I hope your project succeeds, and I hope your life succeeds. Is that clear enough?"

"Where are you going?" he asked as she turned and walked from the room.

"Does it really matter?" she said as she walked out of the townhouse, slamming the door behind her.

CHAPTER
FORTY-FOUR

Stanford Sherman had already called twice by the time Noah arrived at his office just after nine o'clock on Friday morning.

Noah smiled as he read the message the attorney had left: "Tell Mr. Greenspan to call Stanford Sherman. Tell him it is extraordinarily urgent."

Noah placed the call himself. "Stan, I got your message. What's so urgent?"

"I have to get back to Kronheim today, remember?"

"Yes, I remember, but it's only nine o'clock. What's the hurry?"

"I like to strike while the iron's hot. You know he can take the offer off the table any time he wants."

"I haven't made a final decision yet. I'm still thinking."

"Well, what am I supposed to tell Kronheim if he calls?"

"Tell him I'm still thinking."

"Noah, this is a two-hundred-and-ten-million-dollar lawsuit we're trying to dispense with here. That's serious money."

"That's why I'm still thinking."

"Noah, you're going to drive me to drink."

"Don't tell Ed that."

"When will I hear from you?"

"When I've made up my mind."

"Well, don't piss away the day. I've seen more than one settlement evaporate because someone got cute."

"You'll hear from me."

"Any other calls for me?" Noah called out to the reception room.

"Ed Scallion has called twice," Barb yelled back.

"Tell him I'll call as soon as I have something to tell him."

"Noah, did you smoke a joint or something before you came to work today?" Barb asked, leaning into his office.

"Why, yes, how did you know?" he replied facetiously.

"You looked like death warmed over yesterday. I mean, you moped around the office all day. And now you look like you haven't got a worry in the world."

"I've never had more to worry about in my life," he replied. "But up until now, all I could do was worry. Today, we start doing something. The worry phase is behind us, and that's a big load off my mind."

"Would you really go to trial with two hundred and ten million dollars at stake?"

"I don't know. I might."

"But why?"

"Because I don't like the idea of some goddamned lawyer in Philadelphia and his clients, whom I wouldn't know if I stumbled over them, dictating how I'm going to run any aspect of my project. And if I go along with what they're proposing, Yusuf is going to get royally screwed."

"And if they sue you and win, you'll both get royally screwed, along with Ed Scallion."

"Yeah," he sighed. "That's the bitch. I can be as stubborn as I want to be, but the cost to the others involved could be pretty awesome."

"Well, it seems to me that there are three of you involved in this: you, Ed, and Yusuf Salaman. Why don't you just put it to a vote?"

"We already voted at Sherman's office Wednesday afternoon. The vote was two to one to settle."

"So, what's there to think about?"

"I don't know," he shrugged. "Maybe something as simple as right versus wrong."

***

By noon, Stanford Sherman had called back twice, as had Ed Scallion. At one o'clock, Sherman called again. Noah had Barb take messages. At two-thirty, when Barb buzzed Noah to tell him that Mark Caztaneo from the *New York Times* was on the phone, he decided to take the call.

"Greenspan here."

"I see it all worked out for the best," Caztaneo said.

"What are you talking about?"

"The word on the street is that the fix is in."

"What the hell is 'the fix'?"

"You know, a settlement. My sources tell me what's going down is a blue-ribbon jury. You get a new architect or, who knows, maybe the old architect; Kronheim's clients get another shot at the project; and Kronheim and your attorney, what's his name, Stanford Sherman—I love that name! Stanford Sherman gets paid for helping you guys all get your shit together."

"You going to write it that way?"

"Sort of. All but the part about you guys getting your shit together."

"I wouldn't if I were you. I haven't made up my mind yet."

"You kidding me?"

"Nope."

"You've got real balls, Greenspan. I mean real, solid, cast-iron balls. You've got a two-hundred-and-ten-million-dollar suit staring you in the face, and you're still thinking about whether or not you want to settle."

"I know this will sound trite to you, but there are other issues here besides the possible damages."

"You mean, like your buddy Salaman getting shafted?"

"I mean, like any architect having a commission stolen from him."

"You know, the plaintiffs think they've got you against the wall. When's the motion for dismissal being heard?"

"Tuesday."

"Now, if you had real balls, you'd wait until Wednesday."

"Why?"

"Because, if the judge grants your motion for dismissal, you're home free."

"And if he doesn't?"

"They still might settle. All these guys want is another round of competition, with you out of the loop on the decision. Worst case, you go to trial. Even if you lose, I bet the court wouldn't award anything like what they're asking for in damages."

Noah hadn't given any thought at all to the hearing on the motion to dismiss since Stan began urging him to accept the settlement. He was sure it would be a perfunctory procedure, with little likelihood of the court granting their motion.

"I'll tell you, Greenspan, Kronheim must be sweating bullets with you sitting there thinking about it. He's got to be as anxious to avoid that dismissal hearing as he thinks you are."

"You know, I think I'm getting better counsel from you than I am from my attorney."

"Look, all he gets out of this is money."

"And you? What do you get out of all of this, Mark, if I tell them I'm waiting until Wednesday?"

"A lot better story."

"Well, I'll think about it, OK?"

"The bank going to pull your financing?"

"Anything you don't know?" Noah asked.

"I don't know whether or not you're going to accept their settlement offer."

"Don't feel bad," said Noah. "Neither do I."

***

Noah hung up the phone and walked to the window that looked out on the Washington Monument. He stood there for several minutes, mulling over the conversation he had just had with Caztaneo. Finally, he had Barb get Stan Sherman on the phone.

"Jesus Christ, Noah, nothing like a little brinkmanship," Stan said as soon as he heard Noah's voice.

"Stan, have you finished writing the motion for dismissal?"

"No. I haven't even started it. Why?"

"Why haven't you started it?"

"Because if we settle we don't need it."

"Start drafting the motion for dismissal, Stan. And send me a draft as soon as you're finished. I want it to be strong, and I want to see it before we go to the hearing."

"What are you telling me, Noah?"

"Do we have a language problem here, Stan?"

"What about the goddamned settlement?" Sherman bellowed into the phone.

"I'll let you know Wednesday morning."

"Wednesday morning! Are you crazy?"

"We're not settling before Wednesday morning!" Noah answered, leaving no room for debate. "And, Stan, I'd like to see that motion for dismissal first thing Monday morning. I presume it's going to be strong as hell."

Sherman sighed. "OK, Noah, we'll do it your way."

Noah called Yusuf first. Yusuf listened carefully as Noah told him he had decided not to decide on the settlement offer before the following Wednesday. Noah explained the strategy he intended to pursue. They were not going to deal with Kronheim hat-in-hand, Noah said.

Yusuf paused to consider what he had just heard. "You've got real balls, Noah."

Next Noah called Scallion. Ed sounded irritated but didn't argue; he knew there was a time when he could reason with Noah and a time when discussion was futile.

"You're the boss, Noah. I just hope to hell you know what you're doing."

"Ed, there's something I want you to do for me," Noah added as if in afterthought. "I want to hold a press conference at one o'clock Monday afternoon. Can you make the arrangements for me? Maybe we can do it at the National Press Club. I'll need a podium and an easel."

"Sure, I'm a member, I can arrange that. You mind if I ask what you're planning to announce?"

"I'm not entirely sure, but I want to get off of the defensive. Everybody thinks we're dead meat. I have to do something about that."

"Sherman will flip over you having a press conference. You know that."

"Right now, all I want Sherman to do is prepare our motion for dismissal. He can say I told you so until hell freezes over if I blow this, but I'm through letting attorneys think and act for me."

***

Noah was surprised at the large number of journalists who had already shown up for the press conference when he and Scallion arrived at the private dining room Ed had reserved. The dozen or so rows of chairs were all filled, and several television news cameras were already in position. A podium with four or five microphones was set up at the front of the room. Behind the podium and off to the side stood an easel displaying a large aerial view of Yusuf Salaman's Potomac Centre.

"Jesus Christ!" Noah said under his breath. "What did you tell them—that President Johnson was going to appear?"

"Nope," Ed whispered back. "All I did was run off an announcement that you were holding a press conference and left one in everyone's pigeonhole Friday night."

"That's all?"

"I dropped the leftovers on the Press Club bar."

"Noah!" Stan Sherman called as he rushed into the room behind them. "What the hell are you up to?"

"We're going to have a press conference, Stan."

"I know you're going to have a press conference. The whole damn city knows you're going to have a press conference. Why in the hell didn't you tell me?"

"Do you have the motion for dismissal?" Noah asked, ignoring his attorney's frantic query.

"Yes, I've got the goddamned motion for dismissal. Now, do you mind telling me what this is all about?"

"We're running out of time, Stan. Let's see the motion."

"Shit," he mumbled as he balanced his briefcase in one hand while retrieving the motion he had spent the weekend drafting.

"Here, goddamn it, here's the motion. Now tell me what's going on."

"Please, Stan, I want to read this," Noah replied, holding up a hand to silence the attorney.

After what seemed an eternity, Noah looked up and said, "This is really good, Stan. I like it. We'll talk as soon as the press conference is over."

"Noah, clients don't wait until after press conferences to talk to their attorneys when the press conference deals with litigation!" Sherman rasped under his breath.

"Stan, relax, will you. You pass out or have a stroke, and you'll ruin the press conference." Then he turned and walked confidently to the front of the room.

As Noah took his place behind the podium, Yusuf entered at the rear of the room, waved, and took a seat against the back wall. Noah smiled reassuringly at his anxious friend. Then Alexandra came in and, spotting Yusuf, made her way to an empty chair next to him.

"Good afternoon, ladies and gentlemen." Noah's amplified voice traveled across the assembled crowd. "My name is Noah Greenspan, and I am the developer of Potomac Centre. I'm glad you could all join us today. For over a year now, we have been hard at work on the development of Potomac Centre, a project of great promise that will consist of residential, commercial, and office-space development on a scale not previously undertaken in this city. Obviously, we consider Potomac Centre to be one of the most exciting urban development projects in the United States."

Noah spoke in a strong, carefully modulated voice, keeping eye contact with his audience as he continued. Although they seemed focused and interested in what he was saying, no one was taking notes.

"Two weeks ago, the *New York Times* broke a story that the Capital City National Bank, which has provided the financing for Potomac Centre, was unhappy with my selection of Yusuf Salaman as the architect for the project. Incidentally, Mr. Salaman's vision for the Centre can be seen on the easel behind me. Since the appearance of that story, the project has been plagued with difficulty, including a class-action lawsuit filed on behalf of the other architects who had entered the same competition as Mr. Salaman and who allege that the competition was rigged to favor him."

"Excuse me, Mr. Greenspan," a voice interrupted from the front row.

Before Noah could identify the journalist who had spoken, flood-lights on all six television cameras quickly illuminated the front of the room. "Yes?" Noah asked, squinting against the glare.

"I'm Mark Caztaneo of the *New York Times*. Are you taking issue with my report of dissatisfaction at the bank?"

"No, Mark, not at all. The bank was unhappy and remains unhappy. The bank was disappointed that a larger, more prominent architectural firm had not been selected. They voiced the opinion that a big, well-known firm would have attracted more positive attention to the project. Their disappointment was certainly understandable. But the concept for Potomac Centre isn't about architects. It's about architecture. At no time were we judging architects, at least not in the sense of knowing which architect's work we were seeing at the time that each contestant's work was being reviewed. We were judging architecture. I am here today to tell you that those who were involved in the review process— Ed Scallion, publisher of the *Urban Architect*; Miss Karen Rothschild, formerly of my staff; and I—were unanimous in our selection of the winning architecture. It was only after that selection was made and we determined who had submitted the winning proposal that the focus shifted from the architecture to the architect. I'll admit, my colleagues questioned the wisdom of awarding this commission to a relatively unknown architect when we had so many excellent submissions from world-renowned architectural firms. In all honesty, they did more than question the wisdom of making such an award. They opposed it. The issue was compounded when they realized he was also an old friend of mine."

"Mr. Greenspan, I'm Charlotte Hughes of the *Philadelphia Inquirer*. There is a rumor that you have already reached a settlement with the plaintiffs in the lawsuit that calls for the establishment of a blue-ribbon jury to make the selection of an architect for Potomac Centre. Is that true? And if it is, doesn't that suggest that something was, indeed, unfair about the selection of Mr. Salaman?"

"There has been such a settlement offered by the plaintiffs," Noah replied. "Ordinarily, it would be inappropriate to discuss settlement offers, but it seems that someone on the other side has seen fit to talk to the press about it. So, yes, there has been an offer made, and, no, we have not accepted it. We have not accepted it because there was not one iota of impropriety in the way the architect was selected and because, as you put it, accepting such an offer might suggest that something was unfair about the way in which we selected Mr. Salaman. That in itself would be unfair to everyone involved in this project—most of all, Yusuf Salaman."

Noah saw Stanford Sherman roll his eyes and shake his head in disbelief as Noah told the gathered press that he had decided to reject the plaintiff's settlement offer.

"Mr. Greenspan," Mark Caztaneo called out, rising again from his seat, "unless you're much wealthier than any of us imagine, haven't you just announced that you've made a decision to play 'you bet your company'? Are we missing something, or are you betting the farm on Yusuf Salaman?"

"Mark, as far as the architectural concept for this project is concerned, Yusuf Salaman is Potomac Centre. He cannot be separated from this project any more than I can. People may love Potomac Centre, or they may hate it, but they will love it or hate it with Noah Greenspan and Yusuf Salaman irrevocably tied to its future."

Noah's words trumpeted in Alexandra's ears, sending shivers down her spine. The sight of Noah standing in the glare of the television lights blurred as tears welled up in her eyes.

"May I speak?" a voice asked from the middle of the room.

"Yes, please," Noah responded.

"My name is David Wald. I'm a partner in the architectural firm of Fenner, Wald, and Nolan of Chicago, Illinois."

Noah's heart pounded in his chest as he watched the imposing architect, whom he quickly judged to be in his late fifties, rise to continue his remarks. David Wald turned and scanned the room, capturing the attention of the press as he looked from one journalist to the other. He was taller than Noah had imagined, big-framed, with strong, determined features and a mostly bald head that seemed an appropriate repository for the creative genius for which he was known. Well-tanned and dressed in a midnight-blue suit, he commanded immediate attention.

Fire one! Noah thought, watching Wald stare at him as though taking the measure of a target before firing a salvo.

"This has become one of the most controversial architectural competitions I have ever observed during my thirty-five years in practice," Wald began. "As some of you may know, my firm was a contestant in this competition, and that makes us a member of the class that has filed suit. I have watched developments pertaining to this suit very carefully, and when I learned that this press conference was scheduled, I decided to come to Washington to attend it."

"Let me begin by saying that I have reviewed Mr. Salaman's entry to see for myself the concept we lost to. I will tell you, also, that my firm has invested hundreds of thousands of dollars in the Potomac Centre competition. I'll be damned if we would ever sit back while a fix cancels out the work of some of the best architectural minds in the country. We put too much time and effort into this competition to ever let that happen."

Noah tried to maintain his calm as his mind raced for a rebuttal to what he felt sure was coming. For the first time he questioned his decision to call the press conference, and he avoided looking at Stanford Sherman. He was sure he could handle anything the press might have thrown at him. But this? He simply never anticipated that one of the plaintiffs would mount an attack at his press conference.

"As I said," Wald continued, "we've reviewed Mr. Salaman's proposal, and I'm here to tell you what Fenner, Wald, and Nolan thinks about what we have here and what we plan to do about it."

Noah toyed with the idea of interrupting Wald and reestablishing control over the press conference, but he decided to let the architect continue and then try to deal with the damage after he was through.

"What we have here, ladies and gentlemen, is brilliant architecture. What Fenner, Wald, and Nolan thinks about these blueprints is that we wish we had drawn them."

Wald's words all but sucked the breath from Noah. Tears filled his eyes as Wald continued.

"Fenner, Wald, and Nolan will not participate in this class-action suit."

"All right!" someone shouted from the rear of the room. Noah thought, but was not sure, that the excitement came from where Yusuf and Alexandra sat.

"Our profession should be celebrating over Mr. Salaman's sudden emergence on the scene, certainly not litigating over it," Wald said. "It is not our firm's policy or practice to ever work as a subcontractor for any other architect; we outgrew the need to do that many years ago.

But I came here to tell Mr. Greenspan and Mr. Salaman, if he is here, that Fenner, Wald, and Nolan would be proud to provide whatever assistance we can to him and to Potomac Centre. You have planned your project with skill and care from the very start, Mr. Greenspan, and with respect to the architecture, you have chosen well.

"I apologize for interfering with your press conference here today, and I'll end my remarks by calling on every other plaintiff in this case to withdraw before any more damage is done."

Noah never did reestablish control over his press conference. The press flocked around David Wald for quotes and perspective. After several minutes, Noah just shrugged and walked to the rear of the room to join Alexandra, Yusuf, and Scallion.

"This is unbelievable!" Stanford Sherman said as he walked over to Noah. "This is the most fucking unbelievable thing I've ever seen!"

"Tomorrow, it's your turn," Noah said, clasping Sherman around the shoulders. "Tomorrow you get the judge to do the same thing."

"C'mon, Noah, give me a break, will you?" Sherman replied. But he was smiling as he said it.

***

The local evening news was full of coverage of Noah's press conference, and the next morning, Noah, Ed, Yusuf, and Stan Sherman brought copies of the *New York Times*, *Wall Street Journal*, *Philadelphia Inquirer*, and *Washington Star* with them on the eight o'clock train from Union Station to Philadelphia. The coverage was uniformly positive, referring to Wald's statement as a bombshell on the eve of the critical dismissal hearing.

Sherman cautioned Noah that Judge Golden's courtroom could be quite different. "His role is to protect the rights of the litigants. He will look only to the evidence to determine whether the selection process was fair."

"They have no evidence," Noah said as he settled into his seat on the train. "It's all circumstantial bullshit—our word against theirs. You just give it your best shot, OK?"

***

Noah spotted Mark Caztaneo as soon as he entered the federal building. The reporter was waiting for an elevator and waved to them as they approached him.

"What a difference a day makes, huh, Greenspan?"

"Thanks for the story this morning. I thought it was very fair," Noah replied. "So what's the rumor du jour?"

"I'd guess Kronheim is going to be pretty feisty. I heard a few more plaintiffs have opted out of the suit."

"That's great!" Yusuf said.

"It's largely irrelevant," Sherman said. "All Kronheim needs is one plaintiff. Once the class is certified, the number of plaintiffs just determines how the ultimate judgment or settlement is divided."

"So Kronheim doesn't care?" Noah asked.

"I wouldn't think so," Sherman answered.

The courtroom was about half full when they walked in. Noah and Scallion were shown to seats at the defendant's table in the front of the courtroom with Stan Sherman. Yusuf sat directly behind them in the front row. Saul Kronheim and two associates were sitting at another table at the front of the room, just to the side of the defendant's table. Only an aisle separated them.

"All rise!" a voice cried as Judge Golden entered the courtroom from a side door. Golden was older than Noah had imagined and appeared at first glance to be irritable and humorless. When the judge had settled into his seat, the bailiff instructed everyone in the courtroom to be seated. Judge Golden wasted no time getting down to business.

"Gentlemen, let me begin by saying that I don't like reading in the newspapers about settlements offered and settlements rejected on the morning of a hearing in my court."

"If it pleases the court," Stan said, rising to his feet and pausing for a signal from the bench to continue.

"Oh, sit down, counselor! I'm not looking for opening speeches. You'll say you didn't leak word of settlement discussions, and Saul there will make the same protest. Let's not dick around so early in the morning. I have made my point, all right?"

"Yes, Your Honor," Stan replied, taking his seat.

"Saul, you know where I stand?"

"Yes, Judge," Kronheim answered with a smile.

"You both have motions for me to review?"

"Yes, Your Honor."

"Yes, Judge."

"Approach the bench, please."

Stan Sherman and Saul Kronheim both rose to their feet and scurried to the bench to hand Judge Golden their briefs. They stood there for a moment while the judge read both documents. Then, as they returned to their respective tables, Judge Golden got to his feet and walked back to his chambers.

"What the hell's going on?" Noah asked.

"Both briefs are very short," Stan told him. "Judge Golden said he was going to consider them for a half hour and then return to the courtroom."

"Are we supposed to wait here, or can we leave the courtroom?"

"He said, 'Why don't you and your clients go get some coffee or take a leak or something,'" Stan replied.

"Are you serious?"

"So help me, that's what he said."

Exactly thirty minutes later, Judge Golden reappeared as promised. The courtroom grew very quiet as he quickly glanced over the two documents once again and then peered over his wire-rimmed glasses at Noah.

"You ever hear of the reasonable-man principle, Mr. Greenspan?"

"Sorry, Your Honor, I'm afraid not," Noah answered.

Saul Kronheim leaned back in his chair and seemed to breathe a sigh of relief.

"Well, young man, it's sort of a test we apply in these types of cases. We ask what a reasonable man would believe under certain circumstances. For example, I might ask whether a reasonable man would believe that Yusuf Salaman, who happens to have been a boyhood friend of yours, the son of your father's business partner, and who is a relatively inexperienced young architect, could have been expected to beat out sixty-three of the world's leading and most experienced architects in a fair and proper competition. What do you think?"

Noah rose to his feet. "If these reasonable men knew Yusuf Salaman or, for that matter, if they knew me, I'd be confident that they would certainly believe that the Potomac Centre competition couldn't have been anything other than fair and proper."

Judge Golden smiled and nodded. "I like that. That's a good answer. But it would only prevail if the court heard from enough character witnesses to come to that conclusion independently. We'd have to have a trial to accomplish that, wouldn't we?"

"I don't think so, Your Honor," Stan interrupted, rising to his feet. "Everyone is presumed innocent..."

"This isn't a criminal trial, Mr. Sherman."

"But the plaintiffs are accusing Mr. Greenspan of cheating. There is nothing whatsoever in his business experience that would support such a charge. To the contrary, he is a man with an impeccable reputation, as is Mr. Salaman. In fact, the only circumstance on which the plaintiffs base their case is the fact that these two men knew each other as boys and their fathers are business associates. Think of it, Your Honor. Learned counsel for the plaintiffs demands that Mr. Salaman in effect be denied the commission he won because the Greenspan and Salaman families have had a long-standing relationship. There was nothing in the rules of the competition that said acquaintances of the developer could not qualify. I would ask how often acquaintances of the court compete for a favorable judgment in this sacred room."

"Do you think that's a fair analogy, Mr. Sherman?"

"If Mr. Greenspan's acquaintanceship with Mr. Salaman is the primary basis for the complaint in this case—and it is—then, yes, I do think it is a fair analogy."

"Mr. Greenspan, you don't by any chance have Mr. Salaman's renderings for Potomac Centre with you in court today, do you?"

"Your Honor, I must object," Sherman said, jumping to his feet again.

"Why? I only asked if Mr. Greenspan had the renderings with him."

"With all due respect, Your Honor, we are not here to judge Mr. Salaman's work."

"Who said anything about judging Mr. Salaman's work?"

"Your Honor," Noah interjected, "I do have the renderings with me."

"Would you be kind enough to approach the bench with the renderings?"

"Yes, Your Honor," Noah replied, grabbing his briefcase and opening it on the table.

"We're dead!" Stan whispered as Noah pulled the renderings from his briefcase.

"Here they are," Noah said as he approached the bench.

Noah returned to his seat as the judge studied the various drawings.

"These are for Washington, DC?" Judge Golden finally asked incredulously.

"Yes, Your Honor," Noah answered.

The snickering emanating from the plaintiffs' table irritated Noah, but he kept his eyes fixed on the bench.

"I take it you're not one for tradition, Mr. Greenspan."

"Oh, but I am, Your Honor. I believe it is important to acknowledge history. Great architecture allows us to look back on our tradition, but it also allows us to look ahead into the future, to make history. I selected Mr. Salaman's proposal precisely because it provided a look into the future. I think our Founding Fathers provided a look into the future nearly two hundred years ago. Progressive thinking is as American as apple pie. I wanted Potomac Centre to be progressive…to hint at the promise of tomorrow."

"Mr. Kronheim?" Judge Golden said, peering over his glasses, a faint suggestion of a smile evident on his face.

"We don't have anything much to add, Your Honor. We think you understand perfectly well that the odds of the work you're holding in your hands having won over the work of sixty-three of the world's leading architects in a fair and proper competition are exactly zero. Approximately two hundred and sixty architects working for sixty-three different firms labored for over three months. That's over twenty-six thousand man-hours in a competition that we believe was rigged. We are entitled to prove in court that they never had a chance to win this so-called competition and that they are entitled to damages to compensate them for the work they did and for the work they lost while trying to compete in Mr. Greenspan's phony competition, and we intend to ask for punitive damages as well."

"Anybody else have anything to add?" Judge Golden asked, looking to the defendants.

"I do, Your Honor," came a voice from the back of the courtroom.

"Who are you?" the judge asked.

"My name is Karen Rothschild. I worked with Mr. Greenspan and Mr. Scallion on the Potomac Centre competition."

Everyone turned in their seats as Karen walked toward the front of the courtroom. Saul Kronheim, catching Noah's shocked expression, decided not to protest, certain that she was going to be hostile to the defense.

"Does anyone want to object to Miss Rothschild's participation here?" the judge asked.

Stan Sherman started to rise, but Noah placed his hand on his arm to silence him.

"Let her say whatever she has to say," Noah whispered.

"Well, what light do you have to throw on this matter, young lady?"

"Your Honor, I was there the night Mr. Salaman's work was selected."

"Yes?" the judge replied, urging her on.

"I was totally against the selection of Mr. Salaman. In fact, I quit my job over Mr. Greenspan's choice and his refusal to reconsider it."

"Did you think the selection was rigged, Miss Rothschild?"

Noah looked at Karen anxiously; a slight smile began to blossom on Saul Kronheim's face.

Karen sucked in a deep breath as her eyes filled with tears.

"No," she finally answered softly. "We did not know who had drawn the plans until after the selection."

"Your Honor, this is most irregular," Kronheim said, rising to his feet.

"Damn it, sit down, Saul! You had your chance to object before Miss Rothschild spoke," Judge Golden snapped before turning back to Karen.

"Go on, please."

"I was against using Mr. Salaman's work because I knew the turmoil it would cause, and…"

"Yes, please go on, Miss Rothschild."

"…and because I thought it was wrong…unnecessary to give the commission to…"

"Yes?"

"…an Arab," she whispered painfully.

A long and deafening silence followed. Then Judge Golden asked, "Is Mr. Salaman in the room?"

"Yes, Your Honor," Yusuf said as he stood to face the judge.

"What do you think of all this, sir?"

"I never spoke with Noah…um…Mr. Greenspan during the entire time of the competition. We never once discussed Potomac Centre. In fact, I rarely see or talk to Mr. Greenspan now. We live in different cities and travel in different circles."

"Saul?" the judge turned again to the plaintiff's attorney.

"Yes, Your Honor?"

"Why do you think Mr. Greenspan and Mr. Salaman cheated on your clients?"

"Well, Judge, you saw those renderings. You can figure the odds of Mr. Salaman winning over the entire group of plaintiffs."

"No, Saul, I really can't figure the odds. This wasn't a lottery. It was a subjective evaluation of creative effort. I personally don't care for Potomac Centre at all. I don't like all the steel and glass. I like brick and porticos and graceful chandeliers. But I'll tell you this: I think it's creative as hell. It kind of sticks in my craw a little, Saul, that you'd have this court reverse Mr. Greenspan's selection of an architect to design and build his project simply because the architect turned out to be an old friend. Maybe if I found for the plaintiffs, Mr. Sherman here could say it was unfair because you and I have been golfing buddies for over twenty years."

"Your Honor, my clients are among the world's finest architects."

"So what, Saul? I suspect, Mr. Salaman here may be among the world's finest architects too. Maybe not among the world's best-known architects, but I bet he's among the finest. You haven't convinced me of a damned thing here this morning.

"Mr. Greenspan," Judge Golden continued, turning his attention away from Saul Kronheim, "I hope you succeed with your Potomac Centre project. I think you've probably been diverted from your business long enough because of this litigation. The court grants defendant's motion for dismissal. Case dismissed!" With a sharp crack of the gavel, the case was over.

CHAPTER FORTY-FIVE

As soon as the judge closed the proceedings, Noah leaped to his feet, hastily embraced Stan Sherman, and then rushed over to hug and thank Karen.

"That was incredible," he said.

"Let's just say it was the right thing to do," she said with a wan smile.

"Come on with us. We're going out to lunch to celebrate."

"No, thanks. I don't really think I have anything to celebrate."

"Karen…"

"No, please," she said, holding up her hand to stop him. "I've cried enough for one day. You go to lunch with the guys. We'll talk some other time. Let me say good-bye to Yusuf and Ed and leave gracefully."

"You've been a major part of Potomac Centre, Karen. You should continue to be."

"You'd never accept my terms, Noah," she said, smiling.

He stared into her eyes and nodded his understanding.

She paused, hoping he would say what she wanted to hear. But after a moment of heavy silence, she turned and walked away.

***

After calling the Greenspans to tell them about Judge Golden's decision, Noah left with Yusuf, Stan, and Ed to celebrate over lunch at Bookbinder's. It had all ended so quickly. The hearing hadn't begun until eleven o'clock, and they were eating turtle soup at Bookbinder's shortly after noon.

"Well, Yusuf, it's really official now," Noah beamed. "You are the architect for Potomac Centre."

"I have to hand it to you, Noah," Scallion said. "If you hadn't hung in there the way you did, this would have turned out very differently. We'd have had a disaster on our hands."

"This has been the most unbelievable two days I've ever experienced," Yusuf said. "First, we have the surprise by David Wald yesterday, and then today Judge Golden comes through for us the way he did. Who would have ever believed it?"

"I thought we were dead in the water when the judge began by asking whether you knew about the reasonable-man principle," Sherman chimed in. "I glanced over at Kronheim, and he couldn't contain the grin on his face when the judge asked you that question, Noah."

"He caught me totally off guard with that one," Noah agreed.

"You couldn't have answered him better then you did."

"You did pretty well yourself, Stan, with that little speech about how there was nothing about my reputation that justified the charge that I had cheated to give Yusuf the commission."

"Well, gee, Noah, I'm glad you think I did something right with this case," Stan grinned.

"You did fine, Stan," Noah said.

"No, I really didn't," Sherman said, turning serious. "It all turned out fine, but I made some bad calls on this one. You guys were so damned credible, you made my job easy."

"Look, I'll be right back," Noah said, excusing himself. "I want to call my folks, and I promised Alexandra I'd call as soon as we knew anything."

***

The four men hurried through their meal and rushed to the Thirtieth Street Station in time to catch the two-thirty train back to

Washington. Yusuf disembarked in Baltimore, promising to call Noah in the morning. The others said their good-byes in front of Union Station in Washington, agreeing that they would get together within a few days to clear up the remaining loose ends. Noah gave Scallion a bear hug before jumping into a taxi for the short ride back to his townhouse. He asked the driver to detour along the riverfront where Potomac Centre would soon be built and felt wildly happy just passing the property.

As soon as Noah got out of the taxi, he saw Alexandra sitting on the stoop, leaning against one of the columns that framed the townhouse entrance. It was a warm and humid afternoon, and a beige cotton jacket she had carried with her lay across her lap. As he approached, he saw that she had fallen asleep sitting there. Noah squatted down so that his face hovered over hers. Her eyes were closed—angelically, he thought—and her lips were slightly parted, as though awaiting a kiss. He obliged her.

"Huh!" she cried, startled by the touch of his lips against hers.

"Hey, Sleeping Beauty," he said with a smile.

"Noah?"

"You were expecting Prince Charming maybe?"

Alexandra laughed. "I must have fallen asleep. I was dying to see you, to hear all about your glorious victory!"

"Come on in," he said, helping her to her feet. "I'll tell you all about it."

Noah spent the next hour telling Alexandra everything that had happened during the court proceeding, including Karen's surprise appearance.

Alexandra listened anxiously while Noah spoke, wondering and fearing what he might say about his feelings toward Karen, but he revealed nothing.

"Hungry?" he finally asked.

"Uh-huh," she said, nodding.

"Come on, we'll run over to Hogates."

They dined on clam chowder and roast beef au jus and talked of everything and nothing. Noah wasn't offering any more information about his personal feelings, and Alexandra wasn't asking. Then, as the summer sun began to set, he looked through the window over the Potomac and suddenly rose to his feet.

"Come on," he said, throwing onto the table enough cash to pay for dinner and a more-than-appropriate tip. "There's something I want to do."

"Where are we going?" she asked curiously.

"You'll see. But come on, or we'll be late."

"Late for what?"

"You'll see that too," he answered, leading the way from the restaurant.

They walked quickly back to his townhouse, and Noah helped Alexandra into his car. A few moments later they were heading up-town through Rock Creek Park.

"Are we going to my folks' place?" she asked as they turned onto Beach Drive, traveling north toward Blagdon Avenue.

"Close," he replied. Then he slowed down and turned into the park-ing area alongside Pierce Mill.

"Don't tell me we're going to park in the dark," she said, laughing in disbelief.

"Nope, we're not going to park. We're going to climb," he answered and got out of the car.

"We're going to what?" she asked as he opened her door.

"Stop asking so many questions," he said, taking her by the hand and rushing toward the heavily wooded hill that led up to the street level of the city, high above the park.

"Noah?" she whispered, a hint of excitement in her voice as they came to the foot of the path that led up through the brush to the familiar rock outcropping. It had always been their special place, the place they would go to be alone and undisturbed, the place where he had made love to her so long ago.

"Come on. I want to get to the top before it gets dark," he said.

Alexandra tightened her grip on his hand as he led the way up the dirt path, holding back the branches of trees and shrubs for her. When they reached the top of the path, Noah stepped onto the flat rock and gently pulled Alexandra up beside him.

They stood for a moment looking out over the park, which had grown still as dusk descended over the city. The sound of the old paddle wheel at Pierce Mill turning against the rapids below brought back poignant memories. Noah put his arm around her shoulder and squeezed her tightly to his side.

"Look familiar?" he asked quietly.

"Oh God, it brings back such memories," she whispered.

"Do you remember the first time we were here?"

"Of course I do," she answered, then added softly, "and the last."

"The world was all obstacles then."

"The world hasn't changed very much," she said sadly.

"No, but we have," he replied, turning to face her.

"Yes," she agreed.

"My love for you hasn't diminished one bit since the last time we stood on this rock."

"Nor mine for you...oh, Noah!" she cried, throwing her arms around him.

"Alexandra, I'll never let you go," he said, bringing his lips down on hers. They kissed passionately, clinging to each other.

"Is there any more of a place for us now than there was before?" she asked when they broke away, tears in her eyes.

"Yes," he answered.

"Are you certain that we're not about to torture ourselves all over again...certain that we can find a place for ourselves?"

"What I'm certain of, Alexandra, is that we have to try. I know I can't banish you from my thoughts, and I have no intention of ever trying to again. I have longed for you, day after day, week after week, month after month, and year after year. Torture was longing for you, dreaming about you, being obsessed with you while pretending I was happy with someone else."

"All the old conflicts are still with us," she reminded him.

"Yes, they're still here…but so are we."

"And what will it do to you to know that my sympathies are with the Palestinians?"

"I don't know," he whispered honestly.

"And when, someday, you want to visit Israel and I say, 'I can't, it's too painful,' what will that do to you?"

"Make me more sensitive to your pain, but I'll probably go without you."

"Someday, I'll want children."

"So will I."

"What will they be?"

"Our children," he answered.

"You know what I mean."

"If they're anything like their mother, they'll be wonderful," he said.

"They'll have views about all of this. They'll have attitudes that might break your heart…or mine. I mean, what will they learn?"

"Whatever we teach."

"Are we crazy to think we can really make a go of it?" she asked again, breathlessly.

"We'd be crazy not to try."

"Oh, I love you, Noah. I've always loved you," she said.

Noah nodded. "I know," he whispered. "It wasn't us trying to be together that was so maddening. It was us trying to be apart."

"So, we try again?"

"We try again," he answered, embracing her anew.

"I'm frightened."

"Me too."

Noah and Alexandra kissed once again. And when they pulled apart, they saw that the sun had at last disappeared over the horizon. They stood as the day faded, suspended between light and darkness, and looked up into the heavens. Noah took Alexandra's hand in his and squeezed it gently as they together gazed at the full moon that had emerged in the sky above.

Made in the USA
San Bernardino, CA
03 January 2014